Thomas Lefroy

Memoir of Chief Justice Lefroy

Thomas Lefroy

Memoir of Chief Justice Lefroy

ISBN/EAN: 9783337423933

Printed in Europe, USA, Canada, Australia, Japan

Cover: Foto ©Andreas Hilbeck / pixelio.de

More available books at **www.hansebooks.com**

MEMOIR

OF

CHIEF JUSTICE LEFROY.

BY

HIS SON,

THOMAS LEFROY, M.A., Q.C.

DUBLIN:

HODGES, FOSTER & CO., GRAFTON STREET,

PUBLISHERS TO THE UNIVERSITY.

1871.

DUBLIN: PRINTED BY R. CHAPMAN.

PREFACE.

THE following Memoir of the Right Honourable
Thomas Langlois Lefroy, late Lord Chief Justice
of Ireland, has been written, not so much as a
record of his public career as of those traits of
character which, in private life, endeared him to
all who had the privilege of enjoying his society;
and in the hope that the bright example he has
left behind, in the unswerving consistency of his
political principles, the simplicity of his Christian
faith, and his deep humility, may be blessed to
many who knew him not while here. To
those who did know him, it will be interesting
to retrace some of the steps of one who, through
all the arduous duties of professional, political,
and judicial life, seemed to live in constant communion with Him who was the source of that

singularly unruffled peace of mind which characterized his whole career.

I have been often asked by friends who only knew him in the later years of his life, at what period his conscience was first awakened to a sense of his own sinfulness and need of a Saviour, or what were the means made directly instrumental in this work of grace. When I began this memoir I was unable to ascertain anything more than the evidence afforded by his letters as to his having a knowledge of the leading principles of religious Truth at an early age ; but since these sheets went to press I accidentally discovered amongst the papers referred to in p. 342, the following interesting memorandum on this subject written by himself under date of 10th Aug., 1822:

" The papers in this parcel were written at different times from the year 1816, when I first began to have any view of God's true method of salvation for a sinner. I had from the year 1795, more or less, read the Scriptures, but not with faith—nor as a little child—but in the pride of a Socinian spirit, and consequently I remained long in the dark.

As truth began to dawn I was enabled to see many things, but darkly, and therefore in these papers will be observed more or less of error ; but I have preserved them, and mention the circumstances, as a testimony to the great benefit of applying with constancy to this source of all truth, and to glorify the long suffering, the tender mercy, and grace of our Lord God, and at the same time to show what it is that hinders us from reaping the blessed fruits with which the Scriptures abound, as soon as we otherwise should do—namely, leaning on our own poor though proud understandings."

The interruptions arising from other duties, as well as my own inability worthily to fulfil the task, have more than once disposed me, during the progress of the memoir, to abandon its publication ; but friends whose judgment I value have led me to feel its completion as a sacred duty, and therefore I willingly trust to the kind indulgence of those into whose hands it may fall to overlook its many deficiencies, of which no one can be more sensible than the writer.

CONTENTS.

CHAPTER IX.

CHAPTER X.

CHAPTER XI.

CHAPTER XII.

MEMOIR

OF

CHIEF JUSTICE LEFROY.

CHAPTER I.

BIRTH—Early History of his Family—Enters Trinity College when fourteen years old—Letter of Lord Stormont—Letters of his Uncle, Mr. Langlois, to Colonel Lefroy—Proposal that he should read for a Fellowship—His Tutor, Dr. Burrowes, averse to the plan—Anecdote of Mr. Burke—Career in the University—College Historical Society —Dr. Burrowes' anticipations of his future eminence.

THOMAS LANGLOIS LEFROY was born on the 8th of January, 1776. He was the eldest son of Anthony Lefroy, Lieut.-Colonel of the 9th Light Dragoons—the descendant of a Huguenot family, who were obliged to fly from Cambray, at the period of the Duke of Alva's persecution in the Netherlands, and took refuge in England. The following inscription, on a monument in the Parish Church of Petham, Kent, to the memory of Thomas Lefroy, the great great grandson of Antoine Loffroy, who first emigrated from Cambray, fur-

B

nishes an interesting record of the circumstances under which the Lefroy family first came to adopt England as their country:—

𝔖𝔞𝔠𝔯𝔢𝔟 𝔱𝔬

THOMAS LEFROY,

OF CANTERBURY,

WHO DIED THIRD DAY OF NOVEMBER, 1723, AGED 43.

OF A CAMBRESIAN FAMILY,

THAT PREFERRED RELIGION AND LIBERTY

TO

THEIR COUNTRY AND THEIR PROPERTY,

IN THE

TIME OF THE DUKE OF ALVA'S PERSECUTION.*

Lieut.-Colonel Lefroy, the father of the subject of this memoir, entered the army in 1763 as Ensign in the 33rd Regiment, then quartered in Ireland, and at the early age of twenty-three married Anna, daughter of Thomas George Gardner, Esq., of Doonass in the County of Clare ; he subsequently changed into the Cavalry, and served as Captain in the 13th Light Dragoons, and afterwards became Colonel of the 9th Light Dragoons. What a com-

* The following memorandum, which has been transmitted amongst the old family papers preserved at Ewshott House, in Hampshire, the residence of the English branch of the family, is traced back to about the year 1611. . . . . "Antoine Loffroy came from "Flanders about the year 1569, in the time of the Duke of Alva's per-"secution. He brought with him a considerable sum of money and "jewels; but his estate shared the same fate with that of many other "refugees who left France on account of their religion, being confiscated, "and all the family writings, papers, &c., destroyed. His wife was a "Flanderine lady of the first quality, and very rich, of the family of the "Du Hoorns. He had two sons, Isaiah, born in Flanders, and David, "born after his arrival in England. He, finding a number of refugees in "Canterbury, and induced by the convenience of the French church, "resolved to fix there."

plete banishment military service in Ireland was in the earlier years of George III. may be gathered from the fact, that when he obtained the command of the 9th Light Dragoons in 1785, that regiment had been sixty-seven years quartered there, and it remained sixteen years longer before it was recalled. Colonel Lefroy sold out of the army in 1791, and having previously purchased landed property in the County Limerick, he resolved not to return to England, and settled in Limerick, where he resided till his death in 1819. Thomas Langlois, his eldest son, the subject of this memoir, after a private education entered the University of Dublin, on the 2nd November, 1790, at the early age of fourteen. The journey between Limerick and Dublin being at that time a work of three days, even in a coach, which for its rapidity was called "the Fly," it may well be imagined that the selection of a college tutor for a boy of that age, leaving his father's home for the first time, was a subject of no small anxiety to all those who took an interest in his welfare. An opening fortunately offered on the pupil list of the Rev. Dr. Burrowes (afterwards Dean of Cork), who kindly consented to receive him into his family circle, and from their first acquaintance the connection seemed more like that of father and son than of tutor and pupil. Even at that early age the kind disposition and the affectionate heart, which in after life secured the esteem of those with whom he associated, already made him a favourite with all who knew him. ·Many of his English relatives wished that he should be sent to an English University, and Mr. Benjamin Langlois, his grand uncle, who watched over his early course with a father's interest, was anxious that he should go to the English Bar, and promised if Colonel Lefroy would allow him to do so, to exert his influence in obtaining a seat for him in the British Parliament.*   But Colonel

---

* Mr. Benjamin Langlois was son of Monsieur Pierre Langlois, of a Huguenot family of noble rank in Languedoc, expelled from France on the revocation of the Edict of Nantes, and younger brother of Field Marshal Langlois, Governor of Antwerp, and afterwards Commander-in-Chief of Upper and Lower Austria, and Commandant of Trieste, under the Emperor Joseph. Many gratifying marks of the high degree in which he enjoyed the favor and confidence of the Emperor and the Empress, Maria Theresa, have been transmitted as heir looms through his sister, Elizabeth Langlois, who married Anthony Lefroy of Canterbury, in 1738. Mr. Benjamin Langlois was Secretary to the Embassy at the Court of Vienna when Viscount Stormont was Ambassador, and he afterwards sat in Parliament for the borough of St. Germains for eleven years. The following letter, offering the post of Under Secretary of State to Mr. Benjamin Langlois, when Viscount Stormont became Secretary of State for the Home Department in 1789, affords curious evidence of the contrast between the duties of the Home Secretary's office then and at the present time, and shows the esteem in which Mr. Langlois was held :—

London, January 31st, 1789.

MY DEAR LANGLOIS,—I have been so constantly occupied that it has not been possible for me to give you an account of our debates, in which I have taken so large a share, and not unsuccessfully, if I may credit the partiality of my friends. The Ministers continue to procrastinate, yet

Lefroy having resolved to remain in Ireland was unwilling to be separated from his son, and it seemed as if Providence was steering his course to that profession, of which he was destined afterwards to become so bright an ornament; for although from the following letters it is evident that after the idea of his being sent to an English University was abandoned Mr. Langlois' desire was that he should read for a fellowship in the University of Dublin, and we might naturally suppose that the suggestion of so influential a relative, and one who took so deep an interest in his welfare, would have had great weight in such a matter yet nothing turned his attention for a moment from the Irish Bar as the sphere of his future labours.

they cannot delay the business above three weeks longer; the plan of future arrangement is nearly settled, and I write to you upon a subject of great importance to me. I write, my dear Langlois, to invite you, not as formerly, to a share of toil and labour, but to a bed of down. I am to be Secretary of State for the Home Department; I cannot, therefore, invite you to come and *work* with me, for we shall have not more business in a year than we have often done in a single week, but I do most earnestly invite you to come and take your share of this sinecure. It will oblige you to come to town sooner than usual; but it will not prevent your shooting parties in autumn. In that I can see no objection; but if, contrary to my hope, you should find London disagree with you, and should think even this quiet office too much for your spirits, you can then return to retirement. I am most anxious that you should at least make the experiment. I entreat of you, my dear Langlois; I ask it of your friendship; nay, more, I expect it from that long and faithful friendship from which I have never expected anything in vain.

Ever yours most sincerely,

STORMONT.

Immediately after his entering Trinity College
Mr. Langlois writes:—

To COL. LEFROY.

Worksop, Notts., 22nd Nov. 1790.

Your letter from Dublin reached me this morning, and,
having rather more leisure here than in town,—I cannot
help congratulating you on your very great good fortune
in having found so proper a person into whose hands to
confide Thomas, who, I hope, will ever deserve the tender
interest we all take in him. His parts are so promising,
and his character so winning, that I sincerely hope the
gentleman he is with will have a pleasure and pride in
bringing him forward. He is so advanced for his years,
that unless vice and bad example lead him astray, he will,
in all probability, be highly qualified, by the time he is of
a proper age and standing, to be a candidate for a Fellowship. I would wish that to be constantly instilled into
him as the great object of his emulation.

B. L.

It appears from the next letter, that in early
life his eyes were so weak as to cause some
anxiety, though one of the most remarkable proofs
of the vigour of his constitution in the later period
of life was, that at the age of ninety-three he used
to read the newspapers even by candle-light without the aid of spectacles. The following year,
Mr. Langlois writes again, from Welbeck (the seat
of the Duke of Portland),—

To COL. LEFROY.

Welbeck, Notts., Nov. 20th, 1791.

I read with infinite pleasure and satisfaction the account you sent me of the great credit and honour Thomas has acquired in his last examination. If he continues as assiduous, I hope he will not have many competitors, of his own strength, to contend with when he comes to stand for a Fellowship which, I own, is still a favourite object with me. With Thomas's talents and disposition, I think he stands a very fair chance of success. Great as the object is, however, let us not sacrifice those still greater ones to it—health and eyesight; I therefore perfectly agree with you in the propriety of his reading for some time as little as may be by candle-light.

B. L.

The following letter seems to be in reply to one from Col. Lefroy, consulting him as to the prudence of moving his son out of his class, in which there were an unusual number of competitors for honours, and, as from the then delicate state of his health and his weak eyesight it was feared he could not continue his studies, it was proposed to change him into the class of Fellow-Commoners.

TO COL. LEFROY,

Worksop, Notts., Dec. 10th, 1792.

I congratulate you very sincerely on your dear Thomas's
fresh laurels; 'tis very pleasing for me to learn that he still
keeps the lead in so distinguished a class, but I am very
sorry that at this distance it is impossible for me to give you
any advice relative to your idea of changing his gown.
Before you come to any resolution, you would do well to
inform yourself how much longer this severe kind of contest
is likely to last; if his superiority is a very decided one,
he may perhaps be able to maintain it without too much
exertion. You know my favourite object for him has
always been a Fellowship, and his distinguishing himself
so early, has still more confirmed me in the hope of his
being able to attain it. The prospect may perhaps be
precarious; but I take for granted that this change of
gown would put an end to it, and I confess that this consideration, were I to decide, would have great weight
with me. Whatever your decision may be, God grant it
may be for the best; and whatever it is, after you have
given the subject all due consideration, you may depend
on it I shall approve. Thomas has everything in his temper
and character that can conciliate affection. A good heart,
a good mind, good sense, and as little to correct in him as
ever I saw in one of his age.

B. L.

It would seem from the following letter that Dr.
Burrowes' advice was opposed to the plan of his
reading for a Fellowship.

TO COLONEL LEFROY.

Welbeck, Notts., Nov. 3rd, 1793.

I received two days ago your letter of the 22nd of last month with the copy of Dr. Burrowes' letter of Sept. 25th. I really am much perplexed how to answer you, there is something so specious in his arguments that they have a good deal shaken me in regard to the Fellowship which was always my favourite object for Thomas. As to what regards his health I must be perfectly silent. All that I can say is, that if there is a very probable chance of his health being affected by the pursuit,—Le jeu ne vaut pas la chandelle,—'tis the first of blessings, and not to be put to a certain risk. If he has any talent for oratory, I would certainly not discourage it, but first let him lay in sound knowledge, and a good stock of ideas—"*Rem verba sequuntur.*" Where there is a natural good elocution, if the judgment is clear and strong, the words will never be wanting. The matter is the great *desideratum* in a public speaker, and though perhaps it is not the direct object of an Academical Education to acquire such matter, yet from the habit that education gives of examining, weighing, scrutinizing various subjects, and distinguishing true and false ideas, it will so strengthen the understanding that it will be enabled to seize the right side of a question, though the object were entirely new. Therefore, whether he means to stand for a Fellowship or not, let him by all means go on with his academical studies. Let him form his taste upon the great Greek and Roman models.

The great defect at your University is that composition in the latter of these two languages is but little attended to. One of the most eloquent writers as well as speakers that this country has bred, Bishop Atterbury, wrote as elegantly in Latin as in English. Whether as a statesman a man is to draw his knowledge from Aristotle and Thucydides I cannot say ; but, I have been often told that the old Lord Granville besides all his modern literature studied much those two books and knew Thucydides almost by heart. If to a thorough and critical acquaintance with the best authors in the Greek and Latin languages Thomas adds such an acquirement in the sciences as is the purpose of academical education, he will lay in such a store of knowledge as with his natual abilities will ensure his making a figure afterwards.

A learned education, (comprehending what we call in England perfect classical scholarship), ought to be his present object; and trifling as it may appear I would rather he employed his time in making bad Latin verses, if he cannot make good ones, simply with the view of making himself master of Prosody, than in reading Smith's Wealth of Nations at the present moment. It will never be forgotten of that able and eloquent speaker Mr. Burke, that in one of his best harangues he mistook the quantity of *vectigal* and called it *vectigal*.* This little instance of

* In "Harford's Recollections of Wilberforce," we find the following account of the circumstance to which Mr. Langlois here adverts. It was given to Mr. Harford by Wilberforce amongst other anecdotes of Lord North :—"On an occasion when Colonel Barry brought forward a motion on the British Navy, Lord North said to a friend of his who sat next him in the House, ' We shall have a tedious speech from Barry to-night. I dare say he'll give us our naval history from the beginning—not forgetting Sir Francis Drake and the Armada. All this is nothing to me, so let me sleep on, and wake me when he comes near our own times.' His friend at length roused him, when Lord North exclaimed : ' Where are we ?' ' At

prosodaical ignorance would in this country have damned
a *young* speaker for ever, or at least he must have distinguished himself exceedingly afterwards before he could
have convinced his hearers that he had common sense. In
a word what I mean to say is this, that while Thomas is
at the University he should follow his University studies
and apply as closely to them as his health will admit; and
that if any idea is entertained of substituting another
course, and of making him either a lawyer, a statesman, or
an orator, while at the University, he would lose all the advantages of a learned academical education, and come forth
an ignorant, empty, presumptuous prater, contemning and
contemned by everybody. They might almost as well at
the University pretend to teach a man the Graces (in Lord
Chesterfield's phrase), and fit him to shine in the *Beau
Monde* as to qualify him to make a figure at the Bar or in
Parliament. A University education gives strength and
vigour to the mind, and opens those sources from which
knowledge is derived ; but the application of that knowledge to our several walks in the world is quite a different

the Battle of La Hague, my lord.' 'Oh, my dear friend,' he replied,
'you have woke me a century too soon !' . . . ." Mr. Burke, in the
course of some very severe animadversions which he made on Lord North
for want of due economy in his management of the public purse, introduced the well known aphorism :—" Magnum vectigal est parsimonia ;"
but was guilty of a false quantity by saying "vectĭgal." Lord North,
while this philippic went on, had been half asleep, and sat heaving back-
wards and forwards like a great turtle ; but the sound of a false quantity
instantly aroused him, and opening his eyes, he exclaimed in a very marked
and decided manner, "vectigal." "I thank the noble Lord," said Burke,
with happy adroitness, "for the correction, the more particularly as it
affords me an opportunity of repeating a maxim which he greatly needs to
have reiterated upon him," and he then thundered out, "Magnum vectigal
est parsimonia."

branch of study, and to be acquired in active life only, and by the assistance of an intercourse with those who are engaged in the same career with us.

B. L.

During the four years of his University course he attended all the class examinations which were then held quarterly, taking the highest prize of each year ; also a moderatorship, and the gold medal of his class. He was a Member of the College Historical Society, which had been established in 1770, and was broken up in 1794, in consequence of the introduction of debates on subjects of modern politics leading to breaches of College discipline ; amongst its members we find the other distinguished names of Plunket, Pennefather, Jebb, Burrowes, &c. During the years 1793 and 1794, he obtained three medals in the Society, two for Oratory, and one for History.

On the 19th Dec. 1794, he moved the series of Resolutions on which the new College Historical Society was founded ; and in the next year he was appointed Auditor, and delivered the opening address of the Session for 1795. In that Session he obtained a fourth medal from the Society.*

* The Annals of the College Historical Society may be regarded as in some degree interwoven with the history of our National University, and, therefore, as the Resolutions here referred to may be read with

The following letter from his College tutor to his father at the close of his college course, affords a gratifying testimony as to the opinion Dr. Burrowes had then formed both of his principles and his prospects for life :—

TO COLONEL LEFROY.

Dublin, April 21st, 1795.

My DEAR SIR,—. . . . . The satisfaction you express as to the mode which I adopted with regard to Thomas's education, is to me a most welcome gratification, and overpays any efforts I may have made to deserve it For, my dear sir, I will at all times say, that the pleasure I have had in Thomas's society, the delight in his advancement in literature, and the return of his endearing attentions to me and to my family, were a price fully sufficient for any services I could have rendered him. For his great success in College I claim no credit. It was entirely the effect of his own talents and judicious diligence. It must be highly pleasing to you to hear that, within my memory, no young man has left our College with a higher character—none so much respected by all the Fellows, or more regretted by a numerous acquaintance. Of my dear Thomas I cannot speak but with emotion : I feel for him

nterest by Alumni of "Old Trinity," I have inserted them, and the address to the Board which accompanied them, together with the Board's answer to the address in an Appendix. I have also given there a portion of Mr. Lefroy's speech as Auditor, which exhibits his clear and forcible style of speaking even at the age of 19; and in his observations on the benefits which the Society obtained by the adoption of those Resolutions, illustrates the sound judgment and practical good sense which he displayed at that early period of his career.

as a son or a brother. I feel for him as you do ; but I
have such intimate knowledge of his disposition and habits,
that I can look with the most assured confidence to his
great advancement in life, and eminence in reputation.
Though I feel his absence more than his family can do, I
can with more certainty look forward to his future fame
and elevation. Of his conduct in London, however sedu-
cing its idleness and its evils, you need not have the
slightest doubt. He is, in his religious principles, in his
desire of knowledge, and his just ambition, fortified in
every place. I have given him letters, which if I am
not much deceived in the persons to whom I have introduced him, will secure to him most cordial attentions from
them, as I could not possibly write more strongly, and as
I am not at all in the habit of trespassing on my London
friends, I have no doubt of their effect. . . . .

Your affectionate humble servant,

H. BURROWES.

To Lieut.-Col. Lefroy, Newtown Pery, Limerick.

A warm friendship which existed between him
and one of his fellow-students, during their College
course, opened the door for him as an acquaintance
and guest in the family of Jeffry Paul, Esq., of
Silverspring, in the county Wexford, the father of
his fellow-student, and, very soon, an attachment
sprung up between him and Mr. Paul's only daughter. During his stay in Ireland, in 1797, when he
came over from London to be called to the Bar,

but only to return again for his further study of
the Law, he was engaged to be married to Miss
Paul. From that time to their marriage, in March,
1799, he was allowed to carry on a correspondence,
and, when death brought to a close the happy
union, which lasted for more than half a century,
not only this correspondence, but all the letters he
had written to her during their married life were
found preserved with a care which marked them
as sacred in the eyes of her who was the chief
object of his affection. The marriage took place
on the 16th March, 1799, at Abergavenny, in
North Wales, where many of the gentry in the
County of Wexford, sent their families for refuge
when the rebellion broke out in that county, in
May, 1798. Mr. Paul remained in Ireland on
service with his yeomanry corps, and the following
letters, selected from his correspondence with Mrs.
Paul, may be interesting as giving some particulars of the rebellion which have not appeared
elsewhere.

TO MRS. PAUL.

Waterford, Friday, 15th June, 1798.

MY DEAREST JANE,—A horrid conspiracy has been
discovered here, within two days, by the interposition of
God Himself—many are concerned, but amongst those
that are in custody, are Brown, Tom's tailor, Sargent, who
kept "The Hole in the wall," and a number of butchers

and publicans. They had stript all the jails and new buildings of lead, and had made an importation of gunpowder. Sargent was to forward a scheme for a great dinner to be given at his house for the yeomen. Wednesday last was the day,—at a particular hour a number were to rush in and murder all the Protestants, at the same time a false drum was to beat through the town, and on the yeomen opening their doors to enquire for the cause, they were to be stabbed by men stationed at every house. The assassins were then to rush in and put to death men, women, and children, in short, there never was a more horrid or better concerted plan for a general massacre of Protestants. In Kilkenny the same was to have taken place. It was discovered by the death of Flynn, the high constable, and among his papers were found some that led to the discovery,—a decisive engagement is expected shortly to take place at Ballytruckle. The success, under God, we doubt not of, as every measure has been taken by the most experienced generals, to enable them not only to beat, but to annihilate the rebels, for nothing else will do. May God bless you, and my dear Tom and Mary, and if it be His blessed will may we yet see each other.

I am your affectionate Husband,

JEFFRY PAUL.

TO THE SAME.

Waterford, 26th June, 1798.

MY DEAREST JANE,—On my return from Wexford on Sunday night very late I received yours of the 19th. A

party of us marched on Friday night to escort Captain
Burton to the army, who were on their march to retake
Wexford. On our arrival we had the mortification to find
that the rebels had evacuated the town and completely
escaped, a very unfortunate circumstance, for they were
there to a great number, and if they could have been
forced to an engagement it would certainly have been
fatal to them, and probably would have finished the
business in this part of the kingdom; but they are now in
force in many parts of the country; the strong army we
have in pursuit will, I trust, destroy them. We marched
by Vinegar Hill and through Enniscorthy the morning
after the engagement there, and such a sight I hope I
shall never again behold; the town and three miles of the
road almost filled with mangled corpses, promiscuously
lying with dead horses, mules, pigs, &c., and the most
precious furniture of elegant houses. That town is almost
entirely demolished, but Wexford is not; there we found
the Church and buildings safe. The rebels had 500
prisoners at Wexford, all to be sacrificed. When they determined to evacuate, they ordered immediate execution,
and had only time to finish seventy, when they got
information that the army was near. I saw the bridge,
like a slaughter house, thick with the blood of those
seventy Protestants. Sir Wm. Hore, Edward Turner, and
Captain Allen Cox, amongst the number; those three men
they took uncommon pains to torture, by piking them
before, they despatched them, and then stripping them
and throwing them over the bridge into the river. The
women have escaped. Tom Willis who was with us,
found amongst them Harry Willis's wife; she had sailed

C

from Cork for England, and was taken off the Wexford coast by an armed boat of the rebels, and a few hours more would have finished her life. Now for Silverspring, I could not go there though so near it, as that part of the country was not regained by us, and if it had I could not have left my duty. Though I was asked to a good bed at Wilson's in Wexford, we were obliged to lie outside the town in a barn, on a little dirty straw. The house at Silverspring, I am told, is standing, but every article of furniture, beds, wine, &c., taken away and destroyed, mostly by the women of that neighbourhood.

Lefroy has begged of me to write to him ; I did once, and shall again to morrow. I pray for good news to fill my letter. My tenderest love and affections are all yours, Tom's and Mary's.

Yours ever,

J. PAUL.

TO THE SAME.

Waterford, 29th June, 1798.

My DEAREST JANE,—I can now give you joy, and I hope you will all kneel down to the Almighty God, who has deigned to hear our cries. Our enemies have fallen into the deep and cruel pit which they dug for us ; if the battle of Ross had ended against us, all in this town were to be massacred ; but on the court house at Wexford are now placed the heads of Bagl. Harvey, Cornelius Grogan, John Colclough, Genl. Keugh and Roche ; I mention those as the great leaders in that country, but at Wexford they are still hanging numbers continually. The rebels

are surrendering their arms by thousands, and their spirit
is completely broken.   General Johnson marched his army
in here last night,—it was an awful and glorious sight.
The rebels in heart fled into their houses, while we loyal-
ists thankfully welcomed the conqueror with shouts that
you would think were never to end.   John Colclough
and his wife, with Bagenal Harvey, fled to the Galtees,
into a cave which was only to be got into at low water ;
they were found with a quantity of money, plate, and
provisions.   This town has had wonderful escapes,—plot
after plot by poison, etc., is still being discovered, but now
all is over with them.

May, Morris and others, I am told, have written for
the return of their families ; I will not yet do so.   Tom
and I will go to Silverspring in a few days,—and on our
return we shall be better able to judge what to do.

Your ever truly affectionate

JEFFRY PAUL.

CHAPTER II.

MR. LEFROY was called to the Irish Bar in Easter Term, 1797, but did not begin to attend the Courts until 1800, devoting himself in the interval with perseverance to the study of the law, and acquiring a knowledge not only of the general principles of jurisprudence, but of the practical details of legal proceedings. It is evident that he laid in a store of knowledge with which few students ever commenced their professional career, for he has left a large collection of manuscript essays and readings on various heads of Common Law and Equity, written while he was keeping his Law Terms at Lincoln's Inn, that would rank high—even amongst the many valuable Digests now extant. During his stay at the Temple, he resided with his grand uncle, Mr. Langlois, in London, and attended daily at Westminster Hall, where, in the Courts presided over by such men as Lord Eldon and Lord Kenyon, he had an opportunity of imbibing those great fundamental principles of law and equity with which his mind in after life proved to be so richly imbued, and which marked the able judgments he delivered as Baron of the Exchequer and Chief Justice of the Queen's Bench.

His habits of application while at the Temple appear to have borne early fruit, as will be seen by the following letter written in the year after he began to attend the Courts, by a friend who happened to be present when he was arguing an important case in the Court of Error.

TO COL. LEFROY,

Dublin, November 19, 1801,
72, Stephen Street.

DEAR SIR,—I sit down with sincere pleasure to inform you that I was present in Court a few days ago, and heard your son argue a writ of Error before the Exchequer Chamber. He was about two hours speaking, and at the close of his argument he concluded by " lamenting he was under the necessity of taking up so much of their Lordship's time." To which Lord Clare replied, " Mr. Lefroy, you have no reason whatever to lament, for you have argued the case with most uncommon precision and much satisfaction to the Court." All the first lawyers at the bar were present, for the Cause had gone through most of the Courts and had been depending nearly 30 years. Mr. Hobbs has almost spent a life and fortune on it. The argument was received not only by the Court but by the Bar, in the most gratifying manner, and the Chief Baron at a large party on that day said—" It was the ablest argument which has been made at the Irish Bar." Mr. Burston, one of the leading lawyers in Chancery, before going out of Court, went up to Mr. Babington, a most eminent solicitor, and advised him to retain your son for every important cause he had to be argued.

Yours very sincerely,

CHARLES D. HOARE.

An important decision pronounced in the Court of King's Bench, in England, in Michaelmas term, 1798* caused considerable apprehension in Ireland as to the validity of judgment securities, which at that time were more prevalent in this country than any other class of securities in Ireland ; and early in 1802, though then scarcely of two years' standing at the Bar, Mr. Lefroy published a tract on " Proceedings by Elegit for recovery of Judgment Debts," which attracted the attention of two eminent lawyers in Westminster Hall, Lord Glenbervie, better known as Mr. Douglas, Editor of the valuable Reports which bear his name, and Mr. Burton, M. P. for Oxford, and Judge of the Court of Session for the County Palatine of Chester. The former in a letter to Mr. Langlois, strongly advising a republication of the Tract in London, says —" I read over your nephew's Essay, which I

---

* De Costa *v.* Wharton and Dixon, 8 Term, Report 2.

assure you, without any compliment, is, in my opinion, a Tract which does him very great credit, as a sound well grounded lawyer, and a young man of excellent sense and very correct legal understanding. Your's sincerely.

GLENBERVIE."

The latter on the same subject writes thus :—

TO BENJAMIN LANGLOIS, ESQ.

Upper Brook Street, 12th March, 1802.

I can assure you with truth, that I have derived from Mr. Lefroy's Essay on Elegit, both amusement and instruction. In my opinion, it is written by a lawyer, a scholar, and a gentleman. The arrangement is good, the argument solid, and the language perspicuous. I should therefore think that it cannot fail of recommending its author to Lord Redesdale's notice, and of making him known in this country, to his credit and advantage. I beg you will give him my professional thanks when you write to him.

Very sincerely yours,

F. BURTON.

Lord Clare's death, in January, 1802, caused a vacancy in the Lord Chancellorship, and in March, 1802, the Irish Seals were given to Lord Redesdale. It would seem as if Mr. Justice Burton had in consequence of his approval of the Law Tract already referred to, brought his name before Lord

Redesdale, for, a short time after his Lordship's arrival in Ireland, he wrote the following letter which I give at length as I think it will be read with interest for the graphic style in which it describes Lord Redesdale's impressions of this country at that time.

TO FRANCIS BURTON, ESQ.,

Judge of the Court of Session for the County Palatine of Chester.

Ely Place, Dublin,
August 30th, 1802.

My DEAR SIR,—I am much obliged to all my old friends who will have the kindness to recollect that I am in this country, and that in a strange country nothing pleases a wanderer more than to learn from his friends that they are well. It soothes the mind, not only by the intelligence it conveys, but by the little pride which it raises, by persuading the absent man that he is not wholly forgotten. You, my dear Sir, are so good as not merely to give me the chit chat of the day, or intelligence of yourself, but to endeavour to persuade me that I ought to be contented with my situation, whatever regret I may feel at quitting my old friends. But it is much easier to talk of submission to evil for public good than to be content with a situation of mortification through mere consciousness of being usefully employed.

I have been unable either to purchase or rent a place tolerably pleasant or commodious, and have been compelled to purchase a little farm of about sixty English acres, with a small house, very quiet, though only four English

miles from this town. The house is so small that I must
add to it, and there is nothing more dangerous than adding
to or altering a small house to make it larger. It has
annoyed me to think of the outcry which our amiable
brother senator, Mr. Robson, made at my salary. As far
as I can judge from experience, I must be a good econo-
mist, if after six years it should replace me in my former
fortune, that is, if it should give me back the sum I have
expended and lost in the change of country. I doubt
whether six years will be sufficient.

Expenses here are very great, especially to a stranger.
A few articles are cheaper than in England, but an Englishman cannot live like an Englishman at nearly so cheap
a rate in Dublin as in London. If he can adopt the
habits of the country and be content without a thousand
comforts which he has been used to in England, and live
in the true Irish style, he may, perhaps, make something
of external show rather cheaper than he would do in London, but every real luxury and almost every convenience
is cheaper in London, and every article is infinitely better.
The pen I write with, and the paper I write upon, remind
me how execrably bad almost every article of manufacture
is, and how abominably dear it is at the same time. For
tho' I do not pay for these articles, yet, signing an order
for accustomed quantities, I perceive the price is far
beyond the value of the commodity. I am endeavouring
to reconcile myself to all this, and repeat every moment
the old saying, " What cannot be cured must be endured,"
and so I chide myself for grumbling. I must endeavour
to make my farm a comfortable residence, for I cannot
submit to live all the year in the stew and dust of Dublin.

I hope I am not blameable in this, though it may be called extravagance, but to be obliged to spend a great deal for show, which only produces discomfort, and to be allowed to spend nothing to obtain real comfort, would be hard indeed.

The few friends I can find here I wish to see, and I can only see them comfortably when at leisure from business. I think it may be useful to draw about me the young men at the Bar, whose talents and conduct merit protection.

Your friend Mr. Lefroy is a young man who fully answers that description, he is much esteemed here, and I think must get forward.

You give a touch at the Jacobins, and that is, in my poor opinion, a very serious subject. In this country, I am sure, it requires attention—the whole character of the Roman Catholics of the lower class is changed. They are completely Jacobinised, and you may judge how far they are to be depended on, and how far all that was intended at that unfortunate period when we lost the great minister who had preserved us for so many years, and all that has been since talked of, is wise and prudent by considering whether anything of that sort can make the least change in the spirit of Jacobinism. As far as I can judge the whole scheme has been formed by ambitious men for their own purposes; first adopted by folly calling itself liberality, and then pressed on abilities which most astonishingly sink under the influence of minds too contemptible to have been worthy of even a struggle with them. 'Tis a wonderful but melancholy instance of the extraordinary submission of sense to nonsense. If it should be persisted in, I tremble at the consequences. People in

England are generally ignorant of this country and its inhabitants. At this moment they are more than ordinarily ignorant. The French Revolution, the Rebellion, and the Union, have made wonderful changes; and the effect of the Union has been in some degree most rapid. The great thing looked for is purity in the administration of Government. You might as well consult Sir Robert Walpole about the proper method of managing England at this moment as consult any of the modern secretaries, even the manager of the Union itself, about the state of Ireland; he must no longer talk even among Irishmen, of making men amiable—a term which, you will recollect, Sheridan handled with much dexterity in answer to the noble Lord.

Yours, etc.,

REDESDALE.

For some years after his call to the Bar Mr. Lefroy went the Munster Circuit, and appears to have had considerable success, as one of his letters from the Spring Circuit, in 1809, contains an apology for the postponement of his expected return home on account of his being called to the Wexford Assizes as Special Counsel, to conduct a heavy case for Mr. Hardy, with a fee of 100 guineas. This for a junior of only a few years' standing was almost an unprecedented testimony to the appreciation in which he was held.

During the long course of his professional and

judicial career he hardly ever allowed a day to pass while on Circuit without writing home, and the tender affection which breathes through the letters to his wife, as well as the evidence they afford of the earnest devotion with which, from an early age, he applied himself to the study of the Bible, make them deeply interesting as well as instructive. The following is dated from Mountrath, on his journey to join the Munster Circuit, in 1810 :—

TO HIS WIFE.

Mountrath, Friday night.

I put a few lines into the Maryboro' post about 4 o'clock, but lest by any accident you should not get them I send this letter to Mr. Bourne, the coach proprietor, with a request that he may forward it to you, as no post goes into town on Sunday, when it will arrive. We have had a fine though rather dull day, the coach not full, so that I had plenty of leisure and inclination for reading. I spent my day in preparing for Dunne* for the long vacation. I read over and compared most part of the Epistle to the Romans, with all those to the Galatians and the Ephesians, and part of those to the Corinthians; every time I read and compare them new light breaks in, and I am determined I will work on without note or comment endeavour-

* He alludes to the Rev. James Dunne, an eminent Clergyman of that day, with whom he passed much time in the long vacations, and had many discussions on Scriptural subjects.

ing to make out the meaning for myself, which I should think may be done by patience and attention. By taking advantage of all the moments which would otherwise go to waste, great progress may be made in this undertaking besides the new portion of life which it infuses into the work which ought always to be going on within—of detecting the lurking-places of sin and the disguises of selfishness and purifying of the heart. These are, I am sure, the true and primary objects with a view to which we ought to read the Scriptures; but I think these will be greatly aided, when we understand all the bearings and connexion of the several parts of Scripture. There is another great good which results from applying even the shreds and patches of time in this way. It serves to allay somewhat the high relish and excitement which this world and all its pursuits and objects are hourly forcing on the imagination and the heart; it keeps in our view a glimpse, at least, of the true in opposition to the glare of the false treasure which we are for ever pursuing, and between the legitimate and excessive pursuit of which the bounds are so treacherous. I include under the head of false treasure every object of earthly attachment however innocent or even praiseworthy, on which a value is set beyond what any earthly object is entitled to, and yet this is a point upon which we are all most sadly and practically going astray every hour of our lives, and on which nothing can set us right but keeping before us, as if in a magnifying glass, the great and paramount claims to a Christian's regard. I do not say that we are to extinguish the affections which belong to the different relations of life; on the contrary, by the pure and sincere

exercise of them, selfishness is in some degree extinguish-
ed, but the gratification arising from the most delightful
of these affections should not form the stay, and hope, and
prop of life. No; therein consists the excess, and the
abuse; but I'll say no more on this head, lest you should
tell me that nothing but my vanity could suggest the
necessity of sermonizing with you in this manner. I own,
however, it is grounded on a conviction that the sensi-
bility and devotedness of my darling wife's attachment
to a certain degree impair her own enjoyment. But,
remember, I am not willing to part with the least atom of
it to any earthly object; whatever of it ought to be pruned
away, let it be transplanted to that region where we may
hope and trust to enjoy it in-bliss unfading.

T. L.

Nor are we left without abundant evidence that
neither the flush of professional success, nor the
pressure of business ever drove from his mind the
loving anxiety of a father's care for the spiritual
welfare of his children ; for at the same time that
he writes home to his wife from the Assizes at
Limerick, commencing with the natural joy and
pride of the young practitioner—" I cannot tell
you how much in demand I have been ; I have
made fifty guineas, and I have the satisfaction of
feeling that I am rapidly establishing myself in
business, as I have had it from attorneys and
clients of whom I know nothing." He also writes

" Your account of my dear children gives me heartfelt delight. May they be enabled to run the race which is set before them, and may we continue to be so highly blessed." " Tell dear A—— how pleased I am to hear of his reading prayers for me every morning. Make him understand what he is about, and learn to pray from his dear little heart, and not from his lips only."

T. L.

On another occasion we find the following notes to his children, enclosed in a letter, written from the Limerick Assizes, to his wife—

TO HIS DAUGHTER J——.

Limerick, Monday.

My DARLING J——,—Your letter gave me great pleasure; it was fairly written, well worded and no mistakes in the spelling; and I hope, by employing your time regularly between this and the next time I leave home, you'll be able to correspond with me on subjects of more importance. Believe me, my darling girl, there is no progress to be made in anything without steady and continued application, which, besides the advantages it brings in the way of improvement, makes labour pleasant from habit instead of being irksome, as it always is to the idle and irresolute. A saunterer when young, continues a saunterer through life. Nothing has always struck me so forcibly to show the value of order, and precision

in our works, as observing the regularity and exactness displayed in all the works of God, day and
night—summer, winter, autumn, and spring,—the
regular and uniform motions of the almost infinite
host of heavenly bodies. In the same manner in His
kingdom of grace, there is a time and a season for everything. Although a thousand years are in his sight as one
day, nothing is permitted to occur a moment before its appointed time. Our blessed Lord's constant observation
was, "mine hour is not yet come." How is it possible
that we can expect to please God in the neglect of order
and the disregard of stated times for different purposes?
Indeed the event shows it, for He appears in an eminent
degree to send a blessing upon diligence and industry in
every situation of life, and these are necessarily connected
with a regard to time and order. As I am satisfied my
darling J—— has real delight in pleasing me, I thought I
could not do better that tell her a principal mode of doing
so, and what is done from a sense of duty to a Father in
heaven as well as to a father on earth, must yield happiness and improvement.

My dearest J——'s
Truly affectionate father,
T. L.

TO HIS SON A——.

I hope you are a faithful chaplain, and make them all
attend regularly at prayers during my absence, and that
you recollect that to pray as we ought is not merely to
repeat words, and to be thinking of something else, we
must recollect what it is we are going about, and in whose

presence we kneel down, and that He sees our hearts and minds as plainly as we see one another, and that He regards only the prayer that comes from the heart, and in which the mind is engaged. I hope you are attentive to your business, and get your lessons, not merely so as to pass, but so as to understand them as perfectly as you can, and above all things that you don't loiter and waste time. When you play,—play,—but when you read, read and don't play. God bless you, my darling boy.

Your ever affectionate father,

T. L.

TO HIS DAUGHTER A —.

I hope you are very attentive, and that you will have your chapter* as well as usual on my return.   Mind

* During our childhood we used to meet together in his study every Sunday, having read and prepared for examination a chapter in one of the four Gospels ; one Sunday he saw me playing about at the time I ought to have been preparing my chapter, and on his remonstrating with me, I said in a very hasty temper, " It is too bad to have all lessons and no play even on Sunday," when he drew me towards him in the most affectionate and patient manner, and said " Do you forget, dear T——, what David says, ' In thy presence is fulness of joy ; at thy right hand are pleasures for evermore.' (Ps. xvi. 11). Now though we cannot while here have this fulness of joy that we shall have hereafter in God's presence, yet, believe me, even in this world, there is no pleasure half so real or so lasting as is to be found in the reading and meditating upon His Word, if we will only receive it, and rest our souls upon it as the word of Him who cannot lie." I fear my reception of his beautiful and affectionate remonstrance could have afforded him but little comfort, as I remember turning away from him certainly more in a sulky than a grateful mood, but the impression was never effaced from my mind. Often and often in after years when I sat down to my Bible, his sweet counsel came back to my recollection with an influence and pleasure which my original reception of it could but little have led the fond and loving counsellor to expect.

whatever your darling mamma and Miss Clarke say to you, and papa will love you always.

And at a subsequent assizes he writes the following letter to be received by his children on Good Friday—

Limerick,
Wednesday.

MY DARLING CHILDREN,—You will receive this letter on the most wonderful day that comes in the course of the whole year, and as God has been good and gracious in affording you this knowledge, I am anxious, if I can, to lead you to spend it as becomes those who know its value. It was on this day that our Saviour, Jesus Christ, died on the cross, to the end, that all who believe on Him should not perish, but have everlasting life. Let us ask ourselves, not giddily, but with thought and seriousness, what could have induced Him to do this for us, or why should God have required it. The answer to the first question is very plain—it could have been only love to man that could have induced Him to leave the glory and happiness He had with the Father, and to take our nature and suffer all He did whilst on earth; but see what ought to be the consequence of this if we have one spark of gratitude in our heart. Ought it not to be as St. Paul says, that we ought not henceforth to live unto ourselves, but unto Him who loved us and gave Himself for us. If you feel it right because your parents are kind and love you, to love them in return, and to study to please them, and to do what they desire (and no doubt it is so), how infinitely

greater is the obligation to Him who laid down His life for
you, who bore to be mocked and tortured and nailed to a
cross that you and I and all who will come to Him may
escape the misery and the torture of hell. But consider
further, and this leads me to answer the second question
—what was the cause of all this? It was sin, and until
we know what sin is, we know nothing. Sin is a worse
disorder of the soul than putrifying sores are to the body;
it is worse to the soul than the most malignant fever to the
body. Sin can no more dwell in the presence of God than
darkness can dwell with light; sin is misery in the end,
and its wages is death,—and even in this life don't we find
that there is no peace to the wicked, but that they are like
the troubled sea, casting up mire and sand. What then
ought we to think—how ought we to feel towards Him
who came to cure the soul of man and to set it free from
the curse of sin. What would you say to the physician
that cured your body and restored you from pain to live
even a few years longer in this poor world? What then
ought to be our thoughts of Jesus Christ who came to
cure our never-dying souls from the disorder of sin, so
terrible in its effects that the language used to express
them is that which describes the most dreadful suffering
we know of—burning by fire. But the worst of sin still
remains to be told—it makes us insensible to itself. It
makes us blind to our own faults, it even makes us fancy
ourselves what we are not, till at length we become, as the
Bible says, dead in sin—that is, as insensible of our sinfulness as a dead body is of feeling. It blinds, it hardens, it
palsies the soul of man. But the blessed Jesus came to
cure this; whilst upon earth He gave sight to the blind,

and feet to the lame, and power to the decrepid and palsied —as a proof that He could and would also cure the like disorders of the soul for all who come to Him with the same faith and trust as these sick people did—of all of whom you may remember it is said that *Jesus seeing their faith healed them.* How then are we to come to Him? By coming to His own Book the Bible—by believing and receiving and thinking often upon what we there read; by having Him always in view, considering whether what we are doing, saying, or thinking would please Him; by praying for His instruction, that He would send His Holy Spirit into our hearts to make us sensible of their sinfulness, to make us hate sin, and desire as the greatest of all blessings to be delivered from it; to feel love and gratitude for all His love and tenderness; to think often what He has done and suffered for us, and to remember every day in the year this wonderful day on which the Son of God died for sinful rebellious man, bore the punishment we deserve, and procured for us the pardon we stood so much in need of, and the life, and joy, and peace for evermore which God alone can give.

May we so receive all His blessings, my darling children, that they may not turn to judgment against us.

Your ever affectionate father,

T. L.

The same simple and heartfelt expression of strong natural affection, and the same tone of earnest piety breathes throughout all his family letters. Many of those written to his wife, when they might fairly be termed 'an old married couple,' seem more like those of a fond and youthful lover, than of a man fully occupied with professional business, and the duties of public life ; while there is at the same time, a pervading tone of practical good sense and Christian sentiment which exhibits the elevated mind and sanctified feelings o the writer.

The following bears the postmark of Waterford July, 1812.

TO HIS WIFE.

I arrived here yesterday about five o'clock from Kilkenny where I completed all my business. It rained in the night, but the day took up about eleven o'clock; and so fresh was the air, so lively and beautiful all the scene from Kilkenny to Ballyheale, that I was quite in a " *Wicklow trance*"* all the way. To see the blessings of heaven so profusely poured out as far as the eye could reach without a single damaged ear of corn after the threatened danger of a famine, with the sun suddenly breaking out and enlivening the whole scene, made me exclaim as I reached the top of one of those fine hills, How excellent are Thy works, O Lord; in wisdom hast Thou made them all. Oh make me to see and feel in this goodly

---

* This was a household word in our family circle from the great admiration he had for the scenery of the County Wicklow where for many years he spent his summer vacations.

scene of joy and gladness the sure pledge of that greater
glory, though yet unseen, which Thou hast prepared for
those that love and serve Thee; and give me in the contemplation of Thy invisible mercies the same delight I
receive in this manifestation of Thy power and goodness.
How I longed to have you with me and all our dear babes
about us, as we had on our last Wicklow excursion. But
a moment's reflection in that mood served to banish all
repinings. If it be necessary that we should be separated
for a while, we are still living together in His presence—
protected by His power, and watched over by His mercy,
whose goodness is over all ; and, I think, our faith and
dependence on Him would be but the profession of our
lips if we suffer ourselves to doubt that in every dispensation which can or may occur, all takes place under His
providence, and that all things work together for good
(that is final real good) for those who love God. It is not
place, or absence, or presence of friends, that does or can
constitute our essential well-being ; and whilst we are
practically and sincerely persuaded of that great truth, we
must and ought to repose with entire confidence on Him
for the safety and protection of those we love—I mean
their safety and protection in every sense in which these
are permitted to be objects of a Christian's desire.

T. L.

TO THE SAME.

Limerick.
Tuesday.

I find it impossible without hurting my poor father's
feelings to leave him to-day, and he has had such a time

of suffering since I came, that it would be cruel to deprive
him of the opportunity which the abatement of his disorder
affords of enjoying my society a little more than he could
hitherto. But he is satisfied at my setting out to-morrow,
so that I shall, please God, be with you to dinner on
Friday. I received my very dear A—'s letter to-day, which
indeed, gave me heartfelt satisfaction, for he has expressed
himself in a manner that shews me he feels unaffectedly
the deep anxiety which dwells in my heart for his eternal
welfare. With the persuasion I entertain of the truth
and reality of a future never-ending state it is impossible,
if I loved our dear children at all, that I could feel less
concern than I do for their condition with respect to it.
If I do not deceive myself very much (and God knows
how possible this is) the most fervent prayer of my heart
in respect to them is, that I may be able to say at the last
day in giving up my charge, "Of them which Thou
gavest me have I lost none." I confess when compared
with this, my anxiety in respect of their worldly welfare
sinks to nothing ; at the same time, that in its proper
place and degree I am sure that both duty and affection
dictate a reasonable share of attention to objects essential
to their welfare and usefulness in this life too ; and the
sweetest reward of all our anxiety is to perceive that it is
felt and acknowledged by those who are its objects. If
ever my darling children should be led to think that I am
unduly anxious about the concerns of a future and distant
state, let them remember that the day and hour must
come when all the power, riches, or influence of the
whole world, could not purchase back one second of mis-
spent time, and that it is solemnly and distinctly told us,

we shall "give an account of every idle word." If this
be true, and is it not as true as every other word of God ?
what can we say for wilfully spending hours and days,
and years, without the wish or effort at anything better
than "idle words," that is, vain and unprofitable topics,
both of thought and conversation, and yet such is the
strain of the world ; I confess I do wish to raise their
minds and affections above this low standard, and to impart to them, if I could, a relish for better things. It is
for this reason that I think it right to be instant in season
and out of season—to reprove, rebuke, exhort—trusting
that in the end it will please God to bless my work with
a rich harvest ; and such truly will it be, to be all gathered in together to his garner—"no wanderer lost—
a family in heaven." May He, in the meantime, be with
us here to guide us, and to guard our steps in His own
ways. With love to all.

T. L.

TO THE SAME.

Nenagh, 15th September.

As no post left this last night I could not give you any
earlier account of our arrival. We had, though a wet
morning, a very pleasant day, and from our very gratifying and I trust profitable conversation and reading we
rejoiced that a post chaise and not the coach, was our
vehicle. Mr. and Mrs. Bennet received us in the most
cordial and friendly manner. I have written to my
County Limerick tenants to meet me in Limerick on
Wednesday, so that I expect to return here on Thursday,

and to be home, please God, either Friday or Saturday. We have been at a retired but beautifully situated country church, where I was more surprised and delighted than I remember to have been for a long time. We had from a coarse, weather-beaten old man, as sound, as affectionate, as earnest, and animating a Gospel sermon as I have almost ever heard—coming evidently from his own heart, and reaching ours. It was delightful to find, from enquiry, how (let the exterior be what it may) divine truth both purifies and softens the heart, for I find that he has been long valued and esteemed as a worthy, excellent man by those around, most of whom neither regarded nor admired him in the pulpit ; but there he stood like a witness in the wilderness, testifying to all the glorious and animating hope which gilds and gladdens his own setting day. His text was, "looking unto Jesus the author and finisher of our faith, who for the joy that was set before Him endured the cross, despising the shame, and is set down at the right hand of the throne of God." May this be the polar star of our course—and the text written upon our hearts until it quickens into life and action. May He, who is the alone author and perfecter of any good, accomplish in all of us this, His greatest blessing, giving us herein pardon, peace, and love.

T. L.

The following extracts from two letters, written to his wife in the year 1813, in relation to a disappointment he had met with, about a matter on which they were both very anxious, exhibit the earnestness of his desire that complete submission to God's will should be made the ruling principle in his own heart, and the hearts of those he loved ; and also the peace of mind which even then he enjoyed from " cherishing the habit "—to use his own words—of following the path of duty and leaving results to God.

TO HIS WIFE.

Waterford, Monday.

. . . . But all things are for the best, and I hope we shall daily learn more and more so to think and feel. We should thus both have more of that perfect peace which they have, whose minds are stayed on God; doing our part we should cherish the habit of being satisfied with the result, casting all our care on Him who careth for us, and knows and designs better things for us than we could do for ourselves. The comfort and security are inexpressible which result from no longer considering ourselves merely as our own, depending on our own puny strength or foresight, but as objects of Almighty care and love. "He that spared not His own Son, but delivered him up for us all, how shall He not with him also freely give us all things ?" This is plainly unanswerable, if we believe the first part; but there is the sticking point of unbelief; we really do not (as we ought) deeply, fully, and without any reserve, believe that amazing truth, that the Great God of the Universe gave the Son of His love to die for man, a poor worm of the earth. If we believed this as we ought, there is nothing too merciful, too tender, to be expected from love like this. This is the great truth which should therefore be ever present to our hearts. This is the bright and morning star, which will light and guide us on our way through this maze of ignorance and sin. The hearty reception and deep persuasion of this is what St. Paul alludes to as the object of his unceasing labour and striving, if he might by any means ' win Christ and be found in him.' From this, as from the sun in the centre of the system, result steadiness in our course, obedience to the laws of our Creator, light to guide us on our way, warmth to cheer and animate our progress, and love and joy and hope to confer all of happiness which the present scene allows. For what reason do I dwell on this? It is, that we may labour whilst we are apart in seeking after the knowledge of our Lord and Saviour Jesus Christ, and praying to be led of God by His Holy Spirit to this knowledge—for thus we shall come together again for good. Thus shall our union be one which will endure when time shall be no more. I wish we may all think deeply and constantly on these things. Words are very light, easily written, easily read, easily forgotten, and we cannot too soon or too young begin the habit of dwelling on their import and full meaning, especially when they are the words of God. I wish my darling children, especially the older ones, would do this; a few sentences, read and reflected on, are more than chapters or volumes hastily and heedlessly gone over. It is with the soul as with the body, the food taken in must be digested in order to profit us.

T. L.

TO THE SAME.

Mountrath, 31st December.

. . . It is well for us we have crosses and perplexities to remind us what is within us still, and to show us how far our wills are from submission to His who (if we would but believe Him) makes all things work together for our good. There is nothing that shews our practical unbelief more than our readiness to repine at the course of events, when they at all thwart our own designs, although we are invited to cast all our cares upon Him who careth for us. If a fellow creature offered to take all trouble off our hands, and to relieve us from all anxiety on the score of success in some great pursuit, how happy, and how disburdened we should feel, and is it because it is our God and Saviour who makes the proposal that we are to be less influenced by it? But the truth is, that we do not give credit to these gracious declarations, we treat the solemn assurances of Him who is not a man that He should lie, as if they were no more than complimentary speeches of one of ourselves. We should be struck dumb with self reproach on this very subject if we were to accustom ourselves to take up some of the tenderest things which God has said to us, and ask ourselves, what credit have I hitherto given to this? how far have I acted as if it were really true? how far do I repose upon it at this moment as if it were a rock which could not be moved? We should find if we were thus to ponder over a single verse, that there is scarcely one of the most gracious promises or assurances of God which He has given us, either by His prophets or by His own Son, which we have not almost overlooked; I mean in respect to any abiding persuasion of their full import and effect.

T. L.

At a later period under still more trying circumstances we find the same yearning after entire
submission to God's will beautifully exhibited in a
letter written during a dangerous illness of one of
his children, which the late Sir Philip Crampton at
first apprehended to be fatal. He and Sir Benjamin Brodie having subsequently met in consultation, they gave an opinion that the malady was not
incurable, though the case was very precarious, and
in reply to the letter announcing this opinion, the
following was written :—

TO HIS WIFE.

Leeson Street, Nov. 18th.

. . . . . I hope that amongst the many mercies
which we have experienced, this trial may prove the
greatest, for it has brought us so nigh to God, and made
us to know what it is really to look to Him as our help
and refuge in time of trouble, and now let us by His
grace improve it by constant and earnest supplication for
submission to His holy will and pleasure in all His dispensations, that we may learn that His love may as well be
shewn in taking away as in giving. I must, however,
say, that neither you nor any of us need be sorry at feeling ever so distressingly our shortcomings in faith or
thankfulness. This is one of the gracious results of all
sanctified affliction,—it works repentance not to be repent-
ed of, but I think you mistake a little the object of the
faith we are now called upon to exercise. It is not that

God will please to grant the desire of our hearts, but that He will do what is best for us, and for the dear object of our prayers, and our most earnest prayer should be that He may subdue our stubborn hearts and wills, so that we may not murmur at whatever He may in His wisdom and His love appoint. I admit this would be an impossibility to accomplish by any effort of our own, but the things that are impossible with man, are possible with God, and I am sure the more we rely on His help, the more surely we shall find it. At the same time, desiring and praying earnestly to be reconciled to His appointments, ought by no means to deprive us of the enjoyment of hope, or lessen our gratitude for every symptom calculated to cheer us during our trial.

T. L.

While the foregoing extracts evince his earnest effort to cultivate the spirit of submission to God's will under all trials, the next extract from a letter giving an account of the grief in which he found Mrs. ———, who had recently lost her husband, no less clearly and instructively exemplifies his views as to the worthlessness of what is called in the world 'natural strength of mind' to sustain the drooping heart in the hour of sorrow, and also as to the blessings which flow from affliction, when sanctified by being made the means of humbling us, and drawing our hearts nearer to God.

TO HIS WIFE.

Castle Connell,
Wednesday.

. . . . . She is a striking instance how utterly inadequate what is called firmness or strength of mind is to contend with affliction. Nothing can do that but what teaches us that it is good for us that we are afflicted, and makes us see through our very heaviest trouble the merciful purpose of Him who makes us perfect by suffering, but who at the same time that He sends the rod, holds out the staff also. There is in true piety a humility of mind, a bowing down of the spirit, an acquiescence in all that comes, as coming from the source of love, which proceeds from faith to patience, from patience to resignation, and from resignation at length kindles into joy, that holy joy which is allied with peace, the joint offspring of that Holy Spirit who alone can bind up the broken heart and pour oil into those wounds which set human consolation at defiance. If, in prosperity, we prepare for trials, we shall never be taken entirely by surprise; and this I believe is another way by which religion makes good its promises of increased comfort, even in this life.

T. L.

In the year 1817, the late Lord De Vesci, one of the most justly valued of our resident proprietors in Ireland, who took a deep interest in the education of the higher class as well as the poor, determined to found a school for the sons of the Irish

nobility and gentry on the same principle as Eton
or Harrow, so far as secular instruction, but in
which religious instruction should be regarded as
an essential element of the education to be given.
He accordingly built a school-house close to his
own country residence, at Abbeyleix, in the
Queen's County, and appointed the present Bishop
of Cashel and Mr. Lefroy as two of the Governors.
They both entered cordially into Lord De Vesci's
benevolent scheme, and were regular in attending
at the visits of inspection for some years.   The
following letters were written on the occasion of
some of those visits.

TO HIS WIFE.

Abbeyleix.
Monday.

As I hope to see you in a few hours after you receive
this, and as I have so much to do, I shall not write you a
very long letter. My journey was extremely pleasant,
the day delightful, and my companion, at least, as much
so.   We found Robert Daly* here; he preached for us
yesterday in his usual excellent style, and has been our
delight and edification as well out of the pulpit as in it.   I
don't think any place could exhibit a more interesting
scene that I saw yesterday, or one upon which the blessing
of God may more surely be expected. Lord De Vesci
sitting here in the midst of the poor children of his estate,

---

* The present Bishop of Cashel.

teaching them and asking them questions in the New Testament with a childlike modesty and simplicity, and with the interest and tenderness of a fond parent. What a blessing to be led into the society and friendship of such men as those who form our party here at present. The edification I receive is not to be told in observing in such men how that religion is not merely knowledge, and how its genuine fruits are to be found in humility, candour, affection, fervent trust and hope in God's grace for all the good we aim at, and yet an active, sober, regular application of all the powers of mind and body to the object to be attained. It sweetens the honey I thus gather to reflect that it may be of use to those from whom I have no separate existence, and cannot bear for a moment to separate myself in imagination for time or eternity. Our Institution holds out great prospects, because good ones, in respect to all that is essential in education; and I trust it will be a blessing and an humble instrument of promoting the cause of true religion.

T. L.

TO HIS WIFE.

Abbeyleix, October 30, 1820.
Sunday.

You won't expect a long letter, both on account of the day and the hour. As no post went last night, I give you a line to say, that we arrived, thank God, safe and well. I have just returned from a Scriptural examination of our thirty-two boys, which I have been at since church and have only time to get ready for dinner. The answering was, in general, very satisfactory, in some instances

E

astonishing. I'll venture to say there are not thirty-two boys taken in any school in Ireland who would have answered so well, or who know so much of Scripture truth; and though it may not yet live in their hearts, I do trust it will in time do so, and make many living monuments of the blessing of God on our endeavours. It is a blessed and delightful work to be engaged for Him and in His name and dependence on His strength. May He be with you as I trust He has been with us to-day.

T. L.

CHAPTER III.

Early abandonment of Circuit from preference for Equity practice—Reports
Lord Redesdale's Judgments—Gratifying circumstances under which
his appointment to the Serjeantcy was made—Letters to his father—
Declines three times a seat on the Judicial Bench.

HE only continued to go Circuit for a few years,
as the practice in a Court of Equity was far more
congenial to his taste, and as he always found
his truest enjoyment in the companionship of his
immediate family circle, the constant separation
which Circuit necessarily caused was irksome to
him. He had a great taste for gardening in early
life, which induced him soon after his marriage to
take a lot of ground in Leeson-street, (then on the
outskirts of Dublin.) On this lot he built the
house which continued to be his town residence
up to his death, enclosing a garden of about half
an English acre ; and here after he gave up going
Circuit, he constantly spent a great part of his
evenings during the spring and summer months in
pruning his fruit trees and other garden work.

I have still vividly before me our whole merry-hearted group—parents and children sallying forth into the garden after dinner, the youngest as well as the oldest taking share in the busy task of weeding borders, watering flowers, cutting shreds, or sitting at his side while he pruned the fruit-trees, and reading the pretty story book which he had bought on his way from Court in order that the evening might not pass without profit as well as pleasure. He soon acquired such a practical knowledge and skill in gardening that he more than once carried off prizes at the Horticultural Shows from the proprietors of all the suburban villas, many of whom were admittedly amongst the first class of practical amateur gardeners.

Soon after Lord Redesdale's appointment as Chancellor of Ireland, Mr. Lefroy was led to undertake the task of reporting the judgments of his Lordship, whose deep research and extensive acquaintance with every branch of law and equity made it a matter of great importance to the profession and the public, that his judgments should be preserved.

To the industry and accuracy of Mr. Lefroy, in conjunction with his friend, John Schoales, Esq., Chairman of the Queen's County, the public are indebted for the valuable collection of cases which has long been received with so much approbation

by the Bench and Bar, as well in Westminster Hall
as in the Courts in Dublin.   In 1816, having then
risen high in practice, he was appointed King's
Counsel.   In 1818 he was appointed King's Serjeant,
and the circumstance under which this appointment took place are so creditable to him as well as
the Irish Government of that day, that they deserve
a brief notice.   It was well known in the profession
that the Lord Lieutenant (Earl Talbot) was pressed
with applications for the vacant Serjeantcy, from
various quarters, by persons of much influence ; but
desirous to give the preference to the strongest professional claims, His Excellency availed himself of
the opportunity of a Privy Council which was
attended by the Chancellor, the Chief Justice, and
the Attorney-General, to ascertain their sentiments.
To them the Lord Lieutenant submitted the names
of the several candidates, and the appointment of
Mr. Lefroy was the result of their unanimous
opinion.

The following letter to his father containing the
intelligence of his appointment, shews the source
to which alone he looked for help and strength to
enable him to fulfil the daily duties of life.

Leeson-street, November 4th, 1818.

My DEAR FATHER,—You will of course be anxious to
know the certainty of the information I gave you in my

letter of yesterday. I saw the Chancellor to day, who saluted me as Mr. Serjeant Lefroy. He also stated to me the very gratifying circumstances under which the appointment took place; with this addition to what I mentioned yesterday, that though the Lord Lieutenant would have been willing to have taken his opinion alone, the Chancellor desired (lest, as he said, it might be supposed that he had any partialities) that the Chief Justice should also be called upon to assist with his advice, and accordingly he and the Attorney-General were of the Council that made the selection, which, I am happy to say, was unanimous. The *principle* of the appointment (whatever may be thought of the *choice*) does the greatest credit to Government, and must operate as the highest encouragement to the straightforward path of duty. I trust that He who has thus led me to honour will sustain me in a firm and constant upright walk—a prayer in which I am sure you will join with all your heart. I have only time to add our love to all.

My dear father's

Ever affectionate and dutiful son,

T. L.

The next letter, evidently written on the occasion of his mother's death, and those which follow, were found with the preceding letter amongst Colonel Lefroy's papers, and testify to the freshness and tenderness of his filial affection, even when the business of professional life and the cares of his own family might well be supposed to

have weakened the ties of earlier years. Nor can
we fail to observe through them the deep anxiety
he felt for his father's progress in spiritual things,
and his joy at seeing the doubts and difficulties,
that had at first obscured the light of the Gospel,
gradually vanishing away and leaving his father in
the enjoyment of that true peace of mind which
he had so long sought for him at the throne of
grace.

TO HIS FATHER.

Leeson-street, 29th, June, 1812.

"I would not have you to be ignorant, brethren, concerning them which are asleep, that ye sorrow not, even
as others which have no hope, for if ye believe that Jesus
died and rose again, even so them also which sleep in
Jesus will God bring with him." (1 Thes. iv. 13, 14.)

This my dearest father, which is our hope, should be
also our consolation and it is vain to seek elsewhere for it.
We must all go down to the grave, therefore to repine
immoderately at what must necessarily happen, and that
without which we cannot pass to glory, honour, and immortality in the life to come, were practically to deny the very
corner-stone and foundation of our best and brightest hopes.
No, let us rather exultingly cry out, "O death, where
is thy sting? O grave, where is thy victory?" Let us
prepare ourselves for the same passage, so as to approach it
with cheerfulness, for this is the glorious privilege of those
whose hearts are set on things above, and I am sure every

hour's experience testifies to us more and more that the things of this earth are but vanity, yielding no solid comfort or peace of mind, and are therefore utterly unworthy of the first place in our regard. Looking therefore, to the only true Source and Fountain of happiness, let us accept all the dispensations which flow from thence, either in respect of ourselves or those we love, as the best and wisest that could happen, and however the broken ties of long attachment may cry out "if it be possible, let this cup pass from me," let us recollect the occasion on which it was added " nevertheless not as I will, but as thou wilt." I should wish very much to be with you on this occasion, and it has cost me great anxiety to determine what was best to be done. Henry's letter by the day coach, which put an end to any further hope, did not come to me until about eight o'clock last night. I had written to you by the post about two hours before in a state of uncertainty, from which you will have collected that I was then ignorant of the event ; even the mail was gone at the time, and that was the only mode which could have afforded me a prospect of being in time to pay the last tribute of respect and affection to my darling mother. . . . .

T. L.

TO THE SAME.

Leeson-street, April 17, 1817.

MY DEAR FATHER,—I send you two vols. of Bishop Horne on the Psalms. The notes are those of a warm-hearted, pious, humble Christain; like all human productions they are unequal, and may not always be appropriate, but they are in general great helps to the spiritual understanding of David's beautiful and inspired compositions, and in the way of occasional reference, you will, I hope, find them agreeable and profitable, and they will lead you to form a good general notion of the spiritual and hidden reference which most of the Psalms have to our Redeemer, but which we are slow at discerning, though, when seen, it gives the Psalms quite a new interest as well as beauty. I have also put up a volume of Dr. Chalmers' Sermons, just come out ; he is the celebrated Scotch Preacher whom all the great officers of State went to hear in London, but this only describes his least recommendation; his greatest is, that his heart is warmed and exalted by the glorious truth which he preaches, and preaches with a force and clearness which fits him to be of great use to us in enabling us distinctly to apprehend the great leading features of the Gospel, as the dispensation by which it has pleased a gracious God to provide for redeeming a sinful world out of the misery as well as the condemnation of sin ; he is an eloquent and to me very interesting writer, and I hope to hear that you relish him; his sermons are confined to the great fundamental topic, the right apprehension of which is essential to understanding the Bible, or reading it either with profit or pleasure. William Hoare* has just called

---

* He alludes to the late Rev. William Deane Hoare, Vicar General of the Diocese of Limerick, for many years eminent as a preacher and laborious minister in the city of Limerick. He was killed by a fall from his gig, and a monument was erected to him in the Cathedral of Limerick by the inhabitants in testimony of their respect and esteem. The following anecdote, which tradition has handed down in the Diocese, bears honorable testimony to his ministerial zeal and services. Bishop Jebb, the learned and eminent theologian, who presided over the Diocese of Limerick during several years

with your letter and the thermometer, which I will get repaired as soon as possible; but his report of his last interview with you has raised the *quicksilver* of my heart, and driven out all the *air bubbles* that disturbed it about you. I trust you will go on increasing in peace and cómfort, and know with all saints the height and depth and length and breadth of the love of God, manifested to us in Christ our Lord and Saviour.

Ever my dearest father's

Affectionate son,

T. L.

TO THE SAME.

Leeson Street, 21st April, 1817.

My dear Father,—I am indeed sincerely grieved to hear of your sufferings since I left you, and I wish with all my heart I could suggest anything for your relief. God grant that Phœbe may be able in her next to give me a better account of your chest and side. I heard yesterday from Robert Daly*—one of our best men and best ministers—a sermon which I often wished you could have heard. It was on that beautiful Psalm (the 23rd), "The Lord is my shepherd, therefore can I lack

of Mr. Hoare's ministry, and who was well known to have a very strong feeling against the Calvinistic school of divinity, was one day discussing with some intimate friends the state of his Diocese, and after enumerating some other men who were carrying on the work of the ministry with earnestness and efficiency, he exclaimed with great warmth, "and there is that little William Hoare, who, though he is such a Calvinist, is worth all the men in my Diocese for work."

* The present Lord Bishop of Cashel.

" nothing. He shall feed me in a green pasture and lead
" me forth beside the waters of comfort." After a very
just and striking view of the extent of human affliction
and observing that there was no promise even to the most
favoured children of God that they should be exempt
from these trials, he called our attention to the promises
of comfort and support under these trials which are given
to all who make the Lord their shepherd, and look to
Him with faith and patience. He introduced those pathetic
and beautiful passages from our Saviour's addresses.
in which He calls himself "our Shepherd" and calls us
His " sheep " and says to Peter "feed my lambs," language which it is impossible to suppose He would ever
have used if He did not mean to excite cordial and confident trust. Daly also observed that the Christian has no
promise of not being exposed to temptation and sin, but
then he has the promise to which David alludes in this
same Psalm, " He shall convert my soul and bring me
" forth in the paths of righteousness for His name's sake.
" Yea though I walk through the valley of the shadow of
" death I will fear no evil, for thou art with me ; thy rod
" and thy staff comfort me." So that though the Christian whilst he has flesh and blood to contend with will
have to struggle against temptation, he has a promise that
that Saviour whom he loves and trusts will by degrees
strengthen his soul so as to make the struggle less, and
will as assuredly in the end procure for him pardon and
peace ; and all He asks is that we should believe in Him.
Even should our faith be not so lively as we could wish
He has compassion on our infirmities, He is touched
with the feeling of them, and for that, as one gracious

purpose, took our nature upon Him.   Be of good cheer
therefore my dearest father, though we are not to put
our trust in princes or in any son of man ; we cannot too
firmly trust to our God and Saviour.   He was under no
necessity to give us the assurance of His love, which He
has done, and why doubt the utmost extent of what He
has promised.

My dearest father's

Ever affectionate son,

T. L.

TO THE SAME.

Leeson-street, no date.

MY DEAR FATHER,—It was a great relief to hear from
Phœbe that you had got some ease when she wrote, which
I trust has continued.   She mentioned to you my intention of going down immediately on the Courts' rising ;
if you wish for my going sooner you need not hesitate in
expressing your wish, as you will thereby afford me a
much greater and more lasting gratification than the
" rascal counters " I should lose.   I hope our friend
William Hoare continues to call upon you, and that you
receive comfort and satisfaction from his visits.

I am every day more and more convinced that the
tendency of all just views of religion is to give peace and
comfort.   The infinite justice of God is tempered by His
infinite love, a love which is shewn to us in a way that
we know not—frequently by great trials and afflictions,
which if taken in this light becomes like the refiner's fire.
How sweetly David calls this to remembrance in the 71st

Psalm: "Oh what great troubles and adversities hast thou showed me ; yea, and broughtest me from the deep of the earth again." But to us this wondrous love is concentrated in the person and character of Christ, and just in proportion as we receive as little children this gift of God, so shall we feel the length and breadth, and depth, and height of His love. When our blessed Lord said, "I am the way ; No man cometh unto the Father, but by me," He said what every faithful follower to this hour has found verified. They all, like Abraham, rejoiced to see his day, and they saw it and were glad. It has pleased God in his wisdom, to make Christ the medium of all gracious designs towards man, and the least He can expect of His creatures is that they shall receive His blessings in the way in which He sees fit to bestow them. In vain shall we expect to find out God, or to partake of the comforts and consolations of His love, but by Him whom He has given as a pledge and messenger of that love. "God so loved the world, that He gave His only begotten Son, that whosoever believeth in Him should not perish, but have everlasting life."

These are plain words, and why should we not accept them, or fear that God is deluding us with what He does not mean ? Let us but trust Him and we shall find in Christ not only pardon, but peace and holiness. Do we desire to be holy and obedient ? The promise is that the believer shall be so. "I will put my law into their hearts, and their sins and iniquities will I remember no more." I am sorry I must stop. Our united love to all.

Ever my dearest father's affect. son,

T. L.

TO THE SAME.

Leeson-street, November 8, 1817.

My dear Father,—I cannot without tears of gratitude
reflect on the marked and gracious dispensations of a
heavenly Father towards you in making your latter days
days of peace and daily increasing comfort, of brighten-
ing prospects and cheering hope—not resting in imagination or conjecture but upon the plain and clear word of
truth.   An excellent friend of mine made me a present
lately, which I have great pleasure in transferring to you,
especially as I am your debtor for so late a one, though of
a different kind.   It is a beautiful hymn, with which, as I
know you have an old relish for a little Latin verse, you
will, if I mistake not, be much pleased.

> Jesu, dulcis memoria
> Dans vera cordis gaudia,
> Sed super mel et omnia
> Ejus dulcis præsentia.
>
> Nil canitur suavius
> Nil auditur jucundius
> Nil cogitatur dulcius
> Quam Jesus, Dei filius.
>
> Jesu, spes penitentibus
> Quam pius es petentibus
> Quam bonus te quærentibus
> Sed quid invenientibus!
>
> Nec lingua valet dicere
> Nec litera exprimere
> Expertus potest credere
> Quid sit Jesum diligere.
>
> Sis, Jesu, nostrum gaudium
> Qui es futurus præmium,
> Sit nostra in te gloria
> Per cuncta semper sæcula.

You perceive, like all versification of the middle ages, or in imitation of it, there is a sort of rythm, but the beauty and simplicity of some of the thoughts, gives it its peculiar charm, added to the sympathy they find in every Christian breast. I called on the Chancellor since my return, for whose kind intentions towards me* I feel deeply indebted, entirely satisfied as I am to be where and what He chooses me to be, in whose hands I wish to place myself, and all that belong to me, without reserve ; you will, I am sure, believe me when I say that so far from having a feeling of regret or disappointment at not getting the Serjeantcy, it is my constant prayer that I may not be lifted up one step higher in this world unless to make more conspicuous my faith and devotion to a crucified Redeemer, and unless He who can do all things thinks fit to strengthen me to encounter the increased temptations which beset higher rank and station. This must be the wish of every man seeking in earnest for a " better city." In the meantime, doing our duty here, let us with contentment and peace of mind leave results in His hands who makes all things work together for good to those who love Him, not the perishable good of this day or to-morrow, but the good which will never fail. Farewell, my dear father, all about me unite in true love and duty.—Your ever affectionate son,

T. L.

---

* He refers here to Lord Manners' recommendation of him in 1817, for the vacant Serjeantcy, then given to Mr. Burton.

TO THE SAME.

Leeson-street, May 5, 1818.

My DEAR FATHER,— . . . It is true I passed by
that part of your former letter which related to my not
going to the Castle, but I deferred answering it only till
I should have time to go fully into the subject. I confess
to you I am afraid to be anywhere where duty does not
call me, especially in scenes where there is a great deal to
excite and inflame the pride of life ; a man has no business to walk in slippery places if he is very anxious not to
fall, and still more if he wishes to guard all those who
are leaning on him from falling. I do not feel that if I
frequented the Castle, and the line of society in which it
would necessarily involve me, that I could consistently or
reasonably expect our children hereafter to keep out of
that mischievous round of worldly and frivolous pleasures
so utterly inconsistent with the sobermindedness and
purity of the Christian character. I see and know how
many men in my own profession have had their sons
ruined, their expectations blasted, and their talents perverted from usefulness by the example and influence of
the society they have been led into by frequenting the
scenes I am afraid to enter into. I do not say that a
Christian cannot or ought not to go to the Castle ; he
may go there or anywhere if his lawful calling and duty
bring him there, but I don't feel that mine do. I went
when it was proper, to return thanks ; and if I should
again have a like occasion to go there, I shall not fear to
go in discharge of duty. These are the short reasons for

my declining to make one of the gay or fashionable world ; not that I dislike gaiety, for in truth I believe I enjoy more of it than those who seek it in these scenes. All at home join in love with my dear father's

Ever affectionate and dutiful son,

T. L.

TO THE SAME.

Newcourt, Bray, August 6, 1818.

MY DEAREST FATHER,— . . . . It has been a great consolation to me to find that you were freed from the pain in your chest under which you were suffering when I left you. I trust, too, your mind has been more free than it was from the perplexities you spoke of, but even these have their use. They try us, and prove us, and serve to show us to ourselves; after we have seen through them our hearts are warmed with gratitude for being delivered from our enemies, for truly these doubts and perplexities which make us dissatisfied with the ways of Him who cannot do wrong, are not only *God's* enemies, but ours, they deprive us of that perfect peace which we have when our minds firmly repose on God, when we do *indeed* (and not merely by constraint) acquiesce in all that He has ordered. One of the great uses of being familiar with the Word of God is to have it ready to give an answer to all these suggestions which our arch-enemy casts as stumbling blocks in our way. The temptation of our Lord and Master was permitted, and recorded, to teach His followers that they must expect the same thing ; and it is very remarkable that every temptation of Satan is repelled by some

F

word of God ; "*It is written,*" says our Lord, and so should
we be prepared to say when doubts arise in our mind.
Thus in answer to all difficulties in the ways of God, it is
written, " Shall not the Judge of all the earth do right?"
" Let God be true, but every man a liar," that is, although
the alternative should be, that if we believe what God has
said, every man must be a liar—even so—we are to believe
the Lord our God.   In truth it will be found that the root
of all our doubts and difficulties is the evil heart of unbelief;
the cordial adoption of that simple, humble principle, that
' God has said it, and therefore it must be right,' would
remove mountains of difficulties, and that is what our
Saviour means by saying that " If ye have faith as a grain
of mustard seed, ye shall say unto this mountain, remove
hence to yonder place, and it shall remove."

My dear father's

Dutiful and affectionate son,

T. L.

Leeson Street, 13th April, 1819.

MY DEAREST FATHER,— . . . I have found some
formidable heaps of papers waiting for me, but I really
care little for the arrear, as I shall set to work with a light
heart. I have left you in peace—such peace as the power
of man could not give, and which is to me, and I trust to
yourself, a consoling pledge that you " have tasted of the
heavenly gift, and are made a partaker of the Holy Ghost
and have tasted the good Word of God and the powers of
the world to come:" and this we have of the grace and
goodness of God through faith in our Lord Jesus Christ.

In Him, through Him, and for His sake, we must seek
and expect everything, and without Him nothing. May
you and I ever be found in this attitude of looking to and
following after Him, as some beautiful lines of a friend of
mine express it:—

> Dear Saviour everywhere I see
> Thy love,—Oh let me follow thee.
> What vain things once were gain to me
>   May I count loss
> And lie in deep humility,
>   Low at thy cross.*

I have no doubt that your comfort and strength will daily
increase. Don't be alarmed or despond because a cloud of
doubt or mistrust may now and again interrupt the sunshine of your peace and joy. This is only one of the
gracious ways our heavenly Father takes to instruct and
confirm His children in drawing nearer to Him, and learning that upon Him they must depend for their daily bread,
that they can only live in the light of His countenance, and
by continual supplies of His grace, and this is really the
only life worth having or seeking, though alas it is
too often our choice to acquiesce patiently in a lower
degree whilst upon earth. May every day that dawns
brighten up the glorious blessed prospect which has now
broken upon you, my dearest father. Keep your eye
upon Him who is "the bright and morning Star," who
came to lighten every man that cometh into the world,
and who will never cast out those who come to Him.

---

* The above lines are part of a favourite ode from which he used constantly to repeat this and other verses with a delight which plainly indi-
cated how accurately they spoke the language of his own heart. The

Don't be afraid to say to Him with Thomas from the bottom of your heart, "My Lord and my God." All about me join in hearty love and good wishes for your health, peace, and comfort in body and soul.

Your affectionate son,

T. L.

author of the ode was the late Mr. Sankey, of the Irish Bar; and as I don't think it was ever before published, I feel assured it will be read with interest by those who have a taste for sacred poetry.

ODE TO MORN.

Sweet Morn, I love thy early beams
Dancing upon the pebbled streams
In fitful intermitting gleams
     Of broken light;
For then my raptured spirit seems
     To take her flight

From scenes of worldly woes and cares
Where Satan high his kingdom rears
To breathe awhile diviner airs
     And purer gales
Where grief no woe-worn bosom tears,
     Nor sin assails.

No passion there with tempest force
Sweeps o'er the soul its headlong course
Nor in conflicting murmurs hoarse
     The billows roar.
Of wild desire and vain remorse
     For sin that's o'er.

Sweet scenes of heavenly peace and rest
How soothing to the troubled breast
That long hath been in anxious quest
     Of happiness;
Yet finds itself still sore opprest
     With heaviness.

Earth beautiful, more beauteous still
Seems to such soul, who drinks her fill
Of gazing on each wood and hill
              That sunny lies
And thinks of Him who at his will
              Bid worlds arise.

On Him she thinks who chased the night,
Who with a word created light ;
And bid yon orb from heaven's height
              Unceasing pour
The splendour of his radiance bright
              In one wide shower.

Tho' passing clouds may veil his face,
They do not, cannot quench his blaze.
So Jesus shines still full of grace
              And healing power,
Tho' doubts their misty vapours raise
              In gloomy hour.

'Tis He, the leafy groves among,
Tunes every feathered warbler's tongue,
Raises aloft the cheerful song
              From thousand throats,
That with the stream gurgling along
              Mingle their notes.

And He, in sweeter symphony,
Draws out pure strains of melody
From souls redeemed, that gratefully
              Unite to sing,
Whether on earth, or whether free,
              Their glorious King.

Dear Saviour everywhere I see
Thy love,—Oh let me follow thee.
What vain things once were gain to me
              May I count loss
And lie in deep humility,
              Low at thy cross.

Let Jesus shine upon that soul,
Away nights' gloomy shadows roll,
The wounded spirit is made whole
              The blind can see;
And he who mourned o'er sins control
              Rejoices free.

On the resignation of Judge Mayne, in 1820, he was offered the vacant seat in the Queen's Bench, by Earl Talbot, but he declined the offer. Again in the following year, on the resignation of Baron George, he was offered the vacant seat on the Exchequer Bench, by the Marquis of Wellesley, who had then succeeded Earl Talbot in the Lord Lieutenancy of Ireland; and in 1823, on the death of Judge Fletcher, he was offered a seat in the Court of Common Pleas, also by the Marquis of Wellesley. There is probably no other instance, either at the English or Irish Bar, of any barrister, not holding the post of a Law officer, having three times declined the honour of a seat on the Bench, but as he was at that time still a young man, and Lord Wellesley's second offer of a Puisne Judge's place was accompanied by the kind declaration of His Excellency's wish to place him in one of the higher judicial offices whenever an opportunity should occur, it is not surprising that he should prefer his position as a leader at the Chancery Bar to the irksome duties of Circuit, which at that period almost always involved the trial of a large number of capital cases.

CHAPTER IV.

In 1822 he goes the Munster Circuit as Judge of Assize—His Charge to
the Grand Jury of Limerick—Letters to his Wife—Again called to go
Circuit as Judge of Assize in 1824—Charge to the Grand Jury of
Limerick—His efforts to promote a sound system of United Education
for the Poor of Ireland—Interest in Religious Societies—Origin of the
Scripture Reader's Society.

In the year 1822, he was called upon, as first
Serjeant, to take the place of one of the Judges on
the Munster Circuit at the Spring Assizes, and it
would be difficult to name a more critical period
than that at which he had, for the first time, to
discharge the arduous duties which the administration of the Criminal law in the South of Ireland at
that time involved. Notwithstanding the apparent
manifestation of loyalty and attachment which was
exhibited to King George IV. during his visit to
Ireland in 1821, he had hardly left the country
and returned to England, when the spirit of outrage
and rebellion broke out afresh, and the disturbances
in the South rose to such an alarming height that the
Ministry thought it necessary to introduce the state
of Ireland into the Speech from the Throne, and to

recommend the enactment of the Insurrection Act,
and the suspension of the Habeas Corpus Act as
the first measures to be considered by Parliament.

When the Special Commission, under the Insurrection Act, opened in Limerick and Cork in the
month of February, 1822, the Calendar of Crime
presented for trial was appalling. The number of
offenders in Cork alone was 366, of whom 35 re-
received sentence of death, and some of them were
ordered for *immediate* execution, others for speedy
execution. With respect to the remainder, Baron
MacClelland, the officiating judge, intimated that
the infliction of the extreme penalty of the law
would be suspended, and that their ultimate punishment would depend on the future conduct of the
peasantry. If tranquillity were restored, and the
surrender of arms in the district became general,
mercy would be extended to them ; but if no sure
signs of returning peace appeared, their doom was
inevitable. Yet, in spite of this warning, the Spring
Assizes, which followed at a short interval, only
presented a further sample of the terrible extent to
which crime prevailed, and the obstinacy with
which outrages of the worst description continued
to be openly perpetrated.

The following extract from the charge delivered
by him to the Grand Jury of the County Limerick
at that time shows how early he saw that the want

of a sound and enlightened system of education for
the lower order of the Irish people was the true
source of the evils of this country, and that unless
this want were supplied, no amount of legislation
in any other direction could allay the feelings of
discontent and hostility to British rule which prevailed throughout a large section of the people, or
rescue us from the disorganized state of society
which was then retarding, and has ever since continued to retard our social, agricultural, and commercial progress. It must now be admitted by all
those who are acquainted with the history of
Ireland during the period which has elapsed since
this charge was delivered that subsequent events
have only too clearly shown the correctness of his
judgment on this important subject, and too fully
verified his prophetic fears as to the hopelessness of
other remedies so long as the real cure for the
disease was neglected.

Extract from the charge of Mr. Serjeant Lefroy to the
   Grand Jury of the County of Limerick at the Spring
   Assizes, 1822.

Mr. Foreman and Gentlemen of the Grand Jury, the
present are times of alarm and danger, in which the unhappy and demoralized state of your county demands
your active service and zeal, so that to the very utmost of
your power your efforts may be applied to suppress in-

surrection and uphold the law. Nothing short of this will
be found sufficient to meet the dangerous and disaffected
state of the country. Your counsels and deliberations
must be founded upon a calm and temperate judgment to
meet the urgency of the times; and to enable you to do
so with hope, you must hold in view the sight of "Him"
who is always present to direct and enlighten the judgment of those who call upon Him in the discharge of
their duties. With respect to the discharge of your
ordinary duties as Grand Jurors, I feel it would be idle to
trouble you with any remarks; your own experience and
ample qualifications are of themselves sufficient to guide
you in the discharge of these duties, and if anything were
wanting to aid you in the way of information, you have
lately had the best assistance from the highest legal
authorities in this country, and the brightest ornaments
on the bench.* But I will claim your indulgence, gentlemen, for a few minutes, while I observe upon the unhappy disturbances which at present disgrace this county,
and in so doing it is my desire to render any assistance I
can to stem the course of the wide-spreading evil to which
I must call your attention.

First, I would observe that I do not feel the present
disturbances can spring from any peculiar temporary
oppression, arising from rents, tithes, or taxes. My
reason for forming this opinion you will find in a short
extract which I will read for you from the Whiteboy Act
of 1776. It was at first only a temporary enactment, but
was afterwards made permanent in the year 1800, and it

---

* Alluding to the Special Commission which had been held under the
Insurrection Act only a few weeks previous to these Assizes.

will be found a good criterion to enable you to judge
whether the present disturbances arise from any temporary grievance, such as I have referred to. [Here the
learned Serjeant read from the 15 & 16 Geo. III., c. 21,
the recital of the then late increase of crimes, familiarly
known as " Whiteboy offences," including the riotous
assembling, by night as well as by day, of men in arms to
attack and injure the persons, habitations, and properties of
the king's loyal and faithful subjects; the carrying away
of their arms, and compelling them to surrender up their
farms; the imposing unlawful oaths, and serving threatening letters.]. I ask you, gentlemen, if the outrages depicted
in this Act, and committed at the distant period of 1776,
are not similar to those we read of in the daily newspapers at the present time. It is clear, therefore, the evil
lies not in any temporary oppression, nor in the exactions
of the landlord or the clergy, the tithe gatherer, or the
tax collector, for these crimes have existed half a century
ago. It has been stated that to an overgrown population
is to be attributed our unhappy and disturbed state; but
let it be considered that these crimes have existed at a
remote period, when the population was not one third of
its present number; the root of the evil, therefore, lies
not in an overgrown population. If, then, the cause of
the present state of society lies not in any temporary
oppression, it may be asked: What is the source of our
present disturbances? To such a question you will
receive an answer in the very form of any of the bills of
indictment for murder, which will go before you. In each
of these bills you will find it stated that the party charged,
not having the fear of God before his eyes, but being in-

stigated by the enemy of God and man, has committed the awful crime of murder.* This, gentlemen, is the foundation of the evil we have to deal with, that our people have not before them the fear of God; for when that salutary fear is cast away, the fear of man is not found effectual to check crime. The next inquiry is, What cure can be applied successfully to the alarming evil? What remedy fit for the disorder is to be administered? You will not find this remedy, gentlemen, in the law passed for the prevention of this class of crimes, for the law has existed and has been duly carried into execution during nearly half a century.

Certain it is that the law may and does in some measure restrain the progress of crime, but it cannot reach the root of the evil or the source of crime. The law cannot change the nature or the habits of men, and our experience of the operation of the law since the year 1776 is demonstrative of this fact. It is no impeachment of the law that the evil has not been eradicated, nor any reason why we should abandon the law, or cease to carry it into execution. So long as men continue to commit crimes, the law must be shown to be supreme, and punishment should follow crime. But whilst we may naturally be indignant at the crimes which now exist, our feelings of humanity

---

* The Form of Indictment for murder at that time ran thus :—

"The Jurors for our Lord the King upon their oath present that A.B., of the parish of C——, in the county of D——, labourer, not having the fear of God before his eyes, but being moved and seduced by the instigation of the devil on the —— day of ——, with force and arms at &c., upon one J. S. in the peace of God and our said Lord the King, then and there being feloniously, wilfully and of his malice aforethought did make an assault, &c."

ought to lead us to find out, if possible, the source of the evil and its remedy, and we are happily not left without the means of doing so, for Scripture teaches us that the source of the evil lies in the absence of the fear of God, and of the influence of true religion, and we have on the same high authority the true and only remedy for the evil in that divine maxim, which should be impressed upon the minds of all—" Train up a child in the way he should go, and when he is old, he will not depart from it." But, gentlemen, woful experience has proved the converse of this great truth, for it is in the way in which they should not go that unhappily the lower orders of the people are too often trained up. To your own experience, gentlemen, I would put the question, 'What sort of training do the lower orders get?' I am bold to say, that if my own children or the children of any of you whom I have the honour to address were so trained, they would probably become the same pests of society. I do not speak of these things theoretically, as I have made the disturbances of this country the frequent subject of my consideration during the last fifteen years, and I give it as my opinion, that until a well-ordered system of education is introduced, not the mere mechanical art of reading and writing, but a system calculated to impress upon the young mind as far as is in the power of man,—to write upon the young heart, the great truths of Christianity—truths which all sects and parties concur in acknowledging; unless such be done, it is idle to hope for peace, loyalty, or tranquillity in this country; society will, as it is doing at present go on from bad to worse. I trust, gentlemen, that you

whom I now address will take this matter seriously to
heart, in pity, at all events to the rising generation, however you may despair of the reform of those who now
seem hardened in crime. I do not mean to dictate to you,
gentlemen, it would not become me to do so from the
place where I now address you; I direct my observations
to you as country gentlemen, and to you who now have
schools on your estates, I would earnestly suggest the
necessity for improving the present system of education,
and no longer allowing the children of the peasantry to
drink of the poison imbibed at the hedge schools, but to
see that they are at least instructed in the fundamental
truths of the Christian religion, which, you must allow me
to remind you, forms a fundamental part of the law of the
land. Without this, gentlemen, I see no means by which
we can look for the fear of God and the principles of
religion having their due influence upon the rising generation, nor do I see any other means of striking at the
root of the evils which now afflict our unhappy country.

I must now apologize, gentlemen of the grand jury,
for the length of time I have occupied you, if any observations have fallen from me worthy of your consideration,
I hope they will operate for the good of my countrymen,
for it is lamentable to observe that from the crimes which
are daily committed, the name of an Irishman has become
an abomination to the civilized world. I trust as soon
as your public business is terminated that you will apply
your minds diligently and anxiously to the cure of the
evil. It is not my intention that any observations of mine
should supersede the important discharge of your present
duty as Grand Jurors; they are only pointed to the dis-

charge of those private duties as men and as Christians, which I would humbly suggest as tending to tranquillize the country more than the most rigorous administration of the law could do, for we might hope thus to eradicate that spirit which is the source of those crimes that disgrace the character of our country."

The two following letters written from that circuit shew the humility of spirit which formed so beautiful a trait in his character, and which, with all the learning and ability he possessed as a great lawyer, still led him ever to seek from his God the help and wisdom needful for the daily duties of life.

TO HIS WIFE.

Limerick, Friday.

Your very welcome, and to my heart most soothing letter just reached me upon leaving court after having discharged the awful duty of passing sentence of death on seven men at once. When I reflect upon the way I have been enabled to go through the duties which have devolved on me, it opens a new source of gratitude to God in the more distinct experience it has given me of the truth of his gracious promise, that according to our day so shall be our strength. Whenever my heart has been cast down I refer to your text, which I keep in the front page of my note-book for each day, and it gives me new strength and courage. I trust the present occasion, though one of much anxiety, will serve to both of us as a

confirmation of our faith, that instead of having vague
notions only of the help and power and grace of God our
Saviour, we shall have the taste and experience of these
blessings. My friend Pennefather has been indeed as
good as his word. He has been a most valuable as well
as friendly brother judge. His sound judgment and great
experience joined to the most perfect cordiality have
afforded me the greatest assistance and comfort, and I
hope you will express to Mrs. Pennefather what I feel on
the subject. Our business was so heavy that it was
impossible to finish, and we have been obliged to adjourn
the Assizes here till after the Cork Assizes. We had a
most hospitable and friendly reception at Tom Lloyd's;
and besides a large party of visitors we had a regular
police guard in the house. We proceed in the morning
to Tralee with the king's troops, police, sheriff, &c., and
we shall, please God, be at our journey's end about five
o'clock.

T. L.

TO THE SAME.

Limerick, 20th April.

We have got through two days of the work of our
adjourned Assizes here; you may judge of what a description it is when I tell you that in that time there
have been *nine* men capitally convicted before me, and
four before Baron Pennefather. I am not without hopes,
working as we do, that we may finish by Saturday night,
or, at all events, very early in the next week. It is a
great comfort to my mind that the counsel for the Crown

and prisoners, as well as the country gentlemen, all express themselves satisfied,—without losing time it has been my wish to exercise the utmost patience, and I have in answer to my constant prayers to be enabled to discharge my duty faithfully, firmly, and yet mercifully, felt a strength both of body and mind, which it would be actual infidelity not to ascribe to Him from whom cometh down every good gift.

T. L.

He was again called to go the Munster Circuit as Judge at the Spring assizes, in 1824, and the following extract presents the important portion of his charge to the Grand Jury of the County Limerick on that occasion, when after calling their attention to the state of the gaols, and to some matters connected with the discipline and health of the prisoners, he continued:—

" And now, Gentlemen, I will advert to the Calendar. I am gratified to find that it contains much fewer numbers than when last I sat here—the number of offences on the present Calendar is 161; the number on the Calendar for the Spring Assizes of 1822, was 243, in addition to which the supplemental Assizes, held the following Christmas, presented a Calendar of 89, making the total number then 332; the aggregate of capital cases at that time was 152; those on the present Calendar are only 112, and the cases which partake of a more aggravated character are only 59. Gentlemen, on the one hand, we have reason to be

pleased with this comparison, especially as I observe that
the chief portion of the crimes appearing on our present
calendar is not of recent date, which I attribute to your
exertions and firmness; but while I congratulate you on the
good effects they have produced, I would be misleading
you, and you would be deceiving yourselves, were you to
suppose this to be anything more than a mere repression of
crime—the spirit from which the great mass of the crimes
which have been committed in your county proceeds is
still alive; and you, Gentlemen, should not relax in the
active and firm yet temperate exercise of those duties
which, as Jurors, as Magistrates, and as resident Gentlemen, you owe to your country. You should also, Gentlemen, turn your attention anxiously to the consideration
of the means necessary to eradicate this spirit, as to the
continuance of which there can be no more striking
evidence than the sad fact that up to this hour, notwithstanding the numerous crimes which have been committed, we find no disposition on the part of the peasantry to give up the delinquents, or surrender the arms
that have been taken from the loyal and well-conducted
inhabitants of your county.

Let us compare the state of Ireland with that of
Great Britain, and how painful is the contrast. When
a murder is committed in England, the whole mass of
the people appear unanimously to feel a shock, a sensation of horror which impels them to assist in the discovery of the murderer. Here the blood-stain of murder
excites no feeling but one,—the murderer is protected,
or if discovered, the witnesses against him are hunted
down. In England, the murderer endeavours to post-

pone his trial, feeling it difficult to find even amongst
the lowest description of farmers, a Jury not tinged
with the prejudices against him ; here, not a finger is
raised, not a word or hint given to lead to the apprehension of the foulest criminal. This, Gentlemen,
is indeed a melancholy contrast. Neither can I avoid
noticing another circumstance by which the distinctive
features of character in the two countries are painfully
marked,—I mean the frequent examples we have of the
little regard which is paid to the solemn obligation of an
oath, demonstrating a want of all moral sense of shame,
or even a knowledge of the distinction between right and
wrong; proceeding in several cases, I admit, from an
ignorance that should excite, not our indignation, but our
compassion. To remedy these great evils, Gentlemen,
there are two means at your disposal. Firstly, to carry out
with moderation and firmness the preventive measures
which the Legislature has enacted for checking the
progress of crime, and punishing the idle and disorderly
members of the adult population, who encourage and
promote those crimes and outrages by which your county
is disgraced. Secondly, to endeavour to instruct the
rising generation, not by letters alone, but really to
educate them by influencing their minds, moulding their
habits, forming their principles, and training their
faculties.

Believe me, Gentlemen, this and this only can ever form
a solid groundwork for the improvement of our social
and moral condition in this country. I have now only to
add in connection with the subject of education that I have
it in command from His Majesty's Government, to impress

upon you the necessity of attending to your Diocesan
Schools.　On this head, it is gratifying to find that £1400
has been presented—but I also learn, that this sum has not
been applied, owing to some failure on the part of the City.
In this case, gentlemen, you will do well to enquire why
the former presentment has not been acted on, and if
necessary to present a further sum.　Before I conclude, it is
well that I should remind you that so far back as the reign
of Queen Elizabeth* an Act was passed to compel the
building of Diocesan Schools in each county, in order to
bring rude and ignorant people to obey the laws of God

---

* The Act here referred to is the 12 Eliz. c. i. (Ir.) which in quaint but
significant and accurate terms assigns the lawless and uncivilized state of
our unhappy country to its true cause :—viz. The ignorance of the Holy
Scriptures in which the greatest number of the people live, and their not
understanding that God's divine law has forbidden the heinous offences
which they are daily perpetrating.

An Act for the erection of Free Schools.

" Forasmuch as the greatest number of the people of this your Majesty's
realm hath of long time lived in rude and barbarous states, not understanding that Almighty God hath by His divine laws forbidden the manifold
and heinous offences which they spare not daily and hourly to commit and
perpetrate ; nor that He hath by His Holy Scriptures commanded a due
and humble obedience from the people to their Princes and Rulers ; whose
ignorance in these so high points touching their damnation proceedeth
only of lack of good bringing up of the youth of this realm either in
public or private schools, where through good discipline they might be
taught to avoid these loathsome and horrible errors, may it therefore please
your most excellent Majesty, that it be enacted, and be it enacted by
your Highness with the assent of the Lords Spiritual and Temporal and
the Commons in this present Parliament assembled and by the authority
of the same, That there shall be from henceforth a Free School within
every diocese of this realm of Ireland and that the Schoolmaster shall be
an Englishman, or of the English birth of this realm." This Act enacted
that the Schoolhouses should be erected at the cost and charges of the
whole Diocese, but by subsequent Acts Grand Juries were obliged to provide by Presentment for the cost of building the Schoolhouses.

and man, and to make them familiar with the English language in which these laws are written. Yet it is sad to be obliged to say that such is the rude and lawless state of your county at the present time, that one might suppose this Act was passed to meet the wants of our own day instead of those of two centuries past. Had this Act been properly carried into effect we should not now be suffering from the neglect of our ancestors, but I trust that at all events from the errors of the past we may have wisdom to learn a lesson for the future."

He went the Munster Circuit again as Judge at the Summer Assizes in 1825, and the next letter, though not bearing any date, evidently refers to that Circuit.

TO HIS WIFE.

John Bennet's, near Nenagh, Sunday Evening.

Here I am, thank God, quietly enjoying a day of real rest and peace,—all my labours and anxieties ended, and I have experienced nothing but unaffected kindness and respect throughout the whole of the Circuit. I finished on Friday, about half-past four o'clock, and had the honour of being presented at the close of the business in Cork with my Freedom for the city, in a very handsome silver box. It was presented to me on the bench, and in very complimentary terms, so you see I finished my course with honour. Baron Pennefather had a few hours' work for Saturday, and meant to spend another Sunday at the High Sheriff's, but I should be sorry to exchange for it my present peaceful retreat. I

came to Mallow on Friday evening to sleep, break-
fasted yesterday at Charleville, where my western tenants
met me with full pockets. I then came on to Kilmallock,
where I was met by those in that neighbourhood and the
Fanstown tenants, who all behaved as well as possible,
and paid their rents cheerfully. The state of the country
as appeared from our Circuit business, as well as from
every other symptom, is most encouraging, and some of
the measures which have been lately adopted, have succeeded beyond all expectation; I allude to the establishment of the Constabulary Force and the improvement of
the Magistracy. I hope my dear namesake is not forgetting his October Examination; every hour he labours now
is an advance in preparing him for those duties honourable to himself and useful to the public, in which I hope
to see him engaged hereafter, and I can tell him that the
present exercise of his mind and the formation now of
habits of close application is the way to fit him for usefulness and distinction in future life. May God bless
you all, my darling earthly treasures, and may he make
us all sensible of the value of having the Lord for our
God—no imaginary God, but He who has made Himself
known to us in His Word and by His dear Son,—all others
are but idols, and as John says, so say I, " Little children,
keep yourselves from idols."—1 John v. 21.

T. L.

In the years 1827, 1828, and 1829, he was
again called on to take the place of one of the
Judges on Circuit. At the Summer Assizes, in
1829, he went the North-east Circuit, and his letters

describing the *tour of pleasure* which the latter
circuit afforded, when compared with his letters
from the Munster Circuit in 1822, already given,
present a striking proof of the contrast between
the state of crime in the North and South of
Ireland.

About this period we trace his name in connexion with almost all the important religious
and charitable societies in Ireland. He took a
deep interest in the " Society for promoting the
Education of the Poor of Ireland," commonly
known as the Kildare-place Society, which was
established in 1811. It was the first effort to
extend the benefits of a sound united Education to
the children of the poor in Ireland, and the leading
principle laid down in its fundamental rules was to
afford the same advantages for Education to all
classes of professing Christians, without interfering
with the peculiar religious opinions of any.
None of the scholars except those who were
members of the Established Church were required
to learn the Church Catechism or Church Formularies, and the object of the benevolent promoters
was distinctly set forth to be " the establishment
of schools wherein the poor might be instructed in
reading, writing, and arithmetic, on a cheap and
expeditious plan, where the appointment of governors, teachers, and scholars should be uninfluenced

by sectarian distinctions, and in which the Scriptures, without note or comment, should be used to the exclusion of all catechisms and books of religious controversy." Lord Fingall, a leading Roman Catholic nobleman in Ireland, was Vice-President of the Society, and on its Committee were members of the Established Church, Protestant Dissenters, and Roman Catholics, all cordially co-operating in the effort to substitute for the wretched kind of Education carried on in the Hedge-schools of Ireland, a more enlightened system based upon liberal principles.

He was also one of the original Committee appointed at the formation of the Hibernian Church Missionary Society, founded in 1814, and was made a Vice-President in 1822. In the same year his name appears as a Vice-President of the Hibernian Bible Society, and he acted on the Committee from its formation in 1813. Again, we find his name as Life Member of the Sunday School Society, and as Life Member and Vice-President of the Irish Auxiliary to the Society for promoting Christianity amongst the Jews, and also of the Society "for promoting the Scriptural Instruction of Irish Roman Catholics through the medium of their own language," familiarly known as the Irish Society, on the Committee of which he acted from the time of its formation in 1818.

From the year 1813 to 1828 we find him amongst
those who took an active part in the well-known
anniversary meetings of religious and charitable
societies held at the Rotundo, in Dublin ; and his
appearance on the platform was always a signal for
the applause which amply marked the respect in
which he was held, coming, as it was well-known,
not for the sake of personal display, or to fill up a
vacant leisure hour, but hastening from the scene
of his professional labours to give the aid of his
powerful advocacy to the still nobler cause of promoting Christianity at home and abroad. The
Society which most of all enlisted his sympathy
was, The Scripture Readers' Society.

An interesting paper appeared in the " Christian
Examiner"for the month of December, 1853, written
by the late Mr. Henry Monck Mason, whose zeal
and labours in the cause of truth are familiar to
all acquainted with missionary work in Ireland,
and after an account of the efforts made by some
earnest Christians in Dublin in the winter of 1821,
for the spiritual instruction of Roman Catholics, by
sending among them missionaries of a humble
grade. We find the following particulars of the
origin of the Scripture Readers' Society:—

" Thynne, a converted Romanist, who had been sent to
Galway as a missionary, returned, and put into our hands

a deeply interesting journal of the events that occurred during his visit to that town. The present Lord Chief Justice Lefroy, who had contributed towards the expenses of Thynne's mission, perused it with much interest, and in the April following, this eminent and Christian lawyer (at that time a Serjeant and acting as Judge on the Munster Circuit) wrote a letter in the midst of his important occupations, to Viscount Powerscourt, expressing deep Christian feelings towards the misguided and ignorant Roman Catholics with whom he came daily into contact. He felt that the call was imperative for some strenuous effort for their conversion, through the medium of Missionaries or Scripture Readers, adding, that if a Society were formed to promote this object, he would assist it with all his influence, and contribute in the first instance £1000. I was present when the letter was received by Lord Powerscourt, who was at that time presiding at one of the annual Easter Meetings in the Rotundo. He mentioned the subject to several who were on the platform, and invited us to meet when our present business should be over. Amongst these were the Rev. Charles Simeon, of Cambridge, and the Rev. William Marsh, of Colchester,* who were then in Dublin

---

* In the " life of the Rev. W. Marsh " lately published by his daughter we find the following incident given, which occurred shortly before his visit to Ireland on this occasion, and appears to have been the means of greatly deepening his interest in the Jewish cause about this time. "He was staying in London for a few days, when his friend Mr. Simeon, sent for him. 'I am advertised' said Mr. Simeon 'to preach for the Jews' Society, and now I am too ill to leave my bed, would you go for me'? 'Gladly if I knew more of the subject. But although I have subscribed to that Society from the first and like the object, I know too little about it to undertake to preach for it the day after to-morrow.' 'Have you a grain of humility? if you

as a deputation to the Annual Meeting of the Jews' Society. When assembled, Lord Powerscourt read to us the letter he had received from Serjeant Lefroy, and said, that were the projected scheme followed up he would add to Serjeant Lefroy's one thousand pounds, two thousand pounds more. The subscription was soon raised to near £4000 by Judge Daly and several others. A Society was immediately formed for the sending forth of Scripture Readers. A Committee was appointed, and Serjeant Lefroy was chosen Honorary Secretary. This Committee went almost immediately to work, and before a month passed we sent forth three Readers, who were faithful and successful ministers for Christ; and thus was laid the foundation of that valuable Society, which has been now for almost thirty years in most efficient operation."

have, you will preach my sermon!' Mr. Marsh laughed, and said, 'If that be the criterion, I think I have.' On his arrival at Stroud, late on Saturday evening, the portmanteau in which the manuscript of Mr. Simeon's Sermon had been packed, was discovered to be missing. Driven by this accident to give his own thoughts from the pulpit, he spent several hours that night in prayerfully searching the prophecies concerning the Jews, and ended by writing a running commentary on ROM. XI. Just before the Service began on the following morning, a waiter from the Hotel came to the Vestry door, to say that the portmanteau had arrived. "Shall I fetch the Sermon?" asked a lay Secretary of the Society who was aware of the dilemma. "No!" said Mr. Marsh, "Mr. Simeon is not to preach to-day; and I am not to preach; St Paul is to preach!" The Society was the richer for that Sermon, and incalculably the richer for the intense interest awakened in Mr. Marsh's mind by those hours of deep study of the Word of God touching the chosen nation, the present duties of Christians towards them, and the glorious hopes for their future. From that hour he devoted himself with the tranquil and enduring enthusiasm of his nature to the cause of the Society, and to the temporal and spiritual welfare of the Jews.

The original draft of the fundamental rules of the Scripture Readers' Society was found in Mr. Lefroy's own handwriting amongst his papers, with the following endorsement :—" I went the Munster Circuit for the first time as Judge of Assize in the spring of 1822, and the number of capital-cases I had to try of course brought forcibly before me the demoralized state of the population. I wrote to Lord Powerscourt (knowing his Christian zeal), proposing to establish a Society for sending Scripture Readers amongst them, and offering £1000, to which he sent the answer within, and put down his name for double that sum. On my return to Dublin the Society was formed—see prospectus within. I make this memorandum with a gratifying recollection, no doubt, of the share I took in it, but with an humbling and thankful sense of the certainty that it was not of my own heart it proceeded or was carried forward, but of Him, who alone worketh in us to will and to do."

The following is the answer of Lord Powerscourt referred to in the above memorandum :—

Dublin, April 20, 1822.

My dear Serjeant,—I did not receive your letter till yesterday evening, from its being directed to Ely Place, but I lost no time in doing my best on the occasion. I had been thinking of doing something myself, but my thoughts would never have ripened into action if you had not written. I went to-day to George's Church, to hear Simeon preach for the Jews' Society, and such a sermon I never heard, nor any even like it, on Rom. xi. 22-24. I had in the Vestry-room told your plan to such as you desired me, those whom I considered to have a single eye to God's glory, and we met immediately after the Sermon at Matthias's* house. I had previously read your letter to Simeon and Marsh, who both approved of its contents. I send you a list of the people present at Matthias's. They all agreed in the necessity of the thing, and consented to put their names down for money, except ———. We have appointed a provisional Committee, and agreed to meet again when you come to Dublin, to settle particulars. Will you appoint as early a day as you can. You see I have backed you up. May the Lord bless our endeavours, and give us a single eye to His service. I feel for your painful work on Circuit, but I am glad it was the Lord's will that you should be sent for that duty.

Believe me, my dear Mr. Lefroy,

Most truly and sincerely yours,

POWERSCOURT.

---

* The Rev. W. B. Matthias, a highly gifted and popular preacher, was for many years the valued Minister of Bethesda Chapel. It was frequented by most of the noble families and persons of distinction, who visited or resided in Dublin, but was suffered to remain a Conventicle until Dr. Magee became Archbishop of Dublin. His Grace licensed the Chapel in 1828, and relieved its valued and excellent minister from the unpleasant position of carrying on his ministry irregularly as a clergyman of the Church. Brookes, in his Gazetteer, when enumerating the places of worship in Dublin, mentions Bethesda Chapel as the "Cathedral of Methodism."

In the Memoir of the Rev. Charles Simeon, edited by the Rev. William Carus, the following letter appears, written to a friend, immediately on his return to England, and giving an account of the impressions left on the mind of this eminent man by his visit to Ireland on this occasion.

TO THE REV. T. THOMASON.

Oxford, April 26, 1822.

" I am now on my return from Ireland, whither I have been with my dear friend, Mr. Marsh—he for the Gentiles, and I for the Jews. . . . You will wish to hear of my motions now in my climacteric, more especially as my dial has been ' put back ten degrees.' Some of the Prelates of Ireland have withdrawn, and others with them, from the Bible Society and all the religious societies. It appeared to me, therefore, that through the Divine blessing, I might do good by going there. The bugbear in their minds is Calvinism, by which they designate all vital religion. You well know that though strongly Calvinistic in some respects, I am as strongly Arminian in others. I am free from all the trammels of human systems, and can pronounce every part of God's blessed word, *ore rotundo*, mincing nothing, and fearing nothing. Perhaps, too, I may say, that from having published sixteen volumes, and preached for forty years at Cambridge, I may be supposed to give a pretty just picture of the state of evangelical religion, such as it really is. On this account I hoped, that however insignificant in myself, I might be an instrument of good; more

especially, because in the last year I sent to every prelate
there my Sermons on the Conversion of the Jews. It happened, too, that they were anxious to have me to come over
thither: and that Mr. Marsh was actually engaged to go
for the Church Missionary Society. With joy, therefore, I accepted the invitation, being myself most willing
to go; and accordingly I proceeded with Mr. Marsh, on
Monday, April 8th, and got to Holyhead on Thursday,
and we reached our destined home, in good health and
spirits, on the Saturday afternoon.

No sooner were we arrived than Irish hospitality
evinced itself in an extraordinary degree. You, who
know the precise line in which I walk at Cambridge, will
be astonished, as I myself was, to find earls and viscounts,
deans and dignitaries, judges, &c., calling upon me, and
bishops desirous to see me. Invitations to dinner were
numerous from different quarters: one had been sent
even to London, and Cambridge, to engage us to dinner
on the Bible day. But let me enter on what will appear
yet more extraordinary on the other hand. The Archbishop—understanding that foreigners were invited to
preach in Dublin—had said that he had no objection to
Mr. Marsh or myself, but that he expected the minister
to adhere to the canon, which required the exhibition of
our letters of orders, previous to our admission to any
pulpit in his province. Information respecting this had
been sent us, and we came prepared; and the church-
wardens were summoned to the vestry to record and
attest the exhibition of them.

In the morning of the next day I preached at St.
George's Church, to a congregation of twelve hundred, a

kind of preparatory sermon for the Jews; and God seemed
to be.manifestly present with us. In the evening I preached
at a smaller Church in the outskirts of the city; and we had
reason to hope that the word did not go forth in vain. On
the next day (Monday) I dined at the Countess of Westmeath's, and met Judge Daly, and many other characters
of the highest respectability. Tuesday was the Jews'
Society-day. This Society in Ireland takes the lead, and
is carried on with surprising spirit. Their Committee
meets every Monday morning; and they give themselves
to prayer as well as to the ministry of the various offices
that are called for.

The Archbishop of Tuam was in the Chair: we met in
the Rotundo. It is, however, ill-adapted for speaking.
The windows were open on both sides, so that the voice
was carried out by the wind, and those in front could
not hear; I did my best, however, but not without suffering for it for two or three days. They looked to me as
the representative of the Society, and therefore I felt
bound to exert myself to the utmost. It was altogether
a very interesting meeting. The Bible Meeting was the
next day. The Archbishop again was in the Chair,
and his Address was the finest thing I ever heard.
Some of the other Prelates had withdrawn their names
from the Society; the Archbishop of Tuam therefore
stood on very delicate ground. This he stated, but
observed that as they had not declared their reasons
for withdrawing, and he could discover none himself, he
must continue to uphold it. He spoke with a dignity
suited to his rank, yet with the dignity of his Divine
Master. Perhaps Paul before Festus will give you the

best idea of his whole action, spirit, and deportment. I
doubt not but that he will hear of that speech at the day
of judgment. After the reading of the Report I left the
Assembly, for after the exertions of the preceding day I
greatly needed rest. Thursday was the Meeting of the
School Society; that was in a smaller room, and Earl
Roden in the Chair. It was a most delightful meeting;
and my dear fellow-traveller, Mr. Marsh, produced a vast
sensation, as indeed he generally does; such a playful
suavity as his I never heard, on the Friday, at the Church
Mission Society ; the Archbishop of Tuam again presided.
If I could have accepted of all the invitations they would
have lasted almost to this time. On Saturday I preached
my Jewish Sermon to a good congregation, who collected
£114, and my Sermon is printing there; and as I preached
it three days ago before the University of Cambridge, it
is printing here also at Cambridge, where I am finishing
this letter. I will send you a copy. In the note* you will
see perhaps a harder blow at Calvinism, as an exclusive
system, than it has ever yet received. It has been
assaulted severely by enemies, times without number, but
here it is wounded by a friend; and I hope the blow will

---

* The note referred to by Mr. Simeon is the following:—

It is worthy of remark, that whilst Calvinists complain of Arminians as
unfair and unscriptural, in denying personal, though they admit national,
election, they themselves are equally unfair and unscriptural, in denying
the danger of personal apostasy, whilst they admit it in reference to
churches and nations. It is lamentable to see the plain statements of
Scripture so unwarrantably set aside for the maintaining of human
systems. Happy would it be for the Church if these distinctions were
buried by the consent of all parties, and the declarations of Holy Writ
were adhered to by all, without prejudice or partiality !

"The Author's views of this subject are simply these. All good is from

be felt to the restraining of its friends and the reconciling of its enemies to my views.

I believe in final perseverance as much as any of them, but not in the way that others do. God's purpose shall stand, but our liability to fall and perish is precisely the same as ever it was; our security as far as it relates to Him consists in faith; and as far as it relates to ourselves it consists in fear.

But I see that if I go on my paper will not hold half that I have to say, let it suffice therefore to add, that as I was not expected in other parts of Ireland I went no further, but returned on the following Monday to Holyhead.

C. S.

God, dispensed by Him in a way of sovereignty, according to the counsels of His own will, and to the praise of the glory of His grace. All evil, whether moral or penal, is from man; the moral, as resulting from his own free choice; the penal, as the first and necessary consequence of his sins. The Author has no doubt but that there is in God's blessed Word a system; but it is a far broader system than either Calvinists or Arminians admit. His views of that system may be seen in the Preface to this Work."

CHAPTER V.

Requisition to stand for the Representation of the University—Refuses at
first—Reasons for subsequent compliance—Accession of the Duke
of Wellington to Political Power—Roman Catholic Emancipation—
Speech at the Brunswick Club—Resignation of the Serjeantcy.

MR. LEFROY was first induced to enter into the
arena of politics on the occasion of the vacancy
which occurred in the representation of the University of Dublin, by the promotion of the Right
Hon. William Conyngham Plunket to the Chief
Justiceship of the Common Pleas in Ireland. Mr.
Plunket's great talents and eminence in the House
of Commons had long secured to him the support
of that learned constituency, though he was opposed
to many of them in his views of the momentous
question of Roman Catholic Emancipation.

On his retirement from Parliament, the electors of
the University felt anxious to obtain a representative
whose opinions were more in unison with their
own. That their attention should be pointed to
Mr. Lefroy was natural. The reputation of his
distinguished University course, his professional

II 2

success, his political principles, and his private
character, all tended to mark him as the fitting
object of their choice, and soon led to his receiving
a numerously signed requisition to become a candidate.   Mr. Lefroy's tastes and pursuits, his ardent
devotion to his profession, and the deep tone of
religious feeling which had connected him with the
working of so many important religious and charitable institutions in Ireland, led him to look with
extreme reluctance to entering into the turmoil of
political life.   He therefore at first refused to comply with the requisition, but the importance of
obtaining the representation of the University for
the Conservative party being strongly urged by
Lord Manners, Archbishop Magee, Mr. Saurin and
others, whose judgment had great weight with him,
he felt it a duty to sacrifice his own inclination on
the subject.   It was manifest that a canvass, commenced within a few days of the approaching
Election, when so many of the constituents were
already pledged to his opponent,* could not be
successful, but he consented to go forward, as it
was considered desirable that those who wished to
range themselves under the Conservative banner
should have an opportunity of placing their votes
on record, as tending better to secure the represen-

---

* The Right Hon. John Wilson Croker.

tation of the University to the Conservative party at the next election.

It would be difficult to overrate the importance of that chapter of England's political history which opens with this period, whether we regard it as the epoch of that great change which deprived the British Constitution of its essentially Protestant character, by the admission of Roman Catholics to sit in Parliament ; or of that complete revolution in our system of Parliamentary representation which immediately followed the measure of " Catholic Emancipation," the results of which can hardly be looked on as even yet entirely developed.

After Mr. Canning's death in August, 1827, the motley party of his followers, which had only been kept together by his splendid talents, soon fell to pieces. Lord Goderich formed a feeble administration, which only lasted for five months ; its struggles for existence were brought to a close in January, 1828, when the Duke of Wellington, called for by the Sovereign and by the public voice, in obedience to that call, undertook the arduous task of forming a ministry, and Mr. Peel became Secretary of State for the Home Department ; but instead of remaining true to the principles upon which, up to that time, they had acted with reference to the Roman Catholic question, instead of putting down by law the Roman Catholic Association, which had been

declared illegal, and at the same time applying the
energies of Government to improve the social and
material condition of the people of Ireland, the
ministers seemed to be wholly dismayed by the
violent and rebellious attitude which the agitators
in Ireland had assumed, as well as by the conduct
of their opponents in Parliament.

Many of the ablest debaters on the opposition
benches of the House of Commons, while they professed their resolution to support the Established
Church in Ireland, and to maintain the Union,
were yet by their conduct and speeches, furthering
the views of those very agitators, who did not
even affect to dissemble that they demanded what
they called Emancipation, as a preliminary step
towards the overthrow of the Church and the
dismemberment of the Empire.

Ministers saw, or fancied they saw, that the
passing of the Emancipation Bill could no longer
be resisted with success, and instead of resigning
office and casting the responsibility of passing that
measure upon the party by whom it had been so
long advocated, they took that responsibility upon
themselves. It would be difficult to convey any
idea of the sudden dismay and total disruption of
party ties which the course thus adopted produced
at the time, but even now after so long an interval,
and looking back, as we can do, at the events of

that period rather as matters of history than with any party bias, no dispassionate mind can entertain any other feeling than of deep regret at the step then taken by the Conservative Ministry. Had the Emancipation Bill been passed by the great and able men who had long consistently advocated the Roman Catholic claims, the fundamental change in the British Constitution, which was produced by the measure, would, no doubt, have been the same ; and looking at its results, as we now do, in the light which subsequent events have cast upon them, we might wonder at the delusion, and the strange forgetfulness of past history, which could have led such men as Earl Grey, Lord Plunket, Lord Brougham and Mr. Canning, to entertain the idle hopes or hazard the statements with which the speeches of those statesmen at that period abound.*

---

* Extract from Mr. Plunket's speech in the House of Commons on motion for a Committee on the Roman Catholic claims. 28th February 1821.

"We come forward with no attack on constituted authority, no quarrel with existing establishments, ... but an unanimous body, consisting of millions of the king's liege subjects, come before Parliament . . . . petitioning to be admitted to the privileges enjoyed by their ancestors, in order that they and their posterity may enjoy and exercise them, in cordial support of all the Establishments, of all the lawful authorities of the State, according to the well-known principles, and the sound, tried, practical doctrines of the Constitution.   .   .   .   .   .

"I know that there are many persons most worthy, respectable, and liberal, who are quite alive and friendly to the claims of the Roman Catholics, but who, at the same time, have serious apprehensions that the removal of their disabilities might endanger our Establishments in

But however we might have wondered at the delusive grounds on which so important a change in the Constitution was advocated by statesmen of such ability, such experience, and such supposed fore-

Church and State. Could I believe that the measures of redress involved consequences of injury or of danger to these Establishments ; dear to my heart as I hold the interests of my Roman Catholic countrymen, I should abandon their long asserted claims, and range myself with their opponents. . . . . But on behalf of the Roman Catholics, I am bold to say, that though they prefer their own religion to ours, yet that any well-informed Roman Catholic considers the possessions of the Protestant clergy as their absolute property, secured to them as sacredly as the private possessions of any individual are secured to him ; that he abides by the oath which he has taken to maintain that [the Church] Establishment, and that, so far from considering himself under any obligation to subvert it, he holds himself obliged, by the most solemn ties which can bind him to society, as a man, a citizen, and a Christian, to resist all attempts at its overthrow, from whatever quarter they may proceed.—*Life and Speeches of Lord Plunket,* vol. ii., p. 24, *et seq.*

Extract from the Right Hon. G. Canning's speech on the Roman Catholic Relief Bill, introduced by Sir Francis Burdett in 1825.

"This Bill does not tend, as some imagine, to equalize all religions in the State, but only to equalize all the dissenting sects of religion. I am— and this Bill is—for a predominant Established Church, and I would not even in appearance meddle with the laws which secure that predominance to the Church of England. I will not sanction any measure which even by inference could be shown to be hostile to that Establishment."— *Hansard's Parl. Rep.* vol. xiii., N. S. p. 86.

Extract from Mr. Brougham's speech in same debate.

"Grant Catholic Emancipation to the people of Ireland and it will allay all dissensions and disturbances. It will give us their hearts, and in giving us their hearts it will secure our dominion over them, so that a world in arms will not be able to wrest Ireland from us.—*Id.* p. 335.

Extract from Earl Grey's speech on Roman Catholic Emancipation, 4th April, 1829.

"I am myself a member of the Established Church, and I am sincerely attached to it, because I am a firm believer in the superior purity of its

sight, the country would at all events have been spared the evils necessarily flowing from the course adopted by the ministers then in office in taking

religious doctrines, but I am thoroughly convinced that the measure now in progress will not affect the security of the Established Church. It is on the contrary my sincere conviction, that when this Bill shall have been passed into a law the true securities of the Established Church will be greatly strengthened. . . . . Take away the laws of exclusion and you will remove the cause which shuts the ears of the people against its doctrines, and makes them regard it with ill-will and resentment, as creating and maintaining the disabilities under which they suffer. . . . Carry this measure and I have a confident belief that the Protestant Church of Ireland will gain increased influence and security ; defeat it, and my belief is as strong, that its subversion is nearly certain.—*Id.* vol. xxi. N. S. p. 311, *et seq.*

Extract from Lord Plunket's speech in the House of Lords on the Emancipation Bill, 4 April, 1829.

" An honest Roman Catholic cannot choose whether there shall be a Protestant Establishment or not. That is not the question which an honest man asks himself. What an honest Catholic says is, ' I find the Protestant Church Establishment a part of the State for these three hundred years. It has imbedded itself in the Constitution, and is so amalgamated with it, that it cannot be overturned without overturning the State itself, and all the valuable privileges, rights, properties and liberties which we enjoy, and which we expect our family and posterity to enjoy under it. The English Church Establishment is intimately connected and bound up with the Established Church of Ireland ; and neither the English Establishment nor the State authorities in England and Ireland will ever permit the Church of Ireland to be injured, or the Protestant ascendency, in the proper sense of the word, to be destroyed ? My lords, I say, sure I am, that if the alternative were put to him, the Roman Catholic would prefer the Protestant Establishment in Church and State, under which security is afforded to his property, his family, and his life, to the wild and bad, and chimerical attempt to uproot the Protestant Establishment, which could only be done by shaking the foundations of the Empire. The two countries must be separated before that Establishment can be abandoned, and it should not be supposed that the Roman Catholics entertain any wishes for the accomplishment of such an object."—*Id.* vol. xxi. N. S. p. 77.

up a measure, which through their whole political career they had professed, on conscientious grounds, to oppose ; and after standing forward so long as leaders of an opposite cause now suddenly veering round, without one argument advanced to justify their conduct, which had not been again and again confuted.

Without attempting to pronounce any opinion on the question, whether the time had not arrived when political expediency rendered it necessary to pass an Emancipation Bill, no one can deny that subsequent events have furnished a striking comment upon the illusory nature of the securities which were provided for the Established Church in the measure which was passed, and the contempt with which those so-called securities have been set at nought, is now familiar to all. But however men may differ as to the merits of the measure itself, all must agree that the course adopted by those who then, for the first time, undertook the conduct of it, necessarily tended to destroy that reliance which had theretofore been placed upon the opinions and principles of public men. The Emancipation Bill was carried through Parliament against the known inclinations of the Sovereign, against the often recorded vote of the House of Lords, and against the voice of the people, whose petitions were treated with contempt. Ministers conceded everything, not because they thought such concession right and reasonable in itself, but confessedly because they yielded to intimidation ; this too, in despite of the repeated declaration of the agitators, that whatever was conceded they would not be satisfied,—" that they would take each instalment given to them, and demand the residue with greater earnestness."

That Ministers could expect to tranquillize Ireland by thus yielding to an illegal confederacy, is hard to believe, because they well knew that not one of the real miseries of the Irish would be removed or alleviated by the measure. They expected however to conciliate the opposition in Parliament, but when all was done, Ireland (as all who knew its history had constantly foretold) continued to be as it was ; and so far from obtaining the ease for which they looked in Parliament, they discovered, when too late, that they had broken the staff of their strength, in breaking up the Constitutional party.

To one who felt, as deeply as Mr. Lefroy did, the evil of any encroachment upon the essentially Protestant character of the British constitution, the danger of the proposed measure of emancipation was greatly increased by its emanating from the party who had so long professed on conscientious grounds to oppose it. He justly anticipated the

sad effects which this must have, in shaking the
confidence in public men, and opening the door to
that confusion of parties which has since proved
so sadly subversive of the high sense of political
honor and morality, that was long and justly regarded as the peculiar characteristic of British
statesmen. Accordingly, from the very first symptoms that appeared to indicate the approaching
change of policy on the part of the leaders of
the Conservative Party, he felt it his duty openly
to express his views on that which was the
great political question of the day. At the General Meeting of the Brunswick Constitutional
Club of Ireland* he made a speech which
was regarded as one of the ablest delivered in
exposition of the evils of the proposed Bill. In
glowing language he pourtrayed " the singular and
exalted position in which England was placed by
the Act of Settlement, as the only Kingdom
amongst the nations of the earth that made the
maintenance of true religion the first duty of her
Sovereign, and at the same time by connecting it
with the State, declared in the face of the world,
that she considered it as the only sure pledge for
rational liberty, and the true prosperity of a nation ;" and after forcibly describing the effects of the

* The Brunswick Club was instituted in 1828, for the purpose of opposing the proposed measure of Roman Catholic Emancipation.

liberality which had in later years crept into the councils of the nation, " a liberality based in some instances on practical infidelity ; in others, on a perfect indifference to all religion, and a thorough ignorance of the distinction between truth and error," he asks the important question, " Can we doubt that the union between Liberalism and Popery, and the combination of parties which will grow out of such a union must be dangerous to our established Church and its reformed faith ? " Again, when exposing "the absurdity of expecting peace or contentment to flow from concessions wrung from fear and not granted upon principle, extorted by the threats of agitators rather than yielded to the claims of justice," he concludes with these weighty words of warning, " We are told that as the result of the peace and good-will which this measure is to produce, we are to be blessed with a united Cabinet, a united Parliament, and a united Nation ! . but I should like to know what is to be done under the new state of things for the Roman Catholic priests —men who have laboured so industriously and agitated so effectually, to promote the objects of their lay brethren. If they be left without the restoration of their Church property, and of their Church dignities, will there be no rankling sore remaining, no subject for agitation, no object to

give rise to a new ' Catholic Association,' and will
they feel no encouragement to form it from the
signal success of the old one ? "

This manly and open avowal of his political
sentiments rendered him more than ever obnoxious
to Mr. O'Connell and the Irish agitators, and the
same timid policy which had induced the Government to yield to the clamour of that party in
matters of the gravest moment, soon showed itself
in the line of conduct they pursued towards Mr.
Lefroy, in a matter of more importance as affecting
the independence of the Judicial Bench, than as
affecting him individually. During the ten years
that he had held the rank of Serjeant, he had, as
we have already seen, been frequently called on to
discharge Judicial duties on Circuit, in consequence
of the illness or necessary absence of one of the
Judges. No murmur of dissatisfaction had ever
been heard, even from men of extreme views
amongst the Roman Catholics — no imputation of
any political bias warping his judgment, or any
partiality affecting his conduct in the administration
of justice. But the standard of political expediency
had now been substituted for that of principle by
the Irish Executive, and the straightforward line
which Mr. Lefroy had marked out for himself,
in calling public attention to the real source of the
appalling state of crime in Ireland and his un-

swerving firmness in the administration of the law, were well known to be an offence in the eyes of Mr. O'Connell and his party, whose growing influence on the Government was no longer disguised.

It was therefore resolved by the authorities at Dublin Castle, that when a necessity next occurred for sending a substitute for any of the Judges on Circuit, he should if possible be induced to request an exemption from the discharge of that duty. Accordingly, in the Spring of 1830, Baron M'Clelland being obliged by illness to relinquish his post on the Munster Circuit, an un-official communication was made to Mr. Serjeant Lefroy, suggesting that as so many causes still remained unheard in the Chancellor's list, it would be a matter of unfairness, not only to him but to his clients, to nominate him to a Circuit, and that if he were to send a request to Government for exemption from the duty, it would be instantly granted. To this communication Mr. Lefroy replied that, although the Circuit-duty would be to him personally an inconvenience as well as a loss, he felt that it was one of the privileges incident to the office of Serjeant-at-Law, and that for the sake of the profession in which that post gave precedence and honorary rank, he thought it incumbent on him while holding the post, not to abandon any public duty from motives of personal convenience.

This indirect communication having thus failed of its object, a further effort was made by the Attorney-General, at a personal interview with Mr. Lefroy, in which the state of business in the Court of Chancery, was again urged as a reason why he should ask for an exemption from Circuit duty ; but this second effort to get rid of the responsibility involved in the unconstitutional interdict which subsequently issued was as unsuccessful as the former, and only ended in Mr. Lefroy's request that any further communication on the subject should be official and in writing. The following correspondence was the result of his request :—.

FROM WM. GREGORY, Esq.

(UNDER SECRETARY FOR IRELAND.)

Dublin, February 26th, 1830.

SIR,—I have received the Lord Lieutenant's command to acquaint you that he considers your nomination to the provisional exercise of the judicial function as inexpedient in the existing circumstances of this country.

I have the honour to be, Sir,

Your most obedient humble servant,

WM. GREGORY.

Mr. Serjeant Lefroy.

REPLY.

SIR,—I have had the honour of receiving your letter of this morning acquainting me that the Lord Lieutenant " considers the nomination of me to the provisional exercise of the judicial functions as inexpedient in the existing circumstances of this country." Connecting this letter with the communication made to me yesterday morning by the Attorney-General from the Lord Lieutenant accompanied as it was by every assurance of personal respect, I feel it to be due to his Grace to submit to the consideration of his better judgment one or two observations which have occurred to me on the subject of these communications. I confess it does appear to me to be essential to the due administration of public justice, that the officers of the Crown, so far as respects the discharge of their judicial functions, should have the same independence which the law has secured to the judges, so as to place them in like manner beyond the control of popular clamour or existing circumstances. I also think on the part of the profession to which I belong, that I ought not to submit in my person to have the office stripped of one of its most honorable incidents by compromise or acquiescence though inconvenient in its exercise to myself.

I feel therefore compelled to say, that if his Excellency should deem it fit to interdict my going circuit, I should consider it due to the office and myself to request in such case (if this be his Excellency's determination) that he may permit me to resign it altogether. I received the office unimpaired in its privileges; it is admitted I have held it unsullied—and in that state I wish to lay it down, if it is no longer to be enjoyed without mistrust and curtailment.

I have the honour to be, &c., &c.,

THOS. LEFROY.

Wm. Gregory, Esq.

I

Castle, Feb. 27th, 1830.

Sir,—I have received and submitted to the Lord Lieutenant your letter of yesterday's date, and I am directed by his Grace to say that in respecting the independence of others, he cannot consent to forego his own, and that he must abide by the exercise of his own conscientious discretion in the choice of public functionaries. It is satisfactory to his Grace to find that you are aware of the personal respect which he entertains for you, and without attempting to throw any impediment in the course you purpose to pursue, he must express his hope that you will not hastily surrender your professional rank, because he has deemed it prudent in this instance to withhold an appointment which you may consider incidental, but which surely you cannot claim as inseparable from it.

I have the honour to be, &c., &c.,

Wm. Gregory.

Mr. Sergeant Lefroy.

REPLY.

Sir,—I have had the honour of receiving your letter of the 27th, and with the full consideration which I have since felt it my duty to bestow on the subject, I cannot see any ground for altering the determination expressed in my last; but I would beg leave to assure his Grace it is not upon any pretension of questioning the undoubted right of the Government to select its own public functionaries, nor any claim that the judicial functions should be inseparably annexed to the office, that my determination has been founded; but solely on the grounds upon which the separation has been made in this instance. I cannot but feel that under the influence of such a principle impending over the law officer, he never could satisfactorily discharge the judicial duties of the office. My aim and consolation hitherto have been to discharge these duties uprightly, and to the satisfaction of those to whom alone I was responsible, but with total indifference to the judgment or clamour of any party in the country, or any reference to existing circumstances. If, however, the law officers are no longer to be upheld by Government whilst acting on that principle in the discharge of their judicial functions, I must cease to be one of them,

I have the honour to be, &c., &c.,

THOMAS LEFROY.

Wm. Gregory, Esq.

The following extracts from some of the leading journals of the day, evince the public sensation produced by his resignation :—

From the London Morning Journal.

IRISH INTELLIGENCE.

RESIGNATION OF MR. SERJEANT LEFROY.

" Mr. Serjeant Lefroy has resigned his situation, in consequence of the intimation from Government that popular clamour was too great to admit of his going the Circuit, and in consequence of this Mr. Serjeant Blackburne has been nominated to go the Munster Circuit in place of Baron M'Clelland. This unexpected proceeding, which appears to have excited so much interest, does certainly seem a strange way of following up the healing measure.*

The great security we had for the honest administration of justice, in the Judges' places being made certain, is now virtually removed. The demagogues are to say whether the laws are administered impartially, and if they deem them not to be so, they inform Government, with great courtesy no doubt, by asking why they dare to send A., B., or C. on Circuit? Well; Government receives this courteous information with gratitude, and when next occasion requires that one of these proscribed men should fill—what office?—a judicial one!—then a message is sent to say that popular clamour is too great to admit of his administering the law. *O tempora! O mores!* and whom have the Government chosen as the first victim? A man who holds a first place at the bar—who has discharged the judicial duties in the most disturbed times and on the most trying occasions, always with credit to himself as a profound lawyer and an upright man, and with satisfaction to the advocates and to the suitors of the Court—who has several times declined a seat on the bench. Is it to this man they impute the bias of political feeling in the discharge of a duty where the lives and interests of his fellow countrymen are engaged? To remark on the injustice of the imputation would be folly. His character as a Christian and a lawyer is too well known. The fact is—and facts are sometimes unpleasant things—he would not change his conscientious opinions with the times! No; his political character is

* The Emancipation Act, passed shortly before this time.

unsullied by one act of inconsistency or tergiversation ; and this is the man that Government have thus insulted !"

From the Dublin Evening Mail.

" Few circumstances have occurred within our recollection, that have produced such a general sensation as the sudden resignation of Mr. Serjeant Lefroy. Pre-eminent in professional character, sustaining a position at the Bar, at which it has been the good fortune of few to arrive, placed above the ordinary aspirations of his brethren, having frequently declined a seat on the Bench, blessed with great wealth, endowed with talents, and gifted with virtues of the noblest order, his acts are looked upon with a more anxious eye than those of common-place men, and hence, the general sensation to which we have alluded. Several versions have appeared as to the causes which led to the step adopted by Mr. Lefroy ; but, while there is a mixture of truth and misrepresentation in each account that we have seen, there is not a dissentient voice with respect to the high-mindedness and fine sense of honour which actuated the learned personage in the course he adopted. He felt that the profession, of which he was so distinguished a member, was insulted in his person ; that the office he held was sought to be degraded, and the administration of justice itself slighted ; and, so feeling, he sent in his resignation,—not, as some of our contemporaries have it, in pique or in passion, but with a degree of dignity commensurate with his station, and with a consideration becoming his character. A correspondence ensued between Mr. Lefroy and the Government, in which an effort was made to induce the learned gentleman to

alter his determination, or retract his resignation, but in
vain. In the absence of this documentary evidence, it
will be sufficient to state that attempts were made to induce Mr. Serjeant Lefroy to ask as a favour the exemption
from Circuit duties, on the plea of professional avocations
in Chancery, because, as it is triumphantly boasted by the
Popish press, his politics were at variance with those of
Mr. O'Connell and the Radical newspapers. The politics
of a Judge, and Government interference for such an
alleged cause ! what a question does such an association
involve ? What a constructive libel does it contain upon
the purity of justice ?

The public look with an intensity unprecedented to the
production of the correspondence which led to the resignation of Mr. Serjeant Lefroy."

This correspondence he declined to publish at the
time, because he preferred suffering in silence, even
what he considered a great personal injustice,
rather than fan the flame of discontent and excitement raised by the conduct of the Government,
which was regarded by all loyal men in Ireland
as exhibiting a desire to conciliate Mr. O'Connell's
band of professional agitators, and the disloyal party
who followed them, even at the sacrifice of the
independence of the Judges—a principle previously
considered as one of the best safe-guards of our
liberties ; but as those who were responsible for
the act have long since passed away, the reason

for withholding the correspondence no longer
exists, and as the constitutional principles which
induced him to tender and persevere in the resignation of his office are so forcibly put forward
in his own letters to Mr. Gregory, I think any memoir of his professional life would be defective
without them.

CHAPTER VI.

His Election for the University of Dublin—Division on the Civil List in
the House of Commons—Resignation of the Duke of Wellington's
Ministry—Reform Bill—Rapid succession of Ministerial Changes—His
Speech on the Educational Grant for Ireland—Departure in the
working of the System of National Education in Ireland from the
original plan.

AT the General Election which took place on the
death of King George IV., in 1830, Mr. Lefroy
was first elected Representative for the University of Dublin; Mr. North (one of the most
distinguished orators of the Irish Bar) and the
Right Hon. John W. Croker, then Secretary of
the Admiralty, being his opponents. At the same
time his eldest son also successfully contested the
county of Longford, and commenced his Parliamentary career with his father. When they took
their seats in Parliament, the English Tory members
were keenly suffering under the recent desertion
by their political leaders of principles which they
held almost sacred; and it may well be imagined that
the Irish Tory members did not feel the wrong
less acutely. None, therefore, of the members of
the Tory school were much disposed, on the ground

of mere party allegiance, to follow their former political leaders on any question where the merits were at least doubtful.

An occasion soon arose to test the extent to which that feeling prevailed; for the Civil List, proposed by Ministers on the accession of King William IV. to the throne, was one of the first subjects which came on for discussion in the House of Commons in the session of 1830. Loud complaints had long been made by the Members of the Opposition about the heavy charge imposed on the country by the Civil List, which had been settled at the beginning of George IV.'s reign, and they resolved to seize the opportunity afforded by the change of Sovereigns for reconsidering a vote which placed so large an annual grant at the disposal of Ministers, and beyond the control of Parliament, during the whole reign of the existing Sovereign. Accordingly, on the 12th November, 1830, when the Chancellor of the Exchequer moved a resolution "that for the support and maintenance of His Majesty's household, and the honour and dignity of the Crown, there be granted to His Majesty the annual sum of £970,000 during His Majesty's life, and that the said revenue shall be made payable out of the Consolidated Fund," Lord Althorpe announced, on behalf of the Opposition, that they thought it would be requisite to appoint a Select

Committee to examine the details of the proposed
vote.

On notice of a motion to this effect being given
by Sir Henry Parnell, a meeting of the Tory
members, under the leadership of Sir Edward
Knatchbull, was held, at which it was resolved to
vote against Ministers on the question. The division took place on the 15th November, 1830, and
the Government, being beaten by 29, the resignation
of the Duke of Wellington's Ministry immediately
followed, and Earl Grey was called on by His
Majesty King William IV. to undertake the task of
forming a Ministry.

The question of Catholic Emancipation, which for
so many years had formed the *cheval de bataille* between the two great parties in Parliament, being now
out of the way, that of Parliamentary Reform assumed
its place.   The sweeping measure proposed by the
Whig Ministry on that subject soon decided the political course of Mr. Lefroy, and those who shared in
the opinion held by him, that any such measure, if
carried, must sooner or later lead to revolutionary
changes which would endanger the stability of the
British Constitution; accordingly, he and most of
the other Tory members who had voted against Sir
Robert Peel on the question of referring the Civil
List to a Select Committee, resolved to support him
in opposing the Reform Bill.   The second reading

of that Bill being only carried by a single vote, Earl Grey felt it would be impossible to carry the Bill through that House of Commons ; the Parliament was, therefore, dissolved in April, 1831.

Mr. Lefroy was again returned as M.P. for the University of Dublin in the new Parliament, in opposition to the Solicitor-General of the Whig Ministry, and his son was also returned for the County of Longford; but it may fairly be said that the sole business of the new Parliament, which assembled on the 14th June, 1831, was the passing of the Reform Bills for England, Ireland, and Scotland, as the debates on these Bills lasted up to the close of the session in August, 1832, and in the following December the members of the new House of Commons were sent back to their constituents, in order to give all those who had become entitled to the franchise under the Reform Acts an immediate opportunity of exercising their privilege.

The Parliamentary franchise in the University of Dublin, which, previous to the Irish Reform Act, was enjoyed only by the Fellows and Scholars of Trinity College, being now extended to all Masters of Arts, and the University being entitled under the Irish Reform Act to send two representatives instead of one to Parliament, every possible effort was made by the Whig Government to recover for their party this important representation. They again put forward their Solicitor-General, with all the weight of Government influence unsparingly exercised, and along with him was put forward the Honorable Frederick Ponsonby, brother of the Earl of Besborough, who subsequently filled the office of Lord Lieutenant of Ireland under the Whigs. The contest lasted five days, during which the largest number of voters that have ever been polled at the University recorded their votes, and it resulted in the return of Mr. Lefroy and his colleague, Mr. Frederick Shaw, by an overwhelming majority—the numbers at the close of the poll being 1,304 for Lefroy, 1,290 for Shaw, 423 for Crampton, and 390 for Ponsonby.

At the same election Mr. Lefroy's son again contested the County of Longford, but the Whig candidates, having secured the return by the number of fictitious votes which had been placed on the register at the Registry Session held immediately after the passing of the Irish Reform Act, he was obliged to present a petition to the House of Commons against the return ; and after a protracted investigation of some weeks, he succeeded in striking off 74 fictitious votes from the poll, thereby effecting the return of himself and his colleague, Viscount Forbes, in lieu of the Whig candidates.

Those who only look back on the passing of the Reform Act of 1832 as a matter of history, and

who had no part in the public events of the ten
years which immediately followed, can with difficulty realize the rapid succession of political
changes which resulted from that measure ; but it
may serve to give us some idea of the precarious
tenure by which any Minister of the Crown held
his office, or any Member of Parliament his seat in
the House of Commons, when I mention that during
the eleven years for which Mr. Lefroy represented
Trinity College in Parliament, he saw no less than
seven changes in the occupants of the office of
Prime Minister of England, and he was himself
involved in no less than twelve contested elections,
six for the University and six for the county
of Longford.

A short summary of the political history of
that period well exemplifies the sagacity which
prompted the Duke of Wellington, in 1832, to
ask of Lord Grey, " how was the government of
the country to be carried on ?"   For within eighteen
months from the coming into operation of the
Reform Bill by which it was supposed that Lord
Grey had secured the gratitude of present and
future ages, his whole Ministry was broken up, and
his Lordship expelled, almost contemptuously, from
the Cabinet constructed by himself.   And when in
July, 1834, Lord Melbourne was called to form a
Ministry, we find that, notwithstanding the talents

as well as the *pliable* spirit of this amiable and
popular Minister, his Government fell to pieces in
less than six months. Various were the surmises
at the time as to the cause of this sudden disruption
of the Whig Cabinet, which completely took the
country and the Tory party by surprise ; but we
have since obtained a peep behind the scenes,*
which reveals the true history of the break-up
of the Melbourne Ministry, and of what is popularly known as " the Duke of Wellington's Dicta-
torship," under which His Grace held the seals of
office in the most important departments of Government, and discharged the ordinary functions
of the whole Cabinet, for some weeks awaiting Sir
Robert Peel's return from the Continent, where
he was then travelling in the south of Italy. On
the 16th November, 1834, Viscount Palmerston
writes thus from the Foreign Office to his brother
the Hon. William Temple, then British Minister at
Naples :—

My Dear William,—We are all out; turned out neck
and crop. Wellington is Prime Minister, and we give up
the seals, &c., to-morrow, at St. James's, at two. . . .
The Duke, after having saved England in the field, is
destined to be her ruler in the Cabinet. The way this

* See "The Memoirs of Sir Robert Peel, Bart., published by his
Trustees." London, 1856. And "The Life of Viscount Palmerston, by
Right. Hon. Sir Henry Lytton Bulwer." London, 1871.

came to pass is this: Lord Spencer was taken ill ten days ago, and died this day week at Althorp, in Northampton-shire. His death was known in London on Monday last, the 10th. The first thing that Melbourne had to do was to consider who should lead the House of Commons. The Hollands, Ellice, and some other Whigs, strongly recommended John Russell; some thoughtof Abercrombie. Melbourne asked me what I felt about it. I said, it would be inconvenient to me to take the lead with my official business, but that I would do it if the Government wished; and that I would, in short, either take it or leave it alone, as might be most convenient for the arrangements of the Government. On Tuesday or Wednesday Melbourne wrote to the King at Brighton, to say that, as when he first took his present office, he had represented the influence of Althorp in the Commons as one great foundation of the strength of the Government; now that Althorp was removed to the Lords by the death of his father, he deemed it his duty towards the King to ask his Majesty whether he wished him to propose arrangements for sup-plying Althorp's place, or whether he preferred asking advice from other quarters. Melbourne added, that he would never abandon the service of the King as long as it was thought that he could be of any use; and that, how-ever much the Government must feel the loss of Althorp in the Commons, nevertheless, there was no reason what-ever to doubt that we should still retain the confidence of that House of Parliament. " The King appointed Mel-bourne to come down to Brighton on Thursday, as Melbourne in his letter had proposed to do. On Thurs-day he went down, and had a long conversation with the

King that day, before dinner, and on Friday morning
before he left Brighton. The result was, that the King
objected to all the arrangements proposed; stated he could
not agree to the kind of measures about the Irish Church,
which Melbourne said the Government would have to
propose, although those measures were not ripe for being
laid before the King, but were explained to him to be in
principle precisely conformable to what had been stated to
him when Melbourne took office, and to which he had
then agreed. At that time he admitted that the Irish and
English Churches stood upon different grounds, and that
it did not at all follow that, what was right to be done for
one should also be applied to the other; that the Irish
Church required still further reformation, and that no
danger could arise to the English Establishment from correcting the abuses or defects of the Irish. Now, he said
that the two stand upon the same foundation; that one
cannot be touched without endangering the other; that
he is Head of the Church, and bound to uphold it, and
that he could not agree to the sort of measures which
Melbourne said would probably be proposed to him. On
Friday morning the King gave Melbourne a written memorandum, in which he stated shortly the sum of these considerations, and added, that for these reasons, he thought it
better at once to relieve Melbourne from the precarious
situation in which he stood, weakened in the Commons,
and, without any counterbalancing strength in the Lords,
than to charge him with the task of proposing fresh
arrangements; and he added, verbally, that he should
send for the Duke of Wellington. Melbourne came to
town on Friday evening. The Duke went to Brighton on

Saturday (yesterday), and this morning Melbourne heard from the King that the Duke had accepted, and that we were to be at St. James's to-morrow, at two, to deliver up our seals.

At the same time the Duke of Wellington writes to Sir Robert Peel:—

Brighton, Nov. 15, 1834, at night.

My Dear Peel,— . . . . The King asked me to undertake to form a Government for him, on the grounds stated in the papers, of which I have given you the sketch. I told his Majesty that the difficulty of the task consisted in the state of the House of Commons, and that all our efforts must be turned to get the better of these difficulties: that I earnestly recommended to his Majesty to choose a Minister in the House of Commons, and that you should be the person. His Majesty answered, that he would not have hesitated if you had been in England, but that as you were abroad, and it was necessary to act immediately, he had sent for me. I told him that I thought nothing would be more unfair than to call upon you to put yourself at the head of a Government, which another individual should have formed: that it would be injurious to you, and to his Majesty himself. But that, as it appeared to be necessary to take possession of the Government, I was perfectly ready to hold for the present the offices of First Lord of the Treasury and Secretary of State for the Home Department, till you should return home; and that the Great Seal might be put in Commission, Lord Lyndhurst being the first Commis-

K

sioner.　I only request you to return home as soon as you can.　It may be necessary to appoint a Secretary or Secretaries of the Treasury, in order to prepare matters for your elections; but these shall be only temporary.　I don't know of any other appointment that can be necessary.　I enclose a letter from the King.　You shall hear from me at Paris; or if I should have occasion to write, on an early day at Lyons or Turin.

Believe me, &c.,

WELLINGTON.

ENCLOSED LETTER—"THE KING TO SIR R. PEEL."

The King having had a most satisfactory and confidential conversation with the Duke of Wellington, on the formation of a new Government, calls on Sir Robert Peel to return, without loss of time, to England, to put himself at the head of the administration of the country.　In the meantime, His Majesty has appointed the Duke of Wellington First Lord of the Treasury and Secretary of State for the Home Department, in order to hold the Government until the return of Sir Robert Peel.　It will likewise be necessary to put the Great Seal in Commission, and the King has named Lord Lyndhurst the First Commissioner.

WILLIAM R.

Pavilion, Brighton, November 15th, 1834.

The following letter, giving an account of an interview which Mr. Lefroy had with the Duke of Wellington, in the interval previous to Sir Robert

Peel's return to England, well exhibits the unrivalled habits of business and characteristic coolness of the noble Duke :—

TO HIS WIFE.

Eaton Square,
28th November, 1834.

I have just been sitting with that most wonderful of men, the Duke of Wellington, as much at his ease, and as gay, joking about their attacks on " The great Dictator," as if he had nothing to do or to think of; and yet this is not the result of levity, for every particle of arrear in his office was cleared off. Every man who has business gets his answer, and is dispatched, and there is the Duke, having done all that was to do, ready to do anything more that may occur. I met him yesterday in the park, and he was so pleasant and kind that I went to pay him a visit to-day. He mentioned that all was waiting the return of Sir Robert Peel. He said he had sent a warrant for a Commission to Ireland, to take up the great seal, as Lord Plunket had resigned. So you may judge with what truth the gossips reported that " he was invited to hold it, as the Whigs were to return;" indeed, as to all this sort of nonsense you may laugh or smile at it, as you are more or less in spirits; but you may be assured, and may say with confidence, as sure as Sir Robert Peel arrives in England there will be a Government, of which he will be the head, and the Duke a member. So honorable has been the Duke, that he has not spoken even to his most intimate friends (the men who are certain of being in office) from motives of delicacy, and determined

K 2

not to do so. He does not expect Sir Robert till the 8th
or 10th, and I think of going down to Ewshott on Monday, and staying there most part of the week. Don't
mind what the newspapers say; don't read them if you
can't bear anything they may say. I have always disregarded them, and hope I shall be able to do so to the end.

T. L.

When Sir Robert Peel, on his return from the
Continent, consented to undertake the responsibility
of forming a ministry, and was gazetted First Lord
of the Treasury—the fourth within six months—
even his ministry, like Lord Melbourne's, only lasted
a few months, for though enjoying the full confidence of the Crown, the House of Lords, and even
of the people at large, he was forced to give way to
the famous Lichfield House compact, and in
April, 1835, Lord Melbourne became again nominally Prime Minister. I say nominally, because
the coalition of factions which had recalled him to
office deprived him at the same time of independent power. He was from the first forced to
submit to their dictation in matters repugnant to
his own principles and feelings ; and after four
uneasy years, upon the frivolous pretext—not of
losing a vote, but of carrying it by too small
a majority—on an unimportant question relating
to a sugar duty, he threw up the Government on

7th May, 1839. Sir Robert Peel was now again invited to form a ministry, but on some misunderstanding about certain arrangements in the Royal household, Lord Melbourne was restored to office for a time. In this precarious state Lord Melbourne's Government continued for two years longer, but on the 4th of June, 1841, a direct vote of want of confidence afforded a decisive signal of retreat.

The following letter shews the great interest which was excited on the occasion, and the number of members attending on the division which appears to have included nearly the whole House of Commons; it also shews the perfect calmness with which Mr. Lefroy speaks of the results likely to flow from the division, though necessarily again involving him in all the trouble and expense of two further contested elections—one for his own seat in the University, and the other for his son's seat in the County of Longford.

TO HIS WIFE.

5th June, 1841.

At half-past three this morning we divided and beat the Government by one; the votes of members present being 312 to 311, besides 13 pairs. Not a man of our party was absent without a pair, so we shewed a strength of 325, and one man, T——, voted against us on a crotchet, making 326. I think we shall have an election immediately. The Government *Whip* says they have got a man to stand for

Longford against A——. He has no property in the county,
nor any connection with it, and I understand the Radicals
of Longford are divided; if so he may not like to persevere in the canvass, if he meets a cool reception from
any of them, but our desire ought, and I hope will be, to
be satisfied with the result; and as we know that neither
the riches or honours of this life are the things we ought
to set our hearts upon, I trust we shall learn to be satisfied
with the event, let it turn out as it may. Whatever is right
and reasonable should be done by us for A——'s success, and if it fail let us be persuaded it is good for us that
it should fail, if it were only to loosen our attachment to
this low and perishing world. We have the greatest of
earthly treasures in the bond of family love and union
with which we are blessed, and this not as a gift of earth
but sent down from heaven. As soon as I can I shall
rejoice to spread my wings and to flee away to dear home.

T. L.

The ministry did resolve, as he anticipated in the
above letter, to try the effect of a dissolution of
Parliament before resigning, but notwithstanding
all the efforts of the Free Trade party, and in spite
of the full cry of "*cheap bread*" and "*no mono-
poly*," a Parliament was returned, which appears to
have been even less sensible of the merits of Whig
policy than the former one, for immediately after
its assembling in August, 1841, it speedily called
Sir Robert Peel to Downing-street as the pledged
and chosen champion of agricultural protection.

The following letter gives an account of the Longford election which resulted in his son's temporary defeat, but after a tedious and expensive investigation before a Committee of the House of Commons, the sheriff's return was amended, and on the 18th of April, 1842, the Committee reported " that Luke White, Esq., was not duly elected, and that Anthony Lefroy, Esq. was, and ought to have been returned, and that they had altered the poll by striking off 144 persons."*

TO HIS WIFE.

Longford, 16th July, 1841.

We pulled up to-day considerably, but still are beaten by a large majority, owing to the Roman Catholics, who promised to vote for us or stay away, being brought up by the priests in spite of their wishes and polled against A——, as well as from the number of Protestants who were deterred from leaving their houses, by the violence and intimidation of the Priests' mobs. Thank God, we have had a comparatively quiet time within this town, owing to the providential circumstance of having a good High Sheriff, and an effective military force, as well as police. Now that they have obtained their object the priests will suffer the people to be quiet, and had the grace last night,

---

* The uncertainty of the Law as administered by Election-Committees may be judged of by the result of the four Petitions to the House of Commons, prosecuted by Mr. Lefroy, to amend the Sheriff's Return of Representatives for the County Longford; on which two Committees amended the Return, striking off the fictitious votes that had been entered on the Poll; and two refused to open the Register or amend the Return, though the same fictitious votes had been again received by the Sheriff.

when they found what a majority they had, to give advice
to that effect. Our friends from a distance came in nobly,
and we have had the most gratifying testimony of all the
influential resident gentlemen, as to the spirit and determination shewn by A——, in his endeavour to rescue
the county from the dominion of the priests, who now so
completely tyrannize over it. The election is virtually
over, but the Members can't be declared until to-morrow
evening. Henry White has left this, and comparatively few
have been in the town to-day. The poll as just announced
is: for Henry White, 613; for Luke White, 614; plumpers
for Lefroy, 480. On the whole, we have made a very
noble fight, and we expect a few more plumpers to-
morrow. Let us be thankful for the mercies we have
received, in the care of a good and gracious Providence,
amidst all the tumult and violence of the past week, and
let us take as a blessing the disappointment we have met
with, assured that all things work together for good to
the children of God, and such, I trust, we are, not of
ourselves, but by the free and precious grace of Him
who has redeemed us by His own precious blood.

T. L.

The change of Government which took place at
this time brought Mr. Lefroy's parliamentary career
to a close, and he was thus spared the pain of
witnessing the disruption of the largest and most
influential political Party that were ever united
under one Leader in the House of Commons,
caused by Sir Robert Peel's change of policy on
the subject of the Corn Laws. It would be

difficult to exaggerate the sensation produced amongst the followers of this eminent States- man, by this second instance of his sudden aban- donment of the course he had so long previously advocated in Parliament, on questions of such vast public interest, as the admission of Roman Catholics to Parliament, and the maintenance of the laws intended for the protection of our agricultural interest. In the leading Conservative Review we find it referred to in language, which too faithfully reflects the heat of political passion, and which, read by the dispassionate eye of the historian, con- veys a wholesome warning against the uncharitable judgment, too often passed upon the conduct and motives of public men, by contemporary critics:—

" Of all the apostacies that disgrace the political history of mankind, that which Sir Robert Peel exhibited in the fourth year of his second Government is at once the most personally disgraceful and the most nationally deplorable. This unhappy defection was no doubt partly caused by the individual temperament of the man; but also by what in our present view is still more important, his deep-seated doubts whether the ancient constitution of the country could be maintained with such a House of Commons as —notwithstanding his own recent success—he thought futurity was threatened with. He therefore conceived the plan of amalgamating the discordant elements by sacrificing his own friends, who he fancied would not resist, and by adopting the measures of his enemies, whom he looked to conciliate. He accomplished the mischief; but was miserably disappointed in his own expectations. The most important members of his Cabinet dissented; and on the 10th of December, 1845, all resigned."— *Quarterly Review*, vol. xc. p. 571.

But however natural it might be that any inconsistency in the conduct of a leader, of whom his party felt so justly proud, should evoke severe criticisms at the time, I think no unprejudiced mind can doubt that the charges of unworthy motives which were made against Sir Robert Peel, were utterly groundless, and it is only justice to one who long held so prominent a position amongst the public men of our day, to say that it is plain he acted on that occasion, with a full knowledge of the prejudice it was likely to excite against him in the minds of his party, and influenced solely by a conscientious conviction that the public interests demanded a reversal of the policy which he had before supported. If we had no other evidence than the private correspondence which passed between him and several members of his Cabinet, since published in his own Memoirs, these would in themselves be sufficient to convince any fair mind that nothing less than a solemn sense of the duty he owed to his country could have induced Sir Robert Peel to make the personal sacrifices which he knew would follow upon the step he was about to take,—not the sacrifice of power or official position which he could well afford to disregard, but the severance of party connexions which he held so dear, and the suspicions excited in the minds of those whose friendship he valued and with whom he had so long acted in public life. Amongst other letters we find the following from the Right Hon. Henry Goulburn.

My Dear Peel—I have such an habitual deference to the superiority of your judgment, and such an entire confidence in the purity of your motives, that I always feel great doubt as to my being right when I differ from you in opinion. But the more I reflect upon the observations which you made to me a few days since, as to your difficulty in again defending a corn law in Parliament, the more do I feel alarmed at your taking a different course from that which you have previously adopted. An abandonment of your former opinions now would, I think, prejudice your and our characters as public men, and would be fraught with fatal results to the country's best interests. . . . . Under present circumstances, it appears to me that the abandonment of the Corn Law would be taken by the public, generally, as decisive evidence that we never intended to maintain it further than as an instrument to vex and defeat our enemies.

The very caution with which we have spoken on the subject of corn will confirm this impression. Had we always announced a firm determination, under all circumstances, to uphold the Corn Law, it would have been more readily believed, that in abandoning it now we were yield-

ing to the pressure of an overwhelming necessity which
we did not before anticipate. But when the public feel,
as I believe they do, great doubts as to the existence of
an adequate necessity, when greater doubts still are entertained as to the applicability of the abandonment of the
Corn Law, as a remedy to the present distress, they will,
I fear, with few dissentient voices, tax us with treachery
and deception, and charge us, from our former language,
with having always had it in contemplation. So much as
to the effect on our character as public men. But I view
with greater alarm its effects on public interests. In my
opinion the party of which you are the head is the only
barrier which remains against the revolutionary effects of
the Reform Bill. So long as that party remains unbroken,
whether in or out of power, it has the means of doing
much good, or, at least, of preventing much evil. But if
it be broken in pieces by a destruction of confidence in
its leaders (and I cannot but think that an abandonment
of the Corn Law would produce that result), I see
nothing before us but the exasperation of class animo-
sities, a struggle for pre-eminence, and the ultimate
triumph of unrestrained democracy.

Yours, &c.,

HENRY GOULBURN.

In the same volume we find Sir Robert Peel's
vindication of the course he adopted thus given by
himself :—

" It appeared to me that all these considerations,—the
betrayal of party attachments—the maintenance of the
honour of public men—the real interests of the cause of

Constitutional Government, must all be determined by the answer which the heart and conscience of a responsible minister might give to the question—What is that course which the public interests really demand ? . . . . .
I was not insensible to the evil of acting counter to the will of those majorities, of severing party connections, and of subjecting public men to suspicion and reproach, and the loss of public confidence ; but I felt a strong conviction that such evils were light in comparison with those which must be incurred by the sacrifice of national interests to party attachments."

With the exception of the few months for which Sir Robert Peel held the reins of government in 1835, the Conservative party were in the " cold shade " of opposition, during the eleven years that Mr. Lefroy sat in Parliament ; and yet, at the sacrifice of one of the largest professional incomes that any member of the Irish Bar ever realized, he was always found at his post in the House of Commons on the discussion of every question bearing upon Irish interests. His keen sense of injustice was often shewn by the indignation with which he reproved the habit, too frequently indulged in by some members of the House of Commons, of attacking absent persons without any reasonable grounds for the charges brought forward, and without even giving any notice to the accused. It made no difference in such cases with him from what

quarter of the House such attacks proceeded, to
what party the accused belonged, or in what
rank of life they stood, he was always ready and
willing to expose the evils of such a practice, and
to vindicate the characters of those who had no
means of defending themselves. In like manner,
any measure tending to promote the progress of
civilization, or to advance the social welfare of
Ireland, was sure of his cordial support, whether it
emanated from Whig or Conservative. The following extract from his speech in the debate upon
the "Suppression of Disturbances (Ireland) Bill,"
affords an instance of this, while it exhibits the
bold and straightforward way in which he expressed his views as to the system of political
agitation, which he considered to be the bane of
Ireland. After observing upon certain topics
which he thought had been improperly introduced into the debate, he said—

"It is our duty, I think, to satisfy ourselves, our constituents, and the public in general, that we have solid
grounds for passing this important measure. It is impossible that any Member of this House should not deplore
the necessity for such a measure—but so persuaded am I
of this necessity, that I cannot do violence to my conscience by refusing my support to it, though on all other
subjects I have been a most determined opponent of
Government."

He then showed from the statistics of crime in Ireland, the necessity for some such measure, and after answering in detail the several objections that had been urged against the Bill in the course of the debate, he concluded thus—

" We have been told that Ireland has many grievances to complain of, and that these ought to be redressed before measures of coercion are resorted to. It has been observed that she has been misgoverned; but this charge of misgovernment is not intended to have reference to the policy of one administration, or of another, of a Whig, or a Tory Government; but it is intended to bring English authority into disrepute. The object is to destroy the English rule in Ireland, and to excite a feeling against English authority. It is remarkable that this charge always comes from those who are most engaged in exciting the people of Ireland to discontent. To my mind it is perfectly clear, that their object is not the redress of grievances, but the absolute separation of the two countries. In late years there has always been some political nostrum for what are called ' Irish grievances.' We were told that ' Catholic Emancipation ' was a certain panacea for them ; and that if that measure were once passed, there would be an end of all the ills of Ireland—that there would be universal peace and tranquillity. But it is now admitted that none of the benefits which the advocates of that measure predicted as sure to flow from it, have yet resulted, or ever will result from it; what has become of the plighted faith of those for whom the measure was passed ? We now find that the early

friends, and the late supporters of that question, have all
been baffled and disappointed, and Ireland is as much
distracted now as she ever was. We have been told that
this measure was delayed so long that when it was carried
it lost all the effect it would have produced, had it been
carried at an earlier period. But I would ask those who
state this, whether the Roman Catholics of England were
relieved from their disabilities one hour before the Roman
Catholics of Ireland? Were the Dissenters of England
relieved before the Irish Roman Catholics? How comes
it, then, that since the Emancipation Bills were carried,
neither the Roman Catholics nor Dissenters of England
have separated themselves from their fellow subjects, or
manifested this angry discontent, and yet that we find
Ireland just as much disturbed as if that measure of
Emancipation had never been carried. If I may be permitted to state the truth on this subject, it is this, that a
party exists in Ireland, whose object is *nominally* to get
rid of what is called an ' arbitrary Government;' but whose
real object is not the removal of local evils, or personal
disabilities, but rather to bring about a separation between
the two countries. I regret to state that the very worst
spirit prevails in Ireland at this moment, which is constantly
kept up by agitation ; and whilst not only political but
spiritual agitators are allowed to excite and influence the
people, that unhappy country will never be at peace. It
is a remarkable fact which the House should bear in mind,
that the advocates for the separation in Ireland have
always been the advocates for the destruction of the
Church Establishment; well knowing that the Established
Church is the key-stone of that arch which binds the two

countries together. . . . . It was with considerable pain that I heard an Honorable Member opposite state, that if the Honorable and learned Member for Dublin* would only lay aside his phantom of repeal, he himself would be an advocate for all the other remedies proposed by the Honorable and learned Member respecting Ireland —that in short he would give up the Church Establishment and tithes, for the purpose of satisfying the Honorable and learned Member. I must tell the Honorable Member that he would do much better to get rid of his own phantom. If the Honorable Member really supposes that the connexion between the two countries can outlive the destruction of the Establishment, he indulges in a most delusive hope. . . . . Having thus stated the grounds upon which I feel bound to support this Bill—having shewn, as I hope, that a case has been made out by Government to justify them in demanding these additional powers, and that the evidence they have adduced will justify the House in assenting to their demands, I have now only to add, that if His Majesty's Ministers—convinced as they must have been of the absolute necessity of putting a stop to these disturbances—had not brought forward the present measure, or one of equal efficiency, they would not have done their duty to Ireland, they would not have done their duty to their Sovereign or to this Country ; and having made up their minds to the necessity of this measure, if they suffer its details to be frittered away in its progress through this House, they will equally, in my judgment, be wanting to themselves and to the country.

* Mr. Daniel O'Connell.

We have already seen, in his Charge to the
Grand Jury of the County Limerick, delivered in
the year 1822, the strong opinion he entertained
of the importance of providing a system of education based on sound and enlightened principles, for
the lower orders of the people in Ireland, as an
essential element in any scheme for the improvement of their condition. He had personal experience of the willingness with which Roman
Catholic parents availed themselves of the educational advantages supplied for their children by
the Kildare-place Society. He felt that the best
hope for the tranquillization of our country was in
carrying out the two main principles on which that
society was founded, by educating Roman Catholics and Protestants in the same schools, where
they might cultivate habits of friendship and good-
will towards each other, and resting their religious
instruction upon the solid foundation of the Bible,
which formed " the common charter of Christianity," as admitted both by Roman Catholics
and Protestants, while the catechisms of both
Churches and sectarian teaching of all kinds was
carefully excluded. He therefore availed himself
of the first opportunity of calling the attention of
Parliament to a subject which he regarded as of
paramount importance to Ireland.

On the 9th of September, 1831, Mr. Spring

Rice moved in the committee of supply for a grant of £30,000, for enabling the Lord Lieutenant of Ireland to assist in the education of the people; and the late Earl of Derby (then Mr. Stanley), Secretary for Ireland took that occasion to announce to the House of Commons the intention of Government to withdraw the parliamentary grant theretofore given to the Kildare-place Society, on the ground (to use his own words) that "one of . the leading principles of that society was, that without touching on the peculiar doctrines or tenets of any sect, it took as the basis of its operations that in all its schools the Holy Scriptures, without note or comment, should be read by such of the pupils as were competent to understand them." This, however strange it may appear, as coming from the lips of a member of the British Government, was alleged to be "a vital defect in the system of the Kildare-place Society," and rendered it necessary (in Mr. Stanley's mind) to substitute some other means of administering the educational grant for Ireland.

The following speech of Mr. Lefroy's on that occasion expresses his views as to the injustice done by that act to the Roman Catholic children who were enjoying the benefits of the Society's schools; and the statistics he adduces prove that the change then made by the Government was a con-

cession, not to the wishes or feelings of the Roman
Catholic laity, but to a section of the Roman
Catholic clergy, who then, in a milder tone, sought
to assert the right which they now, in a bolder
form, proclaim, of resisting any system of education for the people of Ireland over which they
have not absolute control :—

Sir, I rise to claim the attention of the Committee for
a short time; and it will not, I think, be considered un-
reasonable that I should do so, when I state that the
Society, the doom of which is now about to be sealed,
is one to which I have devoted considerable attention
during a great portion of my public life. It seems to me
that two questions, of very different character, are involved in the discussion. The first is with respect to the
expediency of abolishing the system which at present
prevails in the schools of the Kildare-place Society before
we have established another to supply its place. The
other is, whether, on the principle upon which the Society
has hitherto proceeded, we can expect to obtain the object
which, on all hands, we admit to be desirable, of uniting
the education of Protestant and Roman Catholic children;
or whether, if it cannot be obtained upon the principle
adopted by the Society, it can be secured by the adoption
of any other.

With respect to the abolition of the Society before any
other is established, let me call the attention of the Committee to this important consideration. It is a Society now
in full operation, having under its charge and depending
upon it upwards of 1,600 schools, in which the education

of more than 130,000 children is at this moment going on.
Many of these schools have been raised up and maintained
by large private contributions, amounting to full as large a
sum as the total amount of the Parliamentary grants.
These contributions have been advanced out of the
pockets of individuals upon the faith of the continuance
of Parliamentary aid to this Society; which aid seemed
pledged by an uninterrupted succession of grants for a
period of fifteen years. These grants, too, were made to
the Society under no concealment or disguise of its principles, which were fully and distinctly avowed in the
annual petitions which were presented to this House for
aid; so that the continuance of the grants may be deemed
a recognition on the part of the Legislature of the principles upon which the Society proceeded. If, then, it be
considered right to try the experiment of a new system,
I submit that it is neither just nor politic to the Irish
nation, or to the Society itself, so suddenly to declare
that the Society shall cease at the end of three months.

Let it be recollected that a national system of education
in Ireland must not be moulded merely to meet the peculiar tenets of Roman Catholics: it must also be made
available to members of the Established Church and to
Protestant Dissenters; and when the attention of the
Committee is called to the grounds upon which the Society
adopted the principle on which it acts, I trust it will
appear not only to have been adopted upon reasonable
grounds, but also with a due regard to the prejudices
or prepossessions of every religious sect in Ireland. It
was apparent that the great cause of the unhappiness of
Ireland was its disunion on the subject of religion. The

object, therefore, in establishing a national system of
education, was to find out some common ground upon
which all parties might unite. The Society was fully
sensible of the importance of the principle to which the
right honorable gentleman, who spoke last,* has adverted,
namely, of going together as far as possible, and of only
separating when of necessity they were compelled to do
so. But in a country where all men were so completely
disagreed in their religious views, it was vain to look, in
human compositions, for any common ground upon which
they could unite. The Scriptures, therefore, without
note or comment, including the Douay as well as the
authorized version, were taken as the foundation of
religious education; and it was resolved to exclude all
human additions and interpretations. The right honourable
Secretary has asked of what avail is a religious education
which consists only in teaching the children to read a
chapter or two in the Bible every day? But let me ask,
what is the value of any religious education not founded
on the Scriptures? And how this is to be done under his
system, is an enigma, which remains to be solved. It is
one which the right honourable Secretary proposed to
solve; but he must allow me to say, he has gone a very
short way indeed in giving a solution. The plan adopted
by the Kildare-place Society was, to lay the foundation
in the common charter of Christianity, as agreed upon by
all sects, and to leave to the parents and pastors to raise
the superstructure, which it could not do consistently
with its own principle of union. I admit that some of
the Roman Catholic clergymen object to the system

* Right Hon. Thomas Frankland Lewis.

adopted by the Society. But do we stand here to carry into effect the dogmas of any particular Church? Would any objection to the plan on the part of the Protestant clergy be for one moment listened to in this House? I know that some clergymen of the Established Church do object to the system; but the question for the House is this—is that system acceptable to the people generally, are they willing to receive it, and will they act upon it? I am quite satisfied to try that question by the test of all the evidence that has ever been adduced upon the subject; and I am glad that on this occasion I have not only to appeal to written records to bear out my view, but that I have also a living witness in the right honourable gentleman sitting near me*, who, from his accurate knowledge of the subject as a member of the Royal Commission, will be able to affirm all that I now assert. In the first place, I will appeal to the testimony of these Commissioners, and let it be observed that one of them was a Roman Catholic. I appeal also to the returns made by the Roman Catholic clergy to the Commissioners, by which it appears that, at that time, the number of scholars in the Kildare-place schools was 57,129, and that of these 29,964 were Roman Catholics. I state this from the second report of the Commissioners, in which the details are given. When it appears, then, that more than a moiety of those who are receiving education under this system are Roman Catholics, is it fair to say that the people of that persuasion in Ireland are entirely averse to the mode of instruction which is pursued under it? In

* Right Hon. Thomas Frankland Lewis, a member of the Royal Commission of Irish Education Enquiry, appointed under the Great Seal, dated 14th June, 1824.

the Kildare-place Model School, it appears, by the same
returns, that the number of scholars was 697. Of these,
263 only were Protestants, and the remaining 434 Roman
Catholics. In short, from all the returns it appears that,
wherever the experiment has been tried, whether upon a
large or a small scale, the Roman Catholics are willing
that their children should partake of the advantages of
Scriptural education in common with the Protestants. If
we find that since the establishment of the Kildare-street
Society in 1811 up to the year 1825, when the returns
which I have quoted were made, the Roman Catholics did
partake of this system of education, what foundation is
there for asserting that they will not receive the Scriptures in common with Protestants? And what more
desirable incident could be wished for, in a country torn
asunder, as Ireland has been, by religious dissensions?—
what more rational hope of putting an end to these differences than by the parties meeting on a common ground
to see in what their differences consist?—and whether it
be not possible to reconcile them? It is true, they
might eventually continue to differ, but still they would
disagree the less; for who that believes in the Scriptures
can doubt that their tendency is to soften all the asperities
of our nature, and to teach us mutual forbearance and
charity? I know of nothing more calculated to sow the
seeds of mutual forbearance, and to instil principles of
charity and good-will, than a discreet and judicious Scriptural education. If, unhappily, this truth is not exem-
plified in the conduct of all who have had the advantage
of such an education, it is not, I am sure, the fault of the
Scriptures; nor does the fact in the least impugn the

truth which I advance. It is to be accounted for by the
overbearing temperament of our own unhappy nature,
Now, give me leave to call the attention of the Committee
to one or two further points of evidence. The entire
number of schools for the education of the poor in Ireland.
exclusive of Sunday-schools, amounts to 11,823. In
7,567 of these, Roman Catholic masters are employed.
But now let us see in how many of the 11,823 schools
the Scriptures are read. It appears, according to the
returns, that they are read in 6,059, that in 3,322 they
are not read, and as to the remaining 2,442 the returns
are silent. Out of the 6,059 schools in which the Scriptures are read, only 1,879 schools are connected with any
existing Society in which it can be insinuated that it is in
any degree imperative on the pupils to read the Scriptures;
so that it will be seen that there are above 4,000 schools
in Ireland, mostly under the direction of Roman Catholic
masters, unfettered by the rules of any Society, and
depending chiefly on the parents of the children for their
support, in which the Scriptures are taught. When,
therefore, it is asserted that the Roman Catholics are, as
a body, averse to Scriptural education, I must say that it
is an assumption which is not founded on fact. I agree
with the right honourable gentleman, that the mere circumstance of a child's reading a chapter of the Scriptures
every day, would not alone furnish him with a sufficient
religious education. But the Kildare-place Society affords
an opportunity of further instruction to those who are
willing to receive it out of school-hours, and furnishes
that acquaintance with Scripture without which religious
instruction can be of no avail; and when the right honour-

able Secretary says the Society does not go far enough, I
say it goes as far as it can go in a country circumstanced
as Ireland is, in laying the foundation common to all.
Give me leave also to remark, that it furnishes no small
proof that the system upon which the Society set out was
adapted to the circumstances of Ireland, when I state that
it was originally framed, not by Protestants alone, but by
an union of Churchmen and Dissenters of all descriptions,
including Roman Catholics; and it is remarkable, as affording the first instance in which all religious parties in
Ireland had met upon a common ground, and agreed
upon a common principle. That system has been acted
upon with the perfect good-will, and, I believe, the sincere
approbation, of the generality of the people of Ireland,
although it has undoubtedly been opposed, of late, by the
Roman Catholic clergy. But when we are considering
the prejudices of one religious party in Ireland, are we
entirely to overlook the feelings and judgment of another?
A large body of Protestants will not admit of any system
of instruction in which the study of the Scriptures is not
included; therefore, when the right honourable gentleman
talks of founding a general system of education for Ireland, of which the reading of the Scriptures is to form no
part, the desire to meet the wishes of one particular party
seems to have deluded him into the belief that he is
adopting a principle which will please all. I assure him,
however, that he is mistaken, and that if he should adopt
the system which he has this evening propounded, he will
entirely overlook the wishes of the portion of the community of Ireland whose views and opinions are as much
entitled to respect as those of the Roman Catholics. He

never will be able to found a system excluding the Scriptures which will be acceptable to all parties. I believe, indeed, that he will never be able to adopt any system which will go nearer to unite all parties than that which has already been acted upon for the last fifteen years, and which was acquiesced in by all until the Roman Catholic clergy (many of whom at first supported the Society) thought proper to shift their course. I do not blame these gentlemen, because they are acting only in obedience to the orders of their superiors. They receive their commands from the Court of Rome, and accordingly it appears that in 1821 a Bull was sent to Ireland, forbidding the use of the Scriptures in schools. Upon the arrival of this Bull (and it furnished the first occasion on which the Kildare-place Society was publicly denounced), the honourable and learned member for Kerry* appeared at one of the public meetings, and I hold a report in my hand of his speech on that occasion, from which I will take the liberty of reading an extract. He says:—" The spiritual Head of our Church has issued what may not, perhaps, be obligatory on our consciences, even in spiritual matters, and it is well known that we often oppose him in temporals; but it is, at least, his advice *ex cathedra*. This Bull excludes from Catholic schools the Testament, even with note and comment, though these might be acceptable to Catholics. You say you will afford equal facilities to each persuasion, but, on the other hand, comes the Bull of the Pope refusing to accept this aid." Accordingly, the honourable and learned member goes forth mounted upon this Bull, among the Roman Catholic

* Mr. Daniel O'Connell.

clergy of Ireland, and stirs them up to oppose this institution. Up to that time no man had breathed an objection to the Society; and, on searching the records of this
House, I find that, previous to the issuing of this Papal
Bull, not a single petition was laid upon this table against
the system of education adopted by it. The question
then arises, are we, sitting here, to legislate for the
education of the people of Ireland, in reference to the
Bull of the Pope, or in reference to the wishes of the
people themselves? Parliament is now in precisely the
same situation that it was in the sixteenth century, when
the people of England shook off the spiritual dominion of
the Church of Rome, and insisted on the admissibility of
the Scriptures, and the right of private judgment, and
were sustained by the Parliament in that opposition. If
we are to mould a system of education which shall pre-
clude the children of the Roman Catholics from attaining
any knowledge of the Scriptures, give me leave to say
that we shall be manifesting, in our great liberality and
in the largeness of our toleration for all religions, a total
indifference for any. Thank God, this House, or this
Legislature, or this Constitution, has not yet come to that
point; for though I admit that all the civil disabilities of
Roman Catholics are repealed and gone for ever, we have
not, thereupon, repudiated our Protestant faith, nor re-
nounced our national religion. When, therefore, it is
said that a system is to be devised, which is to inculcate
all creeds, you are attempting to do that which is utterly
inconsistent with common sense, as well as with all religious principle. What should we say to the man in private life who became the teacher of inconsistent doctrines?

And what ought to be said of the Legislature that provided for the teaching of opposite and contradictory
creeds? The proposition is absurd, and I repeat, utterly
inconsistent with all moral and religious principle.

Had the just remonstrances which Mr. Lefroy
then urged against the withdrawal of the Parliamentary grant from the Kildare-place Society been
listened to by the Government, we should not now
be seeking in vain to recover lost ground in the
all important matter of National Education, after
sacrificing the best interests of our Roman Catholic
countrymen, in the idle hope of conciliating an
Ultramontane Hierarchy, and mis-spending nearly
half a century in trying to establish a system which
as at present carried out is admitted to be distaste-
ful to all creeds.

In the debate from which I have extracted
Mr. Lefroy's speech, Mr. Stanley himself admitted
"that the suspicions entertained by the Roman
Catholic clergy, of proselytism being carried on
in the schools of the Kildare Place Society,
were unjust," and that "the number of schools it
had established in the few years of its existence,
and of the pupils who had attended them, was to
him astonishing." And again, in speaking of the
machinery of the Society, he makes the following
admission:—"There is one part of it to which it is

hardly possible to render justice ; I allude to the
model and training-schools, and the arrangement
for printing cheap books. I never heard from the
most zealous Catholic any imputation to the effect
that, through the medium of these books, or any
publications the Society has made use of, there has
been the smallest attempt at proselytism. One of
the best proofs I can give of their freedom from
any attempt of that kind is, that in the schools
under Dr. Doyle* the books published by the
Kildare-place Society are in general use ;" yet,
unfortunately, notwithstanding this candid avowal
by Mr. Stanley of the fairness with which ·the
system of education was carried out, and of
the large measure of success it had attained, he
arrived at the conclusion "that Ireland was to be
looked at, not in a religious but in a political point
of view, that in such a view the influence of the
Priesthood ought not to be diminished, and that as
the Catholic Clergy and Hierarchy were opposed
to the Society, conceiving, *whether rightly or not*,
that one of its fundamental laws was against their
doctrines, the system must be abandoned."

When so earnest a desire was shcwn to satisfy the
scruples of the " Catholic Clergy and Hierarchy,"
we might surely have expected that in the new

---

* Roman Catholic Bishop of Kildare and Leighlin.

system of Education which was proposed, the conscientious convictions of the Bishops and. Clergy of
the Established Church would not have been altogether ignored. Yet from that time to the present
we find the remonstrances of the friends of Scriptural Education, however just and reasonable, have
been always disregarded by the British Government. In 1845 an address was issued by the
Prelates of the Established Church, and re-echoed
by 1,661 Clergymen, from which I have taken the
following extract, as clearly and forcibly exposing
the hardship of the position in which they were
placed as to the education of the poorer members
of the Church by the Rules of the National Board.

" In the former Societies for the education of the Poor,
with which the Clergy were connected, they had, in
accommodation to the unhappy divisions of this country,
consented to forbear from any attempt to teach the Formularies of our Church to the children of Dissenters,
Protestant or Roman Catholic, who attended the Schools
of which the Clergy had the superintendence. But they did
not judge themselves at liberty so to deal with the Word of
God. There was in every School a Bible-class, and all the
- children in attendance took their places in this class as soon
as their proficiency enabled them to profit by the reading
of the Holy Scriptures. But the distinction of the new
system was, that it placed the Bible under the same rule
with books of peculiar instruction in religion, and exclu-

ded it with them, from the hours of general education.
And moreover, this great change was, avowedly, made as
a concession to the unlawful authority by which the
Church of Rome withholds the Holy Scriptures from its
members." . . .

"The Clergy could not doubt that if they connected their
Schools with the National System, and thereby entered
into a compact to dispossess the Bible of the place which
it had hitherto occupied in them, they would be, in the
eyes of the young and of the old of both communions,
practically admitting the false principles of the Church of
Rome, and abandoning the great principle of their own
Church concerning the sufficiency and supremacy of God's
Holy Word. It would seem that the Board to which the
management of National Education is committed, has not
been insensible to the force of this grand and primary
objection, for it changed the offensive but true ground on
which the exclusion of the Scriptures from its Schools
was originally placed, for another which was much more
specious and popular ; and parental authority was brought
in to occupy the post at first assigned to the authority of
the Church of Rome.   Those who were acquainted with
the state of the country, knew that there was no real
objection on the part of Roman Catholic parents, speaking
generally, to read the Bible themselves, or have it read
by their children, but the contrary.   And, in fact, when
ecclesiastical authority was first exerted to put down
Scriptural education in this country, it had to encounter
very stubborn resistance from parental authority,—a resistance which undoubtedly would have been successful if
it had been aided, as it ought to have been, by the State."

" The exclusive appropriation of the Parliamentary Grants for Education, having left the Church destitute of its accustomed aids for the instruction of the children of the poor, the Clergy and Laity, to supply the want which had been thus created, united in forming the Church Education Society for Ireland." . . .

" The very limited resources of the Society, however, being inadequate to the full attainment of its objects, Diocesan and other petitions were presented to Parliament, praying for such a revision of the question of Educational Grants in this country, as might allow the Established Church to share in the funds appropriated to the education of the poor. . . . These appeals have been hitherto un-successful; but we cannot bring ourselves to think it possible that the striking inequality of the measure which has been dealt towards the Established Church of this country in the important concern of Education, and the great hardship of the position in which it has been thereby placed, can fail ultimately to attract towards it such fair consideration as may procure for it due sympathy and redress."

It may be said that this was the expression only of Clerical and not of Lay opinion against the working of the System of National Education. True—but the following Declaration was after-wards signed by several hundred influential Lay-men of the Established Church and Protestant Dissenters, including twenty-five Lay Peers, urging upon the Government the injustice of refusing aid

M

to the Schools of Protestant Patrons because of the Scriptures being taught, when the Schools of nuns and monks were receiving so large a share of the National Grant for Education in Ireland.

DECLARATION PRESENTED TO MR. CARDWELL, THE IRISH SECRETARY, IN MARCH, 1860.

Understanding that it is the intention of the Government to take the subject of Irish National Education into consideration, we, the undersigned Clergy and Laymen, declare it to be our conviction, that such modification of the rules of the National Board might be made, as would enable the friends of Scriptural Education to avail themselves of the system of secular instruction provided out of those public funds to which they so largely contribute; and in the hope of facilitating such an arrangement, and putting an end to the misconception which seems in many cases to exist as to the nature of the claims made by the friends of Scriptural Education, we feel it our duty explicitly to declare our sentiments on the following points :—

1st. We do not seek for denominational grants for education in Ireland.

2nd. We deprecate any modification of the rules of the National Board, which would deprive the public of the benefit of Inspectors appointed by that Board, to test the proficiency of the pupils in all Schools receiving aid from the public funds.

3rd. We are willing to undertake that the Schools under our patronage shall be open to children of all denominations, and to act upon the rules of the National

Board for regulating religious instruction so far as relates to the Teaching of the Articles, Catechisms, or Formularies of the Established Church, or of any sect of dissenters to which we, or any of us, may belong, or any other kind of religious instruction which may be considered to bear a sectarian character, provided only that the patrons of non-vested Schools shall be at liberty to use the Scriptures in their Schools, without being subject to the restrictions now imposed by the rules of the National Board.

4th. We respectfully submit that the objection sometimes urged against granting aid to our Schools, as subversive of parental authority, is shown to be perfectly futile, when it is remembered that such aid will in no way interfere with the vast number of other Schools aided by the National Board, where the children of Roman Catholic parents may, if they choose, receive education without the Scriptures.

5th. We further submit that as long as national aid is granted to the class of Convent Schools, where an officer of the Board admitted, in his evidence before the House of Lords, that no Protestant parent ought to send his children, and where, in fact, they are not sent, so long will impartial justice require that aid should not be refused to our Schools, even if they should not be attended by the children of Roman Catholic parents.

The moderation of tone and sentiment manifested in this Declaration was admitted to be worthy of all praise, yet it also was disregarded by the Government of the day. It only remains to add that a few extracts from the evidence lately given on oath before the Royal Commission of Inquiry into Education will suffice to show that while any concession has been thus peremptorily refused to satisfy the conscientious scruples of Protestant School-Patrons, the State has been for thirty-six years past professing to carry on a system established for the purpose of promoting united Education and yet applying a very large portion of the annual Parliamentary Grant in support of schools where, according to the evidence now on record, "no Protestant child could with safety to its creed attend ;" and that, on the other hand, many thousands of the children of the Protestant poor in Ireland are excluded from any benefit of the Parliamentary Grant by the conditions to which the National Board obstinately adheres.*

In the following extracts I have confined myself to witnesses above all suspicion of any unfair prejudice against the National Board.

---

* The result appears to be that, at the present time, the Members of the Church Education Society, contributing largely as they do to the taxation from which the Parliamentary Grant is made, are also obliged to impose on themselves a tax of £45,619 14s. 6d. per annum to support their schools, in which united education is given to 46,790 Members of the Church of Ireland, 12,160 Protestant Dissenters, and 7,855 Roman Catholics without any assistance from the State; while they see, at the same time, 150 Schools conducted by Nuns and Monks in connexion with the National Board, in which denominational education is given at the expense of the State.

James Wilson, Esq., sworn and examined.

15937. What is your opinion of the working of the National System; is it favourable or otherwise?—I think the National System, if properly managed, and if the principle of united education were strictly carried out, is the only system for Ireland. . . . .

15939. Are there any special points on which you think undue concessions have been made?—The principle of the National system is laid down in Lord Stanley's letter, in which he says: "one of the main objects must be to unite in one system children of different creeds." I consider that to be the true principle upon which the National or united system of education is based. . . . That was the view, which the Commissioners of National Education who were first appointed, took of their duty, but I think that has not been carried out during the last thirty-six years.

15940. Are there any specific points on which you consider that principle has been departed from?—In the commencement of the system it was departed from in the admission of schools under the management of monks and nuns. I conceive those schools are essentially denomina-tional schools

16044. With regard to convent schools, do I understand you to say you regard their connexion with the Board as opposed to the principle of Lord Stanley's letter?—Convent schools are open, like all other schools, to the children of all creeds, if they choose to go; but I consider convent schools must, from their nature, be denominational, and that no Protestant child could with safety to its creed, attend a convent school; not that the ladies of the convent would break any confidence reposed in them; but all the concomitants of the school are denominational.

16045. Have the convent schools any special advantages under the Board?—They have.

16046. What do you regard as their special advantages?—They have this special advantage, that there is no examination of the teachers. A teacher may be wholly incompetent, but the Board ask no questions, whether she is competent or not. They have also an advantage, I think, in their mode of payment. . . In the first place, they have the capitation grant, and in addition to the capitation grant, they have monitors provided to aid the teachers. I made inquiries, and found that, according to the returns of the National Board, there are altogether one hundred and thirty-eight first class female monitors, and I am informed that ninety of these are in the Convent Schools throughout Ireland — that is about two-thirds of the first class female monitors are in Convent Schools.

16048. Does the mode of payment by capitation grant give anything like a fair representation of the amount they receive?—It does not.

Baggot-street convent school has an average of 739; the capitation grant would be £132; the amount actually paid is £460 12s. 6d.

King's Inn Street school has an average attendance of 851, the capitation grant would be £141, the amount actually paid is £556 5s.

In confirmation of the opinion expressed by Mr. Wilson in the foregoing evidence, as to the deno-

minational character of the Convent Schools, I
may add, that Mr. Cumin, one of the Assistant
Commissioners, in his Report says:—

"Nominally the Convent Schools are National schools
because they comply with the rules of the Board, but to
my mind they are thoroughly denominational. That they
are denominational in the eyes of the people and of the
excellent ladies who conduct them admits not of a shadow
of doubt."

And Mr. Brooke, one of the Commissioners, in
his Protest against certain portions of the Report
lately published, says:—

"That the lower classes of Irish Protestants are fully
alive to the danger of those schools is proved by the fact
that, of 73,331 children whose names in the year 1867
were on the Rolls of the Convent schools, only 73 were
Protestants."

In the protest of the Rev. David Wilson, D.D.,
another of the Commissioners against the report
lately published, we also find the startling fact
brought to light, that between the years 1860 and
1868 the Commissioners of National Education had
increased their grants to Convent schools from
£8,044 6s. 9d. to £16,129 6s. 11d.

So also as to the Christian Brothers' Schools, the
Rev. David Wilson, D.D., tells us " that in all these

Schools, emblems, statues of the Virgin, and other
things generally objectionable to Protestants, are
exhibited;" and he then gives a curious incident as
to the Newtown Stackpoole National Schools, male
and female, being a few years ago taken possession
of by the Christian Brothers, who converted the
latter into a barn and the former into a school for
their own pupils: and Dr. Wilson adds this somewhat significant comment:—

" Thus the Christian Brothers possessed themselves of
valuable property, on which a considerable amount of
public money was expended, and the Commissioners of
National Education looked on while this summary transfer
of Schools ' vested ' in themselves was being effected, and
denominational Education was being substituted for
National."

With such evidence before us, it can hardly be
denied that the National Board has hitherto
failed to carry out the principle of United Education which the late Lord Derby avowed to be the
great object of Government in establishing the
present system ; and so long as the British
Government continues to ignore the all-important
truth that Education, in the only sense which
deserves the name, includes the training of the
habits and affections as well as of the head,—the preparation of children not only for the station they

may have to fill in this life, but for the immortal
life which is beyond the grave,—so long, I fear,
shall we see Ireland exhibiting the anomaly she
now does, of a country in which more than three
hundred thousand pounds of public money are an-
nually spent for the purpose of educating the people,
and yet displaying a condition socially and intellec-
tually so far below what might naturally be expected
under such advantages as to suggest the idea that
the Government must be wholly indifferent as to
the progress of civilization in the country or entirely ignorant of the means of promoting it. Yet,
it is sad to find that in the Report of the Commissioners, from whom we looked for some satisfactory
solution of the difficulties connected with the great
question of Irish National Education, we are
threatened with a further advance in the direction
of denominational Education, and if the Roman
Catholic Hierarchy " bring sufficient pressure to
bear" upon the British Government, it is not impro-
bable, that instead of so modifying the present
rules of the National Board, as to admit the Protestant poor in Ireland to share the benefits of the
National grant for Education, they will be left
without any redress, while the Roman Catholic
population of Ireland will be condemned to succumb to a system of Ultramontane Education, as
destructive of any intellectual or moral progress, as

it will be hostile to the continuance of British connexion.

Nor is it unworthy of notice that while Cardinal Cullen, in his evidence before the Royal Commissioners, was advocating the cause of Ultramontanism, and pressing the necessity of committing to the Priests the exclusive management of the education of the Roman Catholics of Ireland, as a measure of *justice to the people*, we have had in one of the ablest works which has emanated on Roman Catholic authority for many years, the important confession—

" That there is already existing within the pale of the Roman Catholic Church a party morally, if not numerically, strong, who are unable to identify the interests of that Church with the advance of Ultramontanism, or rather who cannot but recognize between the two an antithesis to which present facts, no less than past experience, give all the significance of a solemn warning."—" *The Pope and the Council*," by Janus, p. 21.

And in the same able work we find the following wholesome warning given us of what Ultramontanism really is—

" Ultramontanism is essentially Papalism ; and its starting-point is that the Pope is infallible in all doctrinal decisions, not only on matters of faith, but in the domain of ethics, on the relations of religion to society, of Church to State, and even on State insti-

tution; and that every such decision claims unlimited
and unreserved submission in word and deed from all
Catholics." . . . . The very kernel and ruling
principle of Ultramontanism is the consolidation of
absolutism in the Church. . . . . Hence the profound hatred at the bottom of the soul of every genuine
Ultramontane of free institutions and the whole constitutional system."

CHAPTER VII.

Extracts from his Speeches on the Reform Bills for England and Ireland and the Church Temporalities Bill—Letters to his Son the Rev. Jeffry Lefroy on entering the Ministry—Rebuilding of Carrig-glas Manor House—Effects of the Great Hurricane of th January, 1839.

On the question of Parliamentary Reform for England, Mr. Lefroy was rather in advance of many of the political party with which he acted in the House of Commons, for he always looked upon " *the Rotten Boroughs*" as a grievous abuse of the system of Parliamentary Representation which was intended to be provided by the British Constitution. Upon the same principle he felt that the large and important commercial towns of England should have been entitled to send representatives to Par liament, when first that demand was made by the advocates of Reform, but his objection to the measure of Reform proposed by Lord Grey's Government, was that instead of carrying out the constitutional principles of our system of Parliamentary Representation by merely correcting those abuses which the lapse of time and change of circumstances had introduced, the measure departed altogether from the principles of the Constitution, and dangerously increased the democratic element in our political system.

The following short extract from his speech in the House of Commons on the English Reform Bill, shows that such was the ground of his opposition to the Bill, and in this extract we see the views he entertained as to the proper limits of the power possessed by the House of Commons in dealing with questions that involve fundamental principles of the British Constitution, as well as his just appreciation of the blessings which rich and poor alike enjoy under that Constitution, and the danger of rashly abandoning any of those safeguards by which it has protected and secured the rights of all classes.

" It has been said by the right honourable baronet* that the elective franchise must be considered in the light of a public trust, and not as a private right. I do not stand here now to discuss that question. But admitting it to be, as the right honourable baronet asserts, a public trust, to be dealt with by this House as such, I will say that the power of the House so to deal is itself a public trust; one of the primary duties of which is to preserve, according to its principles, that Constitution which is a sacred deposit for the benefit of all—the inheritance and right of all—of the poor as well as the rich—of the low as well as the high;—that Constitution which gives to the rich man the best security for his possessions; to the industrious the best encouragement for his industry; and

* Sir James Graham.

to the poor man, who has nothing else, protection to his poverty from insult, and to his person from oppression. The test, therefore, by which this measure is to be tried is—whether it is a measure consistent with the principles of the British Constitution. If it be, let us adopt it. I am not afraid to follow, indeed it is our duty to follow, whither these principles lead. But if, on the other hand, the measure be found to be contrary to the principles of the Constitution, then ministers themselves cannot consistently persevere in it."

"Much has been said of the danger of refusing this measure, but the danger to our most valued institutions of conceding it is lost sight of; while the sure way to avoid all dangers is by a firm and conscientious adherence to the principles of the Constitution."

In the debate on the Irish Reform Bill he was selected by the leaders of the Conservative party to move the usual amendment for rejection of the Bill, and without attempting to review the principles on which the House of Commons had already decided that a measure of Parliamentary Reform was necessary for England, no dispassionate mind can fail to see the force and soundness of the distinctions which he draws between the two cases.

"In rising to oppose the motion which has just been submitted, I beg to observe that it is my intention to move, by way of amendment to the proposition of the Right

Honourable Gentleman,* that the Bill be read a second time this day six months. In doing so I claim the indulgence of the House, not only on my own account, but from the great importance of the subject. Often as the House has been called upon to legislate for Ireland, never, I am bold to say, was a subject of greater importance submitted to the consideration of the Legislature, not merely with respect to Ireland, but as it affects the empire at large. I concur fully in what has been laid down by the Right Honourable Gentleman, that it is not open to me to dispute principles already recognised by the House; and, therefore, in the observations which I intend to offer, I shall abstain from doing so. My object will be to shew, in the first instance, that the grounds and reasons upon which the English Reform Bill was supported, are not applicable to Ireland; and, secondly that there are circumstances peculiar to Ireland which render the measure not only unsafe for Ireland and her most important institutions, but dangerous also to the kindred institutions of England, and even to the best interests of the whole empire.

"In submitting the measure to the House, the Right Honourable Gentleman slightly glanced at the dangers which are apprehended by those who oppose it. I give him credit for great ingenuity for the manner in which he attempted to make light of those dangers; but if I mistake not, he altogether failed to prove that there was any analogy whatever between the state of the representation in Ireland and that in England, and it is therefore, in my opinion, quite consistent for any gentleman who voted

* Mr. Stanley.

for reform in England to oppose the measure when
about to be extended to the sister country. The great
argument urged in favour of reform in England, was the
enormous preponderance of borough representation over
popular representation. It is also alleged that the borough
representation has departed from the principles of the
constitution, and, therefore, that it is necessary to bring it
back to some real or fancied standard of original purity.
I now beg leave to call the attention of the House to the
state of the representation of Ireland at this moment, and
I would boldly ask does it stand in need of reform on
any of these grounds? At the time of the Union the
Irish House of Commons consisted of three hundred
Members—of these two hundred were swept away—two
hundred be it remembered of the most exceptionable portion of the representation were got rid of—and one
hundred of the soundest part preserved. Now I would
beg leave to say, that was in itself a vast and sweeping
measure of reform. Did the portion which remained
stand in need of any further reform? Amongst the
Members preserved were sixty-four for the counties—all
of course popular representatives—and ten for cities,
popular representatives also, with one Member for the
University, making in the entire seventy-five Members
returned by popular constituencies. Twenty-five therefore, remained, and these were selected at the time of the
Union from places containing the greater amount of population, and were described in the Act of Union as places of
the greatest consideration. Now it is these boroughs which
will be materially affected by the proposed measure,
for I admit, that, with respect to the counties—if it is

necessary to pass a Reform Bill at all which I do not think it is—no very material alteration will take place. Of these twenty-five boroughs seven possess a popular constituency; they have been frequently contested, and have sent to the present Parliament seven reformers; and the present constituency of all is above the standard proposed by the Reform Bill for the newly created boroughs in England. There is another, namely, Coleraine, which, although it possesses a constituency of only fifty-two persons is yet an open borough, and has sent a reformer to the present Parliament after a contest. The representatives of these eight boroughs added to the seventy-five, which I have already stated as being returned by popular constituencies, would give the whole number of popular representatives in Ireland as eighty-three. The constituency of the remaining seventeen boroughs vary from twelve in number up to ninety-four. Some possess a constituency of fifty, some of seventy-five, some of ninety-four; and five or six I am bound to admit, have constituencies of fourteen or fifteen only; but I have already shewn that eighty-three Members are returned for popular representations. The Bill proposes to add five new Members which will make eighty-eight, and in addition to these it is intended to throw open the seventeen boroughs to which I have referred. Of these boroughs there is not one deserving the epithet of "*rotten*" in the sense applied to the English boroughs: there is not one of them a decayed place—they are, in fact, in a more flourishing condition, than when they received the franchise. There is not amongst them a single Sarum or Gatton, but, on the contrary they are all

increasing in affluence and respectability. It is true the
constituency is small, but if it was constitutional to grant
the franchise originally to a small constituency, I cannot
understand upon what constitutional grounds that right
can be now infringed. They are not like the boroughs in
Schedule A of the English Reform Bill which have lost
their constituencies, they are not the boroughs whose
population has departed—their constituencies have not
fallen off—and if these boroughs retain these constituencies I have yet to learn upon what constitutional principle
it is that they are to be deprived of a right which is now
as well merited as the day upon which the Crown bestowed
it. I call on my honourable and learned friend, the Solicitor General for Ireland, to state upon what constitutional
principle it is that these boroughs are to be deprived of
their franchise, merely because the number of their constituencies is so limited. If there be no principle of the
constitution to justify the interference with the rights of
these boroughs—and I defy my honourable and learned
friend to shew that there is—then it can only be justified
upon the ground of expediency, and to that my honourable and learned friend must be driven. But upon what
ground even of expediency can this unconstitutional
interference with the right of these boroughs be supported.
Eighty-three out of one hundred Members have been
proved to be returned by popular constituencies. I would
put it fearlessly to the noble lord opposite, who has introduced the measure of reform for England, whether if the
borough representation in that country bore no larger proportion to the representation of the whole kingdom than
it bears in Ireland, he would have felt himself called upon

or justified in bringing in the measure which he has done?
Would any man in his senses have done so? In Ireland
the proportion of the borough representation is not
quite one-fifth of the whole. In England the supporters of Reform rest their arguments on the necessity
that exists of doing away with the enormous preponderance of the borough representation. But no
such preponderance exists in Ireland, and therefore
there is no ground to justify the application of a
similar measure to that country. The Right Honourable
Gentleman, the Secretary for Ireland, has asked, will you,
while you give a real representation to England, be satisfied with giving the mockery of a representation for
Ireland? I would ask can the present state of the
representation of Ireland be justly called a mockery.
When five-sixths of the representations are popular in the
highest degree, and none of them are open to the objections
which apply to the decayed boroughs in England? Again
it is asked by the Right Honourable Gentleman are we to
put an end to nomination boroughs in England, and to
permit them to exist in Ireland? If the Right Honour
able Gentleman is to legislate for both countries upon the
principle of uniformity, let him carry the principle
throughout the whole Bill, let us have an addition to our
county Members so as to give some counterpoise to property
against the effect of throwing open the boroughs; but
let him not apply a similarity of legislation in one point,
and refuse it in another. If he is not to legislate upon
one principle for England and another for Ireland, I
would call upon him to extend the principle of the Bill,
and the whole Bill to the latter country. The counter-

poising principle of giving to property a fair share in
the representation, is one which Ireland has a right to
demand, and, therefore, if the boroughs are thrown
open, additional Members ought to be given to the
counties.

"Having now, as I hope, shewn the totally different
grounds on which the Reform Bills for England and
Ireland stand, I beg to call the attention of the House
to another reason which makes me feel it a duty to
oppose this Bill. I mean the peculiar danger arising from
the circumstances in which the country is placed—
danger not limited to Ireland alone—danger not merely
threatening that country, but threatening the whole
empire. It has been truly stated that the great objection
to this measure arises from the effect it will have of
throwing the weight into the Roman Catholic interest,
as opposed to the Protestant; but the Right Honourable
Gentleman has been pleased to say that the day is
gone by for that argument—that the distinction of
religion is no longer a ground for giving or withholding
political power—that the Roman Catholic Relief Bill has
put an end to that; What! has the Relief Bill put
an end to the Protestant Constitution? Have we not
still a Protestant King, and an established religion?
What, Sir, if religion be no longer a distinction to be
regarded in reference to political power, what will the
Right Honourable Gentleman say to the title to the
Crown!—does he dare to lay his finger to the foundation
of the throne? Whilst we have a monarchy—and God
knows how long that may be, the King and the Queen
must be Protestants. We have also an established

Church and a reformed religion; and if the Right
Honourable Gentleman attempts to legislate without
a view to these establishments, and without regard
to the principles on which they rest, his legislation
will want the wisdom and prudence, which should .
characterize all legislation. But in answer to this part
of the Right Honourable Gentleman's argument, I
must beg to call the attention of the House to the
grounds upon which the. Roman Catholic Relief Bill
was passed. The King's Speech, in recommending that
measure to the consideration of both Houses, directs
them to ' consider whether the removal of those disabilities
can be effected consistently with the full and permanent
security of our establishments in Church and State—with
the maintenance of the reformed religion established by
law, and of the rights and privileges of the Bishops and
Clergy of this realm, and of the Churches committed to
their charge. These are institutions which must ever be
held sacred in this Protestant kingdom, and which it is
the duty and determination of his Majesty to preserve
inviolate.'

" Both Houses addressed the Throne, echoing these sentiments, and the Right Honourable Secretary for Ireland
joined in the address. The principle was fully recognised
in the Relief Bill itself, by the solemn precaution of an
oath, to guard the interests of the Established Church;
and therefore it is that I take leave to say, notwithstanding the arguments of the Right Honourable Gentleman, if we find a measure fraught with danger to our
Established Church, we are bound to advert to that
danger in order to provide against it. Do Honourable

Members believe that the Established Church in Ireland can long survive the increase of power which this measure will bestow upon the Roman Catholics? If our Church should fall, do Honourable Members think it would fall alone? Can any man divine by what marvel the hand that felled it would be prevented from being uplifted against the sister Church of England? But let us suppose that the Established Church in England should escape, would not the destruction of the Irish Church endanger the connexion between the two countries? The Established Church forms the great connecting link —the bond which binds them together. In proof of this, I would refer to an authority of greater weight than my own—an authority which Honourable Members opposite must respect, coming as it does from an Emancipator, a Reformer, and a Whig. Lord Plunket, in the year 1824, in this House, said he ' had no hesitation to state, that the existence of the Protestant Establishment was the great bond of union between the countries; and if ever that unfortunate moment should arrive when they would rashly lay their hands on the property of the Church, to rob it of its rights, that moment they would seal the doom and terminate the connexion between the two countries.'

"I trust that Noble Lord, if he should come to vote upon this measure in another place, will not forget the opinion which was given by him in this House. But is there no other danger to be apprehended? Is there no other great question pending upon which the Roman Catholic population of Ireland feel intensely, and have formed a determination upon the subject from which nothing can turn them? Has the Secretary for Ireland forgotten the repeal of the Union? He has referred to a document bearing the signature of the Honourable and Learned Member for Kerry. I will refer to another document, a letter, in which that Honourable Member speaks of ' the deep interest which the people of Ireland take in the repeal question—how intense is their anxiety for that measure—how it overpowers every other sentiment of a political nature relative to Ireland.' And then the Honourable and Learned Member for Kerry proceeds to state his own intentions with respect to the measure, in these words: —' I never did—I never will—I never can abandon my anxious desire for a repeal of the Union. I deem that repeal essentially necessary to Irish prosperity. I pledge myself to use every suitable occasion to promote that repeal, and never to omit any available opportunity to advance the interests of the cause of the legislative and constitutional independence of Ireland. If there be any immediate dissolution, be satisfied with returning Reformers to Parliament, without insisting on anything further. Your present preparation for reform will be the best means of hereafter ensuring your Repealers.'

" In other words, the Hon. Member for Kerry says distinctly that he will take reform as a stepping-stone to repeal: and if the present measure should pass, and twenty-five additional Members be placed at the disposal of the populace, and the power of their leader in this House be thereby increased, I ask what Government can long oppose any measure which is backed by such a party. I would appeal to the House, and even to the Right

Honourable Gentleman himself, who has some experience
of the hard measure which the party led by the Honourable Member for Kerry at present in the House have dealt
out to him—of the severe curb with which they ride him—
I would appeal to the Right Honourable Gentleman how
the Government can be carried on if that party be
increased to fifty or sixty Members. They have already
forced the Right Honourable Gentleman to the relinquish-
ment of measures for Ireland, which he introduced to
the House as beneficial to that country. Does the Right
Honourable Gentleman forget the Arms' Bill, to which
he had pledged himself ? There is the yeomanry of
Ireland, too—and I well recollect the meed of praise
which the Right Honourable Secretary bestowed upon
that body on his first going to Ireland—but he was
forced to abandon them at the beck of that party whose
power he is now about to increase. I would beg to
remind him also of the system of national education. As
a man of religious principle, he must have been individually opposed to that measure, but yet he was obliged
to yield it at the dictation of that party. Under these
circumstances, I think it folly in the extreme to augment
that party — to raise up, in fact, a force capable of
thwarting the just and wise resolves of the Government.
It is not, however, merely with reference to their influence on the Government of the day that their power
ought to be viewed. I would appeal to the English and
Scotch Members, whether or not the interests of both
countries must not be materially affected by the existence
of such a party in the House of Commons. That party
will be bound together by a tie that cannot be dissolved.

They will be warned, as they have already been, that their
return to this House again will depend upon their close adherence to their party. Should they falter or hold back,
they will be denounced to the people—their names will be
recorded in the black book of the priests—and they will
suffer at the hustings the penalty for desertion of their party,
in this House. That is the great bond by which they will be
bound together; and on this subject I must avail myself of
the testimony of the Honourable and Learned Member for
Louth on a former occasion, when he warned his Majesty's Government of the precipice on which they would
totter when this party should be reinforced by the accession to their numbers which they would obtain by the
Reform Bill. The Right Honourable Gentleman denies
that the Disfranchisement Bill which accompanied the
Roman Catholic Relief Bill was passed with a view to
abridge the political influence of the Roman Catholic
population. But I must beg leave to differ altogether
from the Right Honourable Gentleman on this point.
The increasing preponderance of the Roman Catholic
constituency, from the time they obtained the elective
franchise in 1793, was such, that by degrees, in most
of the counties in Ireland, property lost its weight and
influence in the elections, and in many places property
was not, in point of fact, represented in the Commons
House of Parliament. It was to meet this that, at the
passing of the Relief Bill, the forty-shilling freeholders
were disfranchised: but the Right Honourable Gentleman
says they were disfranchised, not merely on account of
being subject to the influence of their priests, but chiefly
because they were not independent of their own land-

lords. Is it because he has two objections to them that
he gives us back, in the £10 renters, a worse description
of voters than the exploded forty-shilling freeholders?
The £10 renters in these boroughs will bear no resem-
blance to the £10 householders in England, who pay
rates and taxes by reason of their occupation, and
whose tenement is always worth considerably more
than the rent. The forty-shilling freeholder was obliged
to swear to a profit: the new voter will not be required
to do any such thing; his house need not be worth one
shilling beyond the rent, and drawn, as they will be,
from that class of the people which is nurtured in
strong prejudices against the Established Church, and
equally strong prejudices against British connexion, can
any man doubt that the destruction of the Established
Church, and the repeal of the Union, will be their anxious
hope and object? With such a constituency a representation will indeed be formed, which may well deserve the
Right Honourable Gentleman's epithet of "a mockery"—
a mock representation, so far as property is concerned, but
a real representation of the will of the Priests. If we
have seen all the landlords of a county united together
overthrown by the £10 freeholders, as at present is sometimes the case, how will the matter stand when the influence of the priest is exerted, as it undoubtedly will be,
over the miserable £10 renters? What will, then, be the
state of the Protestant interest in Ireland? I object to
this measure on the score of justice. I desire no more
than the fulfilment of the principle of the Emancipation Bill
itself. It must be admitted that the principle of that Bill
was meant to go no further than to place the Roman

Catholics on an equal footing with the Protestants in the scale of political power; but the present Bill goes to give an overwhelming preponderance to the Roman Catholics. At the time of the Union, the boroughs were preserved, to secure to Protestant property its just weight in the representation.

MR. STANLEY.—We propose to keep all these boroughs.

Mr. LEFROY.—Yes, indeed, the places will remain; the form will exist, but the life and spirit will be gone. It is impossible, if this bill should pass, that the property of Ireland can be represented in this House; in lieu of it the great numerical force of the Roman Catholics will be represented. I will beg now to call the attention of the House to another very important danger connected with the passing of this measure. If it should turn out that Protestant feeling and property should fail to be represented in this House—if the religion of the Protestants should be assailed, and their property menaced—would it not, I ask, be to expect something more than the exercise of human patience, to suppose that they would quietly bear expenses brought upon them by the conduct of the English Government, and yet assist in maintaining the union with a country which had cast them off? Should they throw their swords into the opposite scale, the result would not be problematical. The Union could not possibly be maintained, for it would not be in the power of England to maintain it without the support of the Protestants of Ireland. The Protestants of Ireland are a brave and gallant body of men, disciplined and armed; they form a band upon which England ought to remember that she may securely rely in the hour of peril, and with their aid

she may laugh at the threats of Repeal. But if they
should be cast off by England, and receive neither
that justice which is due to them by national compact, nor that protection which belongs to them as
loyal subjects, they may—and even under these circumstances I should deplore it from the bottom of
my heart—but they may be goaded on, or seduced to
take part with those whose object is to rend asunder
that great bond which now binds the two countries so
closely together. I trust that those English Members,
who, though Reformers, have deeply at heart the welfare of the Empire, will consider this danger, and avert
the possibility of it by withholding their support from
this measure. Its direct tendency will be to increase
the political influence of a party, who for centuries
have been opposed to British connexion, who have shewn
themselves anxious to overturn the institutions of the
country, and to whom the accession of numbers will
only afford greater power to subvert the Church and
repeal the Union. If they should succeed in. overturning the Church in Ireland, let it be remembered
that there are many members in this House, who declare that every man should have his own religion,
as he has his own doctor or lawyer; with these Members the Irish Members will then coalesce; and, having
succeeded in destroying the Irish Church, they will
feel it their duty to do "the same good turn" to the
Church of England. Upon this principle, I appeal to the
English Members, who, though they may be reformers,
have not yet made up their minds to relinquish their
Church or their religion. The House has heard much of

the danger of withholding this measure. If the measure
is one of injustice the House may laugh at threats founded
on an unjust claim. If we receive the cordial support of
Great Britain, the threat of a successful rebellion in
Ireland is vain and illusory, so long as the Protestants do
not concur in it—and I trust they never will."

In his defence of the Irish Church he always
carefully avoided even the appearance of defending
any anomalies to which the lapse of time or altered
circumstances might have given rise in the application of Church funds. On this subject his
views were opposed to many of those with whom
he acted, as he felt that great benefit might be
obtained for our Church, and much of the hostility
which was shewn towards it in some quarters miti-
gated, by such a redistribution of Church property
as would afford more adequate remuneration to the
working Clergy, while he firmly resisted the diver-
sion of any of the Church's property from the
sacred trust under which it was held, for the service
of God and the promotion of true religion in the
land. The following extract from his speech on
the Church Temporalities (Ireland) Bill in 1833,
exhibits the clear and decided tone in which his
warning voice was on all occasions raised, as to the
dangers which must flow from legislating for the
Irish Church on any other principles ; and also
shews his willingness to accept the principle of

Church Reform, where reform was really shewn to be necessary.

"In rising to state the grounds of my opposition to this Bill, I beg to observe that my objections are not made to it for the sake of opposition, but because it appears to me that a dangerous principle is involved in the Bill, and that if it be carried into effect, it will be attended with the most mischievous consequences. I desire nothing but that this House should legislate for the Church in Ireland on the principle of justice—that we should legislate for the Church of Ireland on the same principles upon which we should proceed if we were about to legislate for the Church in England. This has been called "a Bill for the Reform of the Church in Ireland." On the subject of reform, I will say that I do not stand here to defend abuses, nor do I desire that a single abuse should be continued for an hour. I should very ill represent the feelings of the Clergy of the Church of Ireland, if I were to do so, or to resist any fresh distribution of Church property, which would conduce to the promotion of the interests of the Establishment, and the support of the Protestant religion in Ireland. I do stand here, however, to resist any proposition for divesting the Church of Ireland of its property, and devoting it to other than ecclesiastical purposes. I stand here to resist your legislating on principles dangerous in themselves, and tending to injure the rights of all property. And, lastly, I stand here to resist a measure which will raise a most important question as connected with the Coronation Oath."

Here, at considerable length, he examined in detail the various provisions of the Bill for the abolition of First-fruits in Ireland, and the imposition of a new tax on the Clergy in lieu thereof, for the reduction of the number of Irish Bishops, and for the appropriation of the purchase-money to be paid by the holders of Bishops' leases for the perpetuity of their tenures ; and concluded thus :—

"In the course of the last Session, a Commission was appointed for the purpose of inquiring into the state and condition of the Church in Ireland: that Commission has been issued, and has made considerable progress in its inquiry. A great deal of very valuable information has been obtained under it; and I only regret that his Majesty's Government did not think fit to postpone the introduction of any measure of this kind until that information had been laid upon the table of the House. Why this course was not adopted, I am totally at a loss to conceive, unless, indeed, his Majesty's Ministers thought it necessary to propose a measure for the appropriation of Church property, as a set-off for the measure of coercion. It would seem as if Ministers, in creating the monster which they raised up under the Reform Bill, forgot that that monster would require to be fed; and that, alarmed by its cry and clamour, they now feel obliged to satisfy the cravings of its appetite by throwing to it a large portion of the Irish Church property. Ministers, however, are greatly mistaken if they suppose that the voracious creature will be content with this Bill alone. They should remember that the first sacrifice that was made at the commencement of the French Revolution, was of the Church; and they should not forget in how short a time the fall of the aristocracy, the confiscation of property, and the destruction of the monarchy followed that first and insufficient sacrifice. I trust that we are not yet sunk into such a condition as France then was; but I think that if we continue to give way to public clamour—to yield to every demand that an unthinking multitude may make—to consent to violate the standard principles of the law, and to legislate upon such grounds as those upon which many of the provisions of this Bill are founded, it will not be long before we shall arrive at that point at which it will be compulsory upon us to choose, if, indeed, any choice be left to us, between the established institutions of Great Britain, on the one hand, and a thorough democracy, with an agrarian law, on the other. Standing upon the principles of the Constitution, and holding fast to that established religion under which this country has so wonderfully prospered, we may hope that God will yet avert the evil; but when I am assured that we are to go on from one measure of expediency to another, and from the abandonment of one principle to-day, to the abandonment of another principle to-morrow, I feel satisfied that nothing but disaster and confusion can possibly follow!"

In a letter from the Bishop of Ferns (Dr. Thomas Elrington, previously Provost of Trinity College), alluding to a mistake which occurred in the newspaper report of this speech, we find the following gratifying expression of his opinion :—:

The Palace, Ferns, 16th May.

My DEAR SIR,—Premising that I am well aware of the difference between what you say and what you are reported to have said, I think it right that you should be apprised of the latter, when the matter is important. The *Mail* certainly gives a good report of your excellent speech on Monday last, but it makes you say that Dissenters are excluded from vestries for building churches. Now, the fact is, that they are competent to attend and vote. Roman Catholics were not excluded till the 10 Geo. I. c. 6, which recites that their opposition to the building of churches made it necessary to exclude them. By-the-bye, it was very fair to tax them for the rebuilding the churches which had been destroyed by their ancestors. " *Delicta majorum haud immeritus luat.*" If you never had said, and never were to say, anything but your speech of the 13th, I would pronounce that you had repaid the University and the Church for electing you.

Adieu,

Yours faithfully,

THOS. FERNS.

To Mr. Lefroy is to be traced the first step which was taken to facilitate the building of those Chapels of Ease which are now popularly known as Trustee-Chapels, to which we are so much indebted for the progress of evangelical truth in the Church of

O

Ireland within the last thirty years. The 6 & 7 Wm. IV., c. 31,* was drawn up by him, and passed through Parliament mainly by his exertions. But his labours were not confined to the discharge of his public duties in the House of Commons. During the progress of the Irish Reform Bill, the Church Temporalities Bill, the Municipal Corporation Bill, and the Bill for the Amendment of the Grand Jury Laws, he was in constant personal communication with the Primate, the Duke of Wellington, and Sir Robert Peel, upon the subject of those important Bills, and he was one of those whose counsel and judgment on all the important measures that affected Ireland while he remained in Parliament was sought for and esteemed by the leaders of the party and the heads of our Church.

His private letters at this period show us some of the difficulties with which the conservative party had to contend at that time with respect to the legislative measures proposed for Ireland, and they are interesting also as showing that, although the distaste for political life which led to his at first

* Under this Act were erected Trinity Church, in St. Thomas' Parish, Dublin, where the ministry of the Rev. John Gregg (now Bishop of Cork) was for so many years carried on; also St. Matthias's Church, in St. Peter's Parish, Dublin, where the Rev. Maurice F. Day (now Dean of Limerick) carried on his ministry for twenty-four years; and several other churches, which amply testify to the value of the measure.

declining the representation of the University still continued, it never prevented his entering with individual interest and zeal into the duties of his post.

TO HIS WIFE.

Eaton Square,
18th July, 1833.

I am as busy as when the Bill* was in our House, since it is necessary to give every assistance in my power to those who are to fight our battle in the Lords. Don't be surprised at seeing that Government have a great majority on the second reading, nor think that the Lords have deserted the Church. This will arise from its being thought best not to throw out the Bill, but to amend it ; and if the course which I have reason to hope be adopted, it is the wisest and best course. But no person except one on the spot, and acquainted with the real state of political affairs, can judge of the great difficulty of knowing what is best to be done under the circumstances in which we are placed. Here we are every day in consultation, all sensible of the injustice of the Bill, and able to throw it out; yet for the sake of the Church, as well as the State, it must be submitted to. The fact is, if we were to throw it out, the Government would resign; and, as it is impossible for us to form a Government, these men must come back again, and the King would be under the necessity of making peers to swamp the House of Lords, and the last state of things would be worse than the first. Besides this, the Government have kept the clergy of our

* "The Bill to alter and amend the Temporalities of the Church of Ireland."

Church in their power by putting an end to tithe and vestry cess, and yet are determined not to give them a shilling if this Bill does not pass. All our great guns have been reserved for to-night. I have just spent three hours with the Bishop of Exeter, who is going to make (as I expect) an excellent speech.

T. L.

TO THE SAME.

I have now been five successive nights keeping watch for our Church till near daylight. All that could be done has been and will be done. The Duke has worked nobly and is the most devoted friend to Ireland that I have found here ;· he has constantly spent three or four hours over the Bill in the mornings, and afterwards worked in the House for several hours. I spent nearly four hours to-day, completing the amendments to which we got the Government to accede last week, as they are to be all introduced in form on Monday, and on Wednesday the Bill will pass, improved in a great many respects, but with many mischievous provisions still left. There can be no serious opposition attempted on its third reading. The Government have us and the Church in their power ; but as one of their own supporters said to me last night, "Although these men are not yet ripe to be plucked, they soon will, and I shall rejoice to help you to pluck them, but the time is not yet come." And this is truly so. I long to talk over all my pilgrimage of this time with you.

T. L.

TO THE SAME.

Bangor,
Thursday.

I wrote you a few lines from Holyhead, and they were
very few, as I wished to take the letter myself to the
office to make sure of its going by to-night's mail.   Here
I am spending as pleasant an evening as I could do separated from all those I love upon earth.   All nature appears
in its most attractive form—a magnificent setting sun
just over the dark and massy wood stretched along the
opposite bank of the Menai—the air mild as summer, and
the sea, with its unruffled, glassy surface, spread out below.
My window looks out directly on all this beautiful scenery,
but yet my heart is looking back to the scenes I left,
rather than enjoying those before me.   I am not, however, alone.   Your sweet book has served throughout
much of the day to give me a companionship with Him
with whom it is my delightful hope we shall all one day
dwell together.   Often have I thought what a blessing for
time as well as for eternity is a union which has for its
foundation the basis of religion.   Here are you and I, at
the end of thirty-six years, with our tastes more assimi-
lated, our affections more knit together, our sympathies
growing daily more and more perfect ; and this is not by
nature but by grace.   The blessing poured down upon
our united prayers and thanksgivings by the gracious
Spirit which has taught us " to pray together, even when
apart."   Dearest Jeffry will, I hope, take courage in our
family worship, and make such plain observations as I
endeavour to make for the purpose of calling attention to the

principal topics which occur in what he reads, that it may
not glide away like water from leaky vessels.   Let him
ask in simple, hearty earnestness, and be satisfied with
whatever ability or power to do it the Lord may vouch-
safe.   Sometimes God will give more, sometimes less ; the
less is of use to prevent our being puffed up—the more, to
encourage and make us taste of and rejoice in his strength
and gifts.

T. L.

TO THE SAME.

April 8, 1835.

I arrived here yesterday evening, having had a very
pleasant journey, and having, thank God, shaken off all
remains of my cold. . I am very glad that I came, as there
was a pressing note from the Primate to meet Sir Robert
Peel and Lord Stanley to-day, and I have been with
them at his house till now—near post hour.   Nothing
could be more satisfactory than our arrangement for to-
morrow's battle on the Church Bill, in which Lord Stanley
is to lead us into action.   It is quite delightful to observe
how cordially he and Sir Robert Peel do business together.

T. L.

- TO THE SAME.

Library, House of Commons,
16th March, 1836.

Not only every session but every day and hour increases
my distaste for the course I am thrown into here, and
makes me long to flee away and be at rest.   It has, however, one good effect in guarding me from the snare of

falling in love with politics and making me seek for comfort in looking away from all things around and about me, and forward to the things before and above. There, and there only, is a true resting-place for the sick and weary heart. I join you all in the morning around the Throne of Grace, and often feel delight at the thought that though separate in the body we are joined together in the spirit. These are the thoughts upon which my spirit rallies and my heart revives again, and is enabled to make a fresh fight against the onset of discontent. I must hasten away to the House of Commons.

T. L.

The following letters, selected from a correspondence carried on during his busiest periods in the House of Commons, with his son, the Reverend Jeffry Lefroy, soon after his son's entering into the ministry, give us an insight into the subjects on which his heart constantly dwelt, even in the midst of worldly engagements ever so engrossing, and shew us somewhat of the anxiety with which he sought to assist by his counsel, and guide by his experience, those who—to use his own words—" were always in his thoughts ":—

House of Commons,
Monday, March 11th, 1833.

MY DEAREST JEFFRY,—I cannot let my first frank to your new address go without a line from myself, though,

as you may suppose, very busy. But, whilst I feel the
weight and thanklessness of my own labours, it rejoices
me that my own dear Jeffry is engaged in a work which,
whatever be its weight, from its importance, is the work
of a gracious Master—a light burden and an easy yoke
when the heart is in it, and the more it is so, the more
easy and delightful the work becomes ; but even the
labour of this world is lightened by the sweet help which
God's grace ministers, by enabling us to run with patience
and hope the race that is set before us, with our eye and
heart upon Him whose eye and heart, we know, are
towards us.   Dear ——'s society is a great comfort,
and, indeed, a spiritual blessing, as we are enabled to
take sweet counsel together—in conversation, in reading,
and prayer. Believe me, you are never forgotten in our
prayers ; may you know the reality of the power and
blessedness of prayer, of persevering, believing prayer;
may you know the reality and the power of the love of a
gracious God manifested to us in His own dear Son; may
you know the reality of the truth, " that the Blood of
Jesus Christ cleanseth from all sin." Oh ! what weapons
will you then be furnished with to fight the battle of the
Lord against the world, the flesh, and the devil. Dig incessantly in that mine of rich treasure, your Bible, so as
to read it *with understanding ;* that is, first, to ascertain
what the Word says, and then to believe, fearless of consequences, but fearful only of putting man's wisdom in
the place of God's. The Lord has blessed you with great
help where you are, and I trust you will not fail to profit
by it to the uttermost. Aim at nothing less than a full
and clear understanding of the Scriptures, of the *whole*

Word of God, but don't be anxious or precipitate about systems—desire to drink in truth by degrees from the Fountain Head itself, as the Lord, the Spirit, gives it gradually to His babes in Christ—here a little, and there a little—but ever adding line upon line, precept upon precept, that you may be at length " thoroughly furnished unto every good work." By faith and perseverance, we inherit all the promises—amongst the rest, wisdom and knowledge in Divine things. May the Lord bless you, and lift up the light of His countenance upon you, and keep and guide you, is the fervent prayer of

Your ever affectionate father,
T. L.

TO THE SAME.

Leeson-street,
April 8th, 1833.

I was delighted to hear, through T—— before leaving London, that you had made your *debut* in. the pulpit, and trust and pray that you may be kept firm to the anchorage you have taken—Christ and Him crucified—" The power of God unto salvation." Yes, this is the weapon for slaying Satan ; this is the practical, efficient, influential truth for bringing souls to God, whilst your great orators are spending their breath in vain, and scattering their tropes and figures, sowing to the wind, and consequently only reaping the whirlwind. The full, the deep knowledge of Christ, as revealed in the Old as well as the New Testament— shewn forth in the types and figures of the one no less clearly, when they are understood, than in the language of the other,—constitutes the great foundation on which all-effective preaching must be built. As to your style, or rather method, I would give you one caution, that is, to avoid making up a sermon of a collection of observations —having no beginning, no middle, no end, no premises, no conclusion, which might stop anywhere, and might be shaken in a hat, and drawn out as good a sermon as in the order in which it was composed.· The first thing is, to consider what conclusion you wish to establish, and then when you lay before your congregation the point or points you mean to establish, go regularly through your reasoning to establish the conclusion; and let all you say have a drift and a tendency to that point. And if the subject should lead in the discussion to any collateral remark, come back again to your road, and mark that you do so. And, I would add, as much as possible, let your reasonings be such as will unfold Scripture and help to the better understanding of the Bible. Examine well the literal meaning of your text. It is dangerous not to hold by the *letter* as the foundation, before we proceed to the spiritual import or application of language. These are a few of the observations which experience has suggested as helps to me, but labour to become mighty in the Scriptures by the teaching of the Holy Ghost, and you will thus best accomplish your work in the ministry. When you set about a sermon, the Lord will rejoice that you should lay your case before Him, and ask Him boldly for His loving and gracious help, that you may honour His name and His Word, and win souls thereby to His glory. This, my dearest Jeffry, is what we all want. A simple persuasion of the reality of the things that are written, of the literal truth of the promises, and of the invitations given to us *in* the Word and *on* the Word of God, and not to faint or be weary in that belief. Remember the praise and glory of Abraham's faith, that he believed in hope against hope. At the same time his hope was the highest act of reason, because it was founded on God's promise. May the God of Abraham, the Lord Jehovah, bless and guide, and keep and perfect you for His own service.

T. L.

TO THE SAME.

London, Sunday.

The next pleasure to sitting with you and taking sweet counsel with you is *that* I am now about to enjoy. Dear J—— delighted me exceedingly when I sent a message by her. as to the preference I hoped you gave your Bible over all the writings of men, by saying that was exactly your own view. To assist in finding out the true grammatical construction of the words of Scripture, other men's labours may be very useful; but take all your doctrine from the Bible itself. Don't affect to be wise beyond what is written, but don't be afraid to go as far as God has been pleased to go in revealing the counsels of His will. Don't make haste, too, is another good rule; some men affect to have all points of doctrine cut and dry, laid up in store with great exactness; now this may be head knowledge, but the knowledge which will profit both the preacher and the hearer is that which the Spirit of God teaches from the Word of God. These are mighty words though they seem so little—" the Word of God and prayer;" prayer to bring down the guidance and teaching of the Holy Spirit—His teaching alone is

safe and sure teaching, it is gradual, it is that " growth in
grace and in the knowledge of our Lord and Saviour
Jesus Christ," which the apostle Peter earnestly commends
to us in his second epistle; but it is to be had only by
diligent seeking in the Word, with constant, believing
prayer.   The knowledge of the truth is, at the same time,
the instrument or means of personal holiness as well as of
edification to others.   I mean that knowledge which the
searcher after truth obtains in the Word of God by the
teaching of His Spirit. The Scriptures are a mine of
endless riches for the soul when God begins graciously
to open them to us if we follow on to seek; every day
will unfold something more; it is this gradual coming to
the knowledge of the Truth that I covet for you; it is
that alone that can ever make a man a bold, a profitable
preacher; seek for the things which are taught in the
Bible; those who take their doctrine from other men are
for ever carrying on a war of words. The man who
preaches from his knowledge of the Bible speaks of the
things about which the Bible is conversant. He speaks
as a traveller does of a country he has visited and seen.
To explain this by an instance, it is said, " My son, get
wisdom, get understanding."   What a different lesson he
will teach who knows nothing but the word wisdom,
as man knows it, and he who knows that " Christ is made
unto us of God wisdom." When we get Him, that is, the
knowledge of and belief in Him, we then have true wisdom,
and the more we know of Him and trust in Him, the
more we have of it. This realizing of the words of
Scripture, turning the signs into the things signified, is

alone making progress in true knowledge. By close and constant study of the Scriptures only can you learn the peculiarities of Scripture phraseology, which often mislead the novice. Perhaps I was too strict when, at the outset, I confined the assistance to be derived from other writers to mere grammatical interpretations, for it is often useful to see what an able and spiritual man gives as his understanding of a passage in Scripture—not to be implicitly followed, but to be weighed and considered, always keeping in mind that the comparing of Scripture with Scripture is the soundest mode of interpretation. The great safeguard of working out doctrine by a close adherence to the Word is that it avoids fanciful and enthusiastic notions; while, on the other hand, the man who thinks he can find out the truth by the letter only, as a grammarian, without the teaching and guidance of God's Holy Spirit, robs the Spirit of His office of being the revealer and guide to Truth. These, my dearest Jeffry, are a few of the many things which, in a long study of the Scriptures, I have been taught, and which, if I am right in them, I hope may be profitable to you, as helping to put you on the right track in your ministerial work. Remember, too, the value of *pondering*—"whoso is wise will ponder these things, and he shall understand the lovingkindness of the Lord." This, as well as prayer, may be carried on whilst a man is walking about his business. The heart and desires directed to God *in Christ* is the very soul of prayer. May the grace of our Lord Jesus Christ, and the love of God and the fellowship of the Holy Ghost be with you always, and may you know fully the import, and

experience the participation of this blessing. I am sorry
I could not be with you, but it was impossible from all I
have to do here for the next two days.

T. L.

TO THE SAME.

Hobart Place, London,
4th June, 1834.

One of the greatest discomforts of my present un-
settled state is the impossibility of keeping up with
all my dear children the constant intercourse I should
wish, lest it might lead any of you to suppose you were
not always in my thoughts; but I can truly say with
Paul, that God is my witness how dearly I love and constantly pray for you all,—and, indeed, I have a witness
in the grace which I trust He is daily shedding on you all.
I was sorry to learn that all things are not quite according to your wishes in your present situation, but I trust
you will find open ground enough for profitable work, as
respects others, and in the meantime I am sure it will be
well for yourself as it is for us all, to learn to bear with
the crosses and disappointments of this life. It prevents us
liking it too well and helps as a spur to drive us to Him
in whom there is no disappointment, "neither variableness nor shadow of turning." But whilst in respect to the
temporal and personal concerns of your new situation the
state of things may not be all you wish, I rejoice greatly
to hear of the acceptance your ministry has had. After
all, this is the work worthy of the hearts and souls of
those who know what the peace of God in truth is. I
will send you on my return to Ireland a little book which
I think you will find a great help from its luminous

and accurate statement of many of the fundamental
doctrines of the Gospel. It is one of the early works of
Walker, free from whatever aberrations he is said to
have fallen into afterwards, of which, however, I know
nothing. I took it off my chimney-piece where it had
lain for some years to take as a travelling companion, and
it has indeed been a valuable one. It is entitled " Walker's
Address to the Methodists, with his letters to Alex. Knox,
Esq., on the same Subject." It was written in 1803;
perhaps they have it in Lord Mandeville's library. The
great value of it is in unfolding the Bible and exhibiting
Divine truth with simplicity and boldness and at the same
time in a practical view; but this or any other human
work is only of value as a help to the understanding of
God's own precious Book. I am off suddenly to defend
our poor Irish Church, the despoiling of which I am still
in hopes we shall with God's help prevent, and fix it on a
better footing for its ministers than it ever stood.

T. L

TO THE SAME.

Hobart Place, London,
July 7th, 1834.

. . . . You must not be discouraged at the materials you have to work upon in your present flock.
God is able of these stones to raise up children to His
dear Son ; and He who gave sight to the blind and
unstopped the deaf ears, is able to open an entrance
for His Word into their hearts ; and *without Him* we
can do nothing. Don't be disheartened, but go on
preaching amongst them in the spirit of Habakkuk—
" Although the fig tree shall not blossom, neither shall

fruit be in the vines ; the labour of the olive shall fail, and the fields shall yield no meat ; the flock shall be cut off from the fold, and there shall be no herd in the stalls; *yet* I will rejoice in the Lord. I will joy in the God of my salvation. The Lord God is my strength. He will make my feet like hind's feet, and He will make me to walk upon mine high places." Add to your preaching prayer—instant, earnest prayer, that the Word and the grace of God may be glorified amongst your hearers. Recollect it is His glory and not our own,—the good pleasure of His will and not our own—we are to seek, even in the work of striving to win souls to Christ. The more sleepy, stupid, and dull of hearing they may be, the more the power of God and the work of His Spirit is magnified in awakening and quickening them. *You* are to minister the Word—the instrument of His work. *He* is to make it effectual to the pulling down of the strongholds of Satan. He will take His time. He will choose how much or how little shall be done ; but don't be disheartened—work with patience as well as with faith. The dear Master whose, I trust, you are, and whom you serve, is as full of wisdom and power as of grace ; and whilst you show all earnestness and zeal for the conversion of sinners, show also meekness and submission to His holy will, as to the measure of success He may please to give, and sing in your heart the song of Habakkuk. But still go on preaching the Word. Who knows? the Lord may do to-day what He did not see fit to do yesterday. Remember the gracious parable of the unjust judge which was spoken to *this end*—that men ought always to pray and not to faint.—" And shall not God

avenge His own elect which cry night and day to Him ?'
Who answers this query ? The same who is to fulfil
the answer. Oh, how little is our faith! The grain of
mustard seed is not diminutive enough to represent the
faith of the strongest of us. Did we but in our hearts
believe and consider who it is that has promised—and
the proofs he has given us of—His power, His love, His
condescension, what would be our faith, our love,
our zeal, for His work and glory ? In His sight
how infinitely more sleepy, blind, and slow of heart
must we appear, who possess the privilege of access
to His Word, than those poor souls who have scarce ever
heard of Him. Speak of—or rather, I should say, pray
that you may be enabled to lay hold on, and thereby to
speak of—the *things* which are freely given to us of our
God in Christ. The man who knows only the *words* of
his Bible and not the *things*, can never speak to the *souls*
of men. The man who knows the thing which the Word
signifies, it will be in his mouth a word with power.
That's the reason that the study of the Bible must be the
great study of the minister of Christ. I pray for you
that you may be full of zeal and love, ready to spend
and be spent for the Gospel ; that you may be a faithful minister of Christ ; that you may have grace to
adorn the doctrine, and recommend it by your life
and conversation ; that God would crown my years
with this greatest of all honours, by enabling me
to see these things fulfilled in you. I bless Him for
the encouragement He has already given me to go on
seeking and praying for more. Having now poured out
my heart as to spiritual things, I must say a word as to

P

temporal. . . . . Our poor Church is undergoing
severe discipline as to its rights and property, and if a
check be not put to the course now entered upon, it will
be stript of its last shilling by Radicals and Infidels, who
have joined together in the plunder.   America and
France are the models they look to.   In the one there is
no established Church supported by the State ; in the
other, all Churches are paid alike by the State—the one
disclaiming, as a nation, all religion ; the other holding
all creeds alike—Infidelity and Liberalism being the leading principles.   Our comfort and support is that, in spite
of all, Jehovah reigns, and will reign for ever and ever—
Amen. . . . . . You may suppose how tiresome
to be here in such hot weather, fighting incessantly
and always beaten. "O rus quando te aspiciam," I
exclaim constantly, with my eye turned to Carrig-glas.
It's well for the Christians now who can say with the
Christians of old, when threatened with the deserts of
Africa by their persecutors, "You cannot send us any
place where we shall not have our God." May we feel
more and more the truth and value of this blessed
privilege.

T. L.

TO THE SAME.

Hobart Place,
London, 13th July, 1834.

As I always find great profit-in working out the
meaning of passages, by comparing Scripture with
Scripture, I wish to impart to you any good I can

in that way. To give you a sample, I will take
the passage we read in our family worship this
morning—part of our Lord's conversation with the woman
of Samaria. In verse 10 He says:—" If thou knewest the
gift of God, and who it is that saith to thee, ' Give me to
drink,' thou wouldst have asked of Him and He would
have given thee living water." The first thing here is to
ascertain what is meant by " the gift of God." This we
learn in Rom. vi. 23, where St. Paul tells us that " the
gift of God is eternal life through Jesus Christ our Lord."
Next, we ascertain what our Lord meant by " living
water " when we look to John vii. 38, 39, where He says,
" He that believeth on Me, out of his belly shall flow
rivers of living water ;" and the Evangelist adds, " This
spake He of the Spirit, which they who believe on Him
should receive." We also see the beautiful harmony
between the Old and the New Testament, by looking to
Jer. ii. 13, where we find the Lord is called " the fountain
of living waters ;" and in Ezek. xxxvi. 25 He promises to
sprinkle *clean water* upon His people, which in verse 26
is expounded as " a new heart " and " a new spirit."
See also Isaiah xliv. 3. Thus, dearest Jeffry, by searching
after the *things* signified—the *realities* conveyed by the
words, and types, and figures of Scripture, shall we find the
blessed promise fulfilled to us, " Seek and ye shall find." I
may now just add that the faithful preacher of the Gospel
must take care to give God the glory of converting every
soul that believes. It is the office of the Holy Spirit to
enable us to believe on Christ, as much as it is the office
of Christ to be the sacrifice for our sins; and we must no
more rob God the Spirit of His glory, than we should

rob God the Son of the glory of being the propitiation
for our sins. In short, from the beginning of the counsel
of God—the purpose of saving sinners, to the completion
of the work of bringing home to their everlasting rest the
souls that shall be saved—the whole work and the whole
glory must be ascribed (as is most due) to God, "the
Father, Son, and Holy Ghost." There is the agency of men
and instrumentality of the Word, but the work and power
are of God—and well for us it is so. I am sure that the
reason of the small fruit one sees from the preaching of
the Gospel in these days is that it is not preached fully;
many men set forth Christ crucified as the power of
God unto salvation, but they don't go on to shew forth
and claim for God the power and privilege of making
this preaching effectual. They don't praise and bless Him
for sending His Word, and calling men to hear it—they
don't acknowledge this as His doing—they don't shew
forth the need of His Spirit to bring it home to the hearts
of the hearers, so as to make men *feel* the necessity and
value of prayer for the Holy Spirit to quicken their hearts,
so as to make them receive the Word and thirst for more
and more of it.

T. L.

TO THE SAME.

Carrig-glas, Sunday,

Oct. 5, 1834.

It greatly increases the happiness of devoting
part of this day to the contemplation of God's Word
to communicate with you on what occurs to my
mind, with the earnest prayer that, if it be of the

Holy Spirit's teaching, it may be blessed to you as well as to myself. In my last letter, I think, I spoke of what appeared to me to be a *short* preaching of the Gospel, that is, not giving God the full measure of praise and glory to which He is entitled by holding him forth in that portion of His work which is the peculiar office of the Holy Spirit, as well as in His work of atonement and justification, which is the office of His Son, or, in simple language, omitting to point out to men the need of the Holy Spirit to enable them to believe on Christ, and to persevere in that belief to the end, and you will observe that God has as freely promised that needful help, as Ho has freely given up for us His own dear Son. The great doctrine taught in the discourse with Nicodemus, and in the 14th and 16th of John's Gospel, is the necessity of the Comforter coming not only for the purpose of his abiding with the Church, but also for converting the world. See especially on this latter point John xvi. 7—12, and see how remarkably the result of the Spirit's work was shewn. Our Lord had preached and done many wonderful miracles in the presence of the Jewish people, and yet instead of attracting a multitude of believers, even the few who were his followers, forsook Him and fled in the hour of trial, and it was not until after He had breathed on them and said (after His resurrection) " receive ye the Holy Ghost" that the number of the disciples reached even one hundred and twenty. But immediately on the fulfilment of the promise of sending the Holy Ghost to convince the world, we find that the result of Peter's preaching " Christ crucified" to the people was that they were pricked in their hearts, and said immediately to him and to the rest of the Apostles, "Men and brethren, what shall we do?"—*i. e.*, the Holy Ghost convinced them of sin—and the very same people who, a few days before, cried out, "Crucify Him," were now willing to flee to Him for refuge, and at once three thousand souls were added to the Church. How can we doubt that this was done to afford an ostensible evidence that it was by the influence of the Holy Ghost that men's hearts were to be effectually opened to the receiving of the Gospel? The Word and the Spirit must go together— the Word as the instrument, the Spirit as the mighty agent. When we consider man in his natural state, *i. e.*, the world, as dead in trespasses and sins, we see that the three things they want are these which our Lord promises that the Holy Ghost should do, 1st, to awaken them to a sense of their state of sin—*i. e.*, to convince them of sin in not believing on Him; 2nd, to show them the judgment which awaits the world while in this state, and him who is the Prince of the world; and 3rd, to show them the righteousness which is provided in Christ for all those who believe; for it would be of no avail to convince men of the sinful state in which they are, and of the judgment which awaits them in that state, if there were not provided a righteousness in which to stand when brought out of that state. And this work of the Holy Spirit is as much the purchase of Christ's death and offering as any other part of the dispensation of grace for the salvation of sinners. All this is not mere theory and speculation, but is that saving and practical knowledge whereby alone we can serve God acceptably, and glorify Him as we ought.

T. L.

We and Servant feel
Breat Prayer they Kneel
wees & Household Care
Both and Thine by Prayer

Be nger's weary feet
m Kind welcome meet
w is House O'erlook
Tar edy of Thy Flock
He e together Dwell
Be s bearing Still
Ar , nor Angry Strife
Te e of Daily Life.

ed at it—

ctober. 1837.

After his eldest son had for some years represented the County of Longford in the House of
Commons, Mr. Lefroy resolved to rebuild the
Manor House of Carrig-glas with a view to a more
constant residence in the County, and in this as in
every other important step in his life we find his
first instinct was to seek for God's blessing on
what he was about to undertake.   Amongst his
papers was found one of the drawings for the new
house, with texts and hymns written on the back of
the drawing in his own handwriting, of which a
fac-simile appears in plate opposite page 216, and
these abundantly shew the feelings of his heart
on the occasion.

In the year 1837 the foundations of the new
building were laid under the superintendance of
Daniel Robertson, Esq., an English Architect, eminent for the beauty of his designs in the Tudor
style.   On Mr. Robertson's first visit to Carrig-
glas he was so much attracted, in walking through
the pleasure grounds, by a large grove of cedars
of Lebanon (containing some of the finest specimens in the United Kingdom of this rare and
beautiful tree) that he laid out the site of the
new house principally with a view to this important
feature ; but before the house was completed,
the devastating hurricane of 6th January, 1839,
swept with fearful power over the demesne and not

only levelled almost the whole grove of cedars in which Mr. Lefroy took so much pleasure, but destroyed upwards of 4,600 trees in the park and its surrounding woods. Those who remember his enthusiastic admiration of the place will not be surprised to find from the following letters, how acutely he felt upon the occasion, while it is interesting to observe his cheerful submission under what he characteristically describes as "his anguish" in first seeing the desolation which the storm had left behind.

TO HIS WIFE.

Carrig-glas,
April 3rd, 1839.

You will be glad to hear that I have recovered somewhat from my *first anguish*, and am suffering myself to be by degrees led into the dream that though Carrigglas has decidedly lost all its peculiar beauty (at least what constituted its beauty in my eyes) new charms will be unfolded when the wreck and ruin which now strews the pleasure grounds shall be removed, for we shall get views of the distant woods that we had not before, and of the only mountain we can boast of in the county. You can form no idea of the desolation which the storm has made; I could not cross the pleasure-ground from the heaps of trees, but am obliged to walk round to survey the stupendous pile of ruin. A few solitary trees have been preserved by the shelter of the heaps which had fallen around them, but, strange to say, comparatively few of

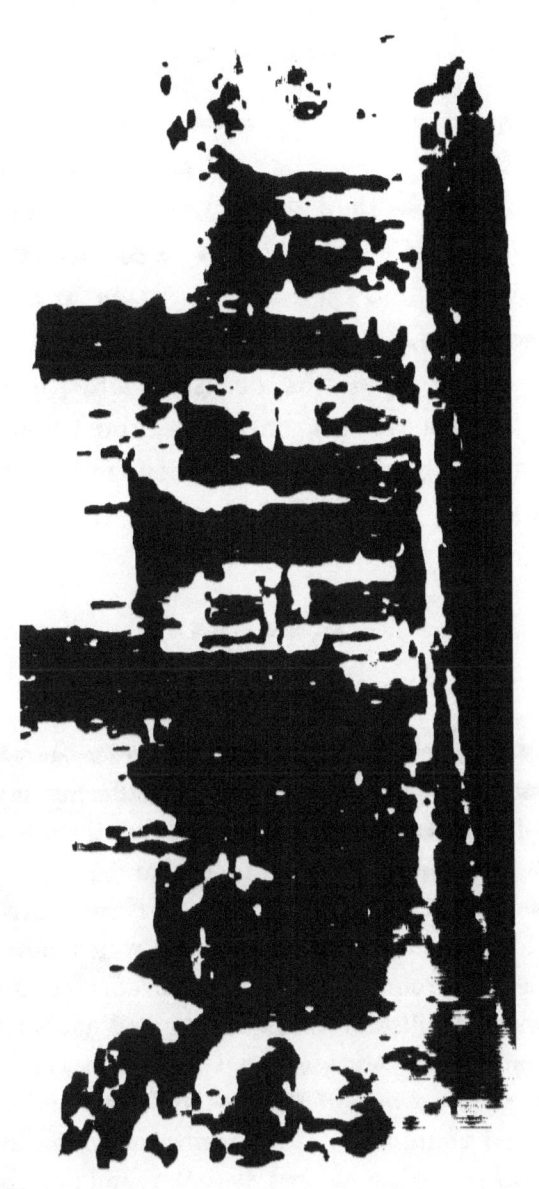

... ... grove of cedars in ... ... but ... ... his ... admission ... ... be surprised to find ... the following ... ... the occasion, which ... to interesting to observe his cheerful submission under what he characteristically describes as "his anguish" in first seeing the desolation which the storm had left behind.

... ...

... ... suffering myself to ... by d... ... the dream that though Carriglee h.. ... lost all its peculiar beauty (at least what constituted its beauty in my eyes) new charms will be unfolded when the wreck and ruin which now strews the pleasure grounds shall be removed, for we shall ... views of the distant woods that we had not before, and ... the only ... we can ... of in the county. You can form no ... of the desolation which the storm has made; I could not ... to ... re-ground from the heaps of trees, but am able ... to walk round to survey the stupendous pile of ruin. A few ... ry trees ... preserved by the shelter of the heaps which ha' been around them, but ... or ... comparatively few of

CARRIG C

the single trees standing out in the more exposed parts of the demesne have been blown down, and almost all the destruction has been either in the woods or close to the house. I am glad dear A—— is not to come here for some time. The new house will be all that a house need be, and I trust will be covered in this autumn, so as to make some compensation for the loss of other beauties before he sees Carrig-glas again.

TO THE SAME.

Carrig-glas,
April 7th, 1839.

I received your affectionate letter filled with the best and truest consolation for what I must in honesty admit to have been a great trial to me here, though I quite feel with you that not only perfect submission, but thankfulness becomes us much more than repining, against which I have prayed and striven. We have just returned from church where we heard our new Rector,* who certainly is a great acquisition. He is a man of very considerable power as a preacher, very faithful and sound in doctrine, and with all the appearance of sincerity and devotedness in his manner. He has not yet taken possession of the Glebe, but I expect to find him a valuable neighbour.

T. L.

* The Rev. John Le Poer Trench.

CHAPTER VIII.

ON Sir Robert Peel's accession to power in
Sept. 1841, public expectation, grounded on Mr.
Lefroy's great professional eminence and long
political services, naturally pointed to him as the
man who would be selected for the Irish Chancellorship, more especially as it was known that
when Sir Robert Peel held the office of Prime
Minister for a few months in 1835 he had accompanied the honor of a seat at the Irish Privy
Council which was then conferred on Mr. Lefroy
by the assurance of his desire to procure for the
public the benefit of Mr. Lefroy's judicial services
as Master of the Rolls, if a vacancy, which was
then expected in that office, should occur. But
the influence of Mr. O'Connell on the action of

Government in Irish affairs, which had been from year to year increasing, was now quite sufficient to raise an effectual barrier in the way of this just recognition of Mr. Lefroy's claims, and the Irish Seals were committed to Sir Edward Sugden. Any attempt to panegyrize so great a lawyer as the present Lord St. Leonards would be super-fluous. Nor could any one deny that the selection was the best which could be made, if the claims of the Irish Bar were to be set aside. But it is not too much to say that the same feeling which has since led to an abandonment of the practice of appointing a member of the English Bar to be Chancellor of Ireland, tended, even in that instance, to lessen the satisfaction with which Sir Edward Sugden's appointment would otherwise have been received ; because it was regarded as involving an unjust oversight of claims admittedly so strong.

We have already seen that after the vote of 4th June, 1841, by which the House of Commons declared its want of confidence in Lord Melbourne's Ministry, his Lordship resolved, before resigning office, to summon a new Parliament; and in the following letter from the Earl of Clare to Mr. Lefroy, on the subject of the elections then pend-ing, we have an incident connected with the appointment of Lord Clare's father to the Chancellor-ship of Ireland in 1789, which shows how different

was the course adopted by Mr. Pitt's Government
from that which both the Whigs and Tories of
1841 thought fit to adopt towards the Bar of Ireland :—

Belgrave Square,

June 25th, 1841.

. . . . . . Your accounts of the College and
City Elections are very cheering, and I really believe the
good cause will be generally successful. The most
moderate members calculate on our having in the new
Parliament a clear majority of thirty, and many think it
will be much more. The job in dismissing Lord Plunket, and in putting Sir John Campbell over the heads
of all the Equity Bar in Ireland, is an outrage which
the profession will very properly resent. The
Whigs talk loudly of justice to Ireland—did a Tory
Government ever offer us such an insult ? In 1789,
Lord Thurlow objected to the appointment of an
Irishman, my father, to succeed Lord Lifford, upon
which Lord Buckinghamshire and the remaining members of the Irish Government sent in their resigna-
tions, saying, if Mr. Fitzgibbon was passed over, they
could not, with credit, remain in office. Mr. Pitt then
sent Major Hobart (the late Lord Buckinghamshire) to
Lord Thurlow. He stormed and roared, but when he
found the ministers firm, he gave way, saying—"If Mr.
Pitt will appoint an Irishman Chancellor, Mr. Fitzgibbon
is the best man he could select." This the late Lord
Buckinghamshire told me in 1815, and contrast the con-

duct of a Tory Government on that occasion to Ireland
with the conduct of a so-called Liberal Government in
1841, in the appointment of Sir John Campbell,

Yours truly and faithfully,

CLARE.

To the Right Hon. Thomas Lefroy, M.P.

Whatever may be felt as to Sir Robert Peel's
conduct in passing by the many eminent men who
then adorned the Equity Bar in Ireland, and giving
the Irish Seals to Sir Edward Sugden, it may be
confidently asserted that the political job so justly
commented on by Lord Clare, in the dismissal of
Lord Plunket and the appointment of Sir John
Campbell (when it was a matter of notoriety that
Lord Melbourne could not many weeks longer hold
the reins of government), stands unrivalled even
amongst the boldest efforts on which Whig Ministers
have occasionally ventured in order to provide
place or pension for their political adherents. Sir
John Campbell was appointed Lord Chancellor of
Ireland on the 22nd June, 1841. The Dublin journals of that period record " that he took his seat for
the first time in the Court of Chancery on the 2nd
July—that he sat in Court the following day to hear
motions, and gave notice that he would not hear
long causes until November!" And the only other
record I can trace of his Lordship's discharge of
the duties of his high office is the following caustic

article, taken from the *Dublin Evening Mail* of Monday, 26th July, 1841 :—

" Lord Campbell, the Lord High Chancellor of Ireland, took his final departure from this country on Saturday last, having during a short sojourn of three weeks, and after sittings continued without intermission for the protracted space of three entire days, earned——a retiring pension of £4,000 a year ! His Lordship's outlay in money, independently of his waste of time and labour of mind in qualifying himself for the enjoyment of this trifling annuity for life, consisted in the expense of a ten days' sojourn at the Bilton Hotel and one dinner to some half-dozen officers of the Court over which he presided with such zeal, talent, and application. 'Plain Jock Campbell' is a lucky man !

It is only justice to Lord Plunket to say that in the interesting volumes lately published by his grandson, the Hon. David Plunket, we have additional light thrown on this transaction, which abundantly proves that to the last his Lordship resisted the attempt of the Government to make him a party to this job. When asked by Lord Melbourne to resign his office for the purpose of appointing Sir John Campbell to succeed to it,* we find that Lord Plunket stated both to Lord

---

* The following is the letter, conveying Lord Melbourne's request, as given in "The Life, Letters and Speeches of Lord Plunket," vol. 2, p. 333 :

(Private.)

"Downing-street, June 6, 1841.

" MY DEAR LORD PLUNKET,—The great friendship which you have

Melbourne and to Lord Ebrington (then Lord Lieutenant of Ireland) " that insuperable objections, utterly unconnected with anything personal to himself, must prevent his being a moving party to such an arrangement." Nor was Lord Plunket's refusal to resign withdrawn until he felt a moral compulsion to yield to the request contained in the following letter :—

(Private.)

Phœnix Park, June 17, 1841.

MY DEAR LORD,—Although, after my communication with you on Monday, I am sensible that, considering what

ever felt and shown personally to myself, and the disinterested anxiety to serve your political friends, and to advance your political principles, by which your conduct has been invariably marked, make me not only hope, but feel confident that you will receive with indulgence the matter which I am now about to open to you. You see the struggle in which we are engaged, and you are aware that many ministerial arrangements must be necessary upon the occasion of the approaching dissolution of Parliament. Amongst these it would be most convenient, and we are most anxious to provide for the Attorney-General, which the present state of the courts of law does not allow us to do in this country. Under these circumstances I have thought it not impossible that you might be willing to seek that retirement and repose, to which your long, able and most distinguished services so well entitle you. I have thought it best, I have thought it the most direct and open course, to state to you at once the object we have in view, and the reasons why we ask it. If it is repugnant to your feelings say so at once, and there is an end of the matter. If you accede you will add to the gratitude which we already owe you for the support and assistance which you have rendered us.

Whatever may be your determination, you will keep the matter entirely secret for the present, and believe me, my dear Lord Plunket, with the most earnest wishes for your health and happiness,

" Yours, ever faithfully,

'MELBOURNE."

was expressed in Lord Melbourne's letter, I have no right to press you further on the subject of his request to you, yet I feel so strongly the difficulty in which both he and the Government will be placed by your refusal that I should not do my duty towards them or myself if I did not endeavour to induce you to recall it, and if, while I fully admit the latitude held out to you by Lord Melbourne, I did not urge on you, so far as you will allow me to do so, as a personal favour to myself your compliance with his desire. Let me add that in so doing I am quite ready to take upon myself the whole responsibility of the arrangement which your resignation is intended to promote, and to make you no otherwise a party to it than in having complied with the request of your friends in the Cabinet, and of myself in particular, by placing your office at their disposal for the purpose of facilitating their Ministerial arrangements.

I am, with great truth, my dear Lord,

Very faithfully yours,

EBRINGTON.

I shall be at home to-day till three, if you should wish to see me.

We also find in Lord Plunket's parting address to the Bar, when alluding to this subject, the following dignified and pathetic vindication of his own honour and of the character of the Irish Bar, as well as his testimony to the eminent qualifications of several of its members for the high office which had been thus prostituted for party purposes :—

" With respect" (says Lord Plunket) " to the particular circumstances which have occurred, and the particular succession which is about to take place in this Court, it will become me to say very little. For the individual who is to occupy the situation I now fill, I entertain the highest political and personal respect; no one can feel it more so. But I owe it as a duty to myself and the members of the Bar to state that for the changes which are to take place I am not in the slightest degree answerable. I have no share in them, and have not directly or indirectly given them my sanction. In yielding my assent to the proposition which has been made for my retiring, I have been governed solely by its having been requested as a personal favour by a person to whom I owe so much that a feeling of gratitude would have rendered it morally impossible that I could have done otherwise than resign.

When I look at the Bar before me, and especially the number of those who might have sat efficiently in this judicial place, I am bound to say that for all those great ingredients which are calculated to enable them to shine as practitioners and as members of the Bar, or as gentlemen, for candour, for courtesy, knowledge, and ability I challenge competition. I challenge the very distinguished Bars of either England or Scotland, and I do not fear that those I have the honour of addressing would suffer in the comparison."

In Mr. Lefroy's letter announcing to his wife the probability of his claims to the Chancellorship being overlooked, we see the truly Christian spirit

Q

in which he was prepared to receive the disappointment.

Carlton Club,
Sept. 3, 1841.

. . . . . Nothing is yet known as to the Irish appointments. Sir Edward Sugden has taken time to consider whether he will go to Ireland, and if he does not go, it will be made a Cabinet question who is to succeed. Thus the difficulty of deciding is to be thrown off Sir Robert Peel by dividing it amongst twelve others. Should anything be known before the post goes I will give you a postscript, but in the present state of things we should be prepared for every degree of disappointment as to worldly matters. Let us not forget the measure of true riches and honour which has been vouchsafed to us which we could not have obtained for ourselves, which no man could give us, and, blessed be the Giver, no man can take away. That sweet truth "The blessing of the Lord maketh rich, and He addeth no sorrow with it," often avails to stay the vexation arising from the ingratitude of politicians. We may depend upon it none of the high stations which would gratify our carnal pride would be free from anxious cares and temptations, and our prayer should be that we may be enabled to submit ourselves to whatever state of circumstances we may be called to. The God of Providence, without whom nothing can befall us, is also the God of grace to keep and guide us.

T. L.

Immediately after Sir Robert Peel's accession to

office, a vacancy occurred on the Irish Judicial Bench in the Court of Exchequer, in consequence of Judge Johnson's resignation, and the appointment of Baron Foster to his place in the Court of Common Pleas. The vacant seat was at once offered to Mr. Lefroy, but he naturally felt unwilling to accept a Puisne Judge's place; he remembered that, before he entered Parliament, he had refused three times the same honour, and after sacrificing, for so many years, one of the largest professional incomes ever made at the Irish bar, in the service of the Political party that had now attained office, after rescuing the representation of Dublin University from the Whig party, and securing to the Conservative party the two seats in the County of Longford, at the cost of thirteen contested elections and three Parliamentary petitions,* to have his high professional claims ignored, and the Chancellorship, for which he was so peculiarly qualified, given to another, was a slight which it was very difficult to endure; many friends, however, by whose opinions he wished to be guided rather than by his own, felt that his refusal to accept office would risk division at a time when the hands of Government required to be strengthened, and that he ought not to

---

* In addition to these, Mr. Lefroy afterwards had another contested election for his son in the County Longford, another Parliamentary petition in 1847, and four contested elections for his son in Dublin University.

shrink from the line of duty which, in the course of Providence, seemed to be marked out for him, though in a post inferior to that in which a more just appreciation of his services would have placed him. The following letter, amongst others of the same kind which he received, confirmed this view:—

Tollymore Park,
5th Nov., 1841.

MY VERY DEAR FRIEND,—I see by the papers that you will accept the post of Baron in the Court of Exchequer. I hope it is true, and long to hear it confirmed by yourself. I can't think that any act of your life will place you higher in the opinion of all good men; or better exhibit your exalted character above the sordid views of most men; and those who have treated you so shamefully must feel the strongest sting of self reproach at your Christian course. I am most anxious about it, and everything that concerns you; for are we not members of one body, bound together in a bond of affection and brotherhood which cannot be broken?

Always most sincerely yours,

RODEN.

We find in two letters written soon after his acceptance of the appointment,—one shortly after he first took his seat in the Court of Exchequer, and the other from his first Circuit, abundant evi-

dence that, however keenly he may at first have
felt what he could not but regard as an injustice
at the hands of Government, yet his Christian principles kept him from long dwelling on it, and
enabled him to feel a happier reward in the useful
discharge of the public duties of his new post than
in any personal honour the Government could
have conferred on him:—

TO HIS WIFE.

Leeson Street,

21st Jan., 1842.

It only required to complete the satisfaction I enjoy
in my new post to find that you feel happy at the
determination to which a gracious Providence led me.
Indeed, it demands from us a thankful acknowledgment of God's goodness in this instance, and calls for
earnest prayer that He will ever order all things for
us after the counsel of His own will, giving us grace to
wait upon Him with patience and submission in all that
He appoints. I have been now sitting a whole week
with Brady and Richards (as Pennefather was sitting
in the Commission Court), and I can truly say that if the
oldest friends I have amongst the judges had been my
companions instead of these my political opponents, I
could not have experienced more unaffected kindness,
cordiality and respect. J—— has told you of Torrens
having chosen the Munster Circuit, in order that he
and I may go together. It is a shame, with such sub-

stantial comforts, to speak of anything like disappointment in a matter which, by the Christian, should be
regarded as, after all, but of little importance.

T. L.

The following letter is written from the first circuit after his accepting the appointment to the Puisne
Judge's place:—

TO HIS WIFE.

Limerick,

March 6, 1842.

Another week's work is ended, and when I consider
the extent of the mercy which has been vouchsafed to
me, truly my heart should burn within me with thankfulness. The four last nights I have been obliged to stay
in court till between nine and ten. Yesterday I sat
eleven hours without once rising from my seat, and
yet I have come home every night as fresh and more in
spirits than when I went out in the morning. In addition
to this, my recollection of the law is actually more fresh
and ready than when I went Circuit as Serjeant and the
respect and deference of the bar increasing every day,
and consequently my ease and comfort in the discharge of
the heavy duty which has, fallen on me increasing also.
Then, again, the cordiality with which my brother judge*
and I work together, and the pleasure which the public
express openly at our determination and exertion, not to

* Mr. Justice Torrens.

leave a single case undecided, is quite cheering. Surely this calls for our all uniting, as with one mouth and one heart, to praise the Lord for leading me by a way I knew not, and now making all so plain and smooth in that way. I hope my dear children will make it part of their daily prayers, (as I know you do) that we may all find grace to acknowledge the mercies I have experienced, and earnestly to supplicate for a continuance of them, so that the whole family shall be found daily gathered around the throne of grace praising the Lord for His goodness, and imploring His guidance and protection for me from day to day. Teach dear little L————, when he prays for grandpapa (as I know he is taught to do), to add that his grandpapa be taught of God to do all that is right and good, for Christ's sake.

T. L.

The attempt on the part of Government to con-ciliate their opponents, by passing over Mr. Lefroy's strong claims to the Irish Seals, met with the re-ward which such a course usually receives, and always deserves; for we find that on the 18th July, 1842, the Right Hon. Richard Lalor Sheil gave notice of a motion in the House of Commons for the correspondence relating to the restoration of Mr. St. George to the magistracy, stating that at the same time he would impugn the general policy of the Irish Government; and in his speech on that motion, one of the specific charges made by him against

Sir Robert Peel was his selection of Mr. Lefroy
for a seat on the *Common Law* Bench.

" If to the Peerage," said Mr. Sheil, " to which his fortune was so adequate,—if to the House of Lords, where,
on Irish appeals, totally unconnected by party, he could,
by his knowledge and his talents, have been eminently
serviceable, in reward for his political services, which I
do not mean to dispute, you had raised Mr. Lefroy, I
should not have complained; his abilities, his acquirements,
his capacity to do good in a proper place, I freely admit ;
but that, with your professions still fresh upon your lips,
the ink in which Lord de Grey's answers were indited
being scarcely dry, you should, from the entire mass of
the Irish Bar, have made choice of a gentleman so conspicuous for the part which he had acted on every
question by which Ireland has been agitated for the last
twenty years, to fill the seat vacated by Judge Johnson's
resignation, was a most extraordinary proceeding. I
bear, I protest, no ill will to Baron Lefroy—I cannot
injure him by an attack ; you cannot hurt him by a
defence. He is beyond the reach of both. If I ran the
risk of doing him the slightest harm, I should abstain
from all reference to his name ; but it is legitimate and
just, where, to the individual in question, no injury can
accrue, to animadvert upon the breach of pledges which
is involved by his promotion. I have no right to condemn
him, but I have every right to censure you ; I doubt not
that he has always acted a conscientious part, but his
appointment is not, upon that account, the less a departure from your engagements, and a violation of those

pledges which no one asked you to make, which were
perfectly voluntary upon your part, into which you
entered without deliberation, and which you have abandoned with discredit."

It is curious, also, to observe how Sir Robert
Peel, in his reply to Mr. Sheil, frankly confesses, not only the expectations of the Irish
Bar as to Mr. Lefroy's promotion to the Chancellorship, but his own conviction of Mr. Lefroy's
eminent qualifications for the office, though he had
not the political courage to act on that conviction.

" Would any man," said Sir Robert Peel, " assert that
a better choice could have been made than that of Mr.
Lefroy?   He (Sir Robert Peel) would say that, at no bar,
and at no period, had there been a gentleman who enjoyed
a higher reputation as an Equity Lawyer. Gentlemen
must remember to have heard Mr. Lefroy in that house,
and no gentleman ever spoke there with less violence, or
in a manner less calculated to unfit him for a judicial
appointment.   Lord Wellesley himself had offered a seat
on the Bench to Mr. Lefroy, and he (Sir Robert Peel),
believed that the offer of Lord Wellesley was the third
offer made to Mr. Lefroy of a judicial office." . . . .
" When it was rumoured that an English lawyer had been
selected as Lord Chancellor for Ireland, most vehement
remonstrances were raised against his appointment, and it
was then admitted that Mr. Lefroy was the most eminent
Equity Lawyer. It was then said that if Mr. Lefroy had

been selected, no complaints would have been heard from the Irish Bar, so that there was no objection to giving Mr. Lefroy an appointment which gave him the control of the whole magistracy of Ireland. Taking these circumstances into consideration, he (Sir Robert Peel) would fearlessly leave it to the House to decide whether any blame could attach to the Government for the appointment of Mr. Lefroy."

It is hardly to be wondered at that Mr. Sheil, looking from his standpoint, should imagine that Mr. Lefroy might bring to the Judicial Bench a strong political bias, from the active part he had taken in public life. Few men in Ireland had ever rendered more zealous service, or made larger sacrifices in support of the political cause which he so long espoused; but it is only justice to Mr. Sheil and his co-religionists to state that, from the outset of Mr. Lefroy's judicial career to its close, none were more cordial than Roman Catholics, whether as jurors, as members of the legal profession, or amongst the general public, in their praise of his eminent qualifications for the Judicial Bench, as well as the inflexible impartiality, and entire singleness of purpose with which he examined and decided every case that came before him. This well-known trait in his judicial character frequently elicited from Roman Catholics of various classes the gratifying testimony that there was no judge on the Irish bench they would sooner select for the trial of any case affecting their property, their liberty, or their lives.

During the early period of his judicial life, the circuit which most frequently fell to his lot was the Connaught Circuit, and, as I was myself a member of that circuit, I can bear grateful testimony to the cordiality with which he was always received by the Bar as well as by the Jurors of each county. That this feeling was quite reciprocal on his part is shown by his private letters as well as by the fact, that although the criminal business of the circuit was, at that time, generally very heavy, he, for several years, availed himself of the opportunity of going westward whenever it was open to him to do so. It is not a little remarkable to see how, in all his letters of this period, we find the same fulness and freshness of home affection which marked the letters written by him as a Junior Barrister on the Munster Circuit more than thirty years before. At the summer Assizes of 1843 he writes to his wife from Galway :—

Galway,

4th August, 1843.

I have finished one day's work here very satisfactorily, thank God, and had the gratification to hear from the Bar that I had done more than in any one's memory had

been done the first day; although I rose soon after five
o'clock, having finished everything that was ready.

I have had a very heavy Circuit, but I have now nearly
finished it, and I have not met with an unpleasant word
or act on the whole of it. The cordiality of the Bar
makes any amount of work comparatively light.

Judge Ball will be able to assist me part of to-day and
to-morrow, so that I am in hopes of getting away in good
time on Monday. I am beginning to feel the quicksilver
rise within me, when I think of getting back to all my
dear ones. I am very sorry to find you allowed yourself
to feel the anxiety you did at not hearing from me the
beginning of last week, as our constant change of
place ought to have accounted for the accident. In addition to this, the post goes from most of the towns on
this Circuit at a very inconvenient hour, during the sitting of the Court; and when I get engaged in business,
it is difficult to watch the hour, or to write at night,
after a long day's work—dining at eight o'clock, sitting
with our guests till eleven, and obliged to be in Court by
half-past nine the next morning—as this has been generally
my case, it's no wonder if I were a very bad correspon-
dent ; but I really have not been so, as, with the exception of one day, I wrote every post last week.

With love to all,

T. L.

In the spring of 1846, he went the Munster
Circuit, and the following extract from his charge
to the Grand Jury of the County of Clare exhibits

the anxiety with which he uniformly endeavoured to impress on all those engaged in the administration of the Law, whether as Grand Jurors, Petit Jurors, or Magistrates, the importance of regarding the duties devolving upon them in these capacities as solemn obligations, which should be entered on and carried out as matters of individual ·and personal interest.

EXTRACT FROM BARON LEFROY'S CHARGE TO THE GRAND JURY OF THE COUNTY OF CLARE.

Spring Assizes, 1846.

Ennis, 24th February.

. . . . . " I am sorry to say that, amongst the cases on the calendar, I find there are three of murder, one of conspiracy to murder, fifteen Whiteboy offences, one case of manslaughter, one case of arson, and seven cases of assaults, all more or less of a serious and dangerous character; but, with respect to the Whiteboy offences and the case of conspiracy to murder, they appear to be of such a character, and committed under such circumstances, that I am compelled to say I cannot see how the law can be upheld, unless some strong and prompt measures are taken to suppress the great prevailing evil which now disgraces certain districts in this country. I allude to a regular system of organisation which appears to exist, for payment of a stipulated sum of money to assassins that are employed to perpetrate the foul deed of murder. It is evident a regular trade has been carried on, for it is quite manifest that those who have been employed for the diabolical purpose of committing murder have gone so far as to make overtures to the party whom they were hired to kill, offering to confess all to him, and to save his life if he would give them a sum of money exceeding that which they were to receive for killing him. Gentlemen of the Grand Jury, if this state of things be permitted to continue, if the taking of human life is to be made a subject of vile trade or barter, and strenuous efforts be not made to put an end to such a trade, I cannot conceive where the evil will end. Let me entreat you, therefore, to adopt some strong measures to counteract this crying evil; if this extortion of money be permitted to continue —if men have not the courage and firmness to resist this sort of overture—if they do not resist it fearlessly and boldly, I repeat it, I do not know where the evil results will end. The case of conspiracy to murder will come before you in the form of an indictment against persons who, as it is alleged, were employed to commit the deed, and I have felt it my duty to make these observations to you, and through you, to everyone in this county, for I address myself to every man who wishes to uphold the law, and live under a well-regulated state of society."

After dwelling at some length on the nature of their duties in sifting evidence, he proceeded to say—

"There is one subject more on which I think it necessary to address you, and I shall merely say a few words—not so much for you, as through you, for other gentlemen in this county, who may be summoned to attend as jurors upon the long panel. When, in the administration of justice and the suppression of crime, so much intimidation is held out as has lately been made use of, it is essential that the intelligent and respectable jurors who have property in this county, who are interested in the welfare of society, and who are returned on the panel, should make it a point of duty to attend; for if those who are possessed of property, men of intelligence, education, and principle, will not perform the duties which the law requires, it is against all reason to suppose that the administration of justice can be carried on vigorously and impartially. If these gentlemen will not take the trouble to attend, in order to assist in the administration of the laws under which they enjoy the property they possess, they will only have to blame themselves if that property should be wrested from them by violence and intimidation. I trust this will not be the case. I hope all gentlemen of this county who are summoned on the panel will attend, in order that we may have the most intelligent, the most independent, and the most impartial jurors—men that will deal out justice without partiality, and with humanity; for I have always found, in the course of my professional and judicial experience, that the most humane verdicts are delivered by jurors of the class to which I have alluded. The importance of their attendance is therefore plain, and I am confident it will have great effect in improving the social condition of your county."

In the two following letters we have an account of his visit to Lord Kingston's Castle, and of the wonders of Lord Rosse's new telescope, which he went to see on his way home from the Munster circuit at that time :—

TO HIS WIFE.

Parsonstown,
Saturday Night.

I fly about, as you will see, with great agility. I slept in Cork on Thursday night, at Mitchelstown Castle last night, and here I am to-night nearly seventy miles on my way to Carrig-glas. I hope to-morrow to spend a quiet day with Lord Rosse, and mount to the skies by the help of his wonderful telescope, but in a better sense also by a quiet Sunday passed as it ought to be in thanksgiving and praise for all the mercies of the last five weeks. I had not intended paying my visit to Lord Kingston until to-day, and worked all Thursday for my brother Judge ; but finding yesterday morning, after working a while, that he had but one record left besides the one he was trying, he agreed with me that I might very well leave and pay my visit to Mitchelstown Castle a day sooner than I had intended ; so I set off and arrived there just as the sun was setting on that magnificent pile of building at the foot of those noble mountains, with its beautiful wooded scenery all around. Its good-natured and hospitable owner received me in the most affectionate manner, though I had come a day before my time, and disappointed him of a good entertainment he had prepared for the next day, to which he had invited a large party, including everybody he thought would be agreeable to me to meet. I would not willingly have done this, but I could not afford the loss of so much time, and I have the gratification to feel that Kingston fully entered into my reasons, and was as much gratified at having me (all to himself) as if I had waited till to-day. Mitchelstown Castle is worth a journey from Dublin, and Kingston has given me the most cordial invitation for us all to pay him a visit, and to T—— and his family in case they go to Youghal. I think you will say I have not done amiss to have written so much after my day's journey, and being up since half-past five this morning. I expect to be at my own dear second home (the first must ever be where you are) on Monday, about two o'clock.

T. L.

TO THE SAME.

Carrig-glas,
March 31, 1846.

Here I am again, thanks be to our gracious Lord, who has been with me at my going forth and my returning, and followed me all the way with His mercy and goodness. Oh, how we ought to desire not to be left to ourselves. I was anxious for the Leinster Circuit, and there is Judge Ball at Nenagh in a murder case since Wednesday, and it is not likely to end till next Wednesday, and then he has three other murders to try, besides a number of minor cases. Again, Baron Richards and Judge Perrin have been obliged to adjourn the Assizes at Roscommon, and are going back there to-morrow, while here am I, with all my work done, fresher by a great deal than when I left just five weeks ago. Yesterday was indeed a most interesting day. Lord Rosse and his wife were as kind to me as possible. The wonders of

R

his telescope are not to be told. He says,—with as much ease as another man would say, "Come and I'll show you a beautiful prospect"—"Come and I'll show you a universe, one of a countless multitude of universes, each larger than the whole universe hitherto known to astronomers." The planet Jupiter, which through an ordinary glass is no larger than a good star, is seen twice as large as the moon appears to the naked eye. It was all true what Doherty* said, that he walked upright in the tube with an umbrella over his head before it was set. But the genius displayed in all the contrivances for wielding this mighty monster even surpasses the design and execution of it. The telescope weighs sixteen tons, and yet Lord Rosse raised it single-handed off its resting place, and two men with ease raised it to any height.

T. L.

In the following charge to the Grand Jury of the County of Roscommon, delivered at the Spring Assizes, 1848, we find the same earnest and anxious desire which was evinced in his charge to the Grand Jury of Clare to impress on the minds of Jurors the necessity of regarding their public duties in connexion with the administration of the law as a matter in which they had an individual interest:—

Roscommon, 22nd Feb., 1848.

"Mr. Foreman and Gentlemen of the Grand Jury, I have had but a short time to look over the calendar laid before

---

* Chief Justice Doherty was more than six feet high.

me; but it has been quite long enough to impress me
with a deep sense of its appalling character. I confess I
scarcely feel adequate to address you, for the heart sickens
and the spirit flags at the contemplation of the apparently
hopeless state of things which is presented to us by the
amount of crime that it records, and the sadly demoralized
state of your county which it exhibits.

But, gentlemen, despair is no remedy for these evils;
the only means by which they can be prevented is by
every man in society doing his duty, and by a firm
administration of justice. Emphatically, I say, gentlemen,
that the state of your county demands that every man
shall be found doing his duty, for that is the only way
by which you can expect to remedy the evils which
now press upon you. The amount of prisoners returned
is one hundred and sixty-six. Of these prisoners there
are forty-eight committed for cases of a serious and
aggravated character; there are six persons committed
under a charge of murder, there are twenty-three under
a charge of conspiracy to murder, there are six for
homicide. Following that of murder, sixty-six are committed for offences perpetrated or accompanied by the
use of fire-arms. If we add where deaths have ensued
the offences perpetrated by the use of fire-arms will
involve the number of seventy-eight. This is the fault
of a mischievous and mistaken encouragement which the
lower order of the people of this county have received to
provide themselves with fire-arms and the still more mischievous facility afforded by the open and public sale of
fire-arms. But gentlemen, we may rejoice that the Legislature, by the recent Act " for the prevention of crime and

outrage in Ireland," have, I trust, put a stop to this mischievous practice. It has been before observed, and it has fallen to my lot more than once to make the observation, that if you take up the English calendar for every county on a circuit and collect all the offences perpetrated by the use of fire-arms, you will not find as many as in some one county in Ireland—a circumstance calculated to show how different the habits of one nation may be from those of another, and how that which is perfectly safe in one country may be most detrimental to the best interests of another.

But, gentlemen, however apparently hopeless any amendment in the state of your county may be, I trust that in reality it will be found that the law has in itself sufficient efficacy for the detection and punishment of the guilty as well as for the prevention of crime, provided those whose duty it is to administer the law avail themselves of the powers conferred on them through its salutary provisions for the purpose. If the law, in its preliminary stages, carried out in the manner as it might and ought to be, I am satisfied you would soon find how efficacious it is for the detection of criminals and the prevention of crime.

And here, gentlemen, I desire to invite your attention to two important Acts of Parliament which seem hardly to be sufficiently known or called into operation. I refer firstly to the 2 & 3 Wm. IV. c. 108, which was an Act passed for the better preservation of the peace in this country, and by which magistrates are empowered to appoint special constables where it is proved on oath that any tumult, riot, or felony has taken place in the county, or may be reasonably apprehended, if the magistrates are of opinion that the ordinary police are not sufficient for the preservation of the peace and for the protection of the inhabitants and the security of property in the county. By that Act the Lord Lieutenant is enabled, on the representation of two magistrates, even to order that persons exempt by law from acting as special constables shall serve, notwithstanding such exemption. Now, gentlemen, the provisions of this Act are most valuable, because by the exercise of the powers here given you are enabled to enlist in the preservation of peace and good order in your county a larger number of persons than those ordinarily engaged in that important duty, and a class of men who are themselves most deeply interested in the careful discharge of that duty.

There is also another statute to which I wish to call your attention, because in the present state of your county I regard its provisions as peculiarly important. I allude to the 50 Geo. III. c. 102. By this Act (section 7) any magistrate in your county is empowered to cause to be arrested and brought before him any stranger sojourning or wandering within it, and to examine such stranger on oath respecting his place of abode, the place from whence he came, his manner of livelihood and his object or motive for remaining or coming into the county, and unless such person shall answer to the satisfaction of the magistrate, or produce sufficient security for good behaviour, such magistrate may commit him to the gaol or house of correction until he shall find such security or shall be discharged by such magistrate. The powers here conferred, gentlemen,

are very properly accompanied by a safeguard necessary
to prevent their being abused, for the magistrate who
commits such stranger is bound without delay to transmit
to the Lord Lieutenant a report of such committal and
the reason thereof, with the amount of bail required, the
examination of the prisoner and the reasons alleged by
by him why he should not be committed, so that such
person may be detained or discharged as to the Lord
Lieutenant may seem right. But with this safeguard, the
power thus vested in magistrates of arresting strangers
found in their county and making them give an account
of themselves will frequently furnish the best means of
detecting criminals who come from a distance to commit
offences and of defeating the attempts to establish con-
cocted cases of *alibi* which are so familiar to all who have
any experience in the administration of criminal law in
this country.* Having thus, gentlemen, endeavoured to
call your attention to some of those powers which the law
has given to magistrates for the maintenance of peace and
order, it only remains for me to remind you of the duty
which belongs to your high and honourable office to
exercise those powers as occasion may require. The law
presumes every man to be acquainted with his legal rights
and duties, and it is positively the duty of magistrates to

* It is much to be regretted that the useful provisions of the 50 Geo. 3,
c. 102, s. 7, referred to in the above charge, were repealed by the 28 Vic.
c. 33, and although in the strangely vacillating spirit in which modern
legislation is too often conducted in matters of grave importance to the
social interests of Ireland, this clause has been re-enacted by the 33 Vic.
c. 9, yet its usefulness has been fettered by limiting its operation to districts under special proclamation, when increased powers for the detection
of criminals ought to have been regarded as essential to the well-being
of the whole country.

be so, as on them lies the obligation of protecting the persons and property of their fellow-subjects."

The following letters written from the Connaught circuit in the years 1847 and 1848 painfully recall to our minds some of the sad results of the Irish famine caused by the potato blight which, in the summer of 1846 appeared so suddenly, that in less than a fortnight the stalks of almost every potato field throughout Ireland were burnt up as if a destroying angel had swept over the land. Unhappily in the two succeeding years the blight reappeared with such virulence that it cut off nearly the whole supply of what then formed the chief food of the labourers and small farmers, and by degrees it dragged into the vortex of misery and desolation, which followed in its wake, most of the better class of farmers and gentry in the West and South of Ireland.

From the Spring Circuit of 1847 Baron Lefroy writes:—

TO HIS WIFE.

Galway,
20th March, 1847.

I have, thanks to our gracious Lord, got through another day's heavy work with great satisfaction, and I have been enabled to afford much relief to the gaol and the unhappy prisoners who were in a wretched state from its over-crowded condition. I have also got a liberal pre-sentment from the grand jury to meet all my wishes for hospital accommodation for the sick, and they willingly adopted my advice to give two day's provisions to each prisoner on his discharge, to take him home. A vast majority of the thefts committed in this county was from the pressure of want.

It is certainly a great gratification to find so much co-operation and good will in every quarter as I have found amongst the gentry here, and to experience the good result of pressing strongly what is right, however reluctant men may seem to be at first to comply with it. Indeed, when I consider that the gentry are comparatively almost as much distressed as the poor, one could hardly be surprised if their feeling for themselves inclined them to be somewhat insensible to the greater wants of others.

T. L.

Again, at the Spring Assizes in the following year, he writes:—

Galway, 20th March, 1848.

" . . . In my experience on this or any other Circuit I never have known so many persons to be tried as appear on the present calendar. There are no less than 696 persons returned for trial, of whom seven men are in custody on charges of murder, but the rest are, generally speaking, to be tried for sheep or cattle stealing, and larcenies committed under the pressure of sheer famine. Besides those to be tried, there are 219 prisoners in the gaol whose terms of imprisonment under former sentences have not expired."

T. L.

The following extract from his charge to the
Grand Jury of the county of Galway at the Spring
Assizes of 1849 may be added, as filling up the
picture given in these letters of the sad state to
which the west of Ireland was reduced at that
period:—

Mr. Foreman and Gentlemen of the Grand Jury, I
deeply lament to be obliged to bring before you the
appalling state of things which the calendar that has been
laid before me presents as existing in your gaol. It
appears that the number of prisoners is no less than 764,
while the building is only calculated to accommodate 110.
As, however, I shall have to call your attention to this
subject at another period of the assizes, I will not now
further dwell on it. The number of prisoners for trial is
423, and from the analysis that has been made of the
calendar, the cases appear to be 259 in number, of which
you will have to dispose. Of this number, there are
fifteen persons committed on charges of murder or manslaughter; but I understand that there are only three of
the cases bearing the character of murder, and they are
not of recent occurrence. There are twenty-four cases of
burglary and robbery. The cases of sheep stealing
amount to 115, the cases of cow stealing to fifty-seven,
and besides these, there are eighty-six cases of larceny.
The number of the sheep and cattle stealing cases is
quite alarming. They might be accounted for, when
want and famine from the sudden failure of the potato
crop overwhelmed the people, but now that so many
efforts are being made to supply the wants of the poor,

this wholesale system of plunder cannot be endured. It is the duty of those to whom the administration of the law is entrusted to see that it be made effectual for the end and purpose of the law, by imposing punishment on the guilty, and thereby deterring others from the commission of similar offences.

He was the first of the Judges of Ireland who had to carry into execution the then new and important provisions of the Treason-Felony Act, at one of the most critical periods of Irish history which has occurred since the Rebellion of 1798. The case was one of such great importance, and his charge to the Grand Jury was regarded as such a clear and able exposition of the law, that the following extracts from the report of the trial could hardly with propriety be omitted from the pages of this memoir.

Commission Court, Green-street, Dublin,
Saturday, May 20, 1848.

Presiding Judges:—The Right Hon. BARON LEFROY and the Right Hon. Mr. JUSTICE MOORE.

———

The QUEEN *v.* JOHN MITCHELL.

———

BARON LEFROY'S CHARGE TO THE GRAND JURY.

Gentlemen of the Grand Jury of the City of Dublin— I am now enabled to address you upon the case which this morning appeared to the Court not ripe for your consideration, for, as I stated to you then, it appeared on the face of the calendar in a very ambiguous light. It is the case of the prisoner John Mitchell; the return made upon the calendar was, that he was committed for publishing a seditious libel; it was impossible, therefore, to ascertain with precision the nature of the charge against the prisoner. It might have been either a misdemeanour for the publication of a seditious libel, or it might have been a charge of felony under the late Act. In either case it was important that the Court should give you their assistance upon it. And we are now enabled to do so, for we have been apprised that a bill for felony, under the late Act, is about to be sent up to you. In the short interval which I have had, I have felt it my duty as far as I could to look into that bill, in order to call your attention to the statute upon which it is framed, with a view to explain the law under that statute, and to make such observations as may guide you, in the application of that law to the facts of the case. I congratulate you, gentlemen, and I think I may congratulate the Court, that the case for your consideration is not such as it would have been if the bill to be laid before you were for misdemeanour for a seditious publication, for, in that class of cases, unhappily, a latitude has of late prevailed as to the topics and the observations which counsel are allowed to introduce, which renders the administration of justice difficult and embarrassing both to the Court and to the Jury. Happily, however, gentlemen, you have to deal with an offence described by the statute to which it is now my duty to call your attention, with an accuracy and precision that will leave you comparatively no difficulty in discharging the duty you have to fulfil. The Statute in question was passed on the 22d of April in the present year. I will first read for you the section upon which the bill to be sent to you is framed, and I will then call your attention in detail to those provisions in the Act upon which you will have to exercise your judgment.

By this Act, after reciting two former statutes relative to the same subject matter, the Legislature proceeds in the third section to enact:—

"That if any person shall, within the United Kingdom or without, compass, imagine, invent, devise, or intend to deprive or depose our most Gracious Lady the Queen, her heirs or successors, from the style, honour, or royal name of the Imperial Crown of the United Kingdom, or of any other of Her Majesty's dominions and countries, or to levy war against Her Majesty, her heirs or successors, within any part of the United Kingdom, in order by force or constraint to compel her or them to change her or their measures or counsels, or in order to put any force or constraint upon or in order to intimidate or overawe both Houses or either House of Parliament, or to move or stir any foreigner or stranger with force to invade the United Kingdom or any other Her Majesty's dominions or countries under the obeisance of Her Majesty, her heirs or successors, and such compassings, imaginations, inventions, devices, or intentions, or any of them, shall express, utter, or declare by publishing any printing or writing, or by open and advised speaking, or by any overt act or deed, every person so offending shall be guilty of felony."

Then follows the fourth section, providing for a case where the indictment shall be framed upon "open and advised speaking only;" but as I find no count in this indictment founded upon that charge, it is unnecessary to trouble you by calling your attention to that section. The fifth section authorizes the insertion in one indictment of any number of matters, acts, or deeds, by which such compassings, imaginations, inventions, devices, or intentions as are mentioned in the third section, shall have been expressed, uttered, or declared ; and then the seventh section provides, that although the matters charged in the indictment or proved upon the trial should amount to high treason, it is not either to vitiate the indictment, or to entitle the party to be acquitted of the felony, as, but for that provision, he might have claimed, on account of the merger of the smaller offence in the greater.

I may now tell you, gentlemen, at the outset, that the indictment about to be sent up to you is framed upon the provisions in the third Section of the Act which I have read to you. Some of the counts are founded on the compassing, imagining, and intending to deprive the Queen of her style, title, honour, and royal name of the Imperial Crown of the United Kingdom; and others upon the compassing, imagining, and intending to levy war against Her Majesty, for the purpose of compelling Her Majesty by force or by constraint to alter her counsels or measures. And the mode in which the indictment charges that utterance and expression was given to these " compassings" or " intentions," is by a publication in a paper called *The United Irishman,* and another journal. There are, besides the counts supported by a reference to the publications in these journals, two counts charging that by divers other publications after the passing of the Act, but before or subsequent to the 6th day of May, which is the day first laid in the indictment for this charge, the prisoner did endeavour to excite her Majesty's subjects to assist in carrying into effect the same felonious compassings, and also did give instructions to the said subjects of Her Majesty, wherein and in what manner such compassings ought to be carried into effect.

Now, gentlemen, I have to observe to you that this law is not altogether new, for the provisions in this Act are to be found in other Acts long antecedent to it, in substance and in terms, but only under a different character and subject to a different penalty. In fact, the matters which by the late Act are made felonies, and punishable by transportation or imprisonment, were, previous to this Act, at least in England, high treason, and punishable, of course, by death. That was certainly the law in England, but a doubt existed whether such was the law in Ireland; and as one of the objects of the present Act was to remove that doubt, perhaps a short history of the law, as it stood before this Act, will enable you better to understand the nature and effect of the Act.

In the year 1796, before the Act of Union, an Act was passed in England, the 36th George III., chap. 7, by which all the matters enumerated in the present Act were made high treason during the life of the then King. That Act was passed in England, and was considered then to be necessary for the protection and better security of the Crown and Government of England, but it never

was enacted in Ireland. In the year 1817, after
the Union, it was thought expedient to make that
Act perpetual which had been enacted only as a temporary
one for the life of George III., and for six months
after the demise of the Crown. Accordingly the 57th
George III., chap. 6, was passed, making the 36th
George III., chap. 7, perpetual, but although that Act was
passed by the United Parliament of Great Britain and
Ireland, yet Ireland is not named in the Act, and thence
arose the doubt as to whether the Act extended to Ireland
or made that which was law in England also law in Ireland.
But whether it did so or not, still, under its provisions, the
offences mentioned in the Act with which we have now to
do would have constituted high treason, and have been
punishable by death. To alter that state of the law this
Act was passed; it applies the same provisions to Ireland
as to England, and deals with such offences not as high
treasons, but as felonies. It is, therefore, neither a new
law, nor can it be looked on as a law of extreme rigour or
severity; on the contrary, it is a law mitigatory, lowering
the character of the offence with which the prisoner in
this case is charged, and mitigating most materially the
punishment which is to attend it under the present Act,
from that which would have attended it under the former
Acts. No jealousy, therefore, gentlemen, can properly be
entertained of this Act as referable to Ireland; nor, if it
was wise and wholesome to continue those provisions for
the protection of her Majesty's government and title in
England, can I conceive that any person will imagine
that it was less necessary and expedient to do so for
Ireland; and it is as part of the law for Ireland that you

are now called upon to give it effect, provided a case is
made out to your satisfaction coming within the provisions of the Act.

That you may be the better enabled to form a correct
judgment upon that subject, gentlemen, I will now ask
your consideration of the two provisions of the Act,
to which exclusively your attention need be applied
—namely, the provision which is intended to guard
Her Majesty's title and right as Queen of the United
Kingdom of Great Britain and Ireland, and the provision
which is intended to guard against the levying of war
against Her Majesty for the purpose of compelling her,
by force or constraint, to alter her counsels or measures.
You will observe, that the Act does not require that these
compassings or intentions should be actually carried into
effect; but it does require that there should be such a
manifestation of the intent as the Act specifies. Not that
any party should, under a mere suspicion of entertaining
any such intents, be convicted or put in danger of being
convicted thereof; but that those purposes or intentions
should be manifested by some writing or publication by
the party charged with entertaining those intentions, or
by some other overt act or matter, evincing clearly that
the party accused did entertain such intents and purposes.
The Act, then, declares that the person so entertaining
any of those intentions, and manifesting them in any
of the ways pointed out by it, shall be guilty of felony.

I shall now call your attention to the course which
the indictment in the present case takes. After charging
these felonious compassings and intentions of the two
kinds to which I have referred, it goes on to state

that the prisoner did publish a certain newspaper, and did publish in that newspaper a certain speech made by himself; and that it appears from that speech so published by himself, that he did entertain the purpose and design ascribed to him by the indictment—of depriving the Queen of her sovereignty over these realms, and of levying war against her, for the purpose of compelling Her Majesty to change her counsels or measures. It will be, therefore, for you to say, in the first instance, whether the publications so set out in the indictment are brought home to the prisoner, as being his publications, published either by him, or by his authority. If you should not be satisfied of that, there will be an end to the case, so far as it depends on the alleged publications charged in the indictment; but if you should be satisfied that the publications were his, or chargeable to him, then you will have to consider whether they manifest the purpose and intent ascribed to him viz., the purpose and intent of depriving Her Majesty of her sovereignty over these realms; or, secondly, the purpose and intent of levying war against Her Majesty, for the purpose of compelling her, by force or by constraint, to alter her counsels or measures. Now, that you may understand the case more clearly, I will take in their order the several provisions of the Act upon which the indictment professes to be grounded.

The first deals with the felonious purpose, or intent to deprive Her Majesty of the style, honour, and royal name of the imperial crown of the United Kingdom. The style and title of her majesty, as sovereign of these realms, is Queen of the United Kingdom of Great Britain and Ireland. You will have to read over attentively the several publica-

tions set out in this indictment, supposing them to be
brought home to the prisoner, and to ascertain in reference
to this first provision, whether you find in these publications evidence of a purpose or intent to deprive Her
Majesty of the sovereignty of these realms as Queen of
the United Kingdom of Great Britain and Ireland.

Here the learned Baron read and commented on
certain passages of the speech which he considered as most expressly manifesting the felonious
intention firstly charged in the indictment, and
after going through these he continued:

You will look through the rest of this speech, you
will see if there be anything in the course of it, tending
to explain, to qualify, or to recall any of these passages
as casual and over-hasty expressions.   But you will
have also to consider therewith, that after having been
made, it is published—an act of deliberation, scarcely
compatible with an over-hasty, sudden, and unintentional
expression of feeling. Of course you may advert to
anything else that may appear to you substantially and
clearly to qualify and take out of these passages their
sting and give the prisoner the benefit if any such appears.
But supposing these passages to stand unmitigated and
unexplained, it will be for you to say, whether any
doubt remains upon your mind of the felonious intention
imputed under this branch of the statute.

The next ground upon which the indictment is sought
to be sustained is that of the intention to levy war against

Her Majesty, with the view to compel her, by force or constraint, to change her measures or counsels. Gentlemen, it is not necessary that this intention to levy war should be carried into effect. The charge here is the compassing, and intending, and avowing the intention to levy war. It is right, however, that before being called upon to ascribe to the prisoner the purpose or intention of levying war against the sovereign, you should understand what, in point of law, is levying war against the Sovereign. It is necessary also to tell you what is *not* necessary to constitute that offence. It is not necessary that an army should be arrayed, should be trained, should be disciplined, or should be officered, with all the usual pageantry of war attending it. The law requires no such thing, in order to constitute a levying of war against the Sovereign. But as this is a very material part of the case, and one upon which there is the most explicit authority, I prefer to state to you what the law is upon the subject from that authority rather than in my own words. I am about to read to you from a work of one of the most enlightened and humane of criminal judges that ever adorned the bench of England, I mean Sir Michael Foster. After observing what I have already stated not to be necessary to constitute a levying war against the crown, he adds:—

" But every insurrection which, in judgment of law is
" intended against the person of the King, be it to de-
" throne him, or oblige him to alter his measures of govern-
" ment, these risings all amount to a levying of war
" within the statute, whether attended with the pomp or
" circumstance of open war or not. All risings, in order
" to effect innovations of a public character and of a

" general concern by an armed force, are in the construc-
" tion of the law high treason, within the clause of levy-
" ing war; for although they are not levelled against
" the person of the King, they are against his Royal
" Majesty, and besides they have a direct tendency to
" dissolve all the bonds of society, and to destroy all pro-
" perty and all government too, by numbers and an
" armed force. Insurrections, likewise, for redressing
" national grievances, or for the reformation of real or
" imaginary evils of a public nature, and in which the
" insurgents have no special interest; risings to effect
" those ends by force and numbers, are by construction
" of law within the clause of levying war, for they are
" levelled at the King's crown and royal dignity."

You are not called upon, gentlemen, to decide in this
case, and it is-not with that view that I have read those
passages to you—that war was levied against the Sovereign.
You are only called upon to say whether the intention to
levy war against the Sovereign was entertained by the
prisoner. But before you can charge a party with that
intention, you must understand what it is to levy war
against the Sovereign; and, therefore, and with that view
only, I call your attention to this, in order that you may
examine the documents before you, and see whether in
any of them you can find evidence of any purpose or
intention which, if carried into effect, would amount to
levying war against the Queen for the purpose of compelling Her Majesty, by force or constraint, to change
her measures or counsels. Gentlemen, when the Act
says to compel the Sovereign by force or constraint to
change her counsels, the Act does not contemplate that

the jury should be obliged to come to the wild conclusion that the prisoner must have designed to have marched an army to London, and there, by actual physical force, to compel the Queen to change her measures or counsels; no, but if you find in these documents evidence of a purpose and intention to stir up a rebellion—to stir up an insurrection, for the purpose of redressing real or imaginary national grievances, or for the purpose of obliging the Sovereign to change her measures or counsels by the constraint which may arise from the circumstance of a rebellion being stirred up in the country, and that (in order to relieve the innocent portion of Her Majesty's subjects from the pressure of such an evil) Her Majesty might be induced thereby to yield that which is demanded of her, rather than persevere in the attempt to resist the demand under pressure of the aggravated afflictions and sufferings of Her Majesty's subjects in the country. If you should find, in the documents before you, anything leading you reasonably to suppose that even in that way it was intended to constrain the Sovereign, it would be within the terms of this Act. But though I am putting this case to you in all its variety, I may be going unnecessarily far; because, if you can find throughout these publications— —if you can find a distinct call to arms—a distinct call to the nation, or a large portion of it, to arm for the purposes suggested, then it will be for you to say whether any doubt remains upon your minds of the intent of levying war against Her Majesty for the purpose of compelling her to change her counsels or measures.

Gentlemen, the two remaining counts of the indictment refer to publications which are not set out in the indictment ; they refer to publications which, if they are brought before you, you will first consider attentively the question whether they have been brought home to the prisoner ; next, you will have to peruse the publications with attention, in order to ascertain whether they contain that which is ascribed to them in these last two counts of the indictment, viz :—excitements to Her Majesty's subjects to give assistance to the carrying into effect these felonious intentions, or whether they point out to them the mode and manner of carrying out those intentions.

I have now gone through all the portions of this Act which appeared to me to be material in respect to the bill about to be sent up to you ; and the summary of what I have addressed to you is shortly this : that you have first to ascertain whether these publications are brought home to the prisoner, next, whether regarding them as expressions and manifestations of intentions by being published, they afford you evidence of the intentions charged ; if they do, you are bound to find the bill, if they do not, you will of course ignore it. The object of the Act, as I have already stated, is not to punish treason, or these felonious compassings when carried out into actual treason ; but the wise, and I would say the merciful purpose of the Act is, to intercept treason, to stop it short while it yet rests in intent, and only in such a manifestation as ascertains the existence of the intent, but before it ripens into all its awful and mischievous effects. The Act, therefore, though it does go to punish the intent, and in that respect might perhaps, be deemed an act of severity, yet when it comes to be considered, is in

truth, an act of mercy and wisdom ; for although punishment may fall upon those who only intend the mischief, yet
it is far better they should suffer for their evil intentions
than to wait till the great body of the public should suffer
under the affliction which must result from those
intentions being carried out into all the calamities in
which the country would be involved by the perpetration
of actual treason.

The Grand Jury, after some deliberation, found
a true bill against the prisoner, and the trial proceeded immediately.   The duty of charging the
Petit Jury devolved on Mr. Justice Moore ; and
after the jury had handed in their verdict of
"guilty," Baron Lefroy passed sentence on the
prisoner as follows :—

John Mitchell, I cannot help expressing the feelings
of regret, in which I am sure my brother Judge par-
ticipates, to see a person in your condition standing at
that bar under the circumstances in which you are now
placed; you have been found guilty upon an indictment
which charges you with feloniously compassing, imagining
and intending to deprive the Queen of the style, honour
and royal name of the Imperial Crown of the United
Kingdom; and with uttering and giving publicity to
those purposes and intentions, by publishing certain
writings in a newspaper, published by you, called *The
United Irishman*.   Those publications are set forth in

detail. There are other counts in the indictment, on which you have also been found guilty of a felonious intent and purpose to levy war against the Queen, for the purpose of compelling her Majesty, by force and constraint to change her measures and counsels, and that this felonious intent and purpose was manifested by a publication made by yourself, in the same newspaper, and under the same circumstances stated in the former counts. These are the charges upon which you were put upon your trial, and upon which the jury have found you guilty. The evidence was furnished by yourself—publications coming out of your own hands, deliberately issued at an interval of time which gave you full leisure and opportunity to consider what you were about, and to reflect upon what might be the consequences of your own acts. The case turned upon the meaning and interpretation of these publications; that meaning and interpretation was equally furnished by yourself, and came from yourself just as the publications themselves have done. The meaning and intent was collected from the language of the publications themselves; not confined to one, but to be collected from the successive publications, so as to leave no doubt upon the words interpreted by yourself, as to the meaning and intent of these publications. The very able and learned counsel who defended you was not able to offer any other interpretation, any other meaning, than that which was assigned to them on the face of the indictment. Upon this evidence, thus furnished by yourself, the jury have found you guilty. With that verdict, therefore, however you may be advised, or think yourself justified in calling it the verdict of a packed jury, thus imputing to twelve of your countrymen deliberate and wilful perjury—

MR. MITCHELL—My lord, I did not impute perjury to the jury—I beg your lordship's pardon.

Mr. BARON LEFROY—I understood that you had stated, in arrest of judgment, that you had been found guilty by a *packed* jury.

Mr. MITCHELL—I did.

Mr. BARON LEFROY—Well, I owe it to the jury to state, that upon the evidence thus furnished by yourself, no juror who had any regard to the oath he had taken, could have come to a different conclusion. What ground of doubt was even suggested with respect to the fact of the publication by yourself, or with respect to the interpretation and the meaning of those publications? As I have observed, not even your own able counsel could suggest a doubt or a meaning different from what is imputed to them; no, not even to suggest an apology, or at least an apology which could be attended to in a court of justice, but an apology amounting to this—that you had a right to violate the law. Well, then, with the verdict establishing your guilt of the offence stated upon the face of this indictment, even you yourself cannot fairly quarrel. And now, what is the nature of the offence of which you have been thus found guilty? I will not say the greatest —but it is next to the greatest offence—it is near akin to the very greatest offence which any subject can be guilty of towards his Sovereign, or towards his country. By the law of England, up to a late period, the offence of which you have been guilty was high treason. At the present moment, both in England and Ireland, it is a

treasonable felony; and I cannot but hope and trust, that notwithstanding the deliberate perseverance in the course, which unhappily you have been pursuing—I cannot but hope and trust that you may yourself one day or other be struck with the awful consequences, the awful results, to which that course must of necessity have led, if it had not been checked in its progress. Surely, to use your own language, "a provisional government taken from a howling mob"—surely a "practical enforcement of an argument sustained by a hundred thousand pikes," must have been attended with the most desolating and appalling consequences to your country. Surely, surely, that must have been the result. Well, then, independently of the nature of this crime, look at the circumstances connected with it. I will not go into any extraneous circumstances, but look at the circumstances which were brought before the Court, and to which we could not shut our eyes, connected with this offence. It originated in a speech. Well, great allowance might be allowed for a speech delivered under excitement; and though the time and the place were badly chosen, upon an occasion where excitement would do more mischief, perhaps, than upon a more sober occasion, however, if it had rested upon that, there might be great allowance and great apology. But, after time for deliberation, you thought fit to publish that speech, so full of exciting and objectionable matter, so charged with these felonious compassings and intentions, which are here stated upon the face of the indictment ; you thought fit, after deliberation, to publish it, to take away from it all the apology of momentary excitement, and to

take away from it all the apology of limited effect; you
put it into a position calculated to give it circulation
through every corner of the land, to diffuse the poison
through every excitable mind in the whole country. The
law makes, even upon the matter of high treason, a great
distinction; it does, indeed, in every branch of it, make a
great distinction between words spoken and words published. You published, deliberately, this first article, upon
which so much has been already said, that it is quite
unnecessary for me to recall or reiterate the highly objectionable passages it contains to sustain both the one count
and the other. But a comparison of the two publications
—of the 6th of May, and of the 13th of May—naturally
suggests this observation, that any possible mitigation
which might arise from the tenor of the· first, or
from anything occurring in it, has been effectually
withdrawn, and done away with in the second. The
second publication, which was at an interval of a week,
leaves it utterly impossible for the greatest stretch
of ingenuity, or the greatest perversion of interpretation,
to protect you. On the second, the charge is (you have expressed it yourself) of intending to overthrow the monarchy,
and to establish in its place a republic in the country: you
have rendered definite what perhaps was vaguely expressed
in the first ; you have taken away what might and would,
no doubt, if the case had rested on that alone, have been
some apology for that publication, or at least a circumstance
of mitigation, that you have in it disclaimed the intention
of a war of plunder or assassination; in the first you
have disclaimed that, and it would have been a disclaimer
which would have been to your credit and advantage if

you had left it to be made use of on your behalf. But
what appears in the second, from the man who disclaimed
a war of plunder, or a war of assassination? He tells his
countrymen, and he tells it by a preface that he is going
to speak plainly, in this second publication that—" There
is growing on the soil of Ireland a wealth of grain, and
roots, and cattle, far more than enough to sustain in life
and in comfort all the inhabitants of the island. That
wealth must not leave us another year, not until every
grain of it is fought for in every stage, from the tying of
the sheaf to the loading of the ship; and the effort necessary to that simple act of self-preservation will, at one and
the same blow, prostrate British dominion and landlordism
together."

Now, how is it possible that advice could be acted
upon in any way, which must not of necessity have led to
plunder and assassination, to the violent taking by force
and arms the property justly belonging to others, or
withholding it from them by force and violence, by the
use of arms? Thus it is, then, that you appear from one
stage to another to have advanced in a bold, deliberate,
determined opposition to the law, in language more and
more unmeasured, and more and more mischievously
exciting. In speaking thus, I beg to assure you it is not
my purpose to hurt your feelings, but merely to discharge
the duty which is now cast upon the Court to admeasure,
in proportion to the nature of the crime, the punishment
which we feel it our duty to inflict. It is, therefore, that
I have of necessity commented strongly on those passages
of the publications, as well as on the deliberation and the
perseverance manifested in the issuing of them, as forming

in part the materials by which we are bound to measure
our judgment, in discharging the solemn duty which we
owe to the law, to the public, and to the peace and welfare
of the country.

And here I cannot avoid observing that there was no
attempt, in the course of this trial, to offer any explana-
tion, any interpretation, any apology for these publications, or anything tending to raise a doubt upon their
bearing the interpretation that is put upon them by the
indictment.

Now, in adverting to the course taken in the defence
made on your behalf, we desire it (and I especially desire
it) to be understood, that the observations I am about to
make—following up the charge of my learned brother, in
every word of which I concur—are not made to aggravate,
in the least, the punishment which it is our duty to impose,
any more than my learned brother's observations were
intended to aggravate the case before the jury; but I
make the observations in respect to the line which was
adopted in order to mark my sense of its irrelevancy, and
that the Court might not appear to acquiesce in a defence
which, though we did not stop it yesterday, we yet felt it
our duty to reprobate, as in our judgment not warranted
by the privilege given to a prisoner's counsel, and which
we believed to be as injudicious with reference to the
prisoner as it was objectionable on other grounds. No
interpretation was offered, no meaning was suggested,
no effort was made, in the least, to show that you
were not guilty in the sense imputed by the indictment.
On the contrary, the line of defence, not only im-
pliedly, but expressly stated, that although you might

be statutably guilty, yet that you were justified in what you did.

MR. HOLMES—What I said, with the greatest respect, my lords, was, that though the prisoner was statutably guilty, he was not, in my opinion, morally guilty.

MR. BARON LEFROY—I should be very glad indeed to find that I had mistaken altogether the drift of that defence; and so far as the learned counsel would desire to correct the view that I was taking of it, I should gladly adopt his correction. I shall say no more upon it. I only adverted to it to absolve the Court from the possible suspicion that we could sit here and acquiesce in a line of defence which appeared to us at the time to amount very nearly to matter as objectionable as that for which the prisoner stood at the bar, though not involving the prisoner in a participation of it.

I have been somewhat withdrawn from the observations which I meant to have confined to your own case, by reference to a subject which I did not think I could avoid adverting to after what had passed yesterday. But to return to your own case. I wish you to understand that we have, with the utmost anxiety to arrive at a right decision upon the measure of punishment which it is our duty to impose, postponed passing the sentence until this morning. We have examined . the case with great deliberation, and with great anxiety duly to discharge the duty we owe to the prisoner, of not awarding a punishment beyond the just measure of the offence; as well as the duty we owe to the Queen, and to the public, that the measure of punishment should be such as should carry with it the effect of all punishment, which is not the infliction of suffering upon the individual, but the prevention of crime—that the punishment should carry with it a security, as far as possible, to the country, that one who appeared so perseveringly and so deliberately a violator of the law, should not be permitted to continue the course he had entered upon for the disturbance of its peace and prosperity, and that the country should have time, if possible, to recover from the infliction which that course had imposed upon it. If this had not been the first adjudication upon the Act, we might have felt ourselves obliged to carry out its penalties to their utmost extent, but taking into consideration that this is the first adjudication, though the offence is as clearly proved, and is almost as enormous as it can be anticipated that any offence of the kind can be proved to be hereafter, the sentence of the Court is, that you be transported beyond the seas for the term of fourteen years.

The following extract from the letter of an eye-witness of the proceedings, represents, as I believe, the impression left on the minds of all who were engaged in or present at the trial.

" . . . Mitchel's trial is over, and the Baron's most anxious friends could not desire more than the universal admiration elicited from men of all creeds and politics by the way in which he conducted the case. His dignity of demeanor, and his resolute firmness, blended with courtesy and patience throughout the whole of this difficult and important trial, were the subject of general observation."

The same impression seems to have been made on the minds of Members of the English Bench and Bar from the following letter :

63, Upper Seymour-street,

May 29, 1848.

MY DEAR BARON,—I cannot refrain from expressing to you the very great pleasure with which I have perused the proceedings on the late trial in Dublin, and the part which in your judicial character you were called upon to take in them. I assure you with the strictest truth that I hear from all our profession, whether on the Bench or at the Bar (and I have seen and heard many of both), one concurring sentiment of the mingled dignity, firmness, and fairness with which the presiding Judge demeaned himself throughout the whole proceeding. But I am more anxious to express to you how rejoiced I feel that the just judgment of the law should have been pronounced by lips unpolluted by former eulogies or succumbing to the author of all the mischief. I could not help thinking to myself (when I read your sentence) this is the Judge whom O'Connell was not only permitted to malign, but whom *others* high in office, and *professing* themselves conservators of law and order, have in consequence of such maligning kept out of that high place in his profession, where his learning and talents had, by the common consent of every candid man in it, long placed him. In haste,

Believe me, my dear Baron,

Yours ever most sincerely,

EDWARD GOULBURN.

CHAPTER IX.

Baron Lefroy's appointment as Chief Justice of Ireland—Congratulatory
letters on his appointment—Sir John Shelley's attack in Parliament
on the Chief Justice and two other members of the Judicial Bench in
Ireland—Addresses from the Grand Juries and from the Bar of the
Home Circuit.

ON the late Earl of Derby's accession to office,
in 1852, Mr. Lefroy had been more than ten years
occupying the place of fourth Baron in the Court
of Exchequer. During that period he had delivered
several judgments which are recognized by the Bar
and the Bench as amongst the ablest expositions of
the Law that we have on record. He showed an
intimate knowledge, not only of the principles of
the Common Law, but of the points of pleading
and practice arising in the daily business of the
Court which neither the members of the profession
nor of the Judicial Bench had at all anticipated from
the number of years that had elapsed since he had
confined his practice to the Courts of Equity; and,
in addition to his learning, there was a feature of

T

his judicial character which attracted universal
observation amongst all who, as suitors, jurors,
or members of the legal profession, were familiar
with his administration of the Law. I allude to
the bold and firm grasp with which he always laid
hold of the main questions on which the merits of
the case at issue depended, and to the mode by
which, in his charges, he kept the attention of the
jury directed to · these questions without suffering
their minds to be distracted by topics irrelevant,
or, though not altogether irrelevant, yet immaterial
to the due decision of the case.

With such qualifications, it was natural that the
Earl of Derby should be anxious to avail himself of
Baron Lefroy's services in some more prominent and
important post; and accordingly, on the vacancy in
the Queen's Bench occasioned by the transfer of the
Irish seals to Chief Justice Blackburne, Baron Lefroy
was promoted to the head of the Common Law
Bench in Ireland. He took his seat as Chief Justice
on the 1st day of Easter Term, 1852 ; and whether
we form our judgment from the congratulatory
letters he received or from the testimony borne in
the daily press, it is not too much to say that his
elevation was hailed with satisfaction by men of all
parties.

He was discharging his duties on the Connaught

Circuit when Lord Derby's letter, announcing his appointment, reached him ; and the following is his letter conveying the intelligence to his wife:—

Sligo, Wednesday,
4th March, 1852.

Just as I am setting off for my next town, I have received Lord Derby's letter announcing that he had submitted my name to the Queen for the Chief Justiceship, and that Her Majesty had been pleased to approve of the appointment, and, with this, I have already got nine letters of congratulation ! I shall be late for the post from Castlebar, so I stop to give you a line from hence, as, no doubt, you have seen other occupants named for the office by the newspapers, and you may wish to know the *real Chief Justice.* May He who has given us this additional earthly honour give us a due sense of all His mercies. Amidst all the gossiping rumours of the last few days these sweet words have kept my mind very quiet: " Peace I leave with you, my peace I give unto you : not as the world giveth, give I unto you—let not your heart be troubled, neither let it be afraid." I cannot delay a moment longer, except to send my love to all the dear ones around you.

T. L.

Amongst the numerous and gratifying letters he received on his promotion to the Chief Justiceship, I select one from those written by his colleagues on the Judicial Bench, and one from those of his private and personal friends ; but all alike testify to the estimation in which he was held by those who had the best opportunities of forming a right judgment upon his public and private character. The Right Hon. David Pigot, who presided as Chief Baron in the Court of Exchequer during a considerable portion of the time for which Mr. Lefroy occupied a seat as fourth Baron, writes from Circuit :—

Castleblayney, 14th March, 1852.

MY DEAR CHIEF JUSTICE,—I am here, on my return from Derry, Sabbath-bound, as I do not travel on Sunday. I may possibly have to cross over to the North of England immediately on my arrival in Dublin to-morrow. I therefore write this lest I may miss seeing you. I suppose I may now address you by the title which I have written above. Much and warmly as I must rejoice on personal grounds, at *any* thing which could in *any* way conduce to your welfare or your honour, and much as I prize the accomplished lawyer who is to succeed you, I feel most deeply how great is the loss which your elevation will occasion to myself, and to the colleagues whose experience of your value has been still longer than mine. I shall ever look back with a satisfaction, allayed only by a sense of what we are now losing upon the five years and a-half, during which I have witnessed and enjoyed the benefit of the learning and experience, the sound, clear, and vigorous judgment, the keen and stern sense of justice, and, with all, the cordial and candid spirit, guiding, while it enhanced those qualities, by which you have done so much in counselling and assisting us in the Exchequer.

I could not forbear to say thus much to you:—Hoping
that, though we shall no longer meet upon our old ground,
we shall often renew our intercourse elsewhere, and wishing, earnestly, every good wish for your honour and
happiness, I shall only add how sincerely I am,

My dear Chief Justice,

Most faithfully yours,

D. P. Pigot.

The next is from Serjeant Goulburn, brother
of the Right Hon. Henry Goulburn, Secretary of
State for the Home Department:—

62, Upper Seymour Street,

March 2nd, 1852.

My dear Chief Justice,—I have just heard a piece
of news, more gratifying (I can say with strict truth)
than any I have heard for many a day, to wit, your being
at length placed in a seat which was your due of
right twenty-five years ago.   Of right, I say, with
reference to your professional character, let who
would reign, and an hundred-fold your right as regards
your political career, in which you have ever so effectively promoted the interests of the party which I hope
have triumphed for good under the old-fashioned banner
"Let right be done." It is odd enough that I should, just
before I heard this good news, have said to Sugden
how I rejoiced that the best lawyer in England, by
common consent, should be placed at the head of
the law in England, and now it seems the same
may be said of Ireland.   I have not a moment to
say more than that which I think you will give me

credit for saying from my heart, God bless you, " Good luck have thou with thy honours," and

Believe me ever,

Yours sincerely,

EDWARD GOULBURN.

The following references to his administration of the law, taken from journals representing Roman Catholic sentiment in religion, and representing, in politics, opinions the very opposite of those held by the Chief Justice, exhibit plainly the respect and confidence which he possessed even amongst those to whom at all events, too partial an estimate of either his principles or his judicial qualities, cannot reasonably be imputed.

From the Connaught Ranger of 10th March, 1852.

THE LORD CHIEF JUSTICE.

It has been our province for a long series of years to be observers of the Judicial conduct of the going judges of assize, and we are confident we but speak the opinion of hundreds who thronged the Crown Court at the Mayo assizes just terminated, when we state a fairer, more just, or humane judge, than Baron Lefroy, never dispensed justice from our Bench. Wherever there was a prisoner unable to fee counsel, there His Lordship was found closely sifting the evidence, to see if he might not be able to elicit something favourable to the accused—and here we see his merciful disposition fully developed. Again, when the criminal, hardened in repeated acts of transgression, appeared before him, the justice and majesty of the law was instantly vindicated by this upright judge, by ridding society of those dangerous characters. View him where religious dissension, alas, prevails—he swerves not to the right hand nor to the left but honestly and judicially proclaims his abhorrence of those who go about sowing the seed of discord among friends and neighbours. May all such persons benefit by the lesson taught them by the Lord Chief Justice at our late assizes.

We care not what his politics may be, whether Tory or Whig, his decisions at our assizes were calculated to gain respect for the laws as well as for the judge who administered those laws.

From The Freeman's Journal of 13th February, 1854.

MISS CANTWELL'S CASE.

The action of Miss Cantwell against Messrs. Cannock and Co. has eventuated in a verdict for the plaintiff on the first issue, after a protracted trial which excited universal interest. The case was scrutinized in the most elaborate way in the criminal prosecution.

We abstain from any allusion to the general features of the trial, but it was impossible to overlook the calmness, the dignity, the firmness, and complete judicial power which the Chief Justice exercised throughout its protracted course. His charge was a very model of perspicuity, and brought home to the minds of the jury the salient features and bearings of the evidence with remarkable clearness, force, and precision.

In the term in which he first took his seat as Chief
Justice, he was called on in the course of his
judicial duties to preside in the Court of Exchequer
Chamber on the hearing of a case which excited
considerable public interest, and involved a very
important question of Constitutional Law. His
elaborate discussion of the authorities bearing upon
the case, and his lucid exposition of the law,
elicited general admiration amongst the profession
at the time, but, as his judgment appears in the
legal reports of that period,* I will only give here
the portion of it which seems to be illustrative of
character, and to exhibit the freedom of his mind
from that weak sensitiveness which so often tempts
even able and upright men to shrink from a public
duty, lest its discharge should be attributed to
selfish feelings or personal motives. The action was
brought by a suitor in the Civil Bill Court of the
County of Galway, against William Deane Freeman, Esq., Assistant Barrister and Chairman of the
Court of Quarter Sessions for that county, charging
a breach of duty on the part of the defendant in
refusing to receive an appeal from a decree which
he had made against the plaintiff. There was no
allegation of malice, and the facts proved on the
trial at Nisi Prius so far as they are important,

* See Ward v. Freeman, 2 Ir. Com. Law Rep. 460.

are sufficiently disclosed in the Chief Justice's Judgment.

Counsel for the defendant at the trial at Nisi Prius, called on the learned Judge (Moore, J.) either to nonsuit the plaintiff, or, if he would not consent to be nonsuited, then to direct a verdict for the defendant, inasmuch as the defendant as such Assistant Barrister was a Judge of a Court of Record, and in refusing to receive the appeal, he had acted judicially, and therefore no action for such act was maintainable against him. Counsel for the plaintiff insisted that the defendant's refusal to receive the appeal was not a judicial but a ministerial act, and therefore called upon the Judge to leave the consideration of the case upon the evidence to the Jury, and to direct them that if they believed the evidence given on behalf of the plaintiff, they ought to find a verdict for him. The Judge refused this application, and directed the Jury to find a verdict for the defendant, expressing his opinion to be that the defendant, acting as a Judge of a Court of Record, was not liable in this action for the breach of duty alleged to have been committed by him, and to this ruling counsel for the plaintiff excepted. The bill of exceptions was argued before the Queen's Bench in Michaelmas Term, 1851, (Blackburne then presiding as Chief Justice) ; the exceptions were overruled and judgment given for

defendant.   On this judgment a writ of error was
brought, and in addition to the main question noted
for argument, counsel for the plaintiff insisted at the
hearing that, assuming the defendant not to be liable
in point of law for the alleged breach of duty, still
there had been a mistrial in consequence of the
Judge at *Nisi Prius* not having left the case
to the Jury.   This is what is referred to in Chief
Justice Lefroy's judgment as " the second point in
the case " and formed the basis of the decision in
the Court of Error, as a majority of the judges
held that there was a mistrial on the above ground,
and unfortunately the more important question was
left undecided, for although the defendant lodged
an appeal to the House of Lords, he died before
any further proceedings could be taken.   The
Chief Justic edelivered judgment as follows :—

This case comes before the Court upon a Writ of Error
from the judgment of the Court of Queen's Bench.   The
question to be decided depends upon the charge of the
learned Judge who tried the case: if his charge was right,
the judgment should be affirmed ; if his charge was wrong,
the judgment should be reversed, and a *venire de novo*
awarded, unless there be some ground independent of
the exceptions, upon which this Court should feel itself
called to give any other judgment upon the whole record.
The first question is, was the direction of the learned
Judge right? and were the premises on which it was
founded warranted in point of law? This assumes four

propositions:—first, that the defendant, as an Assistant
Barrister, was a Judge of a Court of Record; secondly,
that as such he was not liable to an action for the matter
complained of; thirdly, that in refusing to receive the
appeal he acted judicially, and not ministerially; and
fourthly, that this was a case proper for a direction, and
not (as insisted on by the plaintiff's counsel) fit to be
left to the Jury upon the evidence generally.

Here the Chief Justice discussed at great length
the authorities bearing on these propositions, and
proceeded as follows:—

No doubt the Assistant Barrister is required to receive
the appeal, but it is equally clear that certain preliminaries
must be observed; and who is to decide whether these
preliminaries have been performed, or performed in the
manner and according to the object of the Legislature in
requiring them? . . . Has he no judicial discretion?
Does his judicial duty end until he has decided whether
he will grant execution to the party in whose favour he
has decided, or withhold it at the instance of the party
against whom he has decided? The moment he gives
the right to the one to appeal, he is taking from the other
the right to execution; and if the one may bring an action
against him for not receiving the appeal, why may not the
other bring an action against him for receiving the
appeal? Why is it not just as much a judgment for the
one as it is against the other? And if it be a judgment
by which one or the other may be prejudiced—if one is
entitled to bring an action because he did not receive the

appeal, why may not the other bring an action and say,
going through every one of the items, the affidavit was
not full enough, the bail were not solvent enough, the
costs were not deposited as they ought to be, it was for
delay, and you ought to have been aware of that from
what appeared on the trial before yourself; you therefore
wrongfully and injuriously stopped these proceedings, you
did so wrongfully and injuriously, and against your duty?
and thus in every case which the Assistant-Barrister has to
try, he will be subject to the action of the party against whom
he decides, in respect to the discharge of this part of his
duty. . . . It has been argued that he acts judicially
as to a certain part of his duty—that is, in making a
decree; but in giving or withholding execution he is only a
ministerial officer. But what is there in the Act to
warrant that proposition? He is Judge from first to last;
and it is to the Judge the privilege and protection is
given. . . . . It has also been said, that a Judge at
Nisi Prius has only to try the issue in fact joined between
the parties. But what was the issue here? It was whether the defendant was guilty or not guilty of a mis-
feasance. If the issue in fact become dependent upon an
issue in law, does it not become the duty of a Judge to
direct the Jury as to the verdict they should find, with
his opinion that the act complained of could not sustain
an action? Was he to leave it to the Jury on their oaths
to find the defendant guilty? Why put the defendant
to the disadvantage of moving in arrest of judgment
after a verdict, when the Judge is of opinion that there is
no case for a verdict, and the plaintiff desires, as he has a
right to do, to try the validity of that opinion by a bill of

exceptions? And shall he be allowed, if the Court
concur in that opinion, to try back merely for the purpose
of saying the matter should be decided in another form?
I confess this appears to me quite decisive against allowing
this objection now to prevail, even were there an exception
pointed to it, which I do not find there is. But there yet
remains a view of this case which entitles the defendant
to hold his verdict; and that brings me to the consideration of the plaintiff's third exception, namely, that the
Judge should have told the Jury, if they believed the
evidence on the part of the plaintiff, they ought to find a
verdict for him. This supposes the defendant to be
responsible for a breach of duty, and I am willing so to
take it. But I ask, what evidence is there beyond the
mere refusal to receive the appeal, to show such a breach
of duty as is charged by the declaration, "that the defendant, contriving and wrongfully intending unjustly to
injure and oppress the plaintiff, and to prevent him from
appealing, and not regarding his duty as such Assistant-
Barrister, or the statute in that case made and provided,
or the law of the land, absolutely refused to take said
appeal?" What is the evidence? That the Sessions
commenced at Galway on Friday, the 3rd of November,
1851; that the civil-bill business ended on Saturday, and
the criminal business commenced on Monday. We have,
therefore, the acting of the Assistant-Barrister as a Civil
Judge terminating on Saturday. . . . Taking every
tittle of evidence that was given, in conjunction with the
fact that he was as an Assistant-Barrister sworn to act impartially and justly, and therefore entitled to the presumption
that he would so act, what is there in the evidence in this

case on which to leave it to the Jury to say on their oaths
that he acted wilfully and wrongfully, with the design
and purpose of injuring the plaintiff—that such was the
defendant's motive, that it was no mistake, no refusal for
any justifiable reason? I say, therefore, taking the case
on any of the exceptions, there is no ground for
quarrelling with the direction of the learned Judge.

I regret that this case goes out of our hands without a deliberate judgment upon the ruling of the
learned Judge on the main point of the case, and the
more so, because I believe that if judgment had been
given on that point, and had not gone off on what is
called the second point, the judgment of the Court would
have been very different from what it is. It may, however, have been occasioned by a desire to dispose of the
case on any other ground than the privilege of Judges.
But I confess for my own part, though I trust I am not
insensible to that feeling of delicacy, I think we should
not be forgetful of another feeling, and that is, the desire
to uphold a privilege which is for the benefit of the
administration of justice, at least as much as it is for the
protection of the Judges. I am not squeamish on that
subject. I do not hesitate to claim for the Judges who
administer our laws, and I desire to sustain, a privilege
and protection which has existed from the earliest annals
of the law, which has been claimed and maintained by the
brightest ornaments of the Judicial Bench, and its wisest
and most learned sages. I do not desire or feel it
necessary to decline the privilege which has been asserted
and upheld in England by Lord Coke, Lord Holt, Lord
Mansfield, Lord Tenterden, and Lord Lyndhurst; and in

this country by Lord Downes, Chief Justice Bushe, and
though last in dignity, not least in weight and authority,
the late revered and learned Serjeant Warren. I do not
decline to maintain, with the utmost firmness, that high
privilege, nor do I think it will redound to or advance the
dignity or credit of Judges to put them in the
position in which, under the late Act of Parliament,*
they may be placed, by obliging them to descend
from the bench into the witness-box, and there (to use
a vulgar phrase), to clear themselves from the imputation of perjury. I do not, under such circumstances,
desire to strip them of the presumption which the
law makes in their favour, and to which I think they have
shown themselves entitled through a long course of years;
nor can I think that if they are now about to be stripped
of the benefit of this presumption, it will tend in any
manner to improve the administration of the law, or
advance the cause of justice. I hope, though the attaint
of Jurors is gone by, it is not about to be renewed in the
shape of an action on the case against the Judges, and I
should grieve to think that such was to be the result of
this judgment.

Early in the Parliamentary Session of 1856, Sir
John Shelley a member of the Radical section of
the House of Commons moved—" That there be
laid before the House a return of the date of the
call to the Bar of each of the Judges of the Superior
Courts of Law in Ireland ; the dates of their respec-

* Adverting to the 14 & 15 Vic. c. 99, which enabled the parties to an
action to be examined as witnesses in the case.

tive appointments as Judges ; the number of times each has been absent during the whole of any assize, or if absent during a part only, stating what part, and the reasons, if any, given for such absence ; also in how many, and in what instances, substitutes have been appointed by the crown to preside at any assize, or portion thereof, in the absence of any such Judge, giving in each case the name of the town." Under the cloak of this abstract motion, he proceeded to arraign the Chief Justice, Mr. Justice Torrens, and Baron Pennefather, for " continuing to hold their offices when no longer competent from age or infirmity to discharge their public duties ;" but like many of these ebullitions of party spirit in which the zeal of a certain class of politicians generally outruns their discretion the motion of Sir John Shelley resulted in the signal defeat of the object which was designed, for if he had wished to elicit a public expression of the unanimous respect and esteem in which the Chief Justice was held, instead of wishing to disparage him, he could not have adopted a better course than he did.

The able and effective speeches made by the Right Hon. B. Disraeli, the Right Hon. J. Napier, and Sir F. Thessiger, on that occasion fully exposed not only the groundlessness of the allegations, but the dangerous consequences which must necessarily follow if the House were to permit the character of those who were engaged in the administration of the law to be unjustly assailed by *ex parte* statements, while the Constitution had provided a safe and effectual remedy wherever any member of the Judicial Bench could be shown to have neglected his duties or abused the privileges of his office. In the following letter of the Chief Justice to the Lord Lieutenant's Secretary we have the expression of his calm and dignified resolution not to compromise his independence as a Judge by yielding to the adoption of any unconstitutional step by the House · of Commons, while, at the same time, the facts, for which he refers the Lord Lieutenant to the proper sources of information, furnish the most complete refutation of Sir John Shelley's reckless statement, " that if the return he asked for were granted, it would be found that the Chief Justice was constantly obliged to have a substitute to perform his duty, who had to be paid out of the Consolidated Fund."

Leeson-street, 23rd Feb., 1856

SIR,—In reply to your letter of the 21st instant, enclosing a copy of an order from the House of Commons, dated 14th February, 1856, I beg to observe that as the order does not assume to call upon the judges personally to make a return to the House, I of course understand your letter as only expressing his Excellency's desire to

U

be furnished with such information from me as may
assist him in having a return prepared, which will give to
the House the necessary information on the several
matters required, all of which being matters of record,
can be best authenticated by the officers in possession of
these records.   In this view of the subject, I have great
satisfaction in supplying to you, for the information of
his Excellency (but not as a return to be laid before the
House), such particulars as I am about to do.   I was
called to the bar in 1797, which will appear from the
Roll of Barristers in the hands of the proper officer of the
King's Inns.   I was appointed to the Bench as Baron of
the Exchequer in 1841, and the date of my patent, which
was given up on my promotion to the office of Chief
Justice, will be found by the enrolment.   The fact that I
never missed a circuit, or part of a circuit, since I have
been on the bench, can be established most correctly by
the proper officer of the Treasury, certifying to his
Excellency that no charge appears made at any time for
a substitute, to discharge any of my duties on circuit.
From these sources, and these only as I apprehend, can
his Excellency be furnished with such authentic information as will enable him to have a return prepared,
embracing with perfect accuracy all the objects of enquiry
in the order of the House of Commons.

I have the honor to be, &c., &c.,

THOMAS LEFROY.

The following addresses to the Chief Justice,
presented by the Grand Juries of the several

counties in which he presided as Judge of Assize on the Spring Circuit of 1856, afford a gratifying proof of the opinions of those who had the best opportunity of forming a correct judgment as to the truth or falsehood of the allegations brought forward by the Hon. Baronet.

From the Dublin Evening Mail of 3rd March, 1856.

It is our pleasing duty this evening to direct public attention, and particularly that of Her Majesty's Government and of Sir John Shelley especially, to the following address, unanimously agreed to by the High Sheriff and Grand Jury of the County of Westmeath, and presented to the Lord Chief Justice on Friday last. The address truly represents the feelings of men of all parties in Ireland; and, if proof of this were required, we could point triumphantly to the names of the gentlemen who signed the document; and first, as to the High Sheriff, Sir Benjamin Chapman, he is a Whig; Mr. D. H. Morgan, the foreman, is one of the Radical Representatives for the county; Sir Percy Nugent, a Roman Catholic; Mr. Tuite, a Whig, Mr. Henry Parnell, a Whig, Mr. William Chapman, a Whig, and Mr. John C. Lyons, a Whig. Thus men of all classess and creeds, and all men of great property and position in Westmeath, combined to pay a well-merited tribute of respect to one of the ablest and most upright Magistrates that ever adorned the judgment seat.

Address from the High Sheriff and Grand Jury of the County Westmeath, assembled at the Spring Assizes, 1856.

"TO THE RIGHT HON. THE LORD CHIEF JUSTICE.

"MY LORD,—We, the High Sheriff and Grand Jury of Westmeath, assembled at Spring Assizes, 1856, beg to offer our sincere congratulations to your Lordship on your re-appearance in our county, and at the same time to take this opportunity to bear our humble testimony to the great ability with which your Lordship has always conducted the business of our Courts. We congratulate your Lordship and ourselves that advancing years so far from impairing the efficient discharge of your judicial functions, have only added to your Lordship's vast legal experience, from which we have already derived so much advantage.

Sir B. Chapman, *High Sheriff.*	Wm. B. Smythe, *Barbavilla*, D.L.
W. H. Morgan, M.P.	John C. Lyons, D.L.
Hon. Richard Handcock.	J. Fetherstonhough Briscoe, J.P.
Hon. Henry Parnell.	Henry Murray, J.P.
Sir R. G. A. Levinge, Bart., D.L.	Wm. Fetherston H., J.P.
Sir Francis Hopkins, Bart., D.L.	Richard W. Reynell, J.P.
Sir Percy Nugent, Bart., D.L.	John D. Meares, J.P.
Hugh Morgan Tuite, D.L.	Robert Ralph Smith, *Portlick Castle.*
John Malone, J.P.	George N. Purdon, J.P.
Robert Smyth, *Gaybrook*, D.L.	Nicholas Evans, J.P.
George A. Boyd, D.L.	George J. N. Barry.
Wm. Chapman, J.P.	

REPLY.

Mr. High Sheriff, Mr. Foreman, and Gentlemen of the Grand Jury of Westmeath—To receive such an address from a body combining so much of the rank and intelligence of this great county, must at any time be considered a distinguished mark of honour; but at such a moment as this I confess it affords me peculiar satisfaction, when I have been charged with incompetency for the discharge of my judicial functions on the ground of age or infirmity. This testimony from you, who have had such full and frequent opportunities of judging how my judicial duties are performed, is as powerful a refutation of the charge as I could desire, and so strongly marks the injustice and indiscretion of the imputation that it is unnecessary for me to add more. I beg again to assure you that this unanimous testimony of the High Sheriff and Grand Jury of Westmeath expressed in such terms at this time, shall ever be regarded by me as the highest compliment, and with the most grateful recollection.

From the Dublin Evening Mail of 5th March, 1856.

ADDRESS TO THE RIGHT HON. THE LORD CHIEF JUSTICE
OF IRELAND.

We, the High Sheriff and Grand Jury of the King's County, assembled at this Lent Assizes, feel bound by a sense of public duty to address your Lordship upon the occasion of your again presiding in the criminal court of of our county.

In common with all intelligent, independent and impartial persons in the community, we have witnessed with mingled feelings of indignation and alarm the unjust and unseemly attacks that have been made upon your Lordship as well as upon others of our most eminent and venerable judges, whose long and distinguished services and unblemished reputation should have protected them from even the semblance of a slur; and we must express our regret, that on the occasion alluded to, they were not afforded that protection by those whose more essential duty it was to have done so. We look upon the independence of our judges as the greatest security for our lives, our liberties and our properties, and when we see that independence assailed, we consider ourselves bound to come forward and vindicate it to the utmost of our power. This county has had the great advantage of having its criminal court presided over by your Lordship for four successive assizes, and we desire to bear our humble testimony to the great urbanity, distinguished ability, unwearying patience, and, above all, pure love of justice, that have so eminently marked your Lordship's judicial career in this county. We venture to express a hope that this humble tribute to your Lordship's valuable services, may not at this season, be deemed out of place, and we trust that your Lordship may long be spared to come and preside as judge in our county, and that this kingdom at large may long reap and enjoy the great value of your Lordship's distinguished services as Lord Chief Justice of the Queen's Bench; and with every sentiment of the highest regard and esteem, we beg to subscribe ourselves your Lordship's very faithful servants,

W. G. D. Nesbitt, *Sheriff.*
J. Bernard, D.L. *Foreman.*
John H. Drought, D.L.
Thomas Hackett, J.P.
John Lucas, J.P.
John Andrews.
George Minchin.
Ambrose Cox, D.I.
Thomas Mulock.
John H. Burdett, J.P.
John O'Brien, J.P.

D. Thomson, J.P.
James Drought, J.P.
John D. Lawder.
Robert J. Drought.
James F. Rolleston, J.P.
Charles J. Barrow, J.P.
J. W. Tarleton, J.P.
L. Dickinson, J.P.
Dawson French, J.P.
Edward John Briscoe, J.P.

HIS LORDSHIP'S REPLY.

Mr. High Sheriff, Mr. Foreman, and Gentlemen of the Grand Jury, you have indeed accomplished the object you had in view of gratifying my feelings by presenting to me at such a time, this tribute, which I esteem as a mark of honor and respect of the highest value ; I have just had occasion in the neighbouring county to express the peculiar satisfaction it afforded me to receive a similar testimony to that now offered, but how much must the gratification be enhanced by the repetition of a like honor at your hands. Whatever injustice or indiscretion I may have to complain of, it has been more than redressed to my own feelings, and I trust in the sight of the public, by this further testimony calculated as it is so fully to establish that the charge to which you allude is as groundless as it was mischievous and indiscreet ; but, Gentlemen, I am sure you will appreciate the motives which induce me to forbear going further into this subject. There is, however, one topic in your address, to which, as it is of a public nature, and interesting to the community at large, I feel it right to advert. I mean the sentiment you have expressed of the importance of upholding the independence of the Judges, and I trust the time may never come when there will be wanting public virtue and public spirit to maintain and vindicate that truly constitutional principle, the value of which you so well and so fully appreciate. Gentlemen, I must again beg to make my most sincere acknowledgements for this over indulgent estimate of my public services; it will be a further stimulus to me, if any were wanting, to endeavour during the remainder of my judicial life, so long as it may please Providence to continue me the enjoyment of my faculties, to pursue a course which has called forth from you, Gentlemen, so flattering an expression of approval.

From the Dublin Evening Mail of 7th March, 1856.

TO THE RT. HON. THE LORD CHIEF JUSTICE OF IRELAND.

My Lord,—We, the High Sheriff and Grand Jury of the Queen's County, assembled at Lent Assizes, 1856, beg to express the great gratification we feel at seeing you again presiding as one of our Judges of Assize in this County, and at the opportunity it affords us of bearing our humble testimony to the great ability which your Lordship has always displayed in discharging the business of our Courts of Justice. We congratulate your Lordship that advancing years have in no wise impaired your mental powers, or interfered with the efficient discharge of your judicial functions ; and we sincerely hope you may long continue to hold the exalted position you at present occupy, the duties of which you have hitherto so zealously discharged.

Hon. Henry Flower, *High Sheriff.*	Robert Staples, J. P.
Charles H. Coote, Bart., D. L., *Foreman.*	C. H. Bowen, J. P.
A. Weldon, Bart., D.L.	H. D. Carden, J. P.
Robert H. Stubber, D.L.	Robert White, J.P.
William Cope Cooper, D.L.	Chidley Coote, J.P.
Allan J. Walsh, D.L.	Hon. James Butler, J.P.
Louis Moore, D.L.	Edward M. Dunne, J.P.
Matthew S. Cassan, J.P.	Henry Trench, J.P.
George Adair, D. L.	Denis Moylan.
W. W. Despard, J.P.	J. W. B. Scott, J.P.
C. Bailey, J.P.	John R. Price, J.P.
H. White, J. P.	R. Parnell Maillard, J.P.

GRAND JURY-ROOM, MARYBOROUGH, *March* 5, 1856.

Mr. High Sheriff, Sir Charles Coote, and Gentlemen of the Grand Jury,—I thank you heartily and sincerely for this address. I cannot too strongly express the gratification it affords me as I advance through my Circuit, to meet a repetition of the same sympathy, the same generous and willing testimony you and the other Grand Juries have borne as to the manner in which my judicial duties have been discharged ; but, gentlemen, let me not be misunderstood, as if this gratification were merely of a personal or selfish character. Far otherwise. I feel it as much on public as on private grounds, and I will tell you why I do so. The charge which has called forth this and the other addresses, is one which you as a Grand Jury are not only privileged but bound to deal with, and to express your opinion on it. If true in point of fact, that the Judge sent to preside over and direct your proceedings, was a man disqualified by an impaired mind and understanding for the adequate discharge of his duty, it would be yours to complain ; but, on the other hand, if no foundation exist for such a charge (which I am at liberty to assume is the case from the document in my hand) what could be more painful to the judge, or more calculated to bring into contempt the due administration of justice ? You have come forward this day, as high-minded and honorable men, not only to remove the stigma cast upon the individual, but to discharge a duty to the public, by removing the contempt which it was calculated to bring on the administration of justice by the degradation of the office in his person. You have rescued both by your testimony this day, for which I again beg to thank you, and more especially in reference to myself, for the kind wish expressed of again seeing me in your county.

From the Dublin Evening Mail of April, 1856.

"ADDRESS TO THE LORD CHIEF JUSTICE.

" We have received the following address to the Lord Chief Justice, from the Secretary of the Grand Jury of the County Meath ; and we now give it, with his Lordship's eloquent reply :—

" We, the Foreman and Grand Jury of the County of Meath, beg leave to offer to your Lordship our cordial and respectful congratulations on the practical refutation afforded during the present Assizes to the charges by which your Lordship has been assailed. The mental vigour and profound legal knowledge which have hitherto distinguished your Lordship's professional course, are at this moment displayed with undiminished efficiency. We have just now witnessed their exercise, and it is our earnest hope it may please the Supreme Disposer of human events long to spare your Lordship your present undiminished health and vigour of mind :—

Matthew E. Corbally, M. P., D.L.	Henry B. Coddington, J.P.
Foreman.	John Pollock, J.P.
Richard Chaloner, J.P.	James Naper, jun., J.P.
Hon. Hercules Rowley, J.P.	Hans H. Woods, J.P.
Sir John Dillon, Bart.	Gustavus Lambart, J.P.
W. B. Wade, D.L.	Robert Caddall, J.P.
James N. Waller, D.L.	W. Blackburne, J.P.
Samuel Winter, D.L.	Alexander Montgomery, J.P.
Henry C. Singleton, D.L.	Samuel Garnett, J.P.
Robert Fowler, D.L.	Thomas Rothwell, J.P.
John Tisdall, J.P.	Robert Fowler, jun.
Anthony S. Hussey, D.L.	

HIS LORDSHIP'S REPLY.

TO THE FOREMAN AND GRAND JURY OF THE COUNTY
OF MEATH.

Dublin, April 4th, 1856.

GENTLEMEN,—I have just received your address, which has been transmitted by your Secretary to my Registrar. You have, indeed, said in it all that my heart could desire ; and all that, coming as it does now, is sufficient to perfect whatever might be wanting to satisfy the highest and most honorable ambition of any Judge. To find your testimony in unison, as I may now say, with that of all the other Grand Juries (who have done me the like honour) as well as of my own profession, that my administration of the law has been alike satisfactory to every class and description of her Majesty's subjects most competent to form a judgment on the matter, and to be alike testified by all to have been and to continue efficient, upright, and impartial, and in every way deserving of their approbation, is, indeed, an honor and a gratification not to be surpassed. I have further to acknowledge and to thank you most cordially for your earnest and affectionate desire that it may please the great Disposer of all events long to continue to me the blessings of health I have hitherto enjoyed in mind and body. It reminds me, Gentlemen, and it is most suitable to join also my own acknowledgments to Him who has so enabled me to discharge the arduous and anxious duties of the office I fill, as to have attained for me the reward and encouragement of your generous praise, for which allow me again to offer you my most grateful thanks ; and believe me, Gentlemen, your most faithful and obliged

THOMAS LEFROY, C. J.

From the Dublin Evening Mail of 19th March, 1856.

"COUNTY GALWAY.

" We this day complete the round of public approbation elicited by Sir John Shelley's ill-advised attack upon the Irish Bench. We subjoin the Address from the County of Galway to the Lord Chief Justice, with his Lordship's Reply. It will be seen that several Roman Catholic Gentlemen of the highest respectability have joined in the common expression of sympathy with the Bench. Galway has nobly stood forward to vindicate the independence of the Judges of the land, as essential to the impartial administration of justice, as necessary to the honor of the crown, and the security of the rights and liberties of the people.

"TO THE RIGHT HON. THE LORD CHIEF JUSTICE OF THE QUEEN'S BENCH.

" We, the undersigned members of the Grand Jury of the County Galway, assembled at Spring Assizes, 1856, take the opportunity of conveying to your lordship the expression of our unaltered regard and respect. If we depart from the ordinary rule in expressing our opinions with reference to Judges not on our circuit, it is in consequence of the regret with which we have seen the report of Sir John Shelley's motion in the House of .

Commons in relation to the Irish Judicial Bench, the independence of which we consider it of the first importance to maintain. But, my Lord, the many opportunities we have enjoyed of seeing you preside in our Courts, and the grateful recollection we entertain of your Lordship's judicial conduct in tempering justice with mercy during the successive years of famine, when our county was steeped in distress, and stained with the crimes which accompanied it, have entitled us to express our admiration of your character as a Judge, with the duties of which you have happily blended the knowledge and experience of the country gentleman.

We therefore earnestly hope that Providence may long spare you to the country, of which you are so bright an ornament, and to your many friends, by whom you are so deservedly and universally beloved.

J. W. H. Lambert, *Foreman.*	Michael Browne, J.P.
Dunlo.	B. Persse, D.L.
J. Burke, Bart., M.P., D.L.	A. W. Blake, D.L.
T. A. Bellew, M.P.	Anthony O'Flaherty, M. P.
Thomas E. Blake, Bart.	M. S. Kirwan, D.L.
A. A. Nugent.	Charles Lynch, J.P.
Christopher St. George.	James Daly, J.P.
Denis H. Kelly, D.L.	James Galbraith, J.P.
John Martyn, J.P.	John Burke, *Mayor.*
Robert Bodkin, D.L.	Francis Blake, J.P.

"THE CHIEF JUSTICE'S REPLY.

Mr. Foreman, Lord Dunlo, and Gentlemen of the Grand Jury,—The address you have presented to me under such peculiar circumstances, is indeed not only highly honourable in itself, but especially gratifying to my feelings. Your departure from ordinary usage, founded on a just regard for the independence of the Judges, brings to my mind the very important and expressive terms of the Act which was passed for making the Judicial Office permanent, and by which the Legislature has marked its sense of this invaluable principle, by reciting, " that the independence of the Judges of the land is essential to the impartial administration of justice, and highly conducive to the honour of the crown, and the security of the rights and liberties of the people." But, gentlemen, that Act, wisely and nobly as it provided for the independence of the Judges, was not designed to make them irresponsible. I make no such claim for myself or the Irish Bench, and you have not lost sight of the distinction; accordingly the Legislature has by the same Act provided a remedy for securing the responsibility of the Judges by an address to the crown from both Houses of Parliament; but assuredly such a weapon was never intended to be wielded except upon a just occasion, and for an honest purpose, nor, under color of its provisions, to afford an opportunity of making charges unfounded and injurious, not only to the character of the Judge, but to the administration of justice. It is well for both, gentlemen, that your lengthened and varied experience of the judicial duties, which have fallen to my lot in your county, has enabled you—and your generous and independent feelings disposed you—to bear a testimony which must effectually disappoint every such unfair or indiscreet purpose. I heartily thank you for this address, which shall be preserved as one of the most honourable and gratifying memorials of my judicial life.

THOMAS LEFROY, C. J.

From Saunders' Newsletter of 14th March, 1856.

" ADDRESS FROM THE HOME BAR OF IRELAND TO THE
LORD CHIEF JUSTICE.

We, the members of the Bar going the Home Circuit,
having heard that observations have been made upon the
advanced age of your Lordship, as involving unfitness for
the onerous duties of your high office, beg leave to express
to your Lordship our continuing admiration and esteem.
We still view with pride in our Chief Justice the same
thorough knowledge of the principles of law, the same
clear discernment in the administration of justice, and the
same undiminished energy and dignity of character which
have always commanded the respect of the Bar, and we
pray your Lordship to accept this our testimony to your
Lordship's eminent abilities, which were never more conspicuous than during the present circuit. Signed on
behalf of the Home Bar, pursuant to their unanimous
Resolution at Naas, this 13th day of March 1856.

WALTER HUSSEY GRIFFITH,
Father of the Home Bar.

His Lordship having received the address, replied in a
clear, strong tone of voice, which was occasionally broken
by the intense and natural emotion under which he
laboured, and in a manner so impressive, dignified, and
affectionate, that it was impossible for any one who was
privileged to hear him to remain unmoved.

" Father Griffith and Gentlemen of the Home Bar,—
However painful it must be to any man filling the high
office in which I am placed to be charged with incompetency to perform its duties, I may well rejoice at the

occasion which has called forth a testimony so truly
honorable, so gratifying, as that which you have now
presented to me. I may say with great truth I never
felt—no, not even on the announcement of being placed
in that distinguished position—the same gratification that
I do at this moment. That occasion was accompanied by
a just sense of the responsibility of the office I was called
upon to undertake, as well as of the arduous duties to be
discharged. I did not, indeed, anticipate the dishearten-
ing, and, I may now say, unfounded aspersions to which
you allude; but you have by this address at the same
moment dispelled the apprehensions I then felt, and
refuted those unworthy imputations, which were not only
injurious to the character of the judge, but calculated to
bring contempt on the administration of justice in the
person of the judge. The testimony of those so competent
as the men who now stand before me, and with the
opportunities you have had to form a just estimate of the
manner in which the duties of my office have been performed, must be to my own feelings, as well as to the
public, entirely satisfactory. It is the great seal put to
the testimony already borne by the several grand juries
who have done me the honor to present addresses in the
course of this circuit; and yours is in itself a record, which
no disingenuousness, or indiscretion, can venture to
gainsay. It will ever be remembered by me with feelings
of gratitude to you, accompanied by an humble but
thankful acknowledgment of the goodness which has
continued to me the enjoyment of those faculties which
have enabled me in any manner to earn the esteem and
approbation so kindly and generously expressed in your

address. Allow me to express the hope that if any of those whom I have the pleasure of addressing shall ever be placed in a judicial position, and happen to be circumstanced as I now am, he shall have the gratification to receive as flattering and graceful a testimony from the members of his profession as that which I have this day received."

CHAPTER X.

THE efforts of the Whig party to secure for their political supporters the due reward of their services in the shape of place or pension has long been proverbial. We have already seen the means by which the Melbourne Cabinet contrived in 1841, when their continuing in office was no longer possible, to thrust Lord Plunket out of the Court of Chancery, in order to provide for an expectant Attorney-General; and again we have seen Sir John Shelley's attempt to create no less than three vacancies on the Irish Bench in 1856. One might have supposed that the rebuke then received in the general condemnation of the Hon. Baronet's conduct would have been sufficient to prevent the recurrence of a proceeding tending so seriously to lower the character and dignity of the House of Commons, and to impair the independence of the judicial office so essential to the due administration of justice. But in 1866, when a crisis likely to decide the fate of the ministry then in power seemed to be imminent, the temptation of securing for the party such offices as those held by the Chief Justice and the Lord Justice of Appeal, was too great to admit of any effort being left untried ; accordingly, with little regard to the decency of endeavouring to mask the political object, we find, at almost one and the same time, the Marquis of Clanricarde in the House of Lords assailing the Chief Justice, and Mr. Bryan, the member for Kilkenny, in the House of Commons, assailing Lord Justice Blackburne and Chief Justice Lefroy. The reader will appreciate at its just value the exhibition of virtuous indignation displayed by the actors in this scene, when they protested that they were *compelled by a stern sense of public duty* to call the attention of Parliament to the "injury caused to the administration of the law in Ireland," and "to the insult inflicted on the country" by permitting these venerable judges to continue longer on the Bench ; but public opinion, which seldom is far astray on such matters, notwithstanding their protestations, rather

regarded the noble Marquis and his colleague in the
House of Commons as apt instruments chosen to
carry out the object of those who were pulling the
wires behind the scene. At all events, whatever
be the characters they filled, the recklessness of
their allegations and the unconstitutional nature of
the whole movement was effectually exposed in
both Houses. In the House of Lords, Lord
Chelmsford, in his able vindication of the Chief
Justice, replied, that—

"*Prima facie* the noble Marquis was right in saying that a Judge who had arrived at a time of life far
beyond the ordinary period of man's existence could not
be perfectly competent to the duties he had to discharge;
but he would remind the noble Marquis that he must be a
little cautious in measuring the capacity of age. A distinguished ornament of their lordship's House had not
long ago passed away, who had adorned every debate
with the most profound wisdom, and a judicial eloquence
that had never been surpassed. That noble and learned
lord, on the night that he entered upon his ninetieth year,
addressed their lordships in a speech that riveted their
attention for more than half-an-hour, in which the most
perfect clearness, lucidity, and wisdom showed that his
powerful intellect was setting without a cloud. Suppose
that that distinguished person had held a judicial appointment, would it be a justification to call upon him to resign
on the score of his age? And yet, if he understood the
noble Marquis, the whole ground of his accusation against
the learned Chief Justice, was that he had arrived at the

age of ninety. Even if there had been any error or mistake on the part of a judge, that would not be a ground for bringing the matter before the Houses of Parliament, unless it was clear that it arose from the decay of his mental power. But there was not a practitioner in the Court of Queen's Bench who would say that a single decision of the Lord Chief Justice was not what it ought to have been, or that they showed any decay of his mental faculties. From the year 1862 to the present period there had been only four writs of error from the Court of Queen's Bench, and, during the last two years, only one bill of exceptions had been offered to the ruling of the learned Judge. The noble Marquis had asked whether it would be possible that an English Judge of that age would be able to endure the labours of Circuit? For five-and-twenty years the Chief Justice had not missed a single Circuit, or town on any Circuit, except in the year 1847, when he was suffering from low fever, and was obliged to absent himself for six weeks.* He had up to the present moment discharged duties of the most important kind. The criminal business of the Court of Queen's Bench was very considerable; besides which, the important questions connected with the Fisheries Acts all went to the Court of Queen's Bench. The Chief Justice performed his part in the discharge of those duties, and every one of his decisions met with the most perfect approbation. As to the business of the Court of Queen's Bench in Ireland, it was enough to say the amount

---

* It was after completing the Spring Circuit of 1847 that the Chief Justice (then Baron Lefroy) was taken ill ; but he did not miss a single town on any Circuit during the twenty-five years of his judicial life.

recovered in that Court in 1864 was £345,740; in 1865, £445,000; while in the Court of Common Pleas in 1864 the amount was only £148,000; and in 1865, £150,000; in the Court of Exchequer the amount recovered, in 1865, had not been made up; but in 1864 it was only £330,000.

"With regard to the trial of the prisoner King, for the murder of an officer, which took place at the last Assizes for the King's County, and which had been alluded to by the noble Marquis, he did not know upon what authority the facts were stated;* but if he wanted a case which would satisfy him of the strength and vigour of the Chief Justice's intellect, it would be that very case. Their lordships might recollect that a question of law arose in that case with respect to the indictment. By an Act of Parliament in Ireland, if a murder was committed within 500 yards of the boundary of a county, the indictment might be laid either in that or the adjacent county. In the case alluded to, the murder took place not in the

---

* The fact alleged was that the Chief Justice was incompetent even to discharge the formal duty of passing sentence correctly on the prisoner, but the following address delivered by his Lordship, *extempore*, on that occasion after a protracted and anxious trial, furnishes the best comment on the malignity of the statement.

"Lawrence King, you have been found guilty of a murder, the more aggravated by the circumstances under which it took place—circumstances which made it your duty to protect the gentleman who had put himself under your guidance, and made it a treasonable treachery for you to betray that trust. Therefore, when requested by the jury to recommend you to mercy, I refused to do so, and it now remains for me to pronounce that sentence which is not only in accordance with human law, but with that Divine law, which says that ' whoso sheddeth man's blood, by man shall his blood be shed.' " His lordship, assuming the black cap, then passed sentence of death in the usual formal terms, and concluded as follows : " And may that great God have mercy on you, who, for those

county in which the venue was laid, and an objection was taken that it ought to have been stated in the indictment that the murder took place within 500 yards of the boundary of the county. That question was argued before the Chief Justice with very great ability, and he was of opinion that there was no necessity for introducing that averment in the indictment; but the question was so important, especially as the life of a human creature was concerned, that he reserved the point. It was accordingly argued before the Judges, and they decided almost unanimously that the judgment of the Chief Justice was right. The only dissentient was Mr. Justice Hayes, but he differed on a point which did not materially affect the decision of the Chief Justice."

In the House of Commons Sir H. Cairns, in a speech commended even by his opponents for its moderation, begged the House to consider the great injury to the administration of justice which must arise from bringing subjects of this kind in such a manner under the consideration of the House—

who have violated His law, has provided an opportunity of coming before Him, confessing their guilt, humbling themselves, and trusting in that Saviour whom He has appointed to be a substitute for sinners. It is not merely the loss of this life that you have to dread, but that awful death beyond the grave of those who come before Him in judgment hereafter. Yet, even for the vilest sinners, He has provided a way of salvation, if they trust to the mercy of Him who has given His Son to be a ransom for their sins. In adding the words with which this sentence closes, ' May God have mercy on your soul,' I do so most heartily, with all the earnestness of one who is convinced of the efficacy and greatness of that mercy. I earnestly call on you, in coming to God, to look to that means of mercy which He in His love has promised to sinners.—*Extract from the King's County Chronicle.*

" What would be thought (said he) if some English
member were to put a notice of this kind upon the paper—
a notice affecting the Lord Chief Justice, the keeper of
the Great Seal, or some other of the superior judges of
law or equity, and to drag their names before the public
upon mere newspaper paragraphs, which bear upon their
face their own refutation? If there were truth and
foundation in what has been stated, it ought to be put
before the House in the form of a distinct motion, such
as the right hon. gentleman (Mr. Fortescue) has referred
to, and then, as a matter affecting the due administration
of public justice, notice would be taken of the facts by
the House. I speak with as great freedom as any one,
and free from bias or prejudice upon this question; and
as the right hon. gentleman has referred to the propriety,
in a general point of view, of not having judges upon the
bench at very advanced ages, I will state candidly what
my opinion is. I think it would be an excellent question
to be agitated and determined in Parliament, whether
there ought not to be some age beyond which, as a
general rule, judges should not occupy their position on
the bench ; (here the hon. member discussed the arguments *pro* and *con* upon this subject, and then continued); but I think the question of age in public officers
filling judicial situations should be made the subject
of general enactment and not of comment or criticism
in particular cases. We have in England, also, judges
of very advanced years, and I must say that some of them
exhibit to this day proofs of the greatest physical and
mental ability. One of these, the very eminent and distinguished man who fills the position of Judge of the

Admiralty Court, was selected last year by the late Prime Minister as the Judge of all others in this country to whom one of the most important and arduous cases that have arisen of late years should be referred, I mean the case of the Banda and Kirwee booty. At the same time, or nearly at the same time, the eminent Judge of whom I have been speaking was, by the selection of the Government, chosen to act as a member of the Capital Punishment Commission. Now, the Lord Justice of the Court of Appeal in Ireland is about the same age as the eminent Judge to whom I have referred, and it seems to me rather too much to assume that, because he has reached that age, it is impossible that he can fill his position upon the Bench properly. I cannot bear personal testimony to what passes in the Courts of the Lords Justices, but we have constantly brought before the House of Lords appeals from that Court, and, so far from there being a common form of judgment, in which Lord Justice Blackburne says he concurs with the Lord Chancellor, the fact is quite otherwise. Not more than two years ago there was a case in which Lord Justice Blackburne differed from one or two of his colleagues, and his opinion was confirmed by the House of Lords, in opposition to that of the other two Justices.

" The name of the Chief Justice of the Queen's Bench has also been mentioned. I can state from what has fallen under my own observation with regard to that eminent person that not more than three years ago a great case connected with the salmon fisheries was tried before him in Dublin. A number of exceptions were taken to his ruling. They came to be argued

in the Court of Exchequer Chamber in Ireland. Two of
the judges of the Exchequer Chamber agreed with the
Lord Chief Justice, and all the other judges differed from
him.   An appeal was brought to the House of Lords;
the English judges were summoned; they were unanimous, and the law Lords were unanimous, in favour of
the opinion given by the Chief Justice of the Queen's
Bench in Ireland.   I have also very recently read a report
of a trial for bigamy in Dublin, and the question arose
as to the effect of a man's going through the ceremony of
marriage, being a Protestant, before a Roman Catholic
priest.   The prisoner was convicted in the first instance,
but on an appeal to the Court of Exchequer Chamber, the
majority of the judges acquitted him, and I had the pleasure of reading a very elaborate and convincing judgment
from the Lord Chief Justice of the Queen's Bench agreeing
with the majority, in which he seemed to have led his
learned brethren by the cogency of his arguments.
Therefore, it is really a little too much, and it would be
fatal to the independence of the judges in any country;
I say, moreover it must be very injurious to the administration of justice, and to that respect which we all
desire the judicial office should have in the eyes of the
public, to bring forward charges of this kind, which, when
traced out, seem to rest on no proper grounds, and which
are directed against individuals who (however great the
wonder, seeing their advanced age), still appear to possess
their faculties to the fullest degree."[*]

* For the able and effective speeches of the Right Hon. James
Whiteside, Sir George Bowyer, &c., &c., see Hansard's Parl. Rep., 3rd
Ser., vol. 183.

But it was not in the Houses of Parliament alone that this barefaced attempt met with the rebuke it so justly merited. The following epitome of the debate, taken from one of the London Journals, shews the way in which the proceeding was regarded outside the walls of the House of Commons :— · .

" Sir Hugh Cairns was justly severe upon those who had brought this question before the House on the authority of an anonymous paragraph. Mr. Whiteside went into details which completely disproved the asserted falling off in the business of the Queen's Bench, showing that the amount litigated there is larger than in either the Exchequer or the Common Pleas. The learning and ability of the Chief Justice had been shown by the manner in which he had acted in several important trials; his self-reliance by the infrequency with which he had summoned his Puisne Judges to his help; his vigour of mind and body by his vivacity in company and conversation; and his legal acumen, by the fact that not one of his decisions had been reversed by the Court of Ultimate Appeal. As for the charges made against him, they melted away as soon as they became the subject of examination. The story about his inability to pronounce judgment without a written copy of the words turned out to have arisen through his reading from a copy handed to him by the Clerk of the Court in the same way as is done when the youngest Judge upon the Bench passes sentence at the Old Bailey; and the verbal error in giving judgment consisted simply in his having substituted the word 'interred' for 'buried' in the prescribed formula. In

short, the first and patent fact, that the Chief Justice is
ninety-two years of age, excepted, his assailants failed to
show a single plausible pretext for seeking to enforce his
retirement, or to offer anything like an excuse for their
persistent and indecent attacks upon one whom an ex-
Chancellor has declared to be the ablest Judge in
Ireland.

" We trust that we have now heard the last of these
endeavours to compel the learned and eminent persons
whose names were mentioned, to vacate their seats, and
abandon the positions they have so long adorned.
Whether it be desirable to fix a limit of age beyond
which a Judge shall not continue to hold office is a
debateable question into which we need not now enter—
that there will be many inconveniences resulting from it
is, we think, undeniable. As Mr. Whiteside forcibly observed, ' it might as well be said that in age Titian had
lost his genius, Radetski could not win a battle, and
Lord Lyndhurst had become a fool.' Sir George Bowyer
cited additional and equally pertinent illustrations of the
same point, when he referred to the judgments of the
octogenarian Lord Mansfield ; the nonegenarian Dr.
Lushington; to the advanced age Lord Tenterden had
attained when he died in the Central Criminal Court ; to
the ripeness of Lord St. Leonards at the present moment;
and to the vigour of intellect possessed by the American
Chancellor, Kent, who, when in enforced retirement, wrote
those admirable Commentaries which have entitled him
to the honourable appellation of the Transatlantic Black-
stone. We presume that no one would go so far as to
advocate a general adoption of this principle of super-

annuating everybody to whom nature had been bountiful, and whom time has treated tenderly; and we should be indisposed to apply a Procrustean standard of age to our judicial offices, while carefully abstaining from adopting it in any other department of the State. The real reason for these assaults upon certain dignitaries of the Irish Bench is that which was broadly charged, and very faintly denied in the course of Friday night's debate. The Chief Justice's resignation is called for, because a certain officer of Government is anxious to succeed him. But we trust he will have to wait some time longer yet. The old man is not the sick man, and the day of his official demise has not been accelerated by the debates of the last week. Rather has it been abundantly shown that the charges against him are unfounded; the imputations upon him undeserved; the stories of his incompetency myths; the tales of his mistakes exaggerations. We do not envy Mr. Bryan the distinction he has achieved by bringing the subject before the House; but we have no reason to complain of the statements of fact and the expressions of opinion which his ill-advised persistence has been the instrument of eliciting."—*Morning Herald of 14th May,* 1866.

Some of the jeux d'esprit to which the occasion gave rise afforded the Chief Justice himself so much amusement that he more than once said on reading or hearing of them—" It was worth being assailed to bring out these witty articles." The following were amongst those he often adverted to with pleasure: —

From the Belfast Newsletter, of 23rd *April,* 1866.

" Whenever the political weather-glass indicates an approaching storm, we may look out with the utmost confidence for an attack on Chief Justice Lefroy. The Chief Justice is one of the most obdurate men of whom there is any record extant. In the first place, he was born in the year 1776, and is consequently ninety years of age. This in itself is an offence against the decencies of society which no respectable Whig could be expected to endure. Fancy a man who was running about a lively six-year-old when the Volunteers assembled at Dungannon presuming to exist in these modern times, when steam and electricity have become the servants of man! Why, he is thirteen years older than the American Republic. He remembers the old French Monarchy; and in his youth he must have shuddered to hear of the enormities of the Reign of of Terror. And yet he is hardened enough to live on, as though he did not belong to a by-gone age and generation. Then, again, he was called to the Bar in 1797. Why, he must have jostled members of the old Irish Houses of Parliament in College Green about the time when the Union debates shook the framework of society. But the worst of it is the Chief Justice has the audacity to retain his faculties, and to give the utmost satisfaction to the suitors and the members of the legal profession. He has never yet obliged the attentive Whigs by exhibiting a single indication of dotage; and it is more than probable that he lives on for the mere purpose of keeping anxious officials on the tenter-hooks of expectation. It is

really too bad. Depravity so shocking in one so old is
dreadful to contemplate. Why does he not exhibit the
Christian virtue of resignation? If it were only to show
that he is not wholly without charity, he ought to make
way for some rising young supporter of the Government.
And then let any candid person consider that the Ministry
may possibly be put out before the world is a week older.
It is true they expect a majority, and we presume they
will obtain it. But it may happen to be a very narrow
majority, or it may be a negative quantity. . . . . .
Under these circumstances, it was only natural that the
Whigs should, with their accustomed decency, strike at
'the old man eloquent' who still adorns the Bench and
does honor to the profession. Old age, ever venerable
when associated with virtue, ought to be peculiarly
honored when the store-house of its ripe experience
exhibits no signs of decay, when the mind remains unclouded, and the lips have not forgotten to utter words
of wisdom. But Whig rapacity knows no blush."

From the Standard, of 21st April, 1866.

" On Thursday night the Marquis of Clanricarde rose
pursuant to notice, to submit a motion in form directed
against the constitution of the Irish law courts, but in
substance intended to compel the resignation of an
eminent and distinguished ornament of the Irish bench.
The noble lord came forward, not for the first time, in
the character of a Reformer. He had no personal feeling
but he had a public grievance. Could he have consulted
his own wishes, he would have remained silent and

uncomplaining, but a stern sense of public duty constrained him to speak. Therefore, with the firmness of an ancient speaker, he rose to point out the defects in the working of the machinery of the Irish legal system. It is somewhat disappointing to find that a motion prefaced with so much pretence of public spirit, becomes narrowed in the course of a long and elaborate speech, into a complaint against a single individual. The defects in a system mean the retention of office by one particular dignitary, and the zeal for the public service, professed by a partizan of the present Government, subsides into a querulous complaining of the infirmities of Chief Justice Lefroy. Of the learning and ability of the highest common law judge in the sister country Lord Clanricarde makes no complaint. Against his judgment, his acumen, his skill, his patience, he has not a word to say. His attainments he is quite ready to acknowledge—his feelings he would be more than sorry to wound or to disregard. He esteems him, he respects him, nay, he loves him. But, to parody a popular song, he loves his love with a but. He does not say that the Chief Justice is corrupt, for no one would dream of coupling him with some former occupants of the English Woolsack. Nor does he say that he is incompetent, for every one confesses his remarkable ability. . . . But Chief Justice Lefroy has one defect, which every one can find out who looks into a biographical dictionary. He is not so young as he once was, and therefore he ought to make way for somebody else. Not long ago he presided at a protracted and important trial. For more than twenty years he had gone circuit without missing a town, except on one occasion, in 1847, when he was laid up for some weeks with low fever.* But for all that he is old; as old as was Lord Lyndhurst when he astonished and awed the assembled Peers with his speech on the national defences.

. . . . The marquis has no particular complaint against Chief Justice Lefroy; but for all that he wishes him gone. He no more knows the cause of his dislike than did the nameless accuser of Dr. Fell. But that he does wish him out of his place, ' he knows full well,' and so, by way of a gentle stimulant, he brings forward the question in Parliament, and asks the House of Lords to censure the Chief Justice in a vote which shall compel his resignation. We need not follow Lord Chelmsford through his able and-eloquent vindication of Chief Justice Lefroy from the aspersions which the reflections of the Marquis of Clanricarde had cast upon him. In brief, the statements of the ex-Chancellor consisted of a categorical refutation of every charge that had been brought against the Irish Chief Justice by the former Lord Privy Seal."

From the Pall Mall Gazette.

RETENTION OF MENTAL VIGOUR-IN OLD AGE.

" The marquis of Clanricarde originated on Thursday last in the House of Lords an interesting discussion relative to the alleged incompetency of the present Lord Chief Justice of the Court of Queen's Bench of Ireland to discharge, in consequence of his advanced age and bodily infirmities, the important judicial duties assigned to him. This debate raised the interesting questions, At what particular period of life do the mental powers begin to

---

* The mistake in this instance is rectified in the note, *ante*, p. 313.

decline, and when, as a general rule, is first observed the commencement of intellectual decay ? The celebrated physiologist of the University of Montpelier, Dr. Lordat, maintains that it is the vital, not the intellectual, principle that is seen to wane as old age throws its autumnal tinge over the green foliage of life. ' It is not true,' he says, ' that the intellect becomes weaker after the vital force has passed its culminating point. The understanding acquires more strength during the first half of that period which is designated as old age. It is therefore impossible to assign any period of existence at which the reasoning powers suffer deterioration.' Lord Eldon died at eighty-six. He remained in full enjoyment of his wonderful intellect until shortly before his death. Lord Stowell lived to the age of ninety. His mind was vigorous to the last. Lord Mansfield died at the advanced age of eighty-nine in full and unclouded vigour of intellect. A few days before this illustrious judge passed into eternity he heard his niece asking a gentleman who was present as to the meaning of the word ' psephismata,' which occurred in Burke's celebrated work on the French Revolution. The answer was that it was a misprint for ' sophismata.' ' No,' exclaimed Lord Mansfield, ' psephismata is right.' He then, without the slightest difficulty, quoted from memory a passage from Demosthenes in illustration of the fact. Sir Edward Coke died at eighty-two. The last few days of his life were spent in revising his numerous works preparatory to their publication. Sir Isaac Newton published the third edition of his ' Principia,' with a new preface, at the age of eighty-three. Cherubini continued

brilliant in conversation at the age of eighty. Waller
composed when he was past eighty a beautiful poem
entitled, 'A Presage of the Ruin of the Turkish
Empire.' Titian continued to exercise his marvellous
genius as an artist up to the age of ninety-six, when
suddenly he died of the plague at Venice. At the age of
eighty-three, Cumberland, the Bishop of Peterborough,
studied and mastered critically Dr. Wilkin's ' Coptic
Testament.' Numerous other illustrations could be
cited to establish that the mental powers do not necessarily decay as old age advances. We must, therefore,
to repeat the language of Lord Chelmsford, ' be a
little cautious in measuring the mental capacity of old
age.' "

The thin veil by which it was sought to disguise
the impatient thirst for office that prompted this
attack was easily seen through. It is needless to
say that Mr. Bryan never accepted the challenge
thrown out in the debate by Sir Hugh Cairns and
Mr. Whiteside, that "if he could prove his asser-
tions he should adopt the constitutional course of
bringing forward a motion to address the Crown
for the removal of the judges alleged to be no
longer competent for the due discharge of their
duties ;" and happily the attack (which was in
reality a blow aimed at the independence of all
our judges), could not have been levelled at two
individuals less likely to succumb to any indirect
attempt at intimidation, such as that of the noble

Marquis or Mr. Bryan, so that the effort to procure
the coveted vacancies for the Whig party proved
wholly abortive.

Not many weeks elapsed, however, before some
important vacancies of another kind took place;
the great popularity of Lord Palmerston and the
weight of his well-merited influence had given the
Whigs a majority of 75 at the general election
which took place in the autumn of 1865, but the
loss which the country at large, as well as the
Whig party, sustained by Lord Palmerston's death
in October, 1865, soon began to produce its effects
in loosening the political ties which had so long
kept the Liberal party united under his leadership,
and in less then eight months, Earl Russell's
government was broken up by the defeat of
ministers on Lord Dunkellin's amendment as to
the franchise proposed by their Reform Bill, the
ministerial majority of 75 being converted into a
minority of 11 upon that division.

On the 6th July, 1866, the Earl of Derby was
called on by Her Majesty, for the third time, to
take up the reins of government, and on his
Lordship's accession to office, Chief Justice
Lefroy wrote to express his willingness to resign the trust which Lord Derby had committed·
into his hands, whenever it might be found convenient to make arrangements for the appointment

of his successor. The following extract from Lord Derby's reply to this communication, affords honorable testimony of his appreciation of the late Chief Justice's public services:—

Downing Street,
July 11, 1866.

" MY DEAR CHIEF JUSTICE,—Your son sent me, a few days ago, a most kind letter from you, the handwriting of which I should have taken to be that of a man of thirty instead of ninety, in which you express your readiness to surrender into my hands the high office which I had the satisfaction of intrusting to you fourteen years ago, and which you have filled with so much credit to yourself and advantage to the public service. I find it difficult to express the gratification I feel at the cordial and friendly terms in which the offer of your resignation is couched."

His Lordship then expressed his wish that the Chief Justice should, if not inconvenient, arrange to go the summer circuit, which he accordingly did. On hearing from Lord Derby subsequently, that the arrangements as to his successor were completed, he sent in his formal resignation, and on the 24th July, the Right Hon. James Whiteside took his seat as Chief Justice at Tullamore. In his opening address to the Grand Jury of the King's county, we find the following graceful allusion to his predecessor :—

" MR. FOREMAN AND GENTLEMEN OF THE GRAND JURY,—
It has became my duty to inform you that I have been
summoned to complete the labour of this circuit, already
commenced by my venerable predecessor, but I am
happy to be able to say, that his retirement has not been
occasioned by any ill health. I feel some difficulty in
following in the steps of so distinguished a judge. He
begun his professional career when there were many
great men at the Irish Bar, and he soon became conspicuous for the precision of his judgment, the depth of his
arguments, and the solidity of his understanding. He
preserved for us the decisions of one of the most accomplished jurists that ever held the great seal. His temper
on the Bench was serene, his judgment most profound,
and the weight of his character carried with it an
authority which he never was called upon to enforce.
He has left not merely the name of a great judge, but
the example of one whose virtues endeared him to all
who knew him."

Shortly after Chief Justice Lefroy's resignation,
Lord Derby expressed a wish to be allowed to lay
his name before Her Majesty for a Baronetcy, but
he declined that honour.*

The very gratifying and honourable farewell
addresses on his retirement from the Bench, which

---

* On Mr. D'Israeli's succeeding Lord Derby as Premier, the offer of a
Baronetcy was renewed, accompanied by an offer of a seat at the Irish
Privy Council for his eldest son, but both honors were declined.

were presented by the Grand Juries of the Counties of Meath and Westmeath, where he presided for the last time at the summer assizes of 1866, will be found in the Appendix. The ministerial arrangements for the appointment of his successor having been completed before the opening of the summer assizes of the King's County, the Grand Jury of that county were deprived of the opportunity of paying this compliment to the Chief Justice in person, but the following address was forwarded to his residence at Bray. The dignified and caustic reply which it evoked furnishes so good a commentary on the proceedings which took place in Parliament a few months previous, that I think it should not be omitted here.

FAREWELL ADDRESS FROM THE HIGH SHERIFF AND GRAND JURY OF THE KING'S COUNTY.

TO THE RIGHT HON. THOMAS LEFROY.

Grand Jury Room, Tullamore,

26 July, 1866.

" My LORD,—We the High Sheriff and Grand Jury of the King's County, assembled at the summer assizes, 1866, take this opportunity of expressing our sincere regret that we shall no more have the honor of meeting your Lordship in your public capacity, and also our deep sense of the

able and impartial manner in which you have performed
your duties during so long and honorable a career. We
trust that you have many years of calm and quiet happiness
before you, and in conclusion we beg to thank your
Lordship for the kind courtesy you have ever evinced
toward us, and for the ready support which we have
always met with at your hands.

"JOHN LLOYD, *High Sheriff*,
ALFRED BURY, *Foreman*."

REPLY.

Newcourt, Bray,
July 28, 1866.

"Mr. Foreman and Gentlemen of the Grand Jury of
the King's County,—Allow me to express my cordial
thanks for the gratifying address I have just received.
Such testimony as yours to the efficient discharge of my
judicial duties during the long period for which I have presided at the assizes of your county must ever be a source
of honourable pride and pleasure to me. And if under
ordinary circumstances your address would be calculated
to afford me pleasure, I owe it to you to say how much
its value is enhanced by recent events, affording, as it
does, the best refutation of the unworthy and unjust
attack to which I have been lately exposed. Most of you
were eye and ear-witnesses at the trial which was made
the groundwork of that attack. Above all, gentlemen,
you are disinterested witnesses, and this it is which makes
your testimony peculiarly grateful to my feelings. Such
an address from witnesses of your intelligence, rank, and
independence may well compensate for any personal

annoyance I have heretofore suffered from that attack.
But it is on public rather than on personal grounds that
attacks of this kind are to be deplored.   Our law has provided ample security against incompetence or neglect of
duty on the part of those who occupy the judicial seat,
and no one who values the independence of our Judges
can see with indifference those who should be the pro-
tectors of that independence becoming its assailants.   No
one can see without regret the remedy which was intended
to provide against incompetence set aside, and another
course adopted for party purposes, which only tends to
bring the administration of the law into contempt, whilst
it indirectly seeks to effect a different object.   Such a
course might have induced a weaker man to fly from
the post of duty, though in my case it only served to
strengthen my determination never to yield to menace
what a sense of duty had not led me to concede.   But I
forbear to dwell further on this topic, and I should gladly
have avoided it altogether were it not that, on this last
occasion of addressing you judicially, I feel it due to the
Bench and to the law itself, to leave on record my protest
against a course of proceeding as mischievous as it is
unconstitutional.

"I remain, gentlemen,

"Yours most faithfully,

"THOMAS LEFROY."

In the Term succeeding his resignation, the
following farewell addresses were presented to the
Ex-Chief Justice:—

From the Daily Express of 22nd Dec., 1866.

ADDRESS TO THE RIGHT HON. THOMAS LEFROY, PRE-
SENTED ON HIS RETIREMENT FROM THE OFFICE OF
LORD CHIEF JUSTICE OF IRELAND.

" SIR,—We, the undersigned, Members of the Bar of
Ireland, desire to address you on the occasion of your
retirement from the Judicial Bench.

" We express with pleasure our appreciation of the
industry and energy, the logical power, the profound
learning, the great talents and high integrity by which
your long professional career has been illustrated; and
we acknowledge that your distinguished success was the
just reward of these admirable qualities.

" Your Reports of the Judgments of Lord Redesdale
in the Court of Chancery—the first service rendered by
you to the administration of the law,—have found a
becoming sequel in many valuable judgments pronounced by yourself in the Courts of Queen's Bench
and Exchequer, to which the highest authority will be
permanently attached.

" We are persuaded that the Bar of Ireland will long
cherish with pride and gratitude the memory of the
dignity and courtesy which marked your conduct as
Chief Justice.

" We would congratulate you on the many pleasant
memories which will follow you into your retirement—
the recollection of youthful honours won at the
University; of early struggles and exciting triumphs in
your profession; of many genial and distinguished
friends; and lastly, of the admiration and deep respect

achieved by your talents, and the firmness and impartiality with which you administered the law.

" In that retirement we trust that, by the blessing of Divine Providence, you may enjoy a serene old age, adorned by the exercise of private virtue, enriched with the abundance of domestic happiness, and supported by a bright hope of immortality.

" And now, Sir, we cordially bid you farewell.

　　" ROBERT D. MACREDY, *Father of the Irish Bar*.
　　MICHAEL MORRIS, M.P., *Attorney-General*.
　　HEDGES EYRE CHATTERTON, *Solicitor-General*.
　　SIR COLEMAN O'LOGHLEN, Bart., M.P., (*Second
　　　　Serjeant*)."

Here followed the signatures of 247 members of the Bar of Ireland, including sixty Queen's Counsel.

REPLY.

" MR. ATTORNEY-GENERAL,—

" Allow me to express my cordial thanks to you and all those whom you represent for the truly gratifying Address which you have just read, recording, as it does, the sentiments of so many of the most eminent members of the Irish Bar, distinguished for learning, talent, and moral worth. I am well aware that your kindness has led you to overlook many deficiencies, and greatly to overrate my services in discharge of the duties of the important office which I have so long filled; but I can conscientiously say you could not overrate my anxious desire that the law should be so administered in

the Court over which I have had the honour to preside
as to secure the confidence and respect of all those
interested in it; and if I have at all succeeded in this, as
your kind Address would lead me to hope, I gladly take
the present occasion of acknowledging my gratitude to
Him from whom all power flows for the fulfilment of
any duty, and to whom alone we can look for a successful result from any effort of ours. I shall ever retain a
grateful remembrance of the valuable assistance and co-
operation I have received in the administration of justice,
not only from my brethren on the Bench, but from the
members of the Bar, as well from the integrity and up-
rightness, as the ability and intelligence with which they
have at all times discharged the duties that belonged to
them.

"Many of you, no doubt, have already learned for
yourselves that the law of England presents one of the
noblest and most useful human studies to an intellectual
mind; but to those of you who have but just entered on
your professional career, let me say that, after the
experience of a long life, I look back, not only to the
University honours and the professional triumphs to
which you have so gracefully referred, but to the years
of diligent and patient study which I devoted to the
acquirement of a thorough knowledge of the principles
of our law, as one of the most pleasing recollections of
my early life. I now bid you farewell, and, in doing so,
allow me to reciprocate the kindest—the best of your
wishes for me, by expressing my earnest desire for each
and all of you, that, as advancing years roll on, your
earthly path may be lightened by that bright hope of

immortality which can alone give true happiness, or secure to any man a peace of mind that will stand the test of adversity as well as prosperity.

" I remain,

" Yours very faithfully and obliged,

" THOMAS LEFROY."

From the Daily Express of 21st Nov., 1866.

" A deputation from the Council of the Incorporated Law Society of Ireland, consisting of the following gentlemen:—Richard J. T. Orpen, President; Arthur Barlow and Edward Reeves, Vice-Presidents; Robert J. T. Macrory, John H. Nunn, John Fox Goodman, William Read, Henry Thomas Dix, Thomas Crozier, and John H. Goddard, Secretary, waited yesterday upon the Right Honorable Thomas Lefroy, late Lord Chief Justice of Ireland, for the purpose of presenting him with an address, of which the following is a copy:—

"TO THE RIGHT HON. THOMAS LEFROY, LATE LORD CHIEF JUSTICE OF IRELAND.

" SIR,—On behalf of the Attorneys and Solicitors of Ireland, we desire to offer you the expression of our deep respect and esteem upon the occasion of your retirement from the high office which you have long filled with such ability and dignity. It is with much pleasure that we bear our testimony to the profound learning, deep sagacity, and unwavering patience which has ever marked your judicial character; and although we feel that your lengthened public service forms ample reason

for retirement from the onerous duties of the Bench, we
are sensible that, by that event it has lost one of its
brightest ornaments, in whose hands justice was administered, not only with power and impartiality, but also
with that dignity which should ever accompany such
administration, and which secures for it reverence and
honour. We desire particularly to refer to the support
you have uniformly afforded us in endeavouring to
uphold the character and social status of our profession,
for which we tender our grateful acknowledgment.
Trusting that the remaining years of a life so honourably
and profitably spent may be passed in happiness and
peace. We remain, Sir, on behalf of the Council, your
faithful Servants,

" RICHARD J. T. ORPEN, *President.*

" JOHN H. GODDARD, *Secretary.*

" SOLICITORS' HALL, FOUR COURTS, DUBLIN.
" *20th November,* 1866."

REPLY.

" Leeson-street,
" *November* 20, 1866.

" GENTLEMEN,—I find it difficult adequately to express
the gratification I feel in receiving the address you have
presented to me on behalf of the Attorneys and Solicitors
of Ireland. Such testimony, not only of approbation,
but, as you have kindly said, of respect and esteem,
founded upon the discharge of those public duties of
which, for more than a quarter of a century, the
members of your body have necessarily been constant

and watchful observers, may well be regarded as a source
of honourable pride and pleasure; and I beg to assure
you I shall always so. esteem it. Your address refers to
a subject which has long engaged my anxious attention,
and though now withdrawn from the sphere of duty in
which I could effectively assist the praiseworthy efforts
of the Law Society to uphold the character and social
status of that important branch of the legal profession to
which you belong, yet I shall not cease to feel a deep
interest in the subject. My long experience in the
administration of justice has strengthened my early convictions as to the evil of the practice which now prevails
of allowing men to take upon them the duties of your
profession who have neither the education nor the intelligence necessary for the purpose—a practice which is
opposed to the well and wisely established rule in
England, and which deprives the suitors of the security
they ought to have in being represented by those who
have been admitted as members of your profession, and
who, as officers of the Court, are subject to its control.
It seems to me that the interests not only of your profession, but of society at large, require the abolition of
such a practice; and if a remedy cannot otherwise be
provided for the evil, I trust the aid of the Legislature
may be obtained for the purpose.   I remain, Gentlemen,
yours very faithfully and obliged,

                              " THOMAS LEFROY."

CHAPTER XI.

Traits of His Inner Life—His love for the study of Scripture—Extracts from his Portfolio.

THE feature of his character in private life, which was most generally observed by those who enjoyed an intimate acquaintance with him, was his love for the study of Scripture, and the tendency of his mind to lead conversation to the discussion or consideration of Scriptural subjects : and, perhaps, in no way was the closeness of his walk with God so fully manifest, as in the happiness with which he looked forward to the Sunday, and the refreshment he always felt in the religious observances of the Lord's Day. No one who spent that day in his society could fail to observe that he regarded the sacred obligations of its religious duties, not as a tedious burden, but as a high and happy privilege. His earnest devotion in public worship told plainly that he was engaged in no mere form or ceremony, but was enjoying communion with his

God ; and, with the exception of an hour or little more after church, during which he was in the habit of walking into the country with his children, the greater portion of the time which intervened between morning service and his dinner hour was spent in the retirement of his own study. But it was not on the Sabbath alone that he thus enjoyed holding communion with his God in private. He never travelled without having his Bible at hand, in his writing case, and, generally, some of Archbishop Leighton's works, or some book on Prophecy or on the Revelation, which formed the pastime of his journey. The following letter to his wife, giving an account of his journey from London, when returning from Parliament, in the bygone days of coach-travelling, well exemplifies this trait in his character:—

Leeson-street,
Thursday.

We had, thank God, a delightful journey, and the weather in the Channel very fine until we approached Ireland, when it became wet and windy; but we made an excellent passage of six hours and a half. Robert Daly* joined us at Birmingham; and from Shrewsbury he, Jeffry, and I had the coach wholly to ourselves, and so instructive and delightful a day I don't know when I passed. It is remarkable that I laid out the two days

---

* The present Bishop of Cashel.

of this journey for going very minutely into the Prophecies which Lord Mandeville and I had been reading
together, and I made it the subject of earnest prayer that
I might be guided aright, and profit by my search.   The
first day I read through the whole journey, but was more
than ever puzzled.   However, I was so prepared by my
reading to ask questions and receive instruction, that dear
Robert Daly relieved me out of my chief perplexities, and
opened views of the subject so much more clear and
satisfactory than any I had met with, that I consider
myself to have had quite a gracious answer to my prayers.
On landing, Daly came home with us for breakfast, and
read for us in our family worship.   He is indeed a true
servant of God.

T. L.

He never kept any diary, but he left behind him
a large portfolio full of short notes on passages of
Scripture and points of doctrine, jotted down from
time to time as opportunity offered, and in these we
have a clue to the topics which engaged his thoughts
in his hours of retirement.   From their dates
they appear to have been commenced as early as
1816 and were carried on to 1860.   I have
selected some of these papers from the mass, as
they are not without intrinsic value, and afford
interesting evidences of his own practical experience as a Christian.

THE CHRISTIAN'S WALK SHOULD BE WORTHY OF THE CHRISTIAN'S CALLING.

Christians don't recollect as they should the duty they owe to their calling. They are "*the salt of the earth.*" They are the now only visible display of the power of Christ's religion to sanctify the heart unto obedience; and when they are wanting in the circumspection as to their life and conduct, which in this view they are called upon to exercise, they become the means of their Master's religion being blasphemed, and its power doubted or denied. What a solemn and awful subject for reflection, and what a stimulus should it supply to more constant and earnest prayer for the indwelling of the Holy Spirit, which can alone enable us to " walk worthy of the vocation wherewith we are called "—Ephes. iv. 1.

SINCERITY IN RELIGION.

It is very well to lay stress on sincerity in religion, but not in the way in which men often use this phrase— namely, sincerity in the purpose of serving God *according to our own notions.* This is not the sincerity God requires. The idol worshipper might as well plead his sincerity as an acceptable service to God, if he be in earnest in what he is about. The sincerity God requires is sincerity in serving and obeying Him *in the way He Himself has pointed out*—seeking for this with all our heart, and not resting on our own imagination of what is doing God service. If therefore a man wishes to serve God acceptably, he must understand what is the Religion by which God chooses to be served and worshipped,—we

Z 2

know that if the word is to bring forth fruit it must not only be heard but understood (see Matt. xiii. 23), and the reason that men are without understanding in the things pertaining to godliness is that they will not submit to be taught of God—they won't lend their minds to receive the things which God has told them,—nay, they take offence at them, and can't bear patiently to listen to them, much less to take them to heart. They won't understand that it is by the foolishness of the cross that we are made wise unto salvation—their hearts are darkened because they won't become as little children and come to Christ to be taught, and to beg of Him to take them up in His arms and bless them and open their eyes to see the things which we cannot see without Him—to lead them in the way in which we cannot walk without Him, and to teach them the things pertaining to godliness which we cannot know without Him. God has declared that He will have all men come to Him by Christ, it is therefore presumptuous arrogance to rely upon " our sincerity," so long as we are trying to substitute any other way of coming to Him for the specific mode required by Him ; yet how often we find men talking of "a moral life," and relying on that delusive hope of " sincerity in religion," as the means of acceptance with God, forgetting that " without faith it is impossible to please God."—Heb. xi. 6. We must be able to say with St. Paul—the life which I now live in the flesh, I live by the faith of the Son of-God.

THE WAY APPOINTED BY GOD IS THE ONLY WAY OF SALVATION.

The moment I learn from the Most High how He chooses to be served, or to be glorified, there is an end to every suggestion of my own imagination as to any *other* *mode* of serving or glorifying Him. The answer to any other suggestion is, "it may be very good," your course *may* do well, but I am sure of this one, because it is the mode appointed by Him who is to be served and glorified. When, therefore, God has appointed that He Himself is to be served and glorified, *by* serving and glorifying Christ as the appointed *medium* (the Mediator) by and through whom to serve and glorify God, we have nothing to do but to accept entirely and heartily this method of serving and glorifying Him; let us leave to others their general speculations, but let it be our business to walk in the *appointed* path, and not to endeavour to find out a new or a better way. Christ is made unto us wisdom, sanctification, righteousness, and redemption—a *new* and *living* way for coming unto God. Let others take their own ways, and go on to find out other wisdom, other righteousness, and other sanctification; let us look only to *Jesus*, the author and finisher of our faith, the *appointed* Lamb, the *appointed* Redeemer, the *appointed* Sanctifier, *i. e.*, the medium by and through whom the Holy Spirit is granted—who has it in abundance to give; and let it be our study and prayer to find out His way and will, to follow His steps, and to keep His commandments, and to be, in all things, like unto Him. The daily watchword of the Christian should be, " Looking unto Jesus."

THE NECESSITY OF A CHILDLIKE HUMILITY IN READ-ING THE SCRIPTURES—OBEDIENCE THE FRUIT OF FAITH.

The importance of bringing a perfectly childlike mind to the Scriptures, is not half enough insisted upon ; just such as makes a child receive what it is taught on the credit of its teacher without seeing at the time the reason for it ; "what I do, thou knowest not now, but thou shalt know hereafter."—John xiii. 7. In the Scriptures we read that "In Adam all died ;" why, it may be asked, should Adam be permitted to fall, or his sin be imputed to his posterity, or the consequences of it visited on them? To this the childlike mind says, "*I don't know*, this is amongst the deep things of God, which are hid from me, but I'll tell you what I do know, and what is revealed to me—that the same Being who permitted or ordered the fall of Adam, has sent and raised up Christ to the end that all who believe in Him should not perish, but have everlasting life, and has told us by the mouth of His accredited messenger that ' as in Adam all die, so in Christ shall all be made alive.' " The same childlike mind will be satisfied with this, without knowing why man should be forgiven in this way, why should Christ die for the sins of the whole world. He will leave the disputers of this world, who by their wisdom know not God, to spend their time and talents in groping into what St. Paul declared to be a depth of *unsearchable* riches of mercy and goodness, whilst he embraces, enjoys, and is thankful for the gift, and lives upon it in hope and trust, because he " believes Him faithful who hath promised." This is the anchor of his soul in the day of trouble. And this simple faith, this childlike confidence in God's word, not only gives peace to the soul in the hour of trouble and trial, but brings forth the precious fruit of obedience, for obedience is the fruit of Faith as disobedience was the fruit of unbelief. God said to Adam, " In the day that thou eatest thereof thou shalt surely die." " It is not so," said the tempter, and Eve and Adam *disbelieved* the word of God, and disobeyed. So God says to us now, " through this man (*i. e.*, Christ) is preached unto you the forgiveness of sins, and by Him all that believe are justified from all things from which ye could not be justified by the law of Moses." But the devil tempts us to doubt this gracious promise, and so robs us of the peace of mind that God has provided for all them that believe in Christ, and this *un*belief in the promise makes us unwilling to come to God through Christ, the only way in which our coming can be acceptable (Acts iv. 12).

THE LAW AND THE GOSPEL.

The difference between the Law and the Gospel is, that by one is *knowledge*, by the other is *power;* the *Law* teaches what is sin, but goes no further ; the *Gospel* is a dispensation of power to deliver us from sin, though this will only be perfected when we are delivered altogether from the flesh. Of this perfectness, however, we receive even here an earnest, in a growing hatred of sin, and an increasing thirst after holiness and obedience. True it is that the Law is holy, just, and good, but the weakness of our flesh made it a dispensation under which we never could be delivered from sin and misery, for we never

could perfectly obey the Law, and the very nature of a
Law is that to obtain its rewards it must be wholly obeyed,
for it would be idle to give a Law, and not to *expect*
obedience to every part of it, as a Law.

REAL AND NOMINAL RELIGION.

How unmeaning and unintelligible must many portions
of Scripture appear to those who deny that the province
and power of true religion is to work a real change in a
man—a change which the *true believer* is made partaker
of, but which others neither know nor understand—a
change from the love of sin, to the love of God, and
the hatred of sin, as the greatest of all evils. If
religion comprehend nothing more than an outward
profession, what means these words of the apostle Paul,
" Who have *tasted* of the *heavenly gift*, and were made
partakers of the *Holy Ghost*, and have *tasted* the *good
word of God*, and the *powers* of the world to come."—
Heb. vi. 4, 5. Oh, let those nominal Christians who are
satisfied with a *profession* of the name of Christ, search
their hearts and lives and motives, and say whether they
can say they have *tasted* any of these things—whether
they have been made *partakers of the Holy Ghost*—
whether they have *tasted the powers of the world to come*
in any degree, and what is the evidence that they have
done so. Are they mourning more deeply for sin than
before this mighty change took place ? Are they more
sensible of its hideousness ? Are they more smitten and
overwhelmed by the amazing love and tender mercy of
Him who has revealed Himself to us as a God of infinite
holiness, and yet the Saviour of sinners and rebels ? Are

they longing to be delivered from the remaining corruptions and defilements of the flesh ? Do they love to sit at the feet of Jesus and hear His words—do they esteem this "the good part ?" Do they feel the want of a Saviour, and do they find in Jesus all that want supplied? If not, they have not yet learned the elements of that *true religion* which is to deliver us from the bondage of sin into the glorious liberty of the children of God. They are yet reading the Scriptures in the letter, not in the spirit, as if it were a book of *words*, not of *things*— as if it spoke of visions, not of realities.

"SIN SHALL NOT HAVE DOMINION OVER YOU."
Rom. vi. 14.

In contending about the interpretation of Scripture, those who have not experienced the power and reality of the Christian religion, because they have not sought salvation *by Christ*—who have not *by Him* sought to be cleansed and redeemed from the power of sin—too often wish to bring down the declarations of Scripture to the level of their own experience, and because they don't find in themselves or in the *natural* man, proof by experience of the fulfilment of this blessed Gospel promise, they won't allow of its being taken to import what it really does import. But it should be recollected that the promises of the Gospel are made to those who are *believers in Christ Jesus*. They alone have a right to expect the fulfilment of them. To them alone it is said "sin shall not have dominion over you." They alone, indeed, are seeking to be rid of sin—for, to be a Christian, a man must desire to be rid of sin, and desiring to be so, he

comes to God to be cured and healed in God's *appointed*
way—*i. e.*, by coming to Christ.　Who else has ever been
appointed to cleanse or forgive sins ?　Nor has the
natural man any right to complain, for he may, if he
desires to be freed from the dominion of sin, become
entitled to the same privilege by faith in Christ, (1 Cor.
i. 30).

THE PRIVILEGES OF THE CHRISTIAN.

We can never estimate the privileges of the Christian
too highly, nor should we fear in stating them to go as
far as Scripture warrants, for the greatest encouragement
which a man can have to seek after anything which is within his reach is to be persuaded of its superior value and
excellence.　But there are two things which must be
remembered in speaking of the Christian's privileges,
1st, to mark well that to be a Christian is not a *name* but
a *reality*, and that therefore, whoever professes that name,
and has none of the signs of that real change of which
the true Christian is partaker, cannot expect to be partaker of the privileges which belong to the Christian ;
and further, that he who appears to have some signs, and
rests satisfied without seeking for more may well doubt
the genuineness of these signs.　Witness the example of
Paul, who, " forgetting those things which were behind,
and reaching forth unto those which were before,
pressed toward the mark for the prize of the high
calling of God in Christ Jesus," (Phil. iii. 13–14).　The
true Christian will never be satisfied with any measure of
grace he may have already obtained, but will be eagerly
seeking for more grace.　2ndly, In speaking of the Chris-

tian's privileges, we should be careful to show men that great and wonderful as are these privileges, they are promised and secured to all Christ's disciples, and that God has invited every man to come to Him, to hear His Word, that faith cometh of hearing the Word, that by faith man will be made partaker of these privileges, and that if once we are *Christ's own*, He who by His love made us His own will love us to the end, (John xiii. 1). The importance of hearing and reading the *Word of God* should be more dwelt on, as the great outward means appointed of God for ministering salvation to His people; Christ gave Himself for His Church, that He might sanctify and cleanse them with the washing of water *by the Word* (John xv. 3). Coming to the waters is hearing the Word, and hearing the Word shall not be in vain (Isaiah lv. 10–11; and Rom. x. 17). It is of great use to show men that whilst we insist on the whole work being of God, that He has appointed means and channels, in the use of which He has promised that we shall find Him, and find His work done *in* us and *for* us, if we faint not, but persevere in the use of these means.

ON THE EARLY INSTRUCTION OF CHILDREN IN THE SCRIPTURES.

If we sufficiently kept in mind that the word of God is the instrument by which the Spirit does His work, we should see more clearly the immense importance of an intimate acquaintance with the Bible, and therefore the value of teaching it, even in the letter to children so that when they come to have a spiritual understanding of it, their memory may readily supply parallel or illustrative

passages, and thus give confirmation to what would
appear to be the mind of the Spirit in any particular
passage : " In the mouth of two or three witnesses shall
every word be established," (2 Cor. xiii. 1). It is impossible to overrate the value of the mind being thus made
a store-house to furnish a ready supply for confirming and
illustrating truths already learned; or the great reward
which the attentive reader of the Word obtains in this
way for his diligence. Some men object to the utility of
reading the Scriptures until, as they say, a Spiritual taste
and understanding is acquired. It is true that the Bible
is then read with very increased profit, and then for the
first time with true delight—then for the first time the soul
says with David: " How sweet are Thy words—sweeter
to me than honey and the honey-comb."—Ps. xix. 10.
But it should be remembered, that it is by reading the
Word that we are to be taught of God the things which
pertain unto Life Eternal,—it should be remembered
what David says in another Psalm: " Thy words have *I
hid in mine heart that I might not sin* against Thee."—
Ps. cxix. 11. See what Milner says as to the profit which
Jerome and Augustine derived in their later years when
they really began to live from their constant reading of
the Scriptures in early life, under pious Parents, which
lay like seed in the ground covered over with frost and
snow during the winter, but when the spring came it
shot up and brought forth, first the blade, then the ear
and at length the full corn in the ear. We should never
forget the promise, " that faith cometh by hearing "—
and that hearing is of the " Word." There is nothing
to keep us from error but the WHOLE Bible—read care-

fully, patiently, prayerfully, believingly—looking to, and waiting for the teaching of God by His Holy Spirit. Let us attain unto familiarity with the word itself, and we may depend upon it, that by perseverance in hearing and reading the word with prayer, we shall soon be delivered out of all puzzles as to *essentials*, and if there be anything further needful for us, God will reveal that also. I write this not as theory but the result of my own experience.

THE GLORIOUS LIBERTY OF THE CHILDREN OF GOD.

Not the liberty of sin, as they think who don't know the power of the Gospel believed and received into the heart ; but the liberty which making us *unwilling* to sin delivers us from the bondage and dominion of sin. Oh what it is to be brought to know even *so much* of this liberty as to assure us of its reality and to make us sigh and pray for more of it! Oh what a thing to be changed from Satan's bond slave to be God's freedman! To have the carnal heart, which is enmity against God, made WILLING and obedient. What but the power of God could do this ? But *marvel not*, says our gracious Lord. He who hath *said* it *can* and *will* do it for them whom his grace enables to believe it.

"THE LAW IS GOOD IF A MAN USE IT LAWFULLY."
1 TIM. i. 8.

What is the lawful use of the law? *Negatively, not* to be saved by it—for no flesh can so keep it as to be saved by it (Rom. iii. 20). Christ is the appointed Saviour of sinners, and by the law we are all sinners. *Affirmatively,* it is a schoolmaster to bring us to Christ (Gal. iii. 24) by shewing us our sins—our need of a Saviour in whom we may look for forgiveness of sin, and thus bringing us to Him for the salvation which He alone can give.

ON THE EFFICACY OF PRAYER.

There is no inconsistency or uncertainty in God suspending or reversing His decrees in answer to the prayers of His people. It is of the essence or nature of the Divine prerogative that His decrees should be thus dependant or contingent. Even in the human dispensation justice gives way to mercy, under circumstances, and this on a general principle, not subjecting justice to the reproach of uncertainty or variableness. To deny to prayer its efficacy is putting a thing called "fate" in the place of the "will of God," as that which is to govern the world.

FIFTEENTH CHAPTER OF ST. LUKE'S GOSPEL.

What a gracious invitation and encouragement have we here to the sinner to turn and live—and what a perfect exhibition of the nature of true repentance in its fruits, a real and heartfelt sense of sin, not merely as an offence against the second table of the Law, but primarily as "against Heaven;" making the sinner to humble himself before God, and to confess his sins to Him—laying aside all equivocations—all disguise—all apologies—all hypocrisies—just as David did. See Psalms xxxii. 5; li. 3, 4.

The world thinks only of sins of uncleanliness and of the flesh as requiring repentance, they never think of the great call of all men to repentance, as well those who pride themselves on their moral and virtuous lives as the open profligate : " Repent and *believe the Gospel.*" Turning not merely from the filthiness of the flesh, but of the spirit; from unbelief and rebellion against God's mercy in Christ, to faith and acceptance in Him.

The world also thinks that the repentance spoken of is man's own work, whereas it is as much God's work by His Holy Spirit as faith itself. The humbling of himself and the confession of his sins by the truly penitent sinner, is only the fruit of the inward spiritual change wrought by God's Holy Spirit, but the sinner is encouraged, both by example and promise, to pray for this gift— "Create in me a clean heart, O God, and renew a right spirit within me," says David, and our blessed Lord says, " If ye, being evil, know how to give good gifts unto your children, how much more shall God give his Holy Spirit to them that ask them."

"IF WE WOULD JUDGE OURSELVES, WE SHOULD NOT BE JUDGED."—1 Cor. xi. 31.

How partial we are in judging ourselves. What say we to this—is there any one suffering, any one trial not noticed or complained of? yet how many mercies are forgotten, how many overlooked or disregarded in the very daily receiving of them! Alas! if it were judgment and not mercy, the Law and not the Gospel we had to depend upon!

FAITH.

Faith is not the belief of a dogma or of a doctrine merely. Its object is a *person*—the Lord Jesus. It is trust in Him as our Saviour who died for our sins, and rose again for our justification, as One in whom the believer is dead unto sin—*i. e.*, as having in Him suffered the penalty of the death due to sin—and is, therefore, free from its condemnation, and is in Him made alive unto God—*i. e.*, as one living and desirous to live unto God.

"Faith, the substance of things hoped for, the evidence of things not seen," Heb. xi. 1.

This is not a definition of Faith, but a statement of its effect or operation; for by faith a substance, a reality, is, as it were, given to things hoped for, on the authority of God's Word, Rom. i. 18, &c.   It makes evident—*i. e.*, as it were " seen " things not seen.   " By faith he (Moses) forsook Egypt, not fearing the wrath of the king, for he endured as *seeing* Him who is invisible."   Faith is, as it were, the eye of the soul, the faculty whereby it apprehends Divine things.

FULL AND FREE SALVATION.

We are not saved by our works nor by our faith, but by the redemption given in Christ Jesus, our Lord, *to those to whom God gives grace to receive it*, and that none need despair, He has given us in Christ *all the fulness of grace*, that out of that fulness we may receive.   By grace ye are saved *through* faith, and that not of yourselves, it is the gift of God.   *All of Him*, from first to last.   This offends man, because it ascribes all to God.   But this is the salvation of the Bible, and there is none other, and if any one doubts whether there is salvation for him, he has the assurance that God willeth not the death of a sinner, but rather that he should turn and live—*i. e.*, turn from himself to God in Christ, with the further assurance that God so loved the world, that he gave His only begotten Son, that all who believe in Him may not perish, but may have everlasting life. This is full and free salvation.

ON "SANCTIFICATION" AND "JUSTIFICATION."

While men dispute and write what they call learned treatises on the doctrines of Sanctification and Justification, we may effectually as well as simply learn what is "Sanctification" and what is "Justification," by coming to the knowledge of Christ, who of God is made unto us Wisdom, and Righteousness, and Sanctification, and Redemption. This knowledge we attain unto by faith in the revelation which is made of Him in the Bible.

WRITTEN AFTER A DANGEROUS ILLNESS.

Just beginning to have distinct signs of recovery from a severe illness, in which, at least to myself, I constantly stood on the verge of eternity, but never once ceased to have as calm and steadfast a conviction of my safety in Christ as I ever had of the most deliberate judgment at which I arrived in my Court, resting on the Word, and therefore secure from the delusion of imagination. Death had not the slightest terror for me, though I was passing through a fiery trial of bodily suffering, depression and lassitude, but there was a danger which I did fear greatly —*i. e.*, lest I should fail in willing submission to remain here in suffering so long as there might be a need for it; against this danger I needed and found grace to seek for help, and then I remembered that to experience the truth

A A

of the promise, "I will be with you, through the fire and through the water," I must myself pass through the fire of trial, and I was supplied with strength, and I came not only to acquiesce, but in the end to rejoice and be thankful for all I went through! Indeed, I felt as if I had learned more of the truth of the Bible within these few weeks than I had done during the previous part of my life, from the reality of the Word being so established in my own experience of the things promised, and I learned to praise God for having given me the precious Word laid up in the store-house, for new beauties now and again shone out in clear light to my mind, and passage after passage touched some chord of my heart that used to make it overflow with joy and gladness.

ON THE REVELATION OF CHRIST IN THE PSALMS.

The coincidence between the revelation of the true God, as made in the Psalms, and the revelation made of Him in the New Testament, is very striking as a reciprocal confirmation of the Divine inspiration of both. The great value of finding Christ in the Psalms is, that we there see a detail of the sufferings He endured *for us*, by the contradiction of sinners and the enmity of Satan, though *personally* innocent. The very character of the Saviour was emphatically that of "a man of sorrows, and acquainted with grief," Isaiah liii. 3; yet these sufferings are not given in any great detail in the history of His sojourn on earth, and in truth there are some sufferings described in the Psalms which are greater than any recorded in Christ's life, which, as it seems to me, cannot be applicable to any one else than Christ. What individual having

innocency as described in the Psalms, could complain of
sufferings such as there at times described, except Christ?
Surely not David, and if not David, who else is suggested?
Again, if these sufferings were only David's, would God
have caused them to be recorded for His servants, as
examples of suffering for righteousness' sake ?   Or could
God's servants find in them any such example or motive
to enduring suffering on that ground, if only David's,
compared with the influence and effect of them as Christ's
the Righteous One?   There are also things in the Psalms
utterly inapplicable to David or any other being but our
Lord, whereas there is nothing inapplicable to Him in
His humanity; personally innocent, holy, harmless, and
undefiled, but yet taking on Him the burden of the sins
of men, enduring the fruits of sin, of which death was
one, but the contradiction and hatred of sinners as agents
and instruments of Satan, was another, and a very important one; it was thus the Captain of our Salvation
was made perfect by sufferings, *i. e.*, perfect as a Captain
of our Salvation.   But whether we take the Psalms as
giving us the experience of David or of any other believer,
or as a type of our Lord Himself, they furnish the
strongest practical examples of faith and patience re-
warded by the fulfilment of all the promises of God
to those who wait upon Him, putting their trust in
His word.

   These are but suggestions for a train of thoughts which
I should wish to pursue, enlarge upon, and consider
maturely how far they are sound, *i. e.*, scripturally sound,
for there is no other soundness in matters of religion.

THE CHILDREN OF THIS WORLD ARE IN THEIR GENE-RATION WISER THAN THE CHILDREN OF LIGHT."

That is, they *show* more wisdom, not that they have any *true* wisdom, but the children of this world pursue their own temporal interests consistently and persever-ingly, and they know not any higher interest; while the children of light, who know of a higher interest—as much higher as an eternal life is superior to this present perishing life—don't exercise the wisdom of pursuing it with the same earnestness and devotion which the others employ. What a proof is here of man's fall, as to his reason and judgment, as well as his affectious—a proof also of the two natures in the children of light, as shown by Paul in Rom. vii.: "with my mind I serve the law of God, but with my flesh the law of sin." Even the spiritual man too often finds it difficult to prefer his eternal to his temporal interest, and when he ceases to watch and pray, and refresh his soul with God's word, how soon the flesh gains upon him! but those who would seek to win souls to Christ, should never forget that it is vain to talk to the children of this world of despising riches or worldly honour and glory except by bringing them to seek for that which shall give them a taste of the true riches, of true honour, and true glory—viz., the indwelling of the Holy Spirit. It is one thing to stir up Christians to use the gift of the Holy Spirit which they have received, and another to deal with those who have not that gift, as to whom therefore it is calling on the blind to see things which they have not an eye to see. The object with these should be to bring them to Him,

by whom alone the blind can receive the gift of sight, for
when men have once tasted of the good wine, and
"have their senses exercised to discern good and evil,"
they will not relish the counterfeit.

ON SPIRITUAL REGENERATION.

As to the importance of insisting on the necessity of
the Holy Spirit's work to give effect to the preaching of
the Gospel, we have two remarkable proofs in the pre-
cedents set before us in the Bible—1st, When Nicodemus,
the Pharisee, went to our Lord to learn the truth, the
first thing our Lord taught him was the need of spiritual
regeneration. The foundation He laid was this—"Except
a man be born again, he cannot see the Kingdom of God,"
before He taught him the doctrine of the atonement by
His own death, and then having struck at the very root of
the Pharisaic error as to man's salvation being by his own
work, and having shown Nicodemus that the sinner's salvation was God's work, He then shows him what that work
was—viz., the gift of His own dear Son to die for sinners,
that through faith in Him the sinner might be saved.

2ndly, The Apostles were forbidden to go out and
preach the Gospel until "they were endued with power
from on high"—i. e., endued with the gift of the Holy
Ghost, and accordingly they represented themselves
"preaching the Gospel with the Holy Ghost sent down
from heaven" (see 1 Pet. i. 12). This may primarily
refer to the miraculous gifts by which the Apostles were
enabled to give testimony to the truth and authenticity
of what they taught, but it clearly also refers to the effi-

cacy given to the preaching of the Gospel by that accompaniment of the Holy Spirit which brought it home to the heart and understanding of the hearer.

REPENTANCE AND FAITH ARE THE GIFTS OF GOD.

To guard against an abuse of the Doctrine of Salvation by Grace, we should never forget that Repentance itself is the gift of God, that Faith itself is the gift of God, and that no man can presume to say that he will repent when he chooses. If there were any foundation for such a notion as this, the Doctrine of Salvation by Grace might indeed lead to licentiousness by holding out encouragement to continue in sin in the prospect of future pardon. It is, therefore, of great importance not to lose sight of this great cardinal Truth, that Repentance and Faith are the gift of God—that, in short, coming to Christ is the gift of God, or as He Himself said, " no man cometh to me except the Father draw him." Let, then, the sinner who would resolve to continue one moment in sin on the speculation that he would hereafter repent and obtain pardon, take heed how he can expect at a future day of a holy God the gift of repentance and faith, without which he cannot come to Christ. It was a just observance of this that made Shakspeare describe Macbeth's misery as consisting in this—that he could not repent, that he could not pray. The fact is, that every Christian's experience teaches him the truth of what the Bible says, " that *every* good and perfect gift cometh down from above from the Father of lights." The experienced Christian knows that these words are not (as superficial readers of Scripture

suppose) merely figurative. He knows that without the
gracious aid of God's Holy Spirit he could not pray, or
believe, or repent, or have love or charity, or any other
good thing. But we must remember that God teaches
these things to the Believer gradually. The growing
Christian is able as he increases in stature from the fulness
of Christ by degrees to look over the wall that at first hid
from his view the deep things of God, and he who before
read his Bible without really giving credit to many parts
of it, or supposed they were to be taken figuratively, now
sees that they contain actual truths and realities as much
as the plainer parts which he received at once. Thus, for
example, he perceives it is no less true " that no man
cometh to Christ unless the Father draw him," than " that
whoso cometh to Christ He will in no wise cast out."

" DESIRE THE SINCERE MILK OF THE WORD THAT YE MAY GROW THEREBY."—1 PETER ii. 2.

Mark the object the Apostle sets before us in his
exhortation to desire the sincere milk of the word, i. e.,
not for knowledge, but for spiritual growth, that thereby
we may advance in spiritual growth. Until we feel and
know by experience that Happiness is in proportion to
Holiness, or in other words, in proportion to our conformity to Christ, we shall never rightly 'hunger and thirst
after righteousness.' But when the soul feels sin to be a
disease, a misery, and feels conformity to the mind of
Christ—the imbibing of His love—the tasting of His
Spirit, to be true happiness, then the soul begins to gasp
like a parched and thirsty land for the dew of God's grace

to give it of this delight, and to rescue it from its disease and from the burden of sin. They know nothing of the secret of the Lord—of the really divine life—who talk of crucifying the affections and lusts in order to come to Christ, and be partakers of his happiness. These must indeed be crucified that we may be partakers of His happiness, but it is He that must do it. No, no. Begin with winning Christ—Christ first, Christ second, Christ third, Christ to the end. Win Him—dwell in Him—get Him to dwell in the soul, and you'll see presently what will become of the affections and lusts that used to war against the soul. You'll see the temple cleansed, the oxen driven out, and the tables of the money-changers overthrown, and these old marauders flying in all directions. A few more subtle than the rest will lurk behind, but they too shall be driven out in the end by the power of the Lord of the Temple. Come unto me, says Christ, all ye that are weary and heavy laden, and I will give you rest. This is the Gospel! " By grace ye are saved through faith, and that not of yourselves."

PERSONAL HOLINESS THE BEST WAY TO PROMOTE GOD'S GLORY.—CAUSES OF DISAPPOINTMENT IN THE CHRISTIAN'S LABOUR OF LOVE.

Believers are sadly deficient in recollecting the important truth that the first way to promote the glory of God is by seeking to be enabled to possess and exhibit in themselves a proof of what *His Grace* can do in writing His law on their own hearts. This is *shewing forth His own work*. But no man who has thus sought first the kingdom of heaven, when he has *tasted* of the salvation of God for his own soul, can possibly exist without desiring that others should be partakers of it.

In the warmth of this desire, however, he is very apt to forget who it is that alone can bring light into darkness, and to set forward upon a notion that it is only to preach the Gospel to men and they will receive it. He soon finds how vain is that expectation, and he is checked. Still this ought only to be a check to the Christian's self-sufficiency, not to his honest zeal. He ought still to plant and still to water, looking to God only for the increase, by the blessing of the Spirit on his labour, just as the farmer sows his crops, looking to the future rain and sunshine for their growth and prosperity.

THE DOCTRINE OF ELECTION FULL OF COMFORT TO GOD'S PEOPLE.

When the Christian begins to see the vileness of his state by nature, and becomes sensible of his weakness, the apprehension of being drawn back into the bondage of sin would keep him in continued torment, if he had not a new promise then to dawn upon him. 'Tis then he begins to taste and understand the comfort and wisdom of the doctrines of election, predestination, and final perseverance, which, as the article of our Church well says, are full of comfort to the *godly soul*, and which are not to be given up because they may be perverted by ungodly and profane persons who dispute about them without *knowing* anything of them. These are the pearls which ought not to be thrown to swine. The true Christian does so desire

his God to rule over him, and it is so essential to his peace
that God should continue to do so, that if he were not
assured that it was part of the plan of infinite wisdom and
goodness to do so, and had he not a *promise* that it was
so, he could have no happiness, for he has lost all dependence on himself, and he finds, as St. Paul did, that there
is no good thing in himself.

THE STANDARD OF CHRISTIAN MORALS.

The standard of Christian morals and Christian temper
cannot be let down. It must of necessity be high, very
high—for how could a God of perfect holiness assign any
other standard? The Christian is called to keep his eye
fixed on Christ as his model, and his heart knit to Christ
as his strength. But there is a great difference between
the standard of Christian morals and actual Christian
attainment; the first is, and ever must be, the same; the
latter will vary, because there are diversities of gifts, and
these gifts are received and employed in divers measures.
The Believer, however, is not harassed by the fear of
condemnation because he has not attained to the height
of the standard, though taught and bound ever to aim at
it, for " there is no condemnation for them who are in
Christ Jesus," Rom. viii. 1. Not that they are in the least
at liberty to violate the moral law, nay, they are peculiarly
bound and their delight is to observe it in spirit and in
truth; but when a sinner comes to be in Christ, it is not
the fear of condemnation by which he is actuated; it
would be needless to apply to him this motive. The true
Believer's delight and exceeding great reward would be

to attain to the standard set before him, because he knows that the highest pitch of obedience, the highest relish of God's law, and the highest love of God, is and must be his highest happiness. The offerings he desires to be able to make are free-will offerings with an holy worship. He is no longer barely endeavouring to do enough, and thinking how little is the least that will sufficiently please God. His whole heart is deliberately given to God, and his grief is that he cannot attain to perfect holiness. But his very weakness is his strength. He will at times be tried by temptation, to strengthen his faith, to exercise his patience, and to make him watchful; nay, he will be permitted to fall, in order to exercise his humility, and to abase his latent pride and self-dependence, but he will not be cast down, because his trust is fixed immoveably in his God and Saviour, of whom cometh this trust, and to whom it returns again after having accomplished that whereunto it was sent, even the strengthening and refreshing of His servant.

The standard, however, of Christian morals is set before the Christian as a test whereby to try himself; in order to prevent delusion that he may keep his eye upon it as a standard of attainment to be aimed at, and a standard of perfection to show what is the holiness which his God loves. It serves to abate all false notions, as though he had already attained anything, and all pride of heart when he comes to try himself by this standard. Oh the wisdom and the fitness of what the Christian finds in the Bible!—Its adaptation to all his wants and all his requirements; how well it has been said to be written for our learning, to be "profitable for doctrine, for reproof, for correction, for instruction in righteousness," (2 Tim. iii. 16.) The Christian's duty is to apply it *to his own case*, thereby ascertaining his own deficiencies, praying earnestly to be advanced in his attainments and watching thereunto with all carefulness, for it is sad unfaithfulness to pray and not to watch; to watch over ourselves more particularly in those matters in which we feel especial need of prayer, so that we may the more constantly apply ourselves in prayer to God.

PRAYER ON GENESIS xix. 16, 17.

As for me and my house, O Lord, leave us not to ourselves. May we serve Thee, our God, and Thee only. Arise and take us out from the iniquity of this world, that we be not consumed therein. Whilst we are lingering, lay hold upon our hands and hearts, and lead us forth, that we may escape to Thy holy mountain. Let us not look back, nor desire to return into the land from whence Thou hast brought us out. O visit us with Thy salvation, that we may see and know the felicity of Thy chosen, and rejoice in the gladness of Thy people, and give thanks with Thine inheritance. Amen, Amen.

CHAPTER XII.

Habits in the Domestic Circle—Family Gatherings at Easter and
Christmas, and on the Anniversary of His Birthday—Incidents of
His Last Days.

THE consistent witness of his daily walk to the
reality of his Christian profession, hardly needs to
be enlarged upon. Such frequent instances of it
must crowd the memories of all who knew him.
It may truly be said of him that he considered
family prayer to be " the border which keeps the
web of daily life from unravelling." When
holding the first rank at the Chancery Bar, and
overwhelmed with professional business, the duties
of each day were opened and closed by assembling
his whole household for family worship, consisting
of a portion of Scripture which he read and
accompanied with a few practical observations,
concluding with prayer ; and later in life when
occupying a villa some miles distant from Dublin,
he had daily to attend the Courts as Chief
Justice, his morning hours were so regulated as
to secure ample time for family worship before

the departure of the train which carried him to
his arduous and responsible duties. His habitual
dependence on God's providence and love may be
traced in his invariable practice of calling us all
together for united prayer or thanksgiving on
each occasion of separation or re-union. I do not
recollect his ever leaving home to attend Parliament, or for his judicial duties on Circuit, without
assembling the members of his family to ask for
God's assistance and blessing upon the discharge
of his own duties, and committing to his care and
guidance those from whom he was parting.

To the inner circle of his family, and those who
enjoyed the privilege of frequent intercourse with
him, I feel that any memorial of him would be
wanting which omitted to notice his unalterable
cheerfulness under the little every-day crosses of
life. Though the shadow of a cloud might flit past,
it seemed as if it could never long obscure the sunshine of his temper or his countenance. If a wet
day interfered with some cherished plan for a
holiday excursion (and he retained to the very last
an almost childlike enjoyment of such occasions) we
were sure soon to hear some such remark as " well,
only think of the good this gracious rain will do in
the country," or " Really when I come to think of it,
'tis a decided advantage to me to have the day at
home, as I shall have a fine opportunity of mastering

a difficult case I have to look into." There is a tradition amongst us that the only time "Grandpapa" was ever known to be put out by the weather, was on one occasion during his vacation when he had spent some hours the day before in manufacturing a paper kite for two little grandsons which was to be flown on the lawn to-morrow ; but to-morrow was a storm of driving rain, and as the party was to break up the following day, the failure of the cherished scheme seemed an equal trial both to old and young. This habit of always looking at the bright side of everything, arose undoubtedly from his constant realization of the over-ruling Providence of God even in the lesser affairs of every-day life, as in greater things we have already seen the same spirit of cheerful submission ever present.

The intense enjoyment which in earlier life he felt in the companionship of his children, seemed to be revived again in the pleasure that he had in the society of his grandchildren ; and this feeling was quite mutual, for even when he was Chief Justice, and past eighty, his cheerful habits and loving heart so entirely won their affections, that the greatest indulgence which could be offered to them at any time was the promise of " a visit to dear Grandpapa." Nor will the cordial welcome be easily forgotten, with which he used to greet the happy group on our Christmas visits to Carrig-glas, when in the old days of posting, my wife and I used to arrive with our carriage-full of children, each little one eagerly pressing forward as we drove up the avenue, to catch the first look at dear Grandpapa's bright and joyous countenance, and ready before the carriage door was well opened, to jump into his arms.

In 1845, while we were in England for some months, our four children were left with him, and the following letter bears testimony that he did not feel the charge a very irksome one :—

Carrig-glas,
August 25, 1845.

.   .   .   .   . The dear children are enjoying themselves exceedingly.   I had a delightful walk with the four, after Church yesterday.   Dear little "Cuckoo" walking by my hand the whole way.   It is certainly very pleasant when I awake in the morning to hear the little prattle going on in the two next rooms to me. But think of my delight this morning when I was beginning to read with Augustine on my lap, and that I announced the chapter and verse at which we were to begin, he put his little finger on an earlier verse in the chapter, and said quietly "That's the one!"   When I said "Why so !" he answered " because it was there you stopped yesterday !" And he was perfectly right. I don't think you need pity me much when I have such companions."

T. L.

'The same spirit of affection breathes through the following letters, though written at a much later period of his life, and one of them in his ninety-second year :—

Leeson Street,
Feb. 28, 1864.

MY DEAREST T——,—You should have heard sooner and oftener if I thought I could add anything to the consolations you have within and without under your present circumstances.* But though I cannot offer anything of my own, I can direct you to what has afforded to myself the most grateful measure of spiritual edification drawn from the Bible itself. I refer to a book our dear friend Lord Roden, lately gave me,—"The Way of Peace,"—no misnomer as you will find. But go at once to the 3rd chapter on " Sanctification by the Truth," which will make the mourner's eyes overflow with spiritual joy, as he goes on from the inception of the simple but heavenly process to its consummation in glory,—when the blessed saint shall exclaim with rapture, " Oh! death where is thy sting! Oh! grave where is thy victory." I have seldom felt the truths of the Bible brought home with such simplicity and power as in this work, which is indeed well entitled the " Way of Peace." It is by the Bishop of Carlisle (Waldegrave.) The sermons were preached before the University of Oxford, previous to their publication. I know of nothing that could be more acceptable to you under your present circumstances, and

* Written during the last illness of one of my dear children who was taken to her heavenly rest on the 18th March, 1864.

B B

I am confident I need not assure you of the fulness of our participation and sympathy with you all, and our heartfelt prayers for your comfort and support.

T. L.

Leeson Street,
Jan. 9th, 1866.

MY DEAREST JEFFRY,—I have just received the congratulations of yourself, and your dear companions on God's wonderful mercy in permitting me to see the ninetieth anniversary of my birth-day. It fills my heart with joy and thankfulness of no ordinary degree, when I find those I love ascribing praise for all our family mercies, to Him to whom all praise is due. I think I cannot do better in return than pray that the blessing which old Jacob gave to his loved son Joseph, may rest on my dear Jeffry, and his no less dear wife, who may well claim to be "a fruitful bough, and even a a fruitful bough by a well." "May the God of thy fathers keep thee, may He bless thee with the blessings of heaven above, and bless thy progeny to the utmost bounds of the Everlasting Hills." With fondest love from all the dear ones around me to you and yours,

T. L.

Newcourt, Bray,
September 4th, 1866.

MY DEAREST JEFFRY,—How I wish I could see you and Helena with your dear children at Carrig-glas, where

we purpose going (D.V.) next week. I think you might
afford yourselves and us this great enjoyment. A
day would do it by the Cavan train, if I mistake not.
Our gracious Heavenly Father has given me a marvellous
share of health this autumn, amounting to an exemption
from anything deserving the name of suffering by day
or night, and this with the full use of all my faculties
and senses. Come and help us to acknowledge with
thankful hearts His wondrous mercy, grace, and love.
I long to speak to you and dear Helena of your two
boys who have just left us, and the cause for good hope
you have as to their future. May our gracious God
continue and increase His blessings to you, is the heartfelt prayer in which all with me unite.

T. L.

The following letter was written to his grandson
Lieut. in the 45th Regiment, who was at that time
quartered in India :—

Newcourt, Bray,

April 1st, 1867.

MY DEAR AUGUSTINE,—I was greatly interested by
your letter with the account of the present state of the
country where you are now quartered, corresponding, as
it does, with the descriptions in our Bible, by such
infallible signs and landmarks as even if they stood alone,
would verify the truth and accuracy of the latter. I

allude, amongst other things, to the deep wells from which you say they get water for their cattle, reminding us of the interesting conversation between our Saviour and the woman of Samaria; also to your account of the women grinding the corn, and the sowing of the seed by the roadside, all agreeing with our Bible, and verifying every jot and tittle of what is there written as to these things, so as to establish a truth for which I strongly contend; that the Bible is its own best witness and truest interpreter, when we are duly informed as to the nature of the things of which it treats. Your diary of the voyage was not less interesting, and made me thankful to our gracious God, that you and every soul dear to me to the third generation (which is as far as they have gone) have been blessed with the knowledge of His word, and I trust have received it in spirit and truth. I am rejoiced to hear of the prospect of your being in the position of Aide-de-camp, as in this way you will have the benefit of family society, and more opportunity for that which should be regarded as the first and chiefest of duties by us all, than you might have in the ordinary routine of your profession. We have good accounts from your dear sisters in France, and we have to bless God for restoring to us your dear Aunt A—— who was in imminent danger for some time. We were delighted to hear of your brother A——'s nomination to an Office in London, which I trust he will secure by his industry and application for the examination. With united love from all around me,

T. L.

The habit of keeping the Easter and Christmas festivals, as seasons of family re-union, was invariably observed in our Home circle, and wherever the scattered members might be, as Easter or Christmas drew near, no pleasure had sufficient attraction for any of them, and no inconvenience was a sufficient hindrance, to prevent the family-gatherings that used to render these seasons the opportunities for a happy interchange of thought and affection, which seemed equally valued by all. But there was yet another family gathering which year after year brought round, and which will probably remain even more deeply impressed on the memories of all who shared in those feasts of love :—I mean the anniversary of his birthday, when a wide circle of relatives used to assemble on the happy 8th of January, to congratulate him on the completion of another year added to his honored life. One of these anniversaries,—that of the year 1858, is now especially before my mind ; we sat down a happy gathering of thirty-six in number. There were relatives assembled, not only from England, Scotland, and Ireland, but also from Australia and Canada, many of whom had not met for years ; but it was the last on which we met as an unbroken family circle, for in less than a month afterwards the hand of death had taken from amongst us, her whom he that day in his

after-dinner speech so touchingly described as " the
centre round which his every joy was circled,"—
her who was so long endeared to us all by the
tenderness of the tenderest of mother's love. To
this hour, even though the cloud of sorrow for the
missing links of the earthly circle, has cast its
shadow over these happy scenes, their retrospect
seems like a sweet dream awakening old and
precious memories, imparting new life to by-gone
joys, and reminding one of the just and beautiful
description which a modern poet has given of

THE BIRTHDAYS OF A CHRISTIAN HOME.

As festivals of love
Which shed their glow on life below,
And fit for life above.
Soft as the dews of Heaven they fall
Upon the human heart,
Old memories waken and recall
New life to every part.

Nay, still more reminding us of the Christian's
happy privilege to look forward to the day when
we shall once again meet those saved ones who
are "not lost, but gone before,"—a meeting from
which there will be no parting.

His quick sympathy with the varying circumstances of those around him must recur to all who
knew him. One can never forget the face of anxious
enquiry with which in cases of illness or suffering
he would ask how the night had been passed, or

the beaming smile and fervently whispered " Thank
God" with which he would respond to 'tidings of
relief or recovery. When deprived of his usual
carriage exercise by wet weather, and confined to
the house, he used constantly to come from his
study into the drawing-room when it became
dusk, to take what he called "his constitutional," walking up and down leaning on his
daughter's arm ; and to all who shared in them,
those half-hours are specially rich in memories of
him. He seemed to lay aside all cares of business,
and cheerfully conversed with any of us who were
present, either upon some subject which had been
read to him from the newspapers in the morning,
or upon the book he was reading at the time, constantly drawing from his well-stored memory, some
classical allusion *á propos* to the occasion, and never
returning to his own room without a few gracious
words of salutation. And here I am reminded of the
letter of an old and dear friend, received since he
was taken from us, in which she gives an incident
descriptive of this gracious courtesy of manner.
She writes:—

"During the autumn of 1868 I had enjoyed more than
usual opportunities of intercourse with your venerated
father, from which I derived increasing pleasure and profit,
and it was with real regret that (previous to my departure
from Ireland for the winter) I entered his study with the

solemn apprehension that I should probably no more behold his face in the flesh." "Dear Chief," I said, "I am just come to say farewell, as I am now going to live in London:" with equal kindness and courtesy he readily replied in his own ardent and impressive way, "My dear, dear friend, that is the only sentence I ever remember falling from your lips which did not please me!" He then laid his hand upon me and blessed me, solemnly praying that I might be kept from all the evil that was without and within the Church."

The vivid interest which even in extreme old age he took in passing events, was strikingly shewn on the occasion of the Fenian plot in London, when the wall of Clerkenwell prison was blown up. One of his daughters-in-law writes:—

"I was with him at Newcourt when the tidings arrived. He was then within a few days of completing his ninety-second year. I seem to have still before my eyes his face of awe-struck horror as the account of the terrible catastrophe was read to him from the newspaper at the breakfast-table. Seeing how much it affected him we tried to turn from the subject and lead the conversation to other things, but he saw through the attempt at once, and desired to be told all that was known. Through the remainder of that day he was deeply depressed, and frequently alluded to it as a fearful example of the permission sometimes mysteriously given by the Most High to the powers of darkness to triumph amongst men; and when the evening hour for family prayer arrived, and the chapter had been read, although for some months past he had been accustomed, from advancing infirmity, to offer up prayer from his seat on the sofa, leaning forward to a little table that stood before him, on this occasion he seemed compelled to change his posture, and there kneeling upright on the floor, he offered the usual evening petitions, adding to them the most fervent supplications that we might. be kept from the power of the evil one, that the fury of sinful man might be controlled, his cruel devises brought to nought, the sufferings of the wounded and injured relieved, &c., &c.

The following anecdote told to me after his death by the Rev. Achilles Daunt, illustrates the influence which the example of his piety exercised over those he came in contact with: " I was last evening visiting a member of our congregation—Mr. ——, and he told me that for many years he had had strong religious convictions, but his great snare was the difficulty he felt in making an open profession of his religious feelings ; and he then added, ' I can never cease to be thankful for the impression made upon me by the late Lord Chief Justice some years ago when I was resident Magistrate in the County of ——, and had occasion to wait on him at the assizes upon public business ; I found him in his Court-Chamber, reading his Bible, while waiting for the verdict of a Jury in a case he had just tried. When the business on which I had called was over, the Chief Justice took the opportunity of

calling my attention to the personal profit and
pleasure he had derived through life from the study
of the Bible, and I left the room with the feeling
that I had never heard a man speak who showed
the same intimate acquaintance with the Scriptures
or the same experimental knowledge of religion.' "

For some years previous to his death, he found
that in the air of Bray he was less subject to the
bronchial attacks from which he occasionally
suffered than in Longford, and after his retirement
from the Bench he seldom spent any length of time
at his own country seat. In 1866 he rented the
pretty villa of Newcourt, near Bray, where he
resided up to his death on the 4th May, 1869. It
seems to have been the revival of an early taste,
for we find a letter written to his father in the
year 1819, dated from Newcourt, Bray ;* so that
when a member of the Bar, he must have passed
one of his vacations there.

He always enjoyed riding more than any other
exercise, and whenever the weather permitted, he
continued, up to the year of his death, to take his
morning or afternoon ride on a favourite pony
which he had had for more than thirty years. The
instinct with which this little animal recognised his
master's hand was quite extraordinary, and it was a
scource of constant pleasure and amusement to him
to observe this. The little animal seemed to feel

* See this letter, *ante* p. 65.

almost a conscious pride in being reserved solely for its master's use, for whenever anyone else attempted to get on its back, it showed an evident inclination to dislodge the intruder by freely prancing and kicking, while, for his mounting, it stood motionless, and when he was perfectly established in his saddle went off with a measured pace, as if it knew the preciousness of its charge; and on his dismounting it regularly waited for its feed of bread or broken apples which it generally received from his own hand before leaving the hall door. His eldest daughter, whom he playfully called "his guardian angel," was the constant companion of these daily rides; for from the time of our beloved mother's death in 1858, she was hardly ever separated from him even for a day, and with untiring watchfulness and forethought she seemed to anticipate every wish and provide for every want almost before it was felt by the loved object of her care.

In the evenings, his delight was as often as possible to gather round him the whole family group—children and grandchildren. In all these gatherings, the still fresh flow of his natural spirits, the unaffected interest which he took in promoting the happiness and amusement of all around him, ever rendered him the great centre of attraction to young and old, who alike seemed to regard him as the cheerful companion and the

revered parent, and while he never tried to restrain
the light-hearted spirit of youth, he always endeavoured to impart a religious, or at least a useful or
intellectual tone into whatever might be the subject
which occupied the social circle for the time.
The following extract from a letter of Miss Elizabeth Warren, daughter of his much valued friend
Serjeant Warren, was sent to me by the Lady to
whom it was written, and her account of an evening she spent in the Home circle at Newcourt, not
long previous to his death, vividly brings back to
my mind the call so familiar to us all at the close
of our family gatherings—" Now let us have one
of my favorite hymns before we separate ":—

" About six weeks since, I spent a day at Newcourt.
The Chief was remarkably well, and dined with us at 7
o'clock. In the evening the two little H———'s and I
sang hymns for him, sitting round his sofa,—no accompaniment, only our three voices. He chose the hymns
himself—' Rock of ages,' and, ' Look ye saints, the sight
is glorious.' With his hymn-book in his hand, he followed
every word without spectacles, and I shall never forget
his look of rapturous joy as the tears rolled down his face
when we sang the verse,

'Hark! those sounds of acclamation,' &c.

He exclaimed, 'Oh, we have not the spirit of those
lines,—we have not the joy in our Lord's exaltation which
used to be!' and then he read the lines aloud with so
realizing a sense of their meaning!"

Besides the hymns mentioned in this letter, he scemed to take peculiar pleasure in hearing the beautiful hymn by Madan,

"Lo! He comes with clouds descending,"

and the following from a collection of hymns by the Rev. Thos. Kelly, which was a favorite manual of his:—

1.

Why those fears? behold 'tis Jesus
Holds the helm, and guides the ship;
Spread the sail, and catch the breezes
Sent to waft us through the deep
To the regions
Where the mourners cease to weep.

2.

Though the shore we hope to land on
Only by report is known,
Yet we freely all abandon,
Led by that report alone;
And with Jesus
Through the trackless deep move on.

3.

Oh! what pleasures there await us!
There the tempests cease to roar;
There it is that those who hate us
Shall molest our peace no more:
Trouble ceases
On that tranquil happy shore!

On the Saturday evening previous to his death (the last he ever spent down stairs), the hymn that was sung for him was—

"There is a land of pure delight,
Where saints immortal reign."

Whilst listening, his countenance lit up with such holy joy, that one might imagine some slight foretaste of the bliss of heaven had been actually granted to him. When the voices ceased he exclaimed, " Oh, how glorious, how heavenly ;" then turning to his daughter he said "you must allow me to stay up just to hear that once more ;" and he joined in every word of it as it was sung a second time.

To the last he retained a cheerful and patient endurance under suffering which often elicited the astonishment and admiration of those who attended upon him in sickness. I remember in his last illness (only two days before he was taken from us), after he had spent a very wearisome night from want of sleep, and great oppression of breathing, we closed the window-shutters in the morning, in the hope of his getting some sleep ; just then the physician for whom an express had been sent, arrived from Dublin. After feeling his pulse, the doctor asked whether it would annoy him if the window-shutters were opened for a moment, when he replied with a cheerful smile "not at all, doctor, I always like to have light thrown upon a subject."

On the day previous to his death, most of us being assembled at his bed-side, he asked me to

read to him the 17th chapter of St. John, and in a
firm impressive voice, offered up the following
prayer : " Gracious God, grant that we may be
enabled to receive this portion of thy word into
our hearts, that we may be made wise unto salvation, through the grace and knowledge of Jesus
Christ our Lord and Saviour."

The symptoms became more alarming in the
afternoon of that day, and we telegraphed to
London for his eldest son, who was attending his
Parliamentary duties, and to the north of Ireland,
for his third son. The latter reached Newcourt that
evening, and his eldest son arrived the next morning from London, so that there was not a single
member of the family circle missing at that solemn
hour. Though at that time weak and exhausted
having passed a sleepless night, he welcomed each
of us with his usual sweet and loving smile, as we
gathered round his bed ; he then asked his son
Jeffry to read the 51st Psalm, and repeated in a
languid voice, several of the verses as they were
read to him. Afterwards part of the 14th chapter
of St. John's Gospel was read. He repeated the
third verse, " I go to prepare a place for you, and
I will come again and receive you unto myself, that
where I am ye may be also," and then in a distinct
voice added, " yes!—thus making assurance doubly
sure !" and looking upwards as if he had caught

the sweet music of the heavenly chime floating across the waters of Jordan and welcoming him to his heavenly rest, with these words on his lips he entered the mansion prepared for him in his Father's house.

It was hard, indeed, at first to realize the fact that the bright beaming countenance which had so long formed the sunlight of the happiest of earthly homes was never again to cheer our hearts—that the gentle voice which had so often welcomed us with a kind and loving word for each, was never again to be heard amongst us on earth. But where weak nature shrinks, faith steps in, and sees the bright angel pointing upward from the tomb, and saying, "he is not here, but he is risen." The home he gladdened on earth is but a faint type of that brighter, happier home, in which we look for our re-union. Now for a little while separated, we shall then meet to part no more. And if when memory opens the tomb, unbidden tears arise, they shall be chased away by the recollection that, "the righteous are taken away from the evil to come."

> One thought shall check the rising tear,
>   It is—that he is free.
> And thus shall faith's consoling power
>   The tears of love restrain;
> Ah, who that saw his parting hour
>   Could wish him here again?

Triumphant in his closing eye
The hope of glory shone ;
Joy breathed in his expiring sigh
To think the fight was won.

Those who loved him most, may well bow with submission to the dispensation, which, while it has taken from their earthly home its richest treasure, has, at the same time, landed him safely in the haven of everlasting rest.

The following letter, which I received a few days after his death from his old and valued friend the present Bishop of Cashel, justly expresses what should be the feelings of those who, while they may and must feel their own loss, are yet happily assured of " his unspeakable gain ":—

Waterford,
May 7th, '69.

My dear Lefroy,—It has pleased our gracious God to take to Himself the soul of your dear father, and my oldest, most valued friend. We cannot say that He has not done all things well. He lent him for an unusually long time to his children and his friends, and then He said, ' Come up higher.' When we think what He that giveth grace and glory did for him, and what in consequence He is doing for him now, we cannot think of offering the common consolation to those who feel his loss, but must realize his unspeakable gain. No, we say with warm feeling, Blessed be the God and Father of our Lord Jesus Christ, who according to his abundant mercy

C C

hath begotten us again unto a lively hope by the resurrection of Jesus Christ. We bless God on the part of our departed one and ourselves, for the inheritance incorruptible, and reserved in heaven for him and us who are partakers of the same faith. It is promised to us left behind, that we shall be kept by the power of God through faith unto the salvation ready to be revealed, and we greatly rejoice in the prospect; but he is beyond it; we are to be kept for it, but he has been put into possession of it. Shall not we, then, on his account, greatly rejoice, though now for a season we may be in heaviness? He is indeed taken away from evil to come, and from what an extent of evil we do not know. We may well be led to offer up the beautiful prayer of our funeral service, that our God may speedily accomplish the number of His elect, and hasten His kingdom, that we and all those who are partakers of the faith of the Gospel, may have our perfect consummation of bliss both in body and soul in Christ's kingdom.
. . . . I never shall forget the pleasure and profit we had for many successive years in having your father speaking at the meeting of the Wicklow Bible Society, which, by his presence and spiritual addresses, he was instrumental in establishing and confirming. I look back with a most pleasing recollection to a journey I took with him in the Holyhead Mail from Birmingham.* I had come to Birmingham the day before, and had taken a place in the Mail to Holyhead. I went in the morning to the office just before starting, anxious to see what company I should

---

* This seems to be the journey referred to in the letter given in p. 341.

have, and I found your father, and I think one of you his sons, and a stranger and myself. When he came into the coach he had his Bible in his hand, and he put it into the pocket of the carriage at hand for use, and a most delightful searching of scripture we had on the road. He loved his Bible, and I remember a saying of his that struck me much at the time. He said, I sometimes read the Bible on my knees, not that I am making an idol of the book, and falling down to worship it, but I am in a position to say, "Give me understanding that I may see the wondrous things that are in Thy book," Deal with me according to the favour Thou showedst unto Thy people, etc. Will you give my kindest regards to your sisters, who must feel more than any others the gap that has been made. I pray for you all that grace may abound to you through Jesus Christ.

Yours most affectionately

In the Gospel of Christ,

ROBT. CASHEL.

I cannot here omit the following cordial expression of respect and esteem from the pen of one of his much valued colleagues on the Bench, who spoke as well from the long experience of professional life, as of the many years of their judicial life, during which he and the Chief Justice (while Baron of the Exchequer) had sat together in that Court:—

52, Stephen's Green,

20th May, '69.

MY DEAR LEFROY, ... I cannot easily say to you how shocked I was at the sudden announcement of the fatal illness of your lamented and honoured father. I did not hear of his illness, until I was told of his danger. NEVER shall I forget the manner in which HE, with his great antecedents, his high endowments, his vast experience and learning, and his universally acknowledged position, first at the Bar, and then on the Bench, received and treated ME, when I was raised to the first place on the Bench which he adorned. We both lived to see him placed in his proper position, and after years of eminent public service, his large circle of friends saw him sink, respected, loved, and lamented by all of intelligence and worth in his time. These are great consolations to the family and the friends who have survived him, with the far better ones derived from his known and life-long preparation for the great change. Writing to you AT ALL at this time, I could not forbear saying what I have felt. Pray excuse it.

Yours, my dear Lefroy,

Ever faithfully,

D. R. PIGOT.

On Tuesday, the 11th of May, his earthly remains were conveyed from the villa of Newcourt, and were laid in the family vault at Mount Jerome Cemetery. The number of his colleagues on the Bench, of the members of both branches of the

legal profession, and of his fellow-citizens, as well
as the large circle of his private friends, who assembled from various directions to pay their last
tribute of respect on this solemn occasion, afforded
a striking proof of the respect and regard which
were entertained for him by men of all classes and
creeds. The funeral service was performed by the
Very Rev. Maurice F. Day, Dean of Limerick,
from whose address on the occasion the following
is an extract:—

"It is not fitting that we should follow the honored
remains that lie before us to their resting-place, without a
word being spoken concerning the man who has been
taken from amongst us. It shall be only a word. I will
not speak of him as a great lawyer, as the upright poli-
tician, as the eminent judge. In all these ways he was
known to many here better than to me ; but I will say a
word concerning what I knew of him for the last twenty-
five years that I had the privilege of his intimate acquaintance. His career was distinguished—you all know that.
He had all that man could desire—rightly desire—in this .
world. Advancing in an honorable profession from step
to step, the public voice going before him, every honor
was bestowed upon him, and he attained through successive
steps that high position which he adorned, and which he
was enabled to hold to such an unexampled period of
life. All these things are known to you, and there were
better earthly blessings than these public honors. These
were the blessings of home—the blessings of an unbroken

family. Death did not step into that circle until, after fifty years of happy life together, she who walked by his side was taken away ; and at the last the children whom he loved, and who loved him, were gathered every one of them around that parting scene. These were earthly blessings; but, brethren, let me say a word of what was better than all these.

"There were three things that specially struck me in observing his public and private character, and they struck others who had an intimate knowledge of him, as well as me. One was that distinguishing feature of his character—his love—his earnest devoted love—for God's blessed word. I have gone into his study and found him poring over that word, as if he was only now for the first time tasting in all its freshness the sweetness that is in it. I have gone in, and found him at times occupied with other books, but these he would push away from him, and turn, as he delighted so well to do, to speak of some passages of scripture. He loved God's word; it was sweeter than honey to his soul. His delight was in " the law of the Lord," and in His law did he delight day and night. And so the promise was fulfilled: " he shall be like a tree planted by the water side, that bringeth forth his fruit in his season; his leaf also shall not wither, and whatsoever he doeth shall prosper." There was another feature which, perhaps, may surprise some when we look at his honorable course, public and private. That was his deep humility before God. While others may have looked on him and admired him, and while his family looked up to him with love and reverence, he looked at himself before God as the most unworthy of sinners. He lay low in the dust, and that feeling was deeper and deeper in advancing years. The more he knew of God's word,—the exceeding breadth of that commandment,—the more he was humbled in the sight of God at seeing his own manifold shortcomings. And then there was another feature which happily came in with the last—that he gave all the glory of all his hopes, and of all his comforts, to the finished redemption of his blessed Lord and Saviour.

"It was not as a mere intellectual study he loved the word of God. It was not to speculate upon many questions which arise concerning it, interesting in their place; but it was because he found Christ in it, and that his Saviour was precious to his soul. In the deep sense of his unworthiness, he clung to that finished righteousness of Christ as his one standing ground before God. And, brethren, these things, which marked him through the mercy and grace of our God, followed him to the last. That word which he had loved, and which had delighted him in the many years of his long and honored life—that word was the staff on which he leaned when walking down the valley of the shadow of death; and only a few moments before his parting hour, that word was still on his lips, and the comfort of hearing it manifested in his soul. And the other features followed him too—deep humiliation before God. It was only half-an-hour before his going hence that he asked to have read to him the 51st Psalm—that deep penitential prayer of David humbling himself before God as a sinner. And again giving the glory of all his hopes to the Lord Jesus Christ and to His all-sufficient salvation—that likewise was his comfort, and that followed him to the end. It was not five minutes before his spirit went hence, that when a portion of scripture—the word of the Lord Jesus Christ (in the 14th chapter of St. John) was read to him—" I go to prepare a place for you, and I will come again and receive you to myself, that where I am there ye may be also "—the dying lips of Christ's honored servant repeated these words with intelligence, and added the comforting confession, ' thus assurance is made doubly sure.'

"My brethren, I will not detain you by speaking more. I felt bound to say this much, but let me say one word concerning us all. What are all earthly things now, and what is the long and honored professional career, and the high honors which crowned the close of his life ? What are these greater blessings of family peace and happy relationships ? All at an end. But the things that I am speaking of concerning his personal character—his love for God's word, his humiliation as a sinner, his confidence in Christ—these are not gone. My brethren, for ourselves let us think, can we look for more earthly things than he had ? Few of us, perhaps none of us here, will attain to that advanced life. A few, indeed, may attain to the same high eminence in the world, or to the honors that crowned him; but even of those who attain these honors few may have that unbroken family peace and happiness which he had. If we had them all, what would they be ? But, brethren, we all can have these three precious things that I speak of. I commend to you to study that word which he studied, and which the more he read, the more he loved. I commend to you to walk in the light of that word, and to seek in its pages the satisfying and comforting knowledge of God. I commend to

you, dear brethren, to learn—oh! that we all may learn
by the teaching of His Holy Spirit—our sinfulness in the
sight of God, as he was taught. And then I commend to
you that greatest blessing of all—to know Christ—to know
Him not as one heard of, not as one who is merely
acknowledged as the Son of God, and the Saviour of
the world; but to know Him each one for himself as his
own Saviour, making peace with God for you; putting
away your sins, giving you a title to an everlasting inheritance, and making you God's children, and the heirs of
His kingdom. Oh! that we might all learn this lesson
to-day around these honored remains which are in the
midst of us. Oh! that we may all know that Saviour
who never shall separate from us; that, when all things
earthly pass away, we may be found in Him, and that He
may be our portion for ever and ever.

APPENDIX.

MR. LEFROY'S ADDRESS AS AUDITOR IN THE HISTORICAL SOCIETY OF
THE UNIVERSITY OF DUBLIN ON OPENING THE SESSION OF 1795,
TOGETHER WITH THE RESOLUTIONS REFERRED TO IN PAGE 12,
ON WHICH THE SOCIETY WAS FOUNDED.

THE College Historical Society was originally founded in
1770 for the cultivation of History, Oratory, and Composition. It continued to hold its meetings weekly within the
walls of Trinity College for more than twenty years; but
in consequence of the introduction of debates on political
subjects which tended to the breach of discipline amongst
the Students of the University, the Board were obliged
to forbid its meetings being held within the bounds of
the College. The Society then met in a room hired for
the purpose in the city, and many were admitted as
members who were not students of the University; but
from the time it ceased to be under the control of the
Governing Board of the College, it gradually degene-
rated into a political debating club. Many of the members
strongly felt the evil of this departure from the objects
for which it was originally instituted, and resolved to
modify its rules so as to endeavour to obtain the sanction
of the Provost and Fellows to a revival of its meetings
in College. Amongst those who felt strongly the advan-

tage of restoring the connexion between the Historical Society and the University was Mr. Lefroy, and on the 19th December, 1794, the following resolutions, proposed by him, and seconded by Mr. Torrens,* were unanimously agreed to:—

" 1. Resolved,—That we, the undersigned, do hereby associate ourselves under the title of 'The Historical Society of the University of Dublin, instituted for the cultivation of History, Oratory, and Composition.'

" 2. Resolved,—That we adopt as the fundamental bond of our union the following regulations, viz.:—

" No person whose name is not on the College Books shall be admissible into this Society.

" No person shall be permitted to remain a member of this Society after he shall have taken his name off the College Books, except such members as shall have obtained a medal in the Society, or a premium in the undergraduate course, and such are to continue members only till they are of Master's standing. Also all members of the late Historical Society may be admitted, and continue members of this Society, till said standing, upon subscribing these regulations, though they may not have obtained medals or premiums.

" The Fellows of the College shall have a right to attend the meetings of this Society.

" The students shall attend the meetings of the Society in their gowns.

" The books containing the proceedings of the Society shall be submitted to the Board whenever required.

" No question of modern politics shall be debated."

* Afterwards Mr. Justice Torrens.

The following Address from the Historical Society, T.C.D., to the Board, was then proposed by a Committee, and agreed to:—

" We, the Members of the Historical Society associated within the University, are anxious to communicate to the Board our full and perfect acquiescence in their last regulations; we have adopted them as the bond of our union and the fundamental principles of our Institution.

" We are convinced of the great utility of an institution for the more immediate cultivation of History, Oratory, and Composition, and are no less strongly impressed with the necessity of its dependence on the University for a creditable existence.

" We return our sincere thanks to the Board for its kindness in devising regulations which we think will conduce to the permanent well-being of the Society, and we trust that by our adherence to them, and by the general propriety of our conduct, we shall continue to deserve the favour and protection of the Board.

Signed by order,

" JOHN JEBB,* Secretary.
" December 20, 1794."

"ANSWER OF THE BOARD.

" The Senior Fellows have requested the Vice-Provost to signify to the Members of the Historical Society that they highly approve of their Address presented to them this day; that they think very favourably of their characters and conduct, and assure them of every countenance

* Afterwards Bishop of Limerick.

and support of the Institution they are engaged in
which may be consistent with the duty of the Board as
Governors of the College."

"December 20, 1794.

Mr. Lefroy was elected Auditor* at the opening of
the second session of the revived Historical Society, and
on the 28th of October, 1795, delivered the following
address:—

"GENTLEMEN OF THE HISTORICAL SOCIETY,—I congratulate you that we are re-assembled at our post—not
a second time to found our Institution, but certainly to
found the era of its stability. We may now lay aside all
those anxieties and apprehensions by which we were sur-
rounded in our previous course, henceforward to advance
with the cheerfulness and hope of an assured existence.
We are re-assembled, I trust, not relaxed in a single nerve
of our zeal, but strengthened and confirmed in the spirit
of persevering resolution. The very circumstance of
our meeting together in this University, and our being
drawn closer together here, suggests sentiments congenial and favorable to the task we are about to engage
in. If we but a little anticipate the scenes of life to
which we ourselves shall be differently called, in these

---

* In a tract entitled "Brief Statement of the causes which led to the
dissolution of the Historical Society of T. C. D., by a late Member of
the Society, *Dublin*, 1815," we find the Auditor's Office thus described :
"A Member, generally the most distinguished for his talents, was
appointed to open and close each Session with a speech from the chair of
the Society. The speeches on these occasions consisted principally in a
display of the advantages of the Institution, and the excellencies of the
objects pursued in it."

we shall find that much of what experience prompts us
to admire, has received its first culture in the exercises
which this Institution holds forth to our acceptance.
The knowledge of man and his nature in all the varieties
which history exhibits must be for ever interesting and
instructive. The embellishments of composition are
called for by the refinement of literary taste, but above
all here is laid a foundation for that persuasive art which
is alone adequate to speak its own praises and its supreme
influence over mankind.

"Let us, however, consider more minutely the several
objects of our Institution. The first which, by a sort of
established usage, demands our more particular consideration, is the subject of history. Happy am I (however it may narrow my scope) to feel that so obvious and
persuasive have the advantages of historical knowledge
appeared to those who have preceded me, that every
topic of recommendation is become almost trite and exhausted. They have been often presented in the various
lights of instruction, accomplishment, and liberal entertainment, useful and becoming alike in every situation and
every calling of life. But to direct you in your choice
of history, I will beg leave to trouble you with a few more
detailed observations. I submit them to you with diffi-
dence, and I must entreat for them the same indulgence,
the same share of allowance, which I have to ask for all
that I address to you to-night. In your selection of
history, modern history should be preferred to ancient.
This Institution should in as many instances as possible
be supplemental to the course of our academic studies.
Ancient history is generally the object of early instruc-

tion, or at least is sufficiently comprised in the academic system ; modern history cannot be so much so ; this Institution should therefore supply the deficiency. But in the choice of modern history I have often seen you perplexed and wavering. On that subject I have ever maintained but one opinion. I have always considered a course of general history, something in the nature of an epitome, as the most useful we could adopt. In what I propose, too, I should hope to find a remedy for a serious mischief—the irregular attendance of members on our History Bench. Young members I must say, according to our present system, have little inducement to a regular attendance. They come in upon a course of history which has been going forward for some sessions, and perhaps will not draw to a conclusion for two or three more—a course the total of which is so inconsiderable a portion of general history, that a part or as much as could be comprised in a session or two would be trifling and insignificant. Under such circumstances there cannot be much inducement to perseverance, at least there is a plausible excuse for indolence and disinclination. On the contrary, a course such as I have taken the liberty to suggest, which should be completed in one session, which consequently should begin anew with every succession of members; which besides should be in itself a complete course, so far at least as being a tolerably comprehensive outline of general history, would afford an incitement to a regular and persevering attention. Important, however, as the cultivation of history undoubtedly is, serviceable as the lessons of it may prove which are here impressed on the early memory, we should yet have seen but a few and perhaps the most inconsiderable benefits of this Institution were we to rest here.

"I do not hesitate to point out here as a still greater advantage of our Society the opportunity it affords of cultivating public speaking. Perhaps there are some who would differ from me on this point. Of such I would ask, whether, of all the faculties with which nature has endowed us, is one alone to be left to grow wild? Is the art of public speaking, is oratory—and oratory alone—incapable or unworthy of cultivation and improvement? No. I am persuaded that in this, as in every other faculty of our nature, excellence is to be attained by slow and painful toil.

"Let me not be misunderstood as holding forward this institution as a school where the gift of eloquence can be imparted—that rare flight of genius is the portion of but a very few. But may not the first principles of composition and the rudiments of public speaking be acquired here? May not practice in this place teach what is to be had by practice alone—that ease and full possession of himself so necessary to any man who intends to enter into professional or public life. In this place he need not fear that the awkwardness or failure of a first attempt will blast his future prospects in a profession, or stamp on him a ridicule which will go down with him to the grave.

"With respect to any advice on the subject of oratory, I can only say, that in speaking as in writing, " Sapere est principium," &c., our leading rule should be, rather what we are to say than how we are to say it. But neither should this latter consideration be neglected.

Clearness and precision of expression are indispensable rules to be observed by him who desires to attain any eminence as a public speaker. They are improvements in style towards which every man may and ought to make some progress. So necessary is the art of expressing our thoughts with clearness and precision, and so essential to the useful exercise of our other faculties, that without some degree of it we shall find the noblest of them, which is reason, to be miserably maimed and defective.

" I do not mean this evening to allude to the hackneyed subject of modern politics. I hope your good sense and adherence to a solemn compact will allow some rest to that wretched threadbare topic; but I must say a few words against the mistaken ardour which I have observed in this Society for questions, abstract undoubtedly in their terms, and literally not trenching in any degree on your restrictions, but certainly in their tendency political. Frequently have I observed the same eagerness for abstruse and complicated questions of commercial interests as for political questions. I could wish a uniformity in all our system—that the subjects of our debate, in like manner as our course of history, should be suited to an elementary institution. And surely we are as little fitted for political debaters as for philosophical historians. Look with an honest candour on the little progress we have yet made in our lives—the stages of our knowledge and experience from the cradle to the school, from the school to the college, and thence see the mighty stride into the mazes and labyrinths of politics. Believe me you will hereafter be amazed at your rashness in approaching to discussions in which, under our former constitution, you were every night engaged as 'things familiar and acquainted.' You complain that you are not warmed or interested by questions of history—particularly ancient history—that you wish to declaim on interesting and animating topics. Well, I am convinced that, to a duly-ordered mind and well-regulated affections, it requires only to turn to the transactions of Greece and Rome, in order to be both animated and interested, much more shall we be so by those of history which approaches nearer to our own day, and nearer to the temperature of our own feelings. But all historical questions have at least this ground of preference—they are infinitely better suited to our knowledge and situation. I am well aware that I have broached a doctrine which is unpopular, and that I am, perhaps, offending many ears. It is a censure I am not afraid to meet. One praise at least, to balance it, I shall extort from your justice—I have noticed your faults with an honest candour, and with an honest zeal I have laboured to reform them. The consciousness of this will support me under the burden of any such censure; and, what I even more regard, it will vindicate your Society in conferring on me the honor of so important a task as I am now endeavouring to fulfil, however other imperfections may prove me unworthy of your choice.

" Intimately connected with oratory is the subject of composition, but which I regret does not seem to be pursued with an ardour proportionate either to its own importance or to the encouragement held out by this institution. We have, indeed, been presented with a few *poetic* compositions by some of our members. To these gentlemen we owe peculiar obligation and regard. I make no doubt the future celebrity of their lives will make us proud to boast that we have here seen the first exertions of their early genius. But whilst I very gladly bestow on these gentlemen this well merited meed of praise, I must acknowledge a regret, which I am sure their liberality will second, that the tribute of praise is confined to them alone ; that there never yet has been offered for our approbation a single *prose* composition. And yet I can see no ground for supposing that the temper of this Society would not at all times concur with its laws in rewarding this species of merit. I am strongly persuaded that there are around me those in every way qualified for such an undertaking; and I trust that this passing suggestion will make it unnecessary hereafter to revive this topic with more earnestness.

"I have now touched upon the various and useful objects—History, Oratory, and Composition—to which this excellent institution calls our attention, an Institution so essentially serviceable as connected with this University, that I do not hesitate to declare, from the firmest conviction, that to lop off this branch would be a sort of disorganizing and maiming of the academic system. In your present condition every symptom is cheering. You have increased with all the rapidity of vigour and sound constitution. Contrast your situation now with that from which we have lately passed, when an ungenerous rival was endeavouring to crush your feebleness; when every one of the scribbling tribe dipped his pen in gall, and, with the malignity of the wasp, turned against you its envenomed sting. But let not the dread of such attacks hamper us in our excellent undertaking. To be carped at and misrepresented, has been at one time or other the fate of every thing great and good. The utmost purity of intention is not a sufficient guard against calumny and misrepresentation. At the first dawn of virtue these are the vapours which, like the morning sun, its own mighty influence raises up, by which for a while its brilliancy and its light may be interrupted and absorbed, but which vanish and clear away as it advances in its course.

"Never was there a folly more glaring, more mischievous, than separating the interests of this Society from the interests of the University, and representing them as distinct and even contrasted. Thus, instead of regarding this as an elementary institution for the first growth of youthful talent, thriving under the shelter and by the protection of the University, it was put forward as a sort of chartered independent corporation, of extensive rights and immunities, not to be questioned, however abused to the subversion of academic discipline and order. All these evils flowed from the same source, which to have cut off some would endeavour to represent as a hardship; but I trust even the short experience we have already had, has convinced us that to be relieved for the present and secured for ever from an indiscriminate throng of externs, was no less serviceable to this Institution, than absolutely requisite for the good of the University. In such a promiscuous multitude, admitted and retained without restriction, it must and did happen, that there should be some whose depravity this seminary had not corrected, or whose dullness it had not enlightened, who therefore made it their business to deride the restraints of a necessary and wholesome discipline, and to misrepresent the honorable toils of learning, as slavish and degrading. Others, of necessity there were, engaged in the business of life, warmed with its controversies and strife, who sought to introduce into this Society political dissension and a spirit of peevish opposition, which admitted here would prove a firebrand, devouring and consuming all that is amiable and hopeful in youth. Lamentable, indeed, must be the consequences if that respectful submission to their instructors, which marks ingenuous and honorable minds, is to be scouted and exchanged for a petulant and querulous resistance. Let me ask this simple question, What was the original and proper intent of this Institution? Was it intended as an Institution for the students of the University, or a general debating club for men engaged in the various pursuits and business of life? I believe there is little doubt for which common sense and its original promoters designed such a Society.

" To our present restrictions we are indebted for being brought back to this original and just standard of our constitution. In the former state of this Society the very description of men for whom it was least, if at all intended, had it in their power at all times to overturn its existence and pervert all its benefits from its proper objects, for they had at all times a desolating majority to pour in against the feeble efforts of the students.

" Suffer me, in another instance, to contrast your former and your present situation. Next to the great leading view securing its existence, it should be the object of every Institution to provide against any casual interruptions of the benefits it is fitted to produce. Was it consistent with this plain dictate of common sense and ordinary security that under the former state of this Society there existed a description of members inattentive and even averse to its proper pursuits, who had indeed reaped their own share of the profit, but, not content with the generous tranquil pleasure of beholding the younger members advance to participate in the benefit, were for ever interrupting the proper exercises of the institution, for ever perverting it into an amusement better suited to their own taste ? Perhaps our enemies may tell us that the strife of parties had its own use. Whence came it then, let me ask, that there never was an admonitory address delivered in this place which did not reprobate and cry aloud against that poison of the institution, and that the most eloquent and zealous of its members were always the most warm in condemning such practices? We have now cut off the source of all these evils, whether threatening our existence or the interruption of our more proper pursuits. We have provided that there shall always be a majority of those to whom the existence of this Society—suited to its proper intent and the cultivation of its many advantages—will be always dear and desirable; and as an additional security we have set over ourselves a superintending power, not to affect our supremacy farther than is required for our security, nor to circumscribe us in any useful or necessary act of internal regulation—a power to which we may trust ourselves, for we have already experienced its fostering care and favour.

" Such are the advantages your present has above your former state ; such also you have above your present rivals. But, besides, the change of situations has exposed them to many new evils against which you are secured. Reason and experience may convince us that it is not the nature of any debating society, which has no other restrictions on the subject of its debates or the qualifications of its members but what they themselves may choose to impose, to remain for a long time very select either in the one or the other. Youthful ardour, the political drift of the moment, or party feeling may overturn barriers so weakly guarded, yet so absolutely requisite to ensure respectability. Then must ensue all the mischiefs of a factious debating club, such as I myself have seen, where every man is estimated—not by the degree of his talents or information—not by his active exertions or his integrity. No—by his political creed alone is he judged of —by some principle of blind bigotry which in politics, as in religion, would exterminate with fire and faggot all the heresies against a particular mode of faith. The most violent rant of democratic-phrenzy is greeted with the well suited peals of vociferous applause; and the modest, sober judgment, however supported by good sense or adorned by eloquence, is hooted and cried down with the most opprobrious stigma of savage insult and impatience. These are evils from which this Society is for ever guarded, and to which its rival is hourly exposed. But suppose that society to escape this common lot of its condition, and to maintain a purity which never yet was maintained by a similar establishment, unawed by any wholesome control, there is yet another danger which threatens it—that society has lost its primal simplicity of character. The first painful exertions of timid youth are no longer cheered by seeing all around him his contemporaries—the associates of his studies and his intimates in ordinary life. Even more matured talents are overawed and terrified in the presence of a great majority of men distant in age, in habits, and in ordinary occupations —placed in too remote a sphere to share in any common influence with us. Their appearance in our little system can only bring with it terror and dismay. That certainly is not the best or most useful institution which is fitted for the display of great talents alone, or which requires a degree of elaborate preparation incompatible with other necessary pursuits. Far more extensively beneficial is that in which moderate abilities can be advanced by frequent exercise; and, in this, your institution stands most pointedly contrasted with its rival; indeed, as we are contrasted in most things, so we have in most contrasts a manifest superiority.

Little do I regard the circumstance that either fickleness or the artifice of our enemies may have taken a few from our numbers. If any member has forsaken us because he preferred a frivolous pleasure to the welfare of this institution, I am content to lose him. He cannot mix with our hardy toils who passes away the morning of life in pursuit of a butterfly. If any one has forsaken us through a peevish discontent, him, too, I am content to part with. He who would not coalesce in our zeal no longer remains a drag upon our course.

Some, indeed, set up a more plausible excuse for their
fickleness. These gentlemen left us, it is said, because
we had not amongst us great specimens of eloquence, by
which they might have modelled their genius, and become
orators by example. It is true that, although amongst
those I have the honor to address there are to be found
many bright specimens of talent, yet we have not indeed
any prodigies amongst us; nor do I much repine. I
should be sorry we had transplanted into this institution an overgrown genius, to chill by its shade and
impoverish by its bulk the plants that grew beneath it,
absorbing in the luxuriance of its single fame all those
little tributes of applause which should be diffused
amongst all, to invigorate and forward the growth of
general talent.

" We have every reason, then, to be content with our
choice of this institution. The effect of what our enemies
would represent as a hardship in our restrictions will tend
to make this an Institution more for the Students of the
University than for men called into life and to a profession,—for those who may, at the same time with their
academic pursuits, improve other talents before the busier
scenes of life call for their whole and undivided attention. But neither are men engaged in the business of the
world unconditionally excluded. I should be grieved if
they were—if by no means whatever it were possible,
that they, however advanced in life, in age, or in profession,
should continue to share the benefits of this Society : and I
say to every one who professes an attachment to the Institution, and a desire to continue its supporter—' You may
testify your sincerity—the trifling inconvenience will not

for a moment stand in the way of true zeal.'* But I do not hesitate to hope that if at a future time any of our restrictions should be found prejudicial to the interests of this Society, the same parental attention to our welfare which at first dictated those restrictions will be at all times ready to alter and amend. But take the most unlikely and adverse lot which imagination can present— say that even that power by some extraordinary perversion of mind will prove the very reverse of what we have already experienced—that instead of a kind, an indulgent, a *fostering* power, we shall find it hostile, severe, inexorable, even so, I should not repine at our choice. Set against this most remote contingency of evil all the positive substantial benefits of your situation —all of which your rivals want—many of which we ourselves wanted before—in the stability secured to our Institution in the course of our pursuits, uninterrupted by strife or faction; in the assistance already received from the Governors of the University ; but, above all, in the fact that there is in your situation within this sacred asylum something so chaste, something so ingenuous, so open, so contrasted with meeting together by stealth in a *suspected haunt*, that in the single circumstance of your connection with the University there is a consolation and a reward for every hardship.

" Such, Gentlemen, is the mode which appeared to me the best to adopt in the discharge of the honorable and

* His own attachment to the College Historical Society continued steadfast through life, for when Chief Justice, and more than eighty years old, he took pleasure in attending its opening Sessional Meetings, and felt an honourable pride in wearing, on a blue ribbon round his neck, the several medals he had obtained in the Society when he was a student of the University.

important office to which you have called me. I thought it might not be unserviceable to give this comment on our present constitution, and to endeavour to bring it more fully into the view of those who may not have had occasion so maturely to weigh all its advantages. If in doing so I was forced to bring this Institution into a pointed contrast with another, I have really sacrificed my own feelings in order to lay before you what the security and welfare of this Society seemed indispensably to require. In the discharge of my duty to you, whatever personal odium I may bring on myself from the common enemy I little regard.

"But, Gentlemen, I have detained you too long—too long for your patience, too long for my own capacity, too long for everything but my own gratification in addressing a Society to which I feel my affections so linked, from which I believe no ordinary pursuit or pleasure, nothing but the urgent voice of an arduous and honorable calling, should induce me to separate myself, even for a while; but I trust that at no period, in no situation, however occupying or engrossing, shall I forget what I owe to this Institution. At all times shall I be glad to lay at its feet the feeble offering of my exertions; at all times shall I be mindful and proud to boast of the honors it has thought fit to confer on me, but more especially of this last and most distinguished mark of its regard. May the same zeal which has so wonderfully matured this Society to what it is, still speed you in your course, and all through life animate your pursuit of virtue, learning, and honest fame.

"THOMAS L. LEFROY."

FAREWELL ADDRESSES PRESENTED TO CHIEF JUSTICE LEFROY ON HIS
RETIREMENT FROM THE BENCH, BY THE GRAND JURIES OF THE
COUNTIES ON THE HOME CIRCUIT REFERRED TO IN PAGE 331.

From the Daily Express of 18*th July*, 1866.

" Upon the conclusion of the presentments, the Grand
Jury having been discharged, the following address was
presented, and read on their behalf by Thos. St. George
Pepper, Esq., High Sheriff:—

" To the Right Hon. Thomas Lefroy, Lord Chief Justice
of the Queen's Bench.

" We, the High Sheriff and Grand Jury of the County
Meath, assembled at the Summer Assizes of 1866, cannot
allow the last occasion of your presiding at our assizes to
pass by without expressing our regret at the termination
of the long and useful public career which now draws to
a close, and our gratitude for the able and kind manner
in which you have ever assisted us in the discharge of our
duties. We now hope that after so many years of exertion your life may yet be prolonged in the quiet of your
family circle, and the society of those chosen friends to
whom your personal qualities have so much endeared
you."

" His Lordship (who was visibly affected during the
reading of the address) replied as follows:—

"Gentlemen of the Grand Jury,—Such an address
from those who have had so good an opportunity of

forming the opinion you have kindly expressed, must at all times be grateful to the feelings of any Judge; but I will not conceal from you, gentlemen, that at this moment it comes home to my feelings as peculiarly grateful. I say nothing further than this, but I hope you will not, from any defect in my powers to make an acknowledgment in an adequate form,—I hope you will not consider me deficient in any way in gratitude for such a testimonial as you have graciously borne to the discharge of my duty during the long time during which you have had an opportunity of forming an opinion on the subject. I only wish I were master of language adequate to express the feelings under which I receive so kind and gracious a compliment. I bid you farewell, gentlemen. I shall ever remember with satisfaction my intercourse with this county, and the unvarying kindness and effective discharge of their duty which I have always witnessed amongst the Grand Jurors of this county. Gentlemen, farewell, farewell!"

From the Daily Express of 21st of July, 1866.

"COUNTY WESTMEATH.

"Upon the conclusion of the civil business, the Grand Jury having intimated to the Chief Justice their desire to present him with a farewell address, his Lordship returned from his chamber into the Record Court, when the following address was read by W. Pollard-Urquhart, Esq., M. P., the Foreman of the Grand Jury:

" To the Right Hon. the Lord Chief Justice.

" We, the High Sheriff and Grand Jury of the County of Westmeath, assembled at the Summer Assizes, 1866, having learned that your Lordship is about to retire from the Bench, which you have so long and so advantageously occupied in administering the laws of the country, cannot allow this, your last appearance amongst us, to pass without tendering to you the expression of our sincere wishes for your health and happiness, and testifying our admiration of your high legal and judicial attainments. Frequently as it has fallen to your Lordship's lot to exercise your important functions in this county, the better has been our opportunity, as Grand Jurors of Westmeath, to witness your deep legal acumen, and to appreciate the uniform courtesy which you have always extended to us. Again wishing your Lordship the enjoyment of that happiness, in your retirement, to which your long public career so amply entitles you,

" We are, my Lord, &c.,

" Signed for self and fellows,

" W. POLLARD-URQUHART."

" His Lordship (who appeared deeply moved during the reading of the address) replied with great feeling, but with great clearness and distinctness, in the following terms:—

" Mr. Sheriff, and Gentlemen of the Grand Jury,—I have received at your hands so grateful and so complimentary an address, that I cannot find words to express

my feelings—an address which is not only beyond my
expectations, both as to the value and as to the extent of
the approbation you express, but which, from the peculiar
circumstances under which I now receive it, leaves me
utterly at a loss to express my gratitude in suitable language. The routine of duty did not take me into your
court upon the present occasion ; it is therefore the
more grateful to my feelings that you should come into
this court in the manner you have done, for the purpose
of presenting this address. Gentlemen, I trust you will
believe the deep sense I entertain of your kindness ; and
I can only repeat my regret at the inability to reply to
you in adequate terms. I bid you farewell from the
bottom of my heart, and trust that you will enjoy every
blessing, individually and collectively, that Providence
can bestow."

From the Daily Express of 31st July, 1866.

"QUEEN'S COUNTY.*

" We, the High Sheriff and the Grand Jury of the
Queen's County, cannot allow the Right Hon. Thomas
Lefroy, who for the last fourteen years has gone the
Home Circuit, and presided in this civil court, to retire
from the Bench of Ireland without endeavouring to
express to him the high sense we entertain of his cour-

* The Address from the High Sheriff and Grand Jury of the King's
County, with the Chief Justice's reply, has been already given. See *ante*,
p. 331.

tesy, ability, and justice; and we beg to offer him our sincere wishes of health and happiness for many years . yet to come.

"HENRY TRENCH,

"High Sheriff of the Queen's County.

"J. W. FITZPATRICK,

" Foreman, for self and fellows.

"Maryborough, Summer Assizes, July, 1866."

"Newcourt, Bray, July 30, 1866.

"Mr. Foreman, and Gentlemen of the Grand Jury of the Queen's County,—I beg to express my thanks for your kind farewell .address, just received. For many years of my judicial life I have presided in the civil court at the assizes of your county. You have, therefore, had abundant opportunities of observing my discharge of that portion of the duties of the high office from which I have just retired; and it is gratifying to me, at the close of my judicial career, to take with me such unanimous testimony, not only as to the discharge of those duties, but also of kind feelings and esteem from the members of your Grand Jury, consisting as it does of gentlemen of various shades of opinion, both in religion and politics.

" I have the honor to be,

" Yours faithfully,

"THOMAS LEFROY."

E E

From the Daily Express of 13th August, 1866.

"COUNTY CARLOW.

" To the Right Hon. Thomas Lefroy, late Lord Chief
    Justice of her Majesty's Court of Queen's Bench
    in Ireland.

" We, the High Sheriff, and Grand Jury of the County
of Carlow, assembled at Summer Assizes, 1866, beg, on
the occasion of your retiring from the Bench, to express
our high sense of the able, zealous, and dignified manner
in which you have discharged the duties of your office
during the period of fourteen years in which you have
presided over the criminal business of this county. As
Grand Jurors, we feel great pleasure in bearing testimony
to the courteous and painstaking manner in which you
have invariably given us your advice and assistance
whenever we had occasion to consult you on public
matters. We regret not having now an opportunity of
expressing to you personally these our sentiments. In
now retiring into private life, rest assured you carry with
you the sincere wish of the High Sheriff and Grand Jury
of the County of Carlow, that your future days may be
spent in peace, health, and happiness."

"REPLY.

" New Court, Bray, July 31, 1866.

" Mr. Foreman and Gentlemen of the Grand Jury of
the County of Carlow,—I shall ever esteem, as a mark of
honor and respect of the highest value, the very gratifying address which I have just received from your body.

The testimony it contains as to the discharge of my judicial duties for the many years during which I have presided at your assizes, concurring, as it does, with that of the several Grand Juries who have preceded you, may well satisfy the honorable ambition of any Judge. I have further to thank you cordially for the warm expression of your kind personal feeling, which shall always be held in grateful remembrance by yours very faithfully,

"THOMAS LEFROY."

From the Daily Express of 13th August, 1866.

"COUNTY KILDARE.

"RESOLVED,—That the Foreman be requested to forward the following resolution, which was agreed to by the Grand Jury of the County Kildare.

"'To the Right Hon. Thomas Lefroy.

"'We, the Foreman and Grand Jury, assembled at the Summer Assizes of the County Kildare, cannot separate without expressing to the Right Hon. Thomas Lefroy, on his retirement from the Irish Bench, our deep sense of the strict integrity, eminent ability, and unfailing courtesy which always distinguished him when presiding in our county courts; and we beg his acceptance of our sincere good wishes for his welfare and happiness for many future years.

"'Proposed by J. La Touche, Esq.; seconded by C. Colthurst Vesey, Esq.'"

www.ingramcontent.com/pod-product-compliance
Lightning Source LLC
Chambersburg PA
CBHW030952110726
47900CB00004B/1243